THE GIFT

Rachel Newcomb

CreateSpace
Copyright © 2013

* * *

Preface

 Just as some women claimed to know the exact moment of conception, Elise could pinpoint the moment when her desire for children became a commodity. Reading a magazine, her eyes stopped on a stark black-and-white page, where a feminine hand supported a smooth expanse of baby's back, a delicate cranium of wispy hair turned in profile. The mother's face bent down toward this new creature, her awe palpable. *You have waited a lifetime for this.*
 It was insidious for a fertility clinic to play upon her desperation like this, and in the doctor's office, too, where she waited for the results of another endless round of tests to determine why she couldn't conceive. Yet the sentimentality, though perfectly transparent, drew her in with the promise of completeness, the baby connecting a broken circle. Fertility a taunt, something denied her. The people behind the advertisement could help. Their technologies were nothing if not miraculous. The photo infected her suddenly with a fever that obliterated years of believing she did not need a child to be fulfilled. The disconnected fragments of her past, the accumulated weight of ambitions, careers, lovers, sorrows, disappointments, would cease to matter, all dissolving in the new narrative presented by the photograph: simple, perfect, whole.

* * *

 The girl with the ski-jump nose, her pearls and cashmere sweaters advertising a Princeton of an earlier era, was reading from her poetry. Twelve students sat in silent judgment, workshop copies of the poem in front of them. They were all prepared to hate her. Celia fought her own impulse to resent Nicole for the pistachio green Vespa she drove around campus, for the obvious confidence with which she faced the world.
 Nicole said *cah* instead of car, she would be the type who summered at the Cape and had lacrosse-playing boyfriends. But when she read, they all forgot about the accent, stunned at the way the words spun themselves onto the page like honey, their elegance masking the devastation they described, of life as an elegant train wreck. They clung to the images: mothers sleeping through pharmaceutical-drenched afternoons, a solitary child told not to play with her porcelain dolls.

The untouchable dolls cracked open, hatching themselves one by one to give birth to perfect replicas of the child's parents. Celia had no such experiences to write about, only a work-study job that made her miserable, and a drawl that marked her not of the lowcountry of the aristocratic South but the backwoods of upstate South Carolina.

Nicole's incantations even silenced their professor, brought her to a complete, riveted standstill. Usually Carla Lopez-Ibarrez was all motion and bad jokes, her class carefully staged to make the students feel she wanted them to be at ease in the face of her fame (five books, one National Book Award, a close friendship with Oprah), even if she really didn't. Today, something was different. Every swishing, natural fabric-swathed inch of Carla was immobile, the lapis lazuli beads on her chunky necklace no longer clicked together, the constant shuffling of workshop papers had ceased. Some of the students decided not to hate Nicole. Some of them hated her even more than before. Celia wondered how she might become her.

* * *

In his graduate student carrel in the basement of the Firestone library, Peter worked hard to produce the impression of industriousness. Stacked impressively on his desk were the tomes of colonial officials and Muslim sultans, and on a good day his mind ranged easily among the curling Arabic scripts and the longhand accounts of French and Spanish explorers. But today he was daydreaming again, lost in the irretrievable past. A journal description of a Frenchman's welcome home repast had set him off. How simple marriage must have been for those long ago explorers, returning every few months to their part-time wives, women who accepted their long absences without question. He imagined a wife who would be graceful and expectant, gazing at the horizon for her husband's ship from atop widows' walks, a hot *pot au feu* always waiting on the cast-iron stove. What might Elise have for him when he left the library at six? Not a long-simmered stew, rosemary-infused beef and carrots melding together in a rich burgundy sauce, no doubt Peter would be foraging the fridge for hummus and water crackers while she went over the merits of donor eggs or broadsided him with a proposal to outsource the operation to a surrogate in India. Now that the entire core of his wife's being was directed toward self-replication, Peter felt his physical presence amounted to little more than a donation to be sorted out later in a Petri dish.

The blinking cursor on the blank screen of his laptop taunted him; it might have been a traffic light keeping him forever stalled in his tracks. His incomplete dissertation was the obstacle between this dingy carrel and an imagined position in some New England liberal arts college. He could already picture himself there, sitting at a burnished wood table in a well-lit seminar room (snow on the quad just outside the high windows), surrounded by bright young students eager to learn about the rich civilizations of the Middle East. But first, the histories on the desk in front of him needed to yield their secrets, to organize themselves into some coherent narrative. In the right hands, there were stories to be told here, voices from the past that clamored to be heard. On bad days, the books reminded him that sooner or later he would disappoint everyone, once they realized that his academic pretensions carried no substance.

Sometimes he imagined himself escaping. In another daydream he returned to Morocco, this time not as a Peace Corps worker but as a mystic who spent his days praying, bowing his head to the earth so many times his forehead bore the imprints of his devotion. He imagined having Leila as his wife: Leila, whose name meant night. She was also part of the dark, unattainable past, as impossible to return to as the lives of any of his explorers in these books. As he stood from his prayer, she would approach him, almond-shaped eyes set deeply into nut-brown skin, an expression weary but curious, affectionate.

He would surprise everyone who counted on his predictability: his wife, the parents whose money held him hostage, forever indebted. Or, he sighed to himself, he wouldn't, he would prove to them all that he could do this, he was up to the challenge: an illustrious degree, a brilliant career as a scholar, the oak-paneled seminar room and snow drifting from blue spruce trees outside. He furrowed his brow and willed himself to concentrate a little harder.

CHAPTER ONE

Celia hoped that the Professor's illness would allow her to escape into more compelling employment, into a job that was not quite so insulated from life as the work-study position she had held for the past year in the Department of Religion. For fifteen hours each week she had worked for the frail Dr. Crenshaw, who had spent his productive years analyzing the sermons of Jonathan Edwards, a task that required endless descents into the basement of Firestone Library in search of ancient tomes she tried to copy without tearing. Allergic to over ninety-nine species of dust, Dr. Crenshaw could not go to the library himself, but he never demonstrated any gratitude for her assistance. It was clear he had disliked her from the moment she first appeared in his office, unable to name any of Edwards' writings other than *Sinners in the Hands of an Angry God*.

"A staple of high school English textbooks at mediocre academies," he'd grumbled. "Where were you schooled? St. Paul's?"

"Deer Bluff High School. It's in South Carolina?" Celia tried not to drawl.

"And that infuriating way girl students raise the end of every sentence as if it were a question, as if you weren't quite sure if I'd heard of your esteemed home state," he grumbled. "But your lack of a pedigree explains it. The Financial Aid office persists in sending me scholarship students. I don't know why I should not receive an assistant with the rigorous education necessary to understand the subtlety of Edwards' work."

"If your assistants aren't on scholarship, I doubt they would be doing work-study," Celia replied, and the scowl on his pinched face deepened.

The Professor was working on an analysis of Edwards' writings about other world religions, but he would not confirm this, going so far as to make Celia sign an agreement that she would never reveal to anyone which documents, exactly, he asked her to photocopy. In case anyone might be following her, she was also to re-shelve the books herself, which was not always possible, since many of them had to be brought over from another library where Princeton kept the books that nobody read. At the copying machines she struggled with heavy, leather-bound volumes, attempting to size the paper so that all the information would fit onto one page. No matter what she brought him, Dr. Crenshaw complained. The typeface was too big, or it was too small. The paper sizes were wrong. She should have tried to fit everything onto one sheet.

"I'm sorry, sir." Celia found herself apologizing constantly, unable to drop the "sirs" and "ma'ams" that unconsciously fell out of her mouth, a habit that annoyed most adults she'd met in Princeton.

"I am not a master back on the plantation, child. Learn to speak correctly."

Work-study, the phrase itself was an oxymoron. How could she work when she needed to be studying, or studying when she needed to work just to get enough spending money to buy her books? During her first year Celia had spent all her spare time preparing for classes, fearful that she would not measure up to the students who came prepared with the rigorous Northeast boarding school education she lacked. Academics, she discovered, could be mastered, but the more elusive social capital that her classmates possessed was harder to acquire. Before classes, in the dorm, at the campus center, she absorbed snippets of their conversations, about subjects that were completely foreign to her: crew practice, eating clubs, or weekend trips to The City. She kept quiet, afraid of revealing her ignorance, though she studied the other students as carefully as she did her Macroeconomics textbook. But her reticence had a price. Now that she was a sophomore, she realized she was learning nothing about the world outside of books. She was not yet sure how to remedy this, how to live her life a few steps beyond the confines of her dorm room, the library, and Dr. Crenshaw's stuffy office.

Managing Dr. Crenshaw's eccentricities was becoming increasingly taxing. To soothe his arthritis, Dr. Crenshaw required a space heater on at all times, so that the office was always sweltering. A packrat with an incomprehensible method for organizing his materials, he had saved every photocopy made since the 1960s, his office filled with towering stacks of paper, some of them six feet high. It was unclear what he kept inside his filing cabinets, since in Celia's presence he never opened them. The paper towers took up every available space save one foot in front of the portable heater, but even there they loomed close enough to the heat that a slight accident might send the whole building up in flames.

The professor, whose seniority allowed him to make unreasonable demands, would not allow other members of his department to use Celia's services, insisting that he needed her for the entire fifteen hours she worked each week. Whenever she dallied in retrieving library materials (anything to keep from returning right away) he scolded her for being too slow, but when there was nothing to do she was on call in his furnace of an office, sitting across from him in the bench meant for students who never came to his office hours, surrounded by mountains of yellowed paper, curling with age.

One day she came to his office at the usual time to find the door closed. Receiving no reply to her knock, she slipped away, grateful for one day of respite. Returning the next day to find his door closed again, she stopped by the administrative assistant's office.

"Dr. Crenshaw has pneumonia," she announced. "Check back next week." When his condition worsened, the university announced that he would be out for the rest of the semester. Although Celia tried to muster up sympathy at the news, she felt a guilty thrill that she would not have to return to his office. She imagined going back to collect some extra hours, telling the administrative assistant that Dr. Crenshaw had asked for help straightening his papers before he'd gotten sick, and then sweeping the stacks of photocopies into garbage bags and clearing out the place. Princeton offered to let her continue her work-study assignment in the same department. But the prospect of learning to work with another professor, whose demands and oddities might be just as trying as Dr. Crenshaw's, was daunting. She decided to look for a job outside the university, hoping for something unusual, something completely unrelated to academic life.

That week she began scanning the university classifieds. "Attractive female models wanted for artistic venture. Work weekends in your spare time, earn extra cash." "Attractive female models" set off warning bells, but Celia's misgivings were slightly mitigated by "artistic venture." She sized up her level of comfort with this, imagined allowing art students to define her on the canvas. Would it be liberating to disrobe in front of strangers? She wondered whether she'd be able to leave a sheet draped strategically over her body, which was attractive enough, lean from running, her long legs her best feature. She might hide her hips, thinking them a bit too wide for the rest of her, her long, dark hair arranged strategically over her breasts, which she usually concealed under oversize t-shirts. Celia dialed the number listed, and a male voice answered, "Mike's Camera Shop, what can I do for you?"

"The artistic venture you advertised in the Princeton paper, can you tell me more about it?"

"We're doing test shoots for a calendar," the man explained. "A local automotive parts store is looking for hot girls, do you fit the bill?" Celia hung up. She did not want to be the representative for June, in a string bikini or less splayed over a Harley or holding aloft a muffler in a calendar bearing the title *Girls Gone Wild – Ivy League Style*. Anyone could advertise in the campus newspaper, she reminded herself; their motives were not necessarily all honorable.

She tried another ad whose description sounded more respectable. "College students: got food service experience? Help needed." But when her call was routed through three different operators to a woman who asked, "Are you calling in response to the new restaurant concept in Dallas or in Miami?" she hung up. What could it have been but another waitressing job, something she vowed never again to do after the summer she and her father had spent in Key West, just before her senior year of high school.

Anayo Mills had been closed for over a year, and since then, the only managerial job her father had been able to find in Deer Bluff was at the Sonic drive-in. One night Daniel appeared at Celia's bedroom door with a globe of the world and a plan. His newfound spontaneity seemed related not only to his inability to find work but also to the empty fifths of Southern Comfort whose number in the trash increased each week. He'd let his dark hair grow out a bit, his old suits gathering dust in the closet in favor of a new daily uniform of threadbare University of South Carolina t-shirts and Levi's.

Daniel placed the globe on her chipped writing desk. The globe had belonged to Celia's mother and bore the names of exotic places that no longer existed, Zanzibar and Rhodesia, East Pakistan and the Belgian Congo.

"You spin and I'll close my eyes. Wherever my finger lands, that's where we'll go. If we like it, we'll come back here when the summer's over, you'll finish out the school year, and then I'll move when you go off to college."

Celia thought of the application for the state summer arts camp, languishing in the drawer, and waited for him to continue.

"What have we got to lose?" he asked. "You could stand to make some money to put toward college."

The first time she spun, his finger landed in Bucharest. She looked at him, wondering if he was serious.

"We'll have to limit ourselves to the adjacent forty-eight states," he laughed. "So let's keep spinning until we do. I'm aiming to keep my finger pointing south." When the globe stopped spinning in Cuba, he decided Key West was close enough. "Not that I wouldn't mind pitching a few with Fidel," he said, "but the stamp in your passport might not look good when you're running to become the first lady president someday."

Early one morning at the end of May, they packed up the car, following the back roads that sliced across tobacco and cotton fields until they hit Interstate 95 in Florence. From there they stopped only for gas and fast food, until twelve hours later they had left the continental United States behind them, the battered Ford Taurus making its way across the string of narrow islands where Daniel said that God must have dribbled out the last few drops of the continent after he finished making America.

Celia read to him from a guidebook while he drove, about the tiny deer that populated the islands, about how you could stand at the end of Key West and be at the southernmost tip of the nation. He nodded thoughtfully, his green eyes lighting up when she told him a particularly interesting fact. He was still a handsome man, the disappointments of his wife's death and the mill closing showing themselves only in the etched smile lines that had deepened over the past few years, remaining even after his quick grins faded. She wondered if he'd ever taken trips like this with her mother, trips that were filled with so much promise that being in transit was better than anything they might find at their destination. That summer was the last time she was able to believe absolutely in him. Her childlike confidence in the decisions her father made began to be tinged with doubt, and by the end of the summer, the doubt would turn into an all-out atheism.

He found a job showing vacation condos for a local time-share company, and they rented a furnished, two-bedroom apartment at a price Celia knew they couldn't afford. Through the connections of Daniel's boss, Celia also found work. Sparky's Bait & Tackle advertised itself as a favorite haunt of Hemingway, despite its 1982 opening date and a lobby full of kitschy Key West souvenirs: shot glasses, fish magnets, and bottle openers featuring the bearded visage of Papa himself. "Get Yr Worms and Grub On Here," a swinging wooden placard over the entrance claimed, which sounded horribly unappealing to Celia but did not seem to deter customers who came, stayed too long, and left inebriated. That summer Celia and Daniel hardly saw each other, her father working in the daytime while her shifts started at four, just before he came home. The heat of the Florida Keys in July was almost unbearable, and during the day she was too tired even to go to the beach. Sparky's weak air conditioning barely cooled the restaurant for the customers, let alone the steamy kitchen in the back, where the cooks' sweat dripped into the beer batter in which they coated pieces of conch before tossing them into the deep fryer.

Even the rare nights that she brought in over a hundred dollars in tips were not worth the stares boring into the lettering of her too-tight t-shirt ("I got baited at Sparky's"), men's thighs rubbing against hers as she scooted into the booths to take their orders (another indignity ordered by management), their hands always reaching for something. The uniform of short shorts, iridescent tights, and a suggestive t-shirt might as well have been a flashing road sign advertising her body as public property, and she'd been brushed and groped more times than she liked to remember. Her father seldom came by, feigning tiredness after long days of selling timeshares to New Jersey bankers with a fondness for Jimmy Buffett, but she wondered cynically if he knew his daughter worked at a place that, aside from the Hemingway claim, was mainly famous for breasts not of the avian kind.

"This place is not going to work out," Daniel told Celia one Wednesday in early August when she awoke to find him not at work but drinking a Bloody Mary and frying sausages and eggs at the stove. "Too many tourists making demands. I'm tired of taking orders. I'm not cut out to be told what to do." They left two days later, saying little on the drive back, both of them grateful for the sight of the rusty water tower that heralded their arrival to Deer Bluff.

Wincing as she recalled that summer, Celia wrote off the option of anything involving the food service industry. Even the word "food service industry" reminded her of the other work-study students, unfortunate enough to be placed in one of the cafeterias on campus, scooping mashed potatoes onto the plates of their wealthy classmates whose parents paid full tuition. If she asked for a work-study reassignment, this too might be her fate.

Amid more advertisements proclaiming that she would "make thousands selling Spring Break trips to your classmates," she found one that was different from the rest.

Seeking Ivy League woman, 18-24, to serve as ova donor for loving but infertile couple. Caucasian preferred but not absolutely necessary, intelligent, attractive. Ample compensation for your efforts. Send letter to Box 1279 telling us why you'd like to help.

The unassuming simplicity of the ad, the modest entreaty for help at the end, intrigued her. She had heard about a similar ad that had been placed in university newspapers across the Ivy League a few years earlier, demanding a very specific type of donor, high SAT scores, a model's good looks, and athletic abilities verging on Olympiad. But this advertisement seemed different. The writer used "woman" and not the more sterile, anonymous "female," implying respect, the integrity of a real person. Since she'd moved north, Celia had grown accustomed to thinking of herself as a woman, whereas in Deer Bluff, females of any age were always "girls," even if they were ninety years old.

Celia studied the ad. The couple wanted old-fashioned inquiries, sent to a post office box - and not even an anonymous email address. Perhaps this indicated that they were much older. Calculating the word count, the excessive use of "absolutely" in the phrase describing the race of the donor, she guessed the couple must be open minded, and not very concerned about money. The couple was "loving but infertile," together and determined to become parents despite scientific obstacles. The sum of the words, their total effect, convinced her, particularly the phrase "ample compensation," its almost iambic rhythm promising an end to economic hardship.

* * *

Wedged in traffic between a garbage truck and a Mercedes SUV that had pulled within an inch of her bumper, Elise Matthews practiced *sama vritti pranayama* breathing to de-stress. In the rearview mirror, Elise could see that the driver was only a few years older than she, with patrician features and a smooth mane of blonde hair. These women were ubiquitous in Princeton, their mammoth vehicles with the telltale rise of car seats in the back mocking Elise's inability to procreate, taunting her as an ecological dead end. She saw them moving with austere confidence through the aisles at McCaffrey's, their carts filled with twenty-dollar packages of *ahi* tuna filet and organic breakfast cereals, the whining voices of their children rising and falling like sirens as they approached and receded. The women appeared in her yoga classes, on the train to New York, at Banana Republic, and even in her dreams. In dreams they came to take Peter away from her, whisking him off into a crowd that surged like the sea to separate her from her husband.

"We have nothing to do with Princeton society," Peter replied when she related one of the recurring dreams to him. "Just because we live in this world does not mean we're part of it."

But he didn't really get it. She wanted reassurance that she had not become one of those women (minus the children, of course), her biggest fear since she'd stopped working full time to focus on getting pregnant. Would children, assuming they came, turn her into them, or could she still be a person of substance and depth? Elise tried to distinguish herself in small ways: by getting her hair cut at the mall, for instance, or by continuing her advocacy work with the rape crisis center. Her interest in the rape crisis center stemmed from something that had happened long ago, one of the few small badges of suffering she carried, against which she directed an arsenal of therapy, antidepressants, and yoga.

Elise knew, however, that suffering did not cancel out a life marked by advantages, and Peter was even better positioned for success than she was. His father was a successful internal medicine specialist in

Boston, his grandfather a timber magnate whose trust fund enabled Elise and Peter to live out their latest experiment. Though in the past they'd both lived in New York and worked full time, Peter now supported them comfortably well beyond the means of most of his graduate school peers. Peter could have been as a modern-day T.E. Lawrence, a gentleman scholar whose wealth would have allowed him ample time to gain fluency in obscure dialects of Arabic so that he might go out and pilfer the relics of the Pharaohs.

Elise, too, came from money, though only on her father's side. He was a real estate developer already on his third marriage, and although she refused to take any money from him unless it was absolutely necessary, she had allowed him to pay for college and availed herself, on occasion, of some of his vacation properties. The money was there if she needed it, but she had too much pride to ask, remembering the lesson her mother repeated throughout her childhood, "Never find yourself in a position where you have to depend on a man for anything." A child of divorce, Elise had passed the bulk of her youth with her mother, a Baltimore social worker who insisted that she had been unprepared for her college sweetheart's abandonment of his altruism for the ruthless and materialistic world of real estate.

Finally Elise managed to find a parking space next to a Japanese café and wedged her Honda between two other cars. Safely parked, she sat for a moment, her keys in her lap, concentrating on her even, four-count breathing, until her heart slowed its incessant pounding. The yoga breathing was necessitated not only by the late morning traffic but also by the mission: her twice-weekly check of the post office box she had rented for responses to their ad. In the rearview mirror she checked her makeup, rubbing away the small flecks of mascara that had gathered in the dark hollows beneath her eyes. She was disappointed in what she saw: it might have been the face of one of the Princeton moms looking back at her, pretty but on edge from all the baking and soccer practices. Her hair seemed a little too expertly highlighted, her jeans and Ferragamo loafers decidedly preppy. She shrugged off her blazer and pulled on a Patagonia parka that had been floating around in the backseat of the car; at least this mitigated the Stepford wife effect somewhat.

The post office box was the odd hurdle Elise had decided to make her potential donors jump, and it required her to do something, to physically go and check the mail, rather than lounging around the apartment waiting for the addictive beep of an email notification. Actual hard copies of letters (printed! stamped! mailed!) proved the donors' serious intentions, unlike emails that could be jotted off late at night in a dorm room.

So far the responses had yielded little that she would want in the way of genetic material for her child. An editor by profession, Elise loved language and was looking for someone with a literary bent, someone creative enough to craft an ingenious response to the carefully worded advertisement.

She opened the heavy door of the old post office, glancing up at the ancient mural that graced the post office walls, depicting British explorers in an encounter with half-naked Indians, with angels flying above the scene, clearly on the side of the colonizers. The mural was so offensive that Elise wondered why someone had not painted over it. Slipping the small key into the post office box, she was pleased to see that there were several letters waiting. Dropping the letters casually into her messenger bag, she wandered toward the coffee shop where she sometimes did her editing work, a part-time occupation that was now subsumed by the quest for parenthood. Feeling slightly guilty, she thought of her mother's admonition that she should never allow herself to depend on a man, which in effect she was doing now that her work brought in less than Peter's graduate student stipend, and hardly enough to support the expensive fertility treatments they would be undergoing.

The technical term for her body's refusal to conceive was "diminished ovarian reserve," which always made her think of an endangered species, her eggs beneath a nest on a wildlife preserve somewhere, a desolate, scrubby land that conservationists battled to keep away from developers. Sometimes she wished it were Peter's fault and not hers, but his sperm count was presumably robust and would be for another forty or fifty years. Her ovaries had failed her. She blamed herself, wondering if she hadn't inadvertently caused her infertility by starving herself, or by letting in too many of the wrong kinds of men, before Peter came along, anyway. They had tried IVF, but she had only managed to produce, in the doctor's words, "bad eggs." There was a chance, however, that her body would still hold a pregnancy, and before they resorted to traveling to China or Guatemala to adopt, they decided to try to find an egg donor. Or rather, Elise had decided this. Peter felt that the expense of fertility treatments was excessive when there were perfectly good babies available elsewhere, but Elise stubbornly insisted: having control over the prenatal environment was essential. She had other reasons that she did not verbalize. For one, she did not want their families to know that she could not have children. But most importantly, she wanted his child, the perfect little being that would pull him back into the relationship and make him fully hers again. Something was missing. She thought it might be children, though it seemed that the further they traveled down the road of infertility treatments, the more distant he became. Maybe once an actual baby was on the way, they would regain some of the lost closeness they had had, back in the days when they were both working and lived in the city.

Elise ordered a latté and an oversized oatmeal-carob cookie that would be her lunch. Choosing a table in the very back of the café, she drew the letters one by one from her bag, glancing around to make sure that no one was watching. The students, clad in shades of black and brown, were hunched over their laptops or engaged in intense, weighty discussions. Their muted, somber colors did not seem to fit in the café, with its golden wood floors and playful yellow walls decorated with an elementary school art show. For an instant Elise regretted not posting the ad in the Rutgers paper; perhaps the students there did not take themselves so seriously. Who knew—perhaps one of the letter writers was here. Or in the Arabic class where Peter served as a teaching assistant. Later she would show him their names and ask if he recognized any of them.

There were seven letters in all, and like last week's batch, most were disappointing.

I want nothing more than to give the gift of life to another couple, one of the letters read. *If I am blessed to be the one you choose…* The word "blessed" immediately ruled that one out. She folded the letter up and put it back in its envelope.

I've donated in three previous cycles and am comfortable with the procedure, read another. *Both times the doctor retrieved more than ten follicles*. No, too promiscuous. Elise didn't want to share a donor, or to be constantly looking over her shoulder for her own child's siblings.

I am a student athlete and have also been told that I am exceptionally beautiful, a third letter said. What hubris! Who did this girl think she was? Elise read the rest of the letter just out of amusement. *I am enclosing my SAT scores for your consideration; you will note that my verbal score was 770, my math score a bit lower at 750*. Elise laughed, feeling like an admissions counselor. SAT scores would not be enough in this contest.

I won't lie; I could use the money, another letter said. *While I'm not a Princeton student (my boyfriend goes here, and I read this ad in the newspaper while visiting him), I have a 3.8 average at Rutgers*. There was nothing wrong with honesty, and Elise wasn't opposed to looking outside the Ivy League. She continued reading. *I am very healthy, don't smoke or drink, but I am slightly overweight—5'4" and 160 pounds*. Slightly overweight? No way. Elise shuddered, fighting off disgust, the ghost of her former issues with anorexia welling up. She knew it was wrong to be so dismissive, but she could not help it; her belief in the lifelong quest of keeping thin remained unshaken. Peter shared this belief, although with him it was more about self-control.

Her spirits began to sink as she realized there was only one letter left. The letter was typed, though the signature at the bottom, in careful, almost juvenile cursive script, said only "Celia Bishop." Elise read the letter through in its entirety, almost unaware that she had managed to suspend her judgment until the end.

To Whom It May Concern,

That salutation sounds almost too formal and anonymous for a couple whose name I do not know, yet to whom I might give such a profound gift. Without trying to sound presumptuous, I must tell you that "ample compensation" and "donor" are phrases that I find troubling, for what kind of gift is overtly compensated? That said, I am aware (for I am in an anthropology class at the moment and we are reading Marcel Mauss' The Gift,) that the gift is poison, that to give is to enter into a reciprocal relationship with others, and that gifts are never truly unmotivated. Reciprocity, I'm learning, is complicated, and we are always being compensated somehow, even if we claim only altruism as our motive.

Before I've lost your attention, let me tell you that I'm not pretentious, just an eager learner who likes to apply what I'm learning to the little I have experienced of life. I am twenty years old, have never traveled abroad, and am an only child. My father raised me since my mother died in a car accident when I was five years old. This is an early tragedy that may have given me character, but I can't claim it, since I barely remember her. How terrible, I sometimes think, that I was part of her adult reality for five whole years, yet the curse of early childhood is such that my memories are only fragments: the texture of a dress, still hanging in the closet, in which I might have buried my face, or a passing whiff of perfume in a shopping mall, my father casually mentioning that this was a fragrance she once wore. From fragments I try to recreate her image but mostly come up with fiction. My father was the manager of a textile plant in a region of the South whose landscape often looks more like that of an underdeveloped country. I would say we were middle class and falling. My father is, nonetheless, an intelligent and thoughtful man who has always respected my education and encouraged me to live outside my region before I made up my mind that The South was the most perfect place in the world. (I never had such illusions). I use the past tense to describe my father's employment because since the mill closed down two years ago he has been unable to find something equal to his previous level of employment, and he would therefore prefer not to work at all. His hereditary gifts are the one weakness in my application to donate my eggs. I am not a drinker, however, and I don't frequent the party scene.

I am twenty, old for a sophomore (I was held back in kindergarten the year of my mother's death), on full scholarship at Princeton, still unsure of my major, but I am fond of English and creative writing. This semester our writing teacher ordered us to mine our own experiences for our writing, and it occurred to me that I have not had many, so I am seeking more. My health is good, I am a non-smoker, and my hobbies are running and reading. I am of medium height, with brown hair and green eyes. A classmate might describe me as pretty but not a standout, but this is partly due to my reserve. Underneath I am quite ambitious and strong-willed, and although these traits are not visible to most, they got me here.

As to "why I would like to help": I think your advertisement sounds like an interesting proposition, but I would want to meet you both first. I am open to donating to a gay couple if that should be the case. I would like to help for the principle reason that this sounded like an interesting job, a good way to make money while doing something to make others happy at the same time. You can probably guess from what I've said about my family that money is tight at the moment, but this is not a ploy for sympathy. If this doesn't work out, I'm sure I will find some other type of part-time work. At any rate, my email address is below. I look forward to hearing from you.

Elise folded the letter and carefully placed it back in the envelope. The letter had drawn her in, making her forget herself momentarily. Should she read it a second time, or would her editorial instincts kick in, suddenly finding flaws with a document she had initially responded to? In the bottom of Elise's messenger bag was a manuscript she was supposed to be working on; it was due later in the week, and if she didn't finish it soon, she would have to take it into the city herself.

Grudgingly Elise removed the manuscript, a mystery novel with a vague plot involving stolen religious relics, a medieval Scottish castle, and a craggy, discredited New Orleans detective who would, through the course of the mystery, make a sudden comeback, in part due to the help of that hoariest of clichés, the hooker with a heart of gold. Peter often accused her of being no more than a glorified copy editor these days, and she was embarrassed to admit to herself that this was true. Sometimes she missed her more ambitious days of editing serious literary fiction. Opening the manuscript to the page she had last been working on, her own marks over the Times-Roman typeface looked like hieroglyphs, and as she read over new sentences, the words passed through her mind without sticking. No, she would read the letter again; it was the only thing she could think about. What was there to criticize? The letter writer demonstrated a youthful exuberance, but there was no question that she was thoughtful, intelligent, and serious about donating. Copying down the girl's email address, Elise decided to begin a correspondence.

* * *

Peter moved Elise's arm off his chest and switched off the alarm next to the bed at 6:29, one minute before it would begin ringing. The days were starting to turn cold, which always made it harder to get out of bed for his six-mile run. But without a run, the world felt slightly off balance, and days without runs didn't always go as well as he would have liked.

Elise lay sprawled over most of the bed, hair in disarray and half smiling, the pages of the manuscript she was working on scattered across the floor. In sleep she looked much younger, her face free of makeup and the worry lines that seemed to be deepening lately. It wasn't like her to take so long to finish working on a book, and she'd been lugging this particular manuscript around the house for almost a month now. Although she claimed she didn't need the intensity of her former career, he wondered if they might both be happier if they could go back to the way their lives had been when she was working.

In darkness he threw on shorts, a t-shirt, and running shoes, all laid out carefully on a chair the night before. Checking the thermometer outside the kitchen window, Peter decided against a windbreaker. He grabbed his keys and let himself out of the apartment, running down the single flight of stairs to the first floor exit.

The sky began to brighten as he headed off the main road and onto the towpath that ran the length of the canal. Few people crossed his path at this hour, and he loved having the world to himself. Lately he'd found himself longing for an existence where this solitude would last all day: as a monk, perhaps, engaged only in the rhythms of prayer, tending the monastery garden, brewing wheat beer, or whatever monks did all day. He imagined that monastery life might be like the co-op he once belonged to at Brown, minus the celibacy aspect.

The desire for solitude was so strong that Peter sometimes wondered why he had chosen a profession that necessitated so much contact with other human beings. Even serving as a teaching assistant exhausted him. He had assumed that Princeton undergraduates would fall in love with the Arabic language, as he had, but instead they spent more time whining about their grades or expressing their desire to work for the CIA.

Peter concentrated on the sound of his steady breathing, the give of the sandy earth beneath his feet. Running was a time for reviewing the previous day, for preparing for the one that would follow. Those who were not in the academic world did not understand how taxing it could be. His family understood least of all. His parents had hoped he would choose a conventional career, perhaps going into medical practice with his father, but he had passed his college years deliberately avoiding pre-med courses. Even his choice of one of the more eclectic Ivies, Brown, had been suspect in his family's eyes. Although they were not exactly thrilled when he decided, several years later, to attend graduate school, the Princeton name had been a hopeful sign that their only son was moving toward a serious profession.

His interest in the Near East had begun during a Peace Corps stint in Morocco, where he was stationed in a desolate Saharan coastal town to give lessons in health education. His placement in Sidi Maarif as a healthcare worker had happened purely by coincidence, but it was enough to solidify his conviction that the medical profession was not for him. Working alongside a disaffected young doctor from Casablanca, who was completing a mandatory internship from which he could not wait to escape, depressed Peter profoundly. The health problems of their constituents, many of which would have been easily treatable in America, were overwhelming. His father's posh practice in the suburbs of Brookline seemed light-years away, and he knew he could never go into medicine without feeling a paralyzing sense of the world's injustices.

Despite the frustrations of his work, Sidi Maarif and its people, dark-skinned Sahraouis who wore vividly colored batik robes and spoke Arabic laced with Spanish, fascinated him. While most of his fellow Peace Corps colleagues worked in places once occupied by the French, Sidi Maarif had been a Spanish colonial possession, its Arabic name meaning Famous Saint. The saint in question occupied a white-domed tomb on the edge of town, and though various festivals were held in his name, nobody could remember exactly when he lived or what he had done to become famous. Aside from the saint's tomb, nothing of the original Sidi Maarif existed, as the Spanish had destroyed everything to construct their administrative capital. When they finally left in 1969, years after the French had given up their stake in the country, they abandoned an intriguing array of art deco buildings that, now fallen into disrepair, served as a potent reminder of the transience of empires.

After returning from the Peace Corps, Peter considered moving to Washington to find work in a non-profit, but his father discouraged him.

"You did your two years of good deeds," said Barry, "but now you need to start getting serious and thinking about a career. Start justifying the one hundred thousand dollar price tag of that Brown education."

Peter spent a miserable year in a financial consulting job where lunches were delivered to the lead executives on silver carts and shoeshine boys polished their shoes in the hallway outside their offices each day. After a year he defied his father by quitting, following a few of his Brown acquaintances into an Internet start-up. A friend had started a website that dispensed travel advice and allowed expatriates to post cynical but witty articles about their travel experiences. He did not share the certainty of his peers that start-ups would change the world of business forever, with their informal dress codes and Friday afternoon office keg parties. It was work that did not seem like work, but in fact nothing had seemed like work since his days in the clinic in Sidi Maarif, dispensing advice about vitamin supplements to mothers whose severely anemic children had pica, or the desire to eat dirt.

Peter drifted up the ranks of the company, leaving just before the start-up folded. He entered the publishing industry, joining the formerly quaint and tweedy Smyth & Copperfield, now a small cog in the giant wheel of the Viador media empire, better known for turning out Hollywood blockbusters than serious literary fiction. At Smyth & Copperfield he took a low-paying job working on travel guides and met Elise. Elise had started out at the bottom right after college as an editorial assistant at Knopf, jumping from publishing house to house until she arrived at her current position, managing a list of esteemed writers who were known for their social consciousness, their books about topics ranging from sustainable development to the devastation wrought by colonialism. Getting her to date and then marry him had been something of a coup: months of her barely noticing him hovering around her desk followed by a blissful courtship where every little discovery they made about one another (their shared fondness for the music of Fela Kuti, for example, or for Cherry Garcia ice cream) seemed to confirm they were meant for each other. His parents were enamored with her, praising her poise and confidence almost to the point that Peter hoped her drive to succeed might be enough to carry both of them permanently into his parents' good graces.

Elise possessed a headstrong determination that he had once longed to emulate. His inclination to give careful consideration to his every move led him into states of torpor and indecision. He admired her conviction that every decision was the right one, no matter how hastily considered. While his career choices struck him as mere time-fillers, she loved books and publishing and never seemed to tire of her work. When he announced he wanted to go to graduate school to study the Middle East, he hoped this spontaneous plan would be one they could both believe in, something unexpected but not entirely out of the blue, considering his Peace Corps days in Morocco. She agreed, happy he had finally figured out his calling, and together they had moved to Princeton.

Five years later Peter had notched onto his belt of accomplishments a fluency in Arabic (classical, modern, and three dialects), Ottoman Turkish, and a working knowledge of Hebrew. In the department he was praised for his skill with languages. After defending his master's exams the previous spring, he was in the early stages of his dissertation, a study of the encounters between medieval Sufi mystics and Arab explorers. Finding a dissertation topic had not been easy. Peter buried himself so deeply in scholarship that he found a thousand different subjects to be fascinating, each topic worthy of several years of focused study. He could spend an entire day lost in the richness of a single paragraph, tracing the etymology of words no longer in use, recreating the richness of lost empires from the descriptions of long-dead travelers.

Lately he had begun to feel pressure from his wife to hasten his efforts. Elise had been supportive at first, but after several years of commuting to her own job in New York, she hinted that she was tired of the arrangement. She had submitted her resume to the local university presses but received no offers, arranging instead with her boss at Smyth & Copperfield to work on a freelance basis. In Elise's encouragement that he narrow his topic and proceed further along in his writing, he heard only her frustration with the pace of their lives in Princeton. But Peter was uncertain. Why should they be in such a rush to force their lives onward, to march into the respectable adulthood his parents impatiently longed for, when everything had been moving along just fine?

Peter left the canal towpath behind, winding his way toward campus through the back streets with their oversized oaks and stately Victorian houses. He tried to remember if he had a full change of clothes in his gym locker. Sometimes he couldn't bear to make the complete loop back to his apartment. She had always been a great conversationalist, until recently. Now, all their conversations were abbreviated in the handy code words of infertility: IUI, IVF, FSH, BFN, BFP. Despite his best intentions to be supportive he sometimes tuned her out, her words slipping through his brain like so much water, like the thousands of dollars that had already disappeared on tests and ineffective treatments. Much of their time together over the past two years had been spent in well-appointed doctor's offices where they were encouraged to believe they could beat the odds if they just submitted themselves to another costly procedure. The money they'd spent so far could have supported a thousand diabetics in Morocco for a year, or paid for trips for a thousand women to visit the domed shrines of saints known for their powers to bring children to the barren. A couple of graduate students they'd invited over for dinner once had found success with similar methods after Western medicine failed them. Ultimately what worked, the wife said, was a combination of Mayan abdominal massages in addition to treatments from a *curandero* they'd met in Mexico City, who gave them a fertility drink made from reptile parts and bee nectar that was stronger than any Clomid a doctor could prescribe. Elise laughed when he brought it up.

"They were anthropologists," she said dismissively. "Of course they'd believe in some weird method of native folk wisdom."

Although he understood the societal pressure Elise, in her mid-thirties, felt to have a baby, he did not know why she needed to go to such extreme lengths once it was obvious motherhood was not going to come easily. With no biological clock to worry about, why not wait until he finished his dissertation and they could think about adopting?

He thought of the American couple he had known during his Peace Corps days who had adopted in Morocco. Moroccan law required the parents be Muslim, to ensure the child would not be raised out of the faith. But adoption was an anathema to most Moroccans, who believed in the purity of bloodlines. The couple, career expatriates who had lived in Morocco for several years, converted, managing to convince the relevant authorities of their sincere profession of faith and eventually adopting two Moroccan children. At the time Peter had been shocked by the lengths they had gone to obtain children, but now, even converting to Islam seemed easier than what he and Elise were about to do. But he refrained from mentioning his doubts at the fertility clinic, where they were both required to undergo a psychological screening to ensure that they were ready for the rigors involved in contracting an egg donor.

Elise was interviewing a prospective donor this very afternoon. The clinic had suggested they seek an anonymous donor, but she had other ideas. Peter thought they should meet several of their respondents before deciding, but Elise's instincts told her that the girl who wrote the best letter was fated to be their donor. Her latest scheme was a word association questionnaire, a Rorschach test of sorts, which she emailed to the girl before Peter could tell her not to.

"Off the top of your head: give me three words that describe something you either adore or detest," Elise had asked a few nights before.

"Solitude," he answered. "Indecision. Pressure."

"Not conditions," she answered, oblivious to the fact that his three words related to his current feelings about his existence, although maybe they were more opaque than he meant them to be. "Things. Things in and of themselves that you have strong feelings about."

"Sufis. The Sphinx. Sushi."

"I didn't know you were that into pharaohs," Elise said. "Did you choose to alliterate on purpose?"

"I like the Sphinx because it's unreadable. Sufis are obviously my dissertation topic. And you know my favorite food is sushi. What do you expect to learn from this?" But Elise had already hit the send button. Celia was to write down her associations with a list of words or phrases that Elise had strong feelings about, some of which included plastic foliage, Starbucks, baseball, country music and Hemingway. This was certainly going too far, Peter thought, but Elise was pleased with the results. Celia wrote her back the same night.

"Listen, she hates country music, even though she's a southerner." Elise was reading the message she had just received on her laptop.

"Were you worried she carried the gene for liking country music?" Peter said dryly. His wife ignored him.

"For Starbucks, she wrote 'Globalization.' Plastic flowers are 'cheesy.' I knew I liked this girl."

"What did she say about my words?"

"Sufis: 'don't know what that is, just being honest here.' The Sphinx… listen to this, she actually wrote 'unknowable and mysterious.' Isn't that what you said earlier?"

"I said 'unreadable.'"

"But this is interesting. Next to Hemingway, she wrote 'Dad.' She's a reader; I love that. She's alluding to the fact that everyone called him Papa."

"How do you know? Maybe her dad just likes reading Hemingway." But Elise just laughed and continued to go on about Celia, and how they were obviously all meant for one another.

Peter ended his run in front of the gray stone façade of the Dillon Gym. Instead of going home he would shower, get breakfast at the campus center, and head straight to the library. A rare account of a man who had traveled with the great medieval explorer Ibn Battuta awaited him, ready to be scoured for references to Sufis. For eight hours at least he could postpone reality.

CHAPTER TWO

Meeting in the Small World Café, as Elise had suggested, now did not seem like such a good idea. Through the window Celia could see that the café was crowded with other students and professors, and while she recognized none of them, she still felt nervous that a classmate might spot her and wonder what she was planning. Next to her on the bench outside the cafe, a man with a shaved head and three identical hoop earrings sat reading the *New York Times*, a sinewy German shepherd panting obediently at his feet. She could almost hide behind Sinbad's newspaper, peering out at the people walking by to speculate on which one might be Elise. Celia had worn a black pea coat and Elise mentioned that she would be wearing black pants, but these were such indistinct details she was afraid they would not recognize each other.

A woman veered suddenly toward the bench with such purpose that Sinbad's dog lifted his head as if alert to the signs of danger. The woman's red hair tumbled wildly over her shoulders, and she wore a green velvet coat over black, flowing pants, her eyes trained on Celia's. Celia stood up.

"Marco," the woman said. Sinbad folded his newspaper and stood up to kiss the redheaded woman on both cheeks. The university community was full of these assured global denizens, who gave off an air that made Celia imagine they spent their summers in faraway places like Istanbul or Ibiza and their waking hours at Princeton imbibing postmodern social theory. Embarrassed, she pretended she had meant to get up all along, letting the woman take her place on the bench. Looking down at her watch, she saw that it was already several minutes past the hour, and she wondered if Elise might have lost her nerve.

"Celia?" The uncertain voice belonged to a woman about her own height, straight blonde hair cut just below her chin, framing a sharp nose and a china doll complexion. She half-smiled at Celia, offering a firm handshake. But her expressive blue eyes offset the impression of aloofness.

"I thought after I suggested this place that perhaps we should go somewhere else," Elise said. "I might see one of my husband's colleagues here, and I'd have to introduce you."

"That's exactly what I was thinking," Celia agreed.

"Listen to that pretty accent," Elise said, sizing Celia up.

"I'm trying to lose it," Celia blushed.

"Why would you want to do that? It's charming. Hey, why don't we go to the Italian café around the block?" Elise suggested. "I'm dying for a glass of wine."

It was only three o'clock, and as she followed Elise to the other café, Celia thought of her father, how Daniel would always say it was five o'clock somewhere. An upscale Mediterranean-themed place with ropes of garlic hanging from the ceiling, Mediterra was more a restaurant than a café, empty except for two older women, impeccably dressed in perfectly matched powder blue and lavender suits that dated them to the Kennedy era. A half-finished bottle of white wine sat in a silver bucket next to them.

Elise chose a table near the window, the waiter hovering with a pitcher of ice water to fill their glasses as soon as they sat down. A dish of peppery olive oil and a basket of bread seemed to appear magically in front of them.

"I'll have *pinot grigio*," Elise ordered. "They make a great cappuccino here, would you like one?" Celia nodded.

For a moment they both looked at each other, and Celia sensed Elise carefully appraising her features.

"Sorry, I had to get a drink - I've been so nervous about meeting you," Elise said. "You're much more attractive than you described yourself. Celia blushed. She had straightened her wavy, dark brown hair with the blow dryer and taken extra care to apply makeup, something she did not normally do. Next to Elise, however, she knew she lacked polish. Elise looked expensive, with a shimmering diamond on one hand and small diamonds at her ears, her silky beige sweater and black pants setting off a whippet-like figure.

"I'm talking too much," Elise apologized. "I know these are rather strange circumstances we're meeting under. I thought I could tell you more about Peter and me, and anything you might want to know about this whole procedure. Did you read the material I sent you?"

The thick envelope from the fertility clinic contained pamphlets promoting the joys of the gift, emphasizing the time and the expenses involved, not the eggs themselves. They downplayed the negatives, such as the hormone-filled shots she would have to administer herself, and the painful "harvesting" process, the word making Celia think of hayrides and bobbing for apples. Celia had also spent some time looking at infertility blogs, which told heartbreaking stories of women who'd been at it for years, enduring one failed pregnancy or miscarriage after another. She wondered if Elise had one of these blogs, or if she might have been one of the women whose plaintive posts she'd glanced at on the forum that the bloggers all referred to as "the Boards." Brokeneggs37, for example, sent out erudite dispatches from "a township in Jersey." Or maybe Elise was the woman whose blog was titled "Waiting for my Ivy Baby," which documented the torment of attending college reunions and witnessing all the future little Ivy League grads her industrious fellow alumni were producing.

"I did some research," Celia said. "It all seems pretty involved. And the clinic is not so close. I'm not sure how I would get there for the ultrasounds and the, umm, harvesting. I don't have a car."

"We could take you," Elise said. "That is, if we decide to do this. But getting there shouldn't be a problem." The waiter approached their table, bringing their drinks. Celia tore open an oblong package of sugar, watching the sugar crystals dissolve into the golden brown surface of her coffee.

"Is it…. normal to get to know your donors this well?"

"Not necessarily." Elise took a sip of her wine. "But there aren't really any rules... I'm not expecting you would be involved in the baby's life, but I would like to be able to tell my children who their biological mother was. Not just details like your medical history. I want to get a sense of your personality. Oh, and we should also probably discuss compensation."

"Compensation…" Celia repeated. "What did y'all have in mind?"

"We'd like to offer seven thousand dollars. The prices range all over the place, but we also realize that this whole getting-to-know-you process is emotionally and mentally time-consuming, so we think this is pretty generous. And of course you and I both want the option to back out at any time, should we find something not to our liking." From the offhand way Elise offered the amount, it seemed that money meant little or nothing. Embarrassed, Celia changed the subject.

"What does your husband look like?"

"My husband?"

"I'm only wondering because you and I look nothing alike."

"Oh, I'm not a real blonde, if that's what you're thinking," she said. "My hair is actually about the same color as yours. I've been considering letting it go back to its natural color. I used to wear it long, too, which is a very becoming look when you're young. And your eyes are green, but did you know that green is a mutation of the gene for blue? So a blue-eyed parent could have a green-eyed child. My husband has dark hair and dark eyes. Scottish ancestry, but I think there could be some Native American in there too. With your coloring you resemble him a little more than you do me."

"My great-grandma was Cherokee," Celia volunteered. "The rest is pure Carolina cracker."

Elise's eyes widened.

"I don't exactly come from nobility," she continued. "But my family has been in the United States for two hundred years. Scotch-Irish, mostly, ancestors fought in the Civil War. On the wrong side. Where I come from, it's still called the War of Northern Aggression. My parents were the first in their families to go to college."

"Cherokee, that bit is appealing. Trail of Tears and all that. It would explain your high cheekbones." Elise had already drained her glass and was motioning for the waiter to bring her another one. "You know something about your heritage then. Do you have any records, copies of a genealogy, anything like that?"

"No, mostly just what my dad has told me," Celia explained. "My great-grandma, the Cherokee one, died long before I was born."

Elise had already moved on. "I'm hoping you'll agree with the compensation, oh, and you have to meet Peter, too, just as a formality, but I'm sure he'll like you. He's pretty much given me a free hand with this. If you agree with the money, you'd have to have a physical, administered by one of the doctors at the clinic. And then a psychological screening. I guess you read the other details; I hope you're not squeamish."

"I don't think I would have written if I were."

"I did have a few questions about your father's alcoholism," Elise said. Her second glass of wine arrived.

Celia told her how it had started. Daniel had always been a drinker, but he never drank every day, only a couple beers here and there while watching football on the weekends, or the occasional happy hour after work. Still, he had been both father and mother to her, picking her up from the after-school program at 5:30 when she was younger, diligently cooking the same repertoire of four or five different meals for her supper (spaghetti, roast chicken, taco dinner kits, and chili), shuttling Celia to dance practice three nights each week, or later, when she was in high school, remembering exactly what time track practice and literary magazine meetings would end.

"You were a dancer too?" Elise said, delighted. "I did ballet for twelve years. May have contributed to the anorexia I developed in college, but it gave me a certain amount of discipline. Anyway. Go on."

Celia paused, surprised by the intimacy of this revelation, but she managed to recover quickly. "After the mill closed, it was like his life was over. He was devastated; as the day manager, he was one of the highest men at the mill, and he was so invested in his work. The employees criticized him. They blamed him for the plant closing, but losing the mill hurt our whole community. Anayo Mills was the largest employer in Deer Bluff. After that, he just started to fall apart."

"How long ago was that?"

"A few years ago. He drinks pretty heavily now, but he's quiet about it. He never starts fights in bars or anything like that. Mostly he just falls asleep in his chair in front of the TV. We were collecting unemployment for a while. He had one scheme to move to Key West and start over, but that didn't work out." Their family savings, a life insurance settlement after her mother's car accident that was supposed to be for Celia's college education, had by now all but disappeared.

"Well, his alcoholism doesn't sound that dire," Elise said, her face filled with concern. "But I'm really sorry to hear about his job. It must have been tough for both of you."

"I'm not needy or anything," Celia said. "I have a pretty decent scholarship. I'm going to be fine. I just wanted to do this… I had some issues with my work study assignment and I wanted to work outside the university." She told Elise about Dr. Crenshaw, pleased that her descriptions of her former employer finally made Elise break out into laughter.

"There are some eccentrics at the university, that's for sure," Elise said. "In my husband's department there are a few. Like Youssef Kronenberg, formerly Joe Kronenberg of Brooklyn. Once Jewish, now a convert to Islam. Peter says he spends his weekends twirling around in a skirt and chanting the ninety-nine names of God."

"What is it with that number, ninety-nine?" Celia said. "Dr. Crenshaw claimed he was allergic to over ninety-nine different varieties of dust."

"It must be a code you learn when you're hired here," Elise said. "But anyway. You've told me a lot about you. What else would you like to know about me?"

Elise never sat still, her hand constantly tapping on the table or fiddling with her hair or her wineglass, but somehow she still seemed poised. Her nervousness gave the impression that at any moment she might declare the conversation over, jump up and leave the restaurant. Celia wanted to hold her attention. She knew that Elise had grown up in Baltimore, spent four years at NYU, and had worked in publishing ever since college. Her confidence made Celia want to work at saying amusing things that might keep her there a few minutes longer.

"Why did you decide to go with an egg donor?" she asked. "Why not adopt?"

"I want the whole childbirth experience," Elise said. "I want to control the prenatal environment. And I think it will be an experience that will bring me closer together with Peter. He desperately wants to have children."

"How did you meet your husband?"

"We met at a book party for one of my writers. That must have been seven years ago. At the time we were working at the same place. But we were both busy and didn't end up going out until a few months after we met. After that, it was pretty clear we were going to be together. We got married after he started graduate school, and I moved to Princeton from New York. He's been in grad school for five years now. Finally he's started writing his dissertation."

Celia detected frustration in Elise's voice, but she did not offer further details. The quiet of the restaurant was broken only by the murmuring voices of the two older women, still locked in conversation.

"I should be going," Celia apologized. *Always be the first to leave*, she remembered her senior English teacher, Mr. Lenhart, told his students. He routinely left the classroom before them. *It's a way to get the upper hand.* "I have to go study. I'm still interested, so let me know what your husband wants to do." This would give Elise a way out if she decided that Celia wasn't suitable for the job. She hoped Elise would decide in her favor.

Walking back to the library, she wondered if Elise were the kind of person she would have befriended, had they been the same age. Celia had only a few friends at Princeton, mostly other scholarship students like herself. They gravitated naturally toward one another, sharing their inability to afford spring break trips to the Bahamas and the distinction of having been academic standouts plucked from places like Biloxi, Mississippi or Bangor, Maine. But it was clear Elise had not been one of them. Her polish would have come from boarding schools and summers at Martha's Vineyard; she was of the same breed as Nicole Sumner. Celia flew under the radar of students like that, who moved in circles so tightly closed to outsiders there was no way that someone without money could penetrate. By contrast, Celia imagined herself to be a charity case, a curiosity, someone whose lack of money and pedigree made her an untouchable in an almost invisible caste system.

* * *

Expecting Celia to press her more about why she wanted a baby so badly, Elise was surprised that she took it all for granted. Unlike Peter, Celia seemed to think nothing of the lengths to which she was willing to go to have children. Elise liked the way Celia seemed to take her entire situation in stride; she even downplayed her father's alcoholism, their stint on welfare. Her stoicism in the face of such a blow further endeared Celia to her; Elise wanted to help. Even if Celia did not admit it, she clearly needed a mentor in her life. Perhaps this would be another, less tangible way that Elise could compensate her.

She let herself back into their sparsely furnished graduate student apartment. Their apartment was small, but they'd brought a nice mix of functional and classic pieces from their lives in New York, leaving the rest of their furniture in storage for the distant time in the future when they would finally have a real place again. Throwing her bag on the leather sofa, she poured herself a glass of wine and sat down to work on the overdue manuscript while she waited to tell Peter the news about Celia. She was annoyed when he texted her that he was going to a Tunisian film being shown by the Comp Lit department, but at least this gave her more time to work.

By ten o'clock Peter still had not returned, so Elise took a sleeping pill and got dressed for bed, checking her schedule for the next day on the computer. In addition to stopping by the office to meet with her boss, there was the usual appointment with Dr. Geiger. Lately Elise's meetings with her psychiatrist were the highlight of her week. She knew that her fixation with the baby issue drove Peter a little crazy, and talking to Dr. Geiger about Celia would help her figure out where she stood, so she could present her position later to Peter in a clean narrative, free of the anxieties he had little tolerance for. Peter liked certainty, tolerating indecision only in himself. He preferred the less conflicted side she had presented to him in the early stages of their courtship. Uncomfortable with ambiguity, he did better when he was simply presented with decisions as a fait accompli.

"How do you think Celia perceived you?" Dr. Geiger asked the next day. It was the type of question that she wished Peter would ask. But he would not recognize that such a question was essential to sorting out her feelings on a situation, would instead interpret this as an invitation to more navel gazing, his view of therapy in general.

"I don't know," Elise tucked her feet underneath her on the sofa where she sat opposite Dr. Geiger, who reclined in a black leather Mies Van Der Rohe chair. Elise loved the minimalist décor of his office, the only spot of color a shaggy burgundy rug on the floor. She longed for the day when she and Peter could have a house peppered with modernist treasures. "If I were her age, I guess I would be inclined to view myself as hopelessly old."

"Do you really think she saw you that way?" Dr. Geiger said. "What I'm getting at is, do you think there's a conflict in how you presented yourself and how she saw you?"

"No," Elise said firmly. "I know that people have told me that when they first met me, they thought I was charismatic. But I also know that the impression of charisma fades with time, and then I start to become like any other person, full of flaws and insecurities."

"Who has told you that?"

"Some of the most important people in my life. Peter, for example. My best friend Caitlin. They were both drawn to me for my confidence. But over time, I think they realized it was all a façade. That didn't hurt my friendship with Caitlin, but with Peter, I think the marriage has suffered."

"You wanted him to continue to idealize you, then."

"It's not that," Elise protested. "I just want to remain in control."

"Control," Dr. Geiger said. "That word again." He looked down at his yellow legal pad.

"The recurring theme of my life," Elise said. "The response of disordered eating. Why is it that we believe that once you experience something, it becomes a part of you forever? Alcoholics, for example. They're branded for life. They can be clean for thirty years and they still think of themselves as alcoholic. I'm fine, but the anorexia still haunts me in odd ways."

"Fine even though yesterday you skipped lunch and ate only a cookie?" he asked.

"I make trade-offs, just like French women do. You want the wine, you don't get the dessert." He looked at her with one eyebrow raised, an expression that always led her to think a little harder about her decisions.

"I'd like to go back to something you said a few minutes ago." Dr. Geiger read from his legal tablet. "You said a few minutes ago that you wanted to take control of the situation with your donor by choosing to know her. This is interesting, don't you think? Is it the situation you want to control or the girl, Celia?"

Elise crossed and uncrossed her legs, searching for a comfortable position. "I don't know. The situation. Maybe it's as simple as that."

Dr. Geiger nodded and wrote something else down. They were almost out of time. This always happened; just as they were starting to get somewhere, their hour was up.

After stopping at Dean & Deluca's to buy a special walnut oil Peter liked in his salads, Elise went to her office to meet with Diana. Diana was on the phone, but she waved Elise in with one hand, the other hand clicking away at her mouse, deleting a stream of emails on the computer screen in front of her.

"Ida, I'll have to call you back. I've got another meeting." Diana hung up the phone and looked at Elise, taking in her jeans and linen blouse with an expression of disapproval. Diana Berg wore crisp white shirts and dark tailored suits every day, no matter what the season.

"You missed the 10:30 conference call. I was hoping you'd be here. Didn't you get my emails?"

"I'm here now," Elise said. "But I was in another appointment all morning."

"You have a Blackberry," Diana scolded. "Don't you read your emails when they come in?"

An acquisitions editor, Diana Berg had drawn some major names to Smyth & Copperfield in the three years since she began working there. She lived alone and had no children, attachments that might have prevented her from rising so high in her profession.

"You've been a bit distracted lately," Diana said.

"I've never missed a deadline, have I?" Elise sat down, looking at Diana across her desk.

"No, you haven't. But your work has become a little sloppy."

"Sloppy in what way?" Elise asked.

"Well, your editing on the last Chopaholic mystery was a disaster." Elise rolled her eyes. She hated working on the Chopaholic mysteries, with their pink covers, their plucky heroine, Tabitha, and pages full of product placements. The fictional Tabitha hosted a cooking show and solved murders invariably committed with trendy kitchen appliances. "I had to have another editor redo it," Diana said. She clicked on her computer screen. "Page thirty-seven, you missed a glaring run-on. Forty-two, the author repeats a whole paragraph, which you didn't catch. Sixty-three, but you did this for the whole book, you let sentences like this stand: 'Esmerelda reached deeply into the pockets of her Burberry and withdrew what might have been the fuchsia MAC Milan Mode lipstick Esmerelda normally wore, but which Tabitha knew might actually contain the *habañero* pepper spray with which she swiftly immobilized her victims.' Elise, this sentence is terrible."

"Tell me about it," Elise said. "All those adverbs."

"You also left the little dots out of M☐A☐C. Can you imagine what a disaster this would have been if it had gone to print?"

Under normal circumstances, Elise might have been wounded by her boss' scolding, but she was beginning to loathe herself in this role. The indignity of it all! The former editor of Booker prize-winning novels, reduced to copyediting Sex and-the City-rip-off, chic-lit murder mysteries. She offered her boss a conciliatory smile.

"I'm sorry. I've had some family issues lately. But I'll try to be more careful."

"I don't think that's good enough," Diana said. "I know you've been here a long time, which was why I was willing to consider this arrangement. But that was on a trial basis."

"Are you letting me go?" Elise asked.

"Not exactly," Diana said. "I'm telling you that we really need you here in the office. This part-time thing isn't working for me anymore."

Elise considered Diana's proposal. A year before, she would have agreed to anything Diana suggested, would have dusted off her power suits and hopped on the New Jersey Transit first thing the next morning. But she was burned out. If this was apparent from the quality of her work even as a copy editor, then it must be a sign. If only Peter would hurry up and finish so she could find out where she might be next. Hopefully not the Midwest, or, God forbid, the South.

"Elise?" Diana prompted her.

"I'm going to have to offer my resignation. My personal situation has gotten complicated."

"Do you want to talk about it? Your personal situation, I mean." Diana furrowed her eyebrows and affected a look of concern, but Elise didn't believe her. Diana never wanted to hear about anyone's "personal situation."

"No, I just wish you'd give me another chance to work from home."

"In this economy," Diana sighed, "I really can't. We can't afford your mistakes."

"I don't think I can come back." Elise got up from her chair.

"As you like." Diana pressed her lips together in a thin smile. "At least take a day to think about it. It's not something you have to decide here, on the spot."

"I've decided," Elise said. She smiled brightly at Diana.

Diana studied her for a minute. Elise considered telling her about the fertility clinic, the doctor's visits, the endless hours she had to put into researching her options for having a child. But someone like Diana wouldn't understand. She was not the slightest bit interested in children, or, apparently, a personal life.

"Well, then." Diana turned in her chair, already back to her computer screen. She didn't look at Elise. "We'll be sorry to see you go."

Elise walked slowly back toward the subway. Without a manuscript to lug around, her bag felt unbelievably light. Not having the burden of work to worry about was an immense relief. Her mother would be disappointed to hear she wasn't working, but Elise was old enough to make her own choices.

She decided to stop in a café near work, where she ordered a salad and a glass of wine to celebrate. Around her, people on their lunch breaks ate quickly, and she felt inordinately pleased with herself for escaping the everyday world of work, its hectic pace, the mind-numbing sense of routine. She almost wished she could stop by Dr. Geiger's office to talk about it.

Before getting on the train, Elise allowed herself to buy a copy of a pregnancy book that she'd been wanting. *Organic Pregnancy*, the title read. It was a book she hoped Peter would also appreciate, given his health consciousness. The entire first chapter covered the steps she should be taking, even before becoming pregnant. A superstitious fear that she might jinx the pregnancy had prevented her from getting the book until now, but the meeting with Diana clinched her sense of certainty that the current path she was on was fated, inevitable. Celia was the right choice, she was certain.

At the Princeton train station, she picked up her car and drove toward McCaffrey's supermarket, but even the sight of the stay-at-home moms shopping in the middle of the day did not trouble her. *I'll be one of you soon*, she thought to herself. Elise bought a pound of tiger shrimp, fresh tomatoes from Chile, a bunch of basil, a wedge of Saint André, and a baguette. At home she set to work preparing an elaborate shrimp risotto she knew Peter liked, tossing chopped shallots and garlic in butter, stirring the fat grains of Arborio rice into the buttery mixture, adding chopped tomatoes, deglazing the pan with white wine and then adding the chicken broth. While the risotto simmered (she would throw in the shrimp and the chopped basil at the last minute), she checked her computer to see if Peter was online.

"Celebratory dinner at seven," she typed. "I have lots of news."

"I'll be there," he wrote back. She looked to see who else was online. Finding Diana's name, Elise deleted her from her contact list, as well as two other acquaintances from work. Noticing that Celia's name was highlighted, she decided to invite her over for dinner. Peter might as well meet her as soon as possible.

"Want to come over for dinner? I've made shrimp risotto," she wrote. "You could meet Peter."

"What time?" Celia replied. Poor Celia was probably studying alone in her dorm room with no plans for the evening. Elise was certain Peter would love her.

* * *

At 6:30 Peter closed the book he was reading, a weighty book about sea exploration in the fifteenth century. Somehow it must relate to his dissertation, but as of yet he wasn't sure how. He climbed the stairs to the main floor of the Firestone Library, which at this hour hummed with activity, the large reading room with its high ceilings and tall windows packed with industrious students hunched over chemistry notes and history books. Heading to the exit, he passed one of his students from his Introductory Arabic class, a boy with a brush cut and a face dotted with acne who had expressed interest in someday using his Arabic to work for the CIA. Peter had to fight his dislike for Kevin, who saw the Middle East as a hostile, monolithic region and showed no interest in learning more about the beauty or diversity of its people.

"Hey Professor," Kevin said. "I went looking for you after class but you weren't in your office hours. Could we talk for a second?"

"I was in my office hours," Peter sighed. "I must have just been in the bathroom. Actually, I'm running late for dinner, can this wait?" He tried to keep moving, but Kevin matched his stride.

"I wanted to talk about the grade you gave me on my last paper."

Peter stopped in the lobby.

"The paper that was supposed to be about culture?" he asked. "You mean the one where you wrote that Israel is the only civilized country in the region?"

"Yes, you gave me a D. I thought that seemed a little undeserved."

"You didn't respond to the question correctly."

"You mean I didn't answer in a way that pandered to your political views."

"No, you didn't do what the assignment asked. I asked you to write about some aspect of Middle Eastern culture, not a polemic. I didn't ask you to make value judgments. No culture is more or less civilized than any other."

"Depends on your definition of culture. I was defining culture as the elevation of civilization, which Israel has reached. They've got world-class orchestras to prove it. Not like their barbaric neighbors."

"Barbaric?" Peter said. "You can't use words like that."

"I can't call suicide bombings barbaric?" Kevin argued. "Honor killings? Last time I checked, both practices were popular in that neighborhood, except for Israel."

"How about targeted assassinations?" Peter said, wanting to bite his tongue but finding himself unable to do so. He tried to keep his voice low, but the security guard was listening with interest. "How about torture in the prisons?"

"Terrorists don't play by the rules, so why should we have to when we're dealing with them? These are exceptional times."

"Hitler claimed that, too." Peter knew he was on dangerous territory.

"Well, it seems obvious to me that I got a D because you didn't like my subject, not because of the grammar, which was acceptable. I had Dr. Thomas look it over and he had no problems with it. He said he would have given it an A."

"Dr. Thomas is neither your professor nor your teaching assistant," he responded. "And whether you're writing in Arabic and English, the subject matter is just as important as the grammar and style. You did not write about culture. You wrote a political polemic. Had you written about Israeli wedding ceremonies or Bedouin goat herding practices, you would have been on safer ground. Just remember the parameters of the assignment next time."

"I certainly will, Doctor… or wait, you're not a doctor yet, are you." He smirked. "I'll definitely keep this in mind." Kevin looked at him pointedly then turned to go back into the library.

Peter stepped out into the chilly September air. He had no interest in bringing politics into the classroom and only wished that he could teach without feeling that students cared only about their grades. If only they were there to learn Arabic because of their love for the language's unconventional beauty, and for the region's rich and compelling history! He was used to students complaining about their grades—this was Princeton, after all, and the students were competitive—but Kevin made him nervous. The professor he was assisting as a teaching assistant, a Lebanese expert on 19th century Levantine social history, would back him up here. He would have to tell her about all of this before Kevin went to her, if he hadn't already.

His discussion with Kevin made him late for dinner. Elise wouldn't care, but Peter preferred order, and for his own sanity he liked to parcel the day out into planned tasks, just to make sure they were completed. The run at six thirty each day, shower and breakfast, and on campus no later than eight thirty, ensconced in his carrel. Teaching from eleven to twelve on Mondays, Wednesdays, and Fridays, followed by a lunch, sometimes brought from home or else in the student union. Back in the library from one until three, a coffee break at the hour when he was most likely to get drowsy, then more work again until at least six o'clock. Office hours on Wednesdays from three to five.

The dissertation would only be completed if he were meticulous about his ordering of time. Inspiration without discipline was nothing. At night he could be more spontaneous, going out for the occasional dinner and a movie, or, if Elise were out of town, a beer at the grad student bar. Arranging his life this way offered just enough comfort to prevent him from other excesses that might afflict him if he dropped his insistence on routine. Sometimes even the slightest deviation from the schedule led to chaos, and when this happened he might find himself needing to spend a good hour arranging his books, first by descending order of size, then alphabetically, then by publication date. Without the routine, other troubling behaviors threatened to appear, operating beyond his volition.

Unlocking the door to their apartment, he breathed in the smell of seafood. Seated at the functional wooden IKEA table drinking wine with Elise was a girl he didn't recognize. He wondered if Elise had started working at the rape crisis center again. When she did, it was not uncommon for him to come home to find unfamiliar faces around the dinner table, fellow activists, or girls whom Elise was helping to get through difficult times. He suspected she had boundary issues, so he'd been relieved that she was not volunteering as much lately.

"Peter, this is Celia," Elise said. She stood up to shake his hand. For a minute her name did not register, and Peter tried to recall where Elise might have met her. A friend from yoga class, maybe? Suddenly he remembered where Elise had been yesterday, and why he had avoided coming home until the last possible instant, when she was already asleep.

"This is…" he stalled, reaching out his hand to shake Celia's as she stood up to meet him, her face slightly flushed, whether from the wine or the awkwardness of the meeting, he wasn't sure. She seemed so young; she could have been one of his students, one of the masses of slender, elfin girls who populated the Princeton campus, with perfect, television-commercial hair and shiny white teeth. She wore the requisite long hair over her shoulders, jeans, and a t-shirt from a bar that claimed to be in Key West but was probably the creation of a marketer at Old Navy. She looked at him expectantly.

"I'm sorry, I didn't know I'd be meeting you this soon," he said. "Elise didn't mention…"

"She caught me just as I was about to leave for dinner," Celia said. "Risotto sounded a lot better than the usual fare they serve in the cafeteria."

"What are they serving in the cafeterias these days?" Elise said. "When I was in college, I avoided the cafeteria assiduously. But then, I avoided food in all its guises, institutional or otherwise."

After a few drinks, Elise became expansive, her personality a little more outsized. He knew she was planting the comments about food on purpose. *Ask me about my eating disorder.* But Celia was diplomatic, not falling for the bait.

"I bet the food is the same from when you were in college; they've just updated the names. Like calling something *penne arrabiata* changes the fact that it's really just spaghetti and tomato sauce with a dash of Tabasco."

Peter smiled and sat down at the table.

"Wine?" Elise lifted the bottle in his direction, already half finished.

"Just a bit," he said. "What kind of cheese is that?"

"Your favorite—St. André triple cream."

"How decadent. What's the occasion?" he asked. Elise angled her head in Celia's direction.

"Celia's agreed to help us out," she said, placing her hand over his. "She's going to help us have a baby."

"Well," Peter said, unsure how to respond. She had not even consulted him—wasn't he supposed to have met Celia first? First to approve Elise's choice, and then to get the business over with in a clinic, with as little contact with the donor as possible? But here she was in their home, as if Elise intended to adopt her in the process.

"I told her you still needed to approve, so she knows we haven't fully decided, but I think we're almost there." Elise put her other hand on Celia's in a gesture that seemed rehearsed. "But we're very grateful she's agreed to help if we decide to go through with this."

He could not wrap his mind around the immensity of this situation: half the genetic material of his future son or daughter might be sitting across from him. The other half he would be expected to produce with characteristic good humor in a private room at the clinic, thumbing through magazines that had been God knows where, touched by God knows how many other men who had been subjected to this indignity, maybe even men who had simply walked in off the street because they needed the cash. He imagined explaining to people, years down the road, how they had conceived their child, and how people would snicker inwardly to think of his role in the whole affair. Heat flooded his body. Loosening his collar he took a long sip of wine.

"I know you still need to talk it over with your wife," Celia said. "So don't worry, I won't be offended if you want to back out of the arrangement."

"How about some salad?" Elise jumped up from the table. An awkward silence passed between him and Celia, and he tried to think of something to say to her. His wife returned with a wooden salad bowl filled with baby lettuce, Feta cheese, cucumbers, and tomatoes. "I made the vinaigrette with that walnut oil you like, Peter. I got it today at Dean & Deluca's."

"So you're a graduate student?" Celia placed some salad on her plate. Her wine glass sat full in front of her.

"Yes, in Near Eastern Studies. Ever taken a class in that department?"

"No. I guess I should learn more about that part of the world. It's hard being at a place where there are so many great classes to take. I've still got a lot to learn."

"That's refreshing, actually, that you're willing to admit what you don't know. I have a number of students who think they know everything." To keep the conversation away from the baby topic for now, to pretend as if this were just a normal dinner party, he decided to tell them about his latest run-in with Kevin.

"You should never argue with students," Elise said. "You'll lose your authority. It sounds like he's going to come out of that conversation having the opposite impression of what you meant to say."

"I don't usually let them get to me," he said. "But he was so confrontational. I think the era of political correctness is finished—you can get away with saying or doing whatever you want now, and anything is justifiable with the war on terrorism. Fifteen years ago you could never call another culture 'barbaric.' But fifteen years ago you would have only gone into studying the Middle East if you loved the culture. Now there are a lot of people who are motivated by money, or by wanting to know the enemy before they bomb the hell out of them."

"And what are you motivated by?" Elise asked. Peter ignored the question, pushing the last of the lettuce around in the dressing on his plate.

"I bet he was just mad about his grade," Celia said. "I'm shocked at how the students challenge the teachers' authority. That would never fly back where I come from."

"Well, Princeton is still a pretty genteel place, as things go. But I have a bad feeling about this student. I am pretty sure he's out to get me."

Elise rolled her eyes. "Peter can be rather paranoid." She took away their salad plates and brought the risotto steaming to the table in a ceramic bowl.

"This looks delicious," Celia said, her eyes widening. "You must like to cook."

Elise laughed. "I cook dinner about two nights each week. The rest of the time, I make Peter fend for himself. If I cooked like this every night, I would balloon up like a whale."

"Hardly," Celia said, looking at her admiringly. "You're in very good shape."

"I keep my weight down because I don't eat much," Elise explained. "Peter's better than I am about exercising. I do yoga, but that's about it. Peter, on the other hand, runs every day."

"You do?" Celia said. "I run, too. I was on the cross country team in high school."

"Peter doesn't miss a day," Elise continued. "Six miles, without fail, and on the weekends, ten or more."

Both women looked at him. He took a bite of his risotto and closed his eyes, each grain still holding its shape, perfectly infused with the aromatic broth and basil.

"This is delicious," he said. "Elise is a very good cook when she has the time."

"Which now I'm going to have more of." She looked at him significantly.

"What, you're planning to devote all your time to incipient motherhood?" he said jokingly.

"Hasn't it been clear I've been moving in that direction?" Elise replied. "When I stopped by work today, Diana told me I couldn't work from home anymore. She asked me to come back full time."

"And you didn't agree?"

"Are you kidding? Go back to the commute when all this is going on? I don't think so."

"What about your rule?" he asked. He looked at Celia. "Elise has always been resolute that women should never let men support them. Loses all the gains of the feminist movement."

Elise put down her fork and poured herself another glass of wine. She had hardly taken two bites of the food, but Peter knew she would not eat much more.

"We can talk about this later."

"You brought it up," he said. Celia pretended to be fascinated by her plate.

After dinner, Elise offered to drive Celia back to her dorm.

"You don't need to drive," Peter said. "I'll take her."

"I can walk," Celia offered. "Or take the shuttle. It's not very far."

"Yes, but it's dark," Elise said. "Let Peter take you."

Peter opened the door for Celia before walking around to his side of the car. When he turned the key in the ignition, music poured out of the speakers at full volume—one of the righteous, tormented folk singers Elise listened to when she was alone. He turned the volume down. In the quiet and dark of the car, Peter began to relax.

"This must seem weird to you," he said as he turned out of the apartment complex. "She just wants to get to know you. I know how

Elise is, she probably decided she needed to see you in an informal setting where you didn't feel like you were on the spot."

"Elise has been amazing," Celia said. "We've had some really frank talks. I'm sure she told you everything about me. My father's an alcoholic. But I don't drink. I mean, I accepted a glass of wine tonight because it's rude not to, if your host is drinking, but I don't like to drink."

"You don't have to apologize for anything," he assured her. They arrived at her dorm, and he pulled up to the curb to let her out. For a moment she didn't seem to register that they had stopped. Then Celia turned to him and put out her hand.

"It was nice to meet you." She shook his hand awkwardly. "I just wanted to tell you that I'm not high maintenance."

"What?"

"I mean, I know this whole issue must be weird for you, too—you're desperate for a child and Elise can't give you one. I don't know your wife very well, and I'm not one of those people who assumes just because I know a few details about her life, that I can pretend to know her. But I can tell that this whole situation is tough for her. I just wanted you to know that I don't have a lot of issues. I'm ready to help, no strings attached."

Peter didn't know what to say.

"She told you I wanted a child and she couldn't give me one?"

"She said you desperately wanted children."

"I don't know that I would use the word 'desperately.'" he said. Celia drew back, surprised. "I mean, I wanted to start a family too. I was hoping for better timing --I'd like to be further along in my dissertation. But the doctor says we need to be aggressive."

"You didn't think about adopting?"

"I'm all for it, but she wanted the child to have the genes of at least one of us." He looked out the window. It was embarrassing how much this stranger already knew. "Celia, remember you can back out of this too. It's not like we have a contract or anything."

"I think I can handle it," she said, finally stepping out of the car and wishing him good night. He drove home slowly, thinking of what he would say to Elise when they were alone. Discussing all this was going to prevent him from getting to sleep at a decent hour, which would undoubtedly unsettle his routine, but it was time for a talk.

CHAPTER THREE

Nicole Sumner, when asked by someone in Celia's creative writing class where she found the ideas for her unsettling poetry, had announced simply, "From life." Her response had impressed Celia, especially since she knew her own life was still a blank book, or at best, a collection of children's stories. Nicole's poems and stories narrated the darkness that lay behind affluence, the kinds of jaded experiences Celia imagined wealthy, neglected kids must pursue during their teenage years to draw attention to themselves, to make their families aware of their existence. The words from Nicole's writing hovered in Celia's mind, making her feel she knew the girl, even though they had barely spoken to each other. In her poems, disorders like anorexia and cutting became desirable somehow, a way "to wake/from torpor/to prove that I am of your blood/drawing shards of myself out/shimmering/to show you I'm alive/but only just so." Parents did unspeakable things to one another, and as her poem "Magdalena" revealed, Nicole's father was having an affair with the live-in Brazilian maid. The poem's ending had made the other students draw in their breath: "Magdalena's expensive breasts/which he bought for her/stay hard/even when she's on her knees/doing the work/my mother refuses."

It was impossible to hear her read without being stunned that these poems could be uttered by someone so beautiful, the rawness of the words such a dramatic contrast to her golden, delicate features. Celia also envied Nicole the copious vocabulary that seemed to be her birthright, her knowledge of yachting terminology or Greek mythology, for example, or the ability to employ multiple names for flowers. Her poems were full of random pieces of the world Celia hardly knew existed. Even her knowledge of wildflowers was impressive: *larkspur, lantana,* or *foxglove.*

Celia reviewed the landscape of her own life: the depressed South Carolina mill town, a single-parent upbringing, an uneventful, studious high school career. Her father's situation was the only thing from her past that could have passed for tragic, but writing about him seemed a cheap shot, one that she had exploited before (in the admissions essay that got her into Princeton), and she still felt guilty about turning her father's problems into fodder for personal essays. But she'd written about more mundane topics as well, and nearly everything she did had earned copious praise from her high school

English teacher, Michael Lenhart. In Deer Bluff the stakes were much lower. Princeton writing classes seemed to require a certain world weariness that she knew she did not have yet.

Nicole excelled at confessional poetry, and what did Celia have to confess? She longed to be more conflicted about something. The moral ambiguities, the situations that were neither clearly right nor wrong: she needed to be more attentive to those. She had no intention of developing her own disorders just to have something to write about, but she wanted something to happen, something that would make others gasp at her words, to be shocked that they could flow from such a tranquil exterior.

She had only just met Peter and Elise, but what they were planning seemed a little unorthodox, a possible new source for experience. She wanted more than anything for this to work out, she realized, not just for the money but because it would be the first interesting thing to happen to her in some time. Celia turned on her laptop and tried to start a poem. The cursor winked from the blank screen in front of her, and she tried to conjure up the face of a child that was both hers and not hers. No words came to mind, so she decided to write down her first impressions of Elise and Peter, typing out the details of the evening as it had unfolded, from the impulsive hug Elise had given her as she walked in the door to the stunned expression on Peter's face when he realized who she was. Their apartment was the kind of place she'd like to live in someday, filled with tasteful, understated furniture, as modern and sophisticated as the couple that had decorated the place. A few touches from their travels made the place distinctive: a bright red Moroccan kilim on one wall, an abstract painting on another, framed. Celia had stupidly asked if the artist was one of Elise's friends.

"That? Heavens, no, it's a reprint of a Rothko," Elise laughed. Celia's face burned.

Around his more vivacious wife, Peter was subdued, reticent where Elise was forthcoming, his reserve a trait that gave Celia little to write about but made her want to know more about him. She tried to describe his physical traits: he was conventionally handsome, his dark hair cut in a way that seemed classically male, a hard-won smile that, when it appeared, revealed perfect white teeth. Though Peter and Elise both tried to convince her that graduate students were of a different breed than the undergraduate population, Peter looked like he would have been at home on a lacrosse field or in an investment firm. In short, he fit well at Princeton. Together Elise and Peter made a striking couple, but something was off between them. There was obvious affection in the care Elise took with the food, and Peter's murmur of approval, the way their eyes met as he took his first bite. Otherwise, they seemed on the verge of having a fight that they were holding off since a guest was present.

The risotto was delicious, possibly the best thing Celia had eaten in weeks. What was it she'd put on the salad? Walnut oil. Another new experience to tell her father about, although then she would have to invent a story to explain who had invited her to dinner. In the past Daniel used to be able to see through her lies (always small, always white), though he was less attentive these days, and on the phone there was no doubt she would be able to get away with making something up about how she had made their acquaintance.

She wrote down the detail of Elise's lack of interest in her food. Although the anorexia was the obvious explanation, in a story or novel this could be evidence that she was poisoning her husband slowly over time and did not want to eat the food she gave him. But that was not the kind of novel Celia saw herself writing. Perhaps there was no such thing as a normal, uncomplicated couple. Even happy families possessed a wealth of oddities and dysfunctions that made them, despite what Tolstoy had claimed in *Anna Karenina*, unique. Peter and Elise might therefore be as normal as anyone else, alternating between bickering and affection. However, his disinterest in having a baby struck her as odd, since Elise had insisted he desired it with as much fervor as she did. Perhaps he was simply embarrassed to be speaking directly to a stranger about these matters.

Then there were Peter's fumbling efforts to explain his side of the story in the car. He would be a sympathetic professor, one of those teachers whose earnestness about their field could be touching but difficult to comprehend. In another setting she might have taken one of his classes, or even had a small crush on him, until one day when she would have seen him with his attractive wife and realized he had a whole other life outside of campus, as half of a sophisticated, successful couple. They were the kind of people who would read the *New Yorker* as if it were addressed directly to them, whereas Celia still studied its pages like an anthropologist, wondering what she could do to become an insider. Perhaps she needed to shop for walnut oil.

After writing for a while, Celia closed her computer. Her roommate was out, her bed neatly made. Stacy's boyfriend lived off campus, and she seldom spent more than one or two nights in the room each week. Although Celia often thought guiltily of the money Stacy's parents were losing for the unused space, she enjoyed being alone. During freshman year, her previous roommate, Erin, had entertained a number of male visitors in their room, usually while Celia was present. She had told her father about it, resulting in a mortifying episode during Freshman Parents Weekend. Celia and Daniel had been invited to stop by Erin's family's tailgating tent at the Princeton-Cornell game (she was a legacy), where Daniel had too much to drink and made references in front of Erin's family to their daughter's frequent gentleman callers. Erin was livid, and shortly thereafter had requested a transfer to a single room.

Celia turned the ringer of her cell phone back on, noticing that she'd missed several calls from her father.

"Cee, this is Daddy," her father's voice said in the first message. "It's 6 o'clock here. You're probably at dinner. I was just thinking about you. You won't believe what I did today. Give me a call."

Celia deleted the message, listening for the second one.

"Hey, little June bug. It's eight o'clock, and you're still not there. I wanted to tell you that I saw your old English teacher, Mike Lenhart. He asked about you. He was delighted when I told him you'd decided to major in English. I told him you were coming home for fall break in a few weeks. Maybe you can stop by the school to see him. Anyway. I'll talk to you later. 'Bye."

"Hi June bug, it's a little after nine and I…" The message stopped. Fourth message.

"Sorry, baby doll, got cut off there. I'll just tell you in case I don't get a chance to talk to you. I'm pretty tired. You know why? Because I worked today. I signed up with a landscaping company. They had me planting sod pallets. It's not what I went to college for, but at least it's an honest day's work. I can't tell you how long it's been. So call me."

The final message sounded stern. "Celia, this is your father. Call me back whenever you get in. That's an order."

She dialed her father's number, the line ringing seven or eight times before he finally answered.

"Where were you, June bug?" His voice was fuzzy with sleep. She could picture him dozing in his recliner, the glass on the TV table at his side beaded with condensation.

"I was invited to dinner, Dad. Some graduate students I know."

"Graduate students? Wouldn't they be a little old for you?"

"You always said I was mature for my age, remember? Anyway, you would have liked the meal. Shrimp and rice, and this unusual salad. The dressing was made with walnut oil." She was careful not to say "risotto," as she knew her father was on the lookout for any Ivy League affectations she might be developing. Risotto might be one of them. Why eat risotto when Uncle Ben's boil-in-the-bag would do just fine?

"That's great, Cee, did you get my message?"

"I did, Dad. All five of them."

"Five? I didn't leave you five."

"So, that's good news about your work," she said, trying to sound encouraging. "How did that come about?"

"Well," he said proudly. "You know our neighbor down the street who owns King's Landscaping? I swallowed my pride and asked him if I could do a little work for him on the side. I just couldn't stand to be idle another day."

"I'm proud of you," she said, although he had started other jobs like this before, only to work at them for a few weeks before deciding they were beneath him. "Sleep good tonight so you can be fresh tomorrow."

"I was just about to head off to bed when you called. I love you, baby doll. I'll see you soon."

Celia put the phone back down on the hook. What would her father say if he knew what she might do with Elise and Peter? She wondered if he even knew that egg donation was something people actually did. She was used to telling him most of the details of her life, even about the people she had dated. Unlike most fathers, he was not jealous. He trusted her.

In high school, she'd had one boyfriend, Steven, a quiet, artistic boy originally from Charleston who also ran for the cross-country team. They became a couple their senior year. One night, riding in the school van on the way home from a cross-country meet, he had lifted her face to his and kissed her.

She was not surprised; he was her closest friend, and it seemed natural that relationships transpired this way. The absence of lightning bolts, of passion, or of whatever delirious sentiment romance was supposed to inspire, comforted her. Her other classmates' romantic relationships, by contrast, were not bargains struck between good friends but magnetic attractions to be exploited in a show for others. Against the backdrop of lockers and bleachers, other high school students conducted their couplings and break-ups in front of everyone, as if to affirm in a public morality play that men and women would always be adversaries, forever inhabiting different planets. Since neither she nor Steven went in for much drama, Celia never understood this. He was ethereal and not quite of this world, his style as a cross-country runner that of a slender, graceful animal, golden hair pulled back from his face in a smooth ponytail.

At the time she attributed his almost feminine, other-worldliness to his origins outside Deer Bluff, but during her freshman year of college, when she began to meet fellow students who were openly gay (an orientation not permitted at Deer Bluff High School), she began to wonder. They had slept together a few times with little ardor, both curious to experience sex in the protective cocoon of their relationship.

But unlike the students who panted over each other at school dances, or the articles she read in magazines about the desires of boys her age, Steven had little interest in the physical aspect of their relationship. This was almost a relief, since Celia did not like to follow the crowd, and already she had seen the visible effects of such early transgressions in the swelling bellies of two of her high school classmates.

At the end of senior year they parted amicably, deciding not to continue the relationship into college. Between the University of North Carolina at Chapel Hill, where Steven ended up, and Princeton, they managed to talk on the phone or exchange emails once in awhile, but their former closeness evaporated with the distance. At Princeton she had dated no one. Falling in love might shake her resolve to succeed, and Princeton itself was already enough of a shock. During her first few weeks at the university the previous year, she had walked around in a daze under the high canopy of ancient oaks, in love with the idea of Princeton, its noble stone architecture, the unusual black squirrels that scampered about the campus. She could not believe that she had actually pulled off such a coup, and now her only fear was that she wouldn't measure up, would be unable to perform well enough to stay there.

Celia put on her pajamas and got into bed with Zora Neale Hurston's *Their Eyes Were Watching God*, which she was reading for a women's literature class. Already she was deeply immersed in the story, in the unconventional character of Janie, who meandered among men who were by turns charismatic and controlling, finally slipping from their grasps like some elusive, exotic fish. Was it possible to become like the characters one read about and admired, to construct one's personality in homage to their strengths and eccentricities? Or to study another person and learn how to affect their mannerisms, despite their different backgrounds and histories? She read a few pages before putting the book down, switching off her bedside light to stare up at the glow-in-the-dark stars some previous inhabitant of the room had affixed carefully to the ceiling in the shape of actual constellations. She pretended to be lying on the grass, far outside of any city whose lights would have dimmed the light of the stars, imagining what it would be like to gaze up at the immensity of the universe with someone at her side.

Mentally she composed a personal ad, thinking of how she would phrase what she hoped to find someday in a partner. She would strive to write sentimentally, yet completely without clichés. *You are a person who can share the sky's infinite distance without needing to be reassured that as a couple we can somehow defeat the fact of our ultimate solitude.* Her lover would recognize that both the annihilation of sex and the desire to reproduce were myths, invented by humans in their rush to create the illusion of unity and eternity. *You are comfortable with the knowledge of my inherent separateness, you know that unity is only an illusion, and that realizing this creates a stronger bond between us.* Solitude was comforting; people were too likely to drift away, die, or otherwise disappoint her. Then she thought of her father, alone in the house where he'd raised her, sleeping in his chair to the hum of late night talk shows, surrounded by furniture his wife had bought some twenty years before, the living room a museum of objects from a mysterious, long-forgotten civilization. Celia remembered nothing of her parents' marriage. Having no examples to guide her suddenly made her wonder if everything she'd just imagined she wanted in a partner was wrong. Probably personal ads had to be predictable. *Enjoys running, reading, and long walks on the beach,* was more like it. Who didn't enjoy long walks on the beach? *Candlelit dinners. Looking for that special bachelor to give me a rose.* She wondered what had drawn Elise and Peter to one another, aside from looks. She would ask Elise the next time she saw her.

The stars on the ceiling began to lose their charge, dimming into the flat, neutral plane that was only the generic, impersonal ceiling of a dorm room. Celia closed her eyes, trying to hold the fading impression of stars on her eyelids, and waited for sleep to come.

* * *

The dinner dishes had been washed and put away, the pots were scrubbed to a shine, and the kitchen was completely clean by the time Peter came home. Elise knew how he detested disorder, and at least he would not be able to hold this against her when he confronted her. It had taken him much longer than the fifteen or twenty minutes she expected, but that gave her time to compose herself. She put on a nightgown of pale green silk that she had not worn before, wondering if the way it poured over her figure might be seductive, distracting Peter from the matter at hand. Inviting Celia to dinner had seemed like a good idea at the time, but the look of horror that spread across his face when he understood who was in their apartment made her realize she had made a terrible mistake. That, coupled with her offhand revelation about quitting her job (she blamed this on the wine, as it clearly was not the right moment to reveal this), would undoubtedly have infuriated him, but he would be too polite to say anything until they were alone.

When he finally opened the door, she was on the sofa reading one of his Middle East Studies journals.

"Did you see your advisor's article in here?" Elise said. "He's got an interesting argument about the decline of the Ottoman Empire."

"Don't try to change the subject." With determination he took the journal out of her hands and dropped it on the coffee table. She had casually placed the copy of *Organic Pregnancy* on the table, but he ignored it. Instead of taking a seat next to her on the sofa he pulled over a straight-backed chair from the dining table.

"When were you going to tell me about all this?" he asked. "I thought I was supposed to be a part of this decision, too."

"You didn't like her?" Elise sat up, smoothing out her nightgown. He looked away.

"It's not a question of whether I liked her or not. I couldn't refuse now even if I wanted to."

"Why would you want to refuse? There's nothing wrong with her."

"It's not that I'd want to refuse. It's just that I wanted some say in the matter."

"You told me to handle all this," Elise said. "You said you were so busy that I should choose someone and then have you meet her. That's what I did."

"I didn't expect you would ambush me with her in my own apartment without telling me she'd be there."

"I wanted to ask you last night," she said, "but you came home so late. You didn't even ask about how my meeting with her went."

"I guess the answer to that is obvious."

"Peter, both on paper and in person she's the perfect candidate. She's extremely bright, motivated, healthy, and attractive, what more do you want? And she's agreed to accept seven thousand dollars to help us out."

"That's a lot of money to be making such a quick decision."

"Well, I wanted to offer her more. She's a scholarship kid, and she doesn't have much. She's a southerner. Her father's on welfare."

"You're being awfully casual now with my money."

"Oh, so now it's your money?" Elise could feel the tears welling up in her eyes. "How can you say that? I'm your wife. You always said what's mine is yours, what's yours is mine."

His eyes flashed with anger. "And you always said that you never wanted to take money from a man, even me. You used to say your work and your independence were so important. Was that just something you thought I wanted to hear?"

"People change," she tried to explain. "You might not, but the rest of us aren't always capable of being so consistent."

She was crying now, the words coming out between sobs. Crying made him uncomfortable, she knew, but historically it had been a proven technique for getting him to retreat.

"I just wonder sometimes about your timing." Peter sighed. "This is really sabotaging my concentration. Sometimes I wonder if you're trying or derail me from my own work."

"Derail you? Why should this derail you? We've been married five years. I'm thirty-five years old. That was supposed to be the magic year when my fertility declined, but as we know, fertility left the building a long time ago. There is never going to be a perfect time for a baby, Peter, not after your dissertation is finished, not when you get started with a new job, not now." She'd gained control of her tears, and he seemed to be calming down.

"Please, Peter. I'm asking you to take a leap of faith here," she continued. "I'll take care of the baby while you finish. You can still spend your entire day in the library. If the baby keeps you up at night, you'll wear earplugs. Or we'll get a bigger place. Or if you have deadlines, I'll go stay with my mother for a few weeks. Then when we get settled in a few years, I'll go back to work."

"People in my department are going to wonder," he protested. "They're going to want to know how I support a family when I'm just a graduate student."

"Lots of graduate students have babies."

"The foreign ones, maybe. The ones who are comfortable living on a fixed income and not out buying expensive cheeses and walnut oil from Dean & Deluca."

"Who cares what people think? It's nobody's business what we do; that's the last thing we should be worried about here. Don't let your studies distract you from what's really important. You're not living in the real world here. Don't forget that."

She could tell he was losing his resolve. He wouldn't know what to say to her now, and by this point he was beginning to second-guess himself. All day he was buried in ancient texts, and by now he would be questioning whether he truly had forgotten what it was like to live in the real world. He got up and walked past her into the bedroom. In a minute she heard the water running; he would be getting ready for bed.

The lights were already out when she entered their room a few minutes later. Wordlessly she crawled in bed beside him, his back turned to her, his body as far away from her side as it could get. Although she knew there was a chance he would reject her, she edged over to his side and wrapped her arms around him. His body stiffened at first but there was nowhere else for him to go, save out of the bed, which would have escalated the hostilities to a whole new level. Then he relaxed, a second later putting his hand over hers. It was a gesture she interpreted as solidarity, and she wondered if she should try for more. Conciliatory sex, maybe. It had been a few weeks since they had even tried, and maybe the argument would lead to something.

Since the specter of pregnancy had complicated their relationship, sex had become difficult. At first Peter made love to her whenever she announced she was ovulating.

"Now we're making a baby, not just going through the motions," he had joked. He didn't seem to mind. On her fertile days, she'd send him a coded email message from work. *Ala rising*, it would say. Ala was the Nigerian goddess of fertility, an allusion they both knew from the writings of Eric Babu, an author Elise had worked with. On those days, Peter would come home early. Sometimes she would greet him at the door, jumping into his arms and twining her legs around his body as he carried her into the bedroom, kissing each other hungrily the entire way. Other times dinner would be waiting on the table, and they'd draw out the evening over wine and conversation on all the events of the day, until finally he would brush up behind her while she rinsed their wine glasses in the sink, slipping his hands around her breasts and burying his face in her neck.

As time passed and nothing happened, Elise began to grow worried. Then the doctors' visits started, the endless clinical examinations she endured without complaint. The doctors examined her body's innermost recesses as if Elise were absent, saying nothing about what they saw, about the secrets that her body was keeping from her. She was subjected to tests, procedures, and failures. When their first session of IVF had failed to produce "good quality eggs," and the doctors told her that even with drugs, her body would never produce them, the news had sent her spiraling into a funk. She confessed her infertility to no one except Dr. Geiger and Peter, who was sympathetic but strangely, did not seem particularly concerned.

"It doesn't matter," he had said. "Honestly, I never cared whether or not we had children."

"But this is devastating," she protested. It was not the response she was hoping for. "You were just as excited about having a baby as I was."

"That was when I thought it would be easier. And what if this doesn't work, what will we try next? Surrogacy?" And then he brought up the Peace Corps story again, that tired old saw. Life was always simpler in the Peace Corps, and there was a story with a moral for nearly everything. "In Morocco people in the countryside just visit the tombs of special saints known for their fertility. Why do we have to live in a world this complicated?"

"It's complicated there, too," she reminded him. "Remember what you told me about the woman in your Peace Corps village whose husband left her because she couldn't have children?"

"That doesn't always happen," he said. "The husband just had a particularly forceful family, and he was their only son. They wanted grandchildren, heirs."

But the story had stayed with her. How had that unknown Moroccan woman felt, and what were her chances that anyone would remarry her now that she was tinged with a reputation for barrenness? Peter was an only son, too, his sister unmarried and over forty (and, they suspected, a lesbian, though she hadn't come out to anyone in the family and lived in Seattle, where her private life was too far away to scrutinize). Peter was his parents' sole hope for heirs.

A few months before, she had dreamed of their future life without children, living someplace with a reputable but isolated liberal arts college. They were at a party, and Peter was talking intimately with another woman, a fiery professor of Spanish Literature (her presence in the dream undoubtedly the product of an Almodovar movie Elise had watched the previous night). Peter disappeared with the other woman for a while, reappearing later to announce to Elise that he was moving to Mexico and giving up academia for a career as a fisherman, to live in a hut on the beach where he and the woman would soon be surrounded by children of their own.

Waking with a start, she nudged Peter awake and told him about it. Half asleep, he grunted and told her they would both be lucky if he even managed to get a job, the academic market was so tight these days. But in the light of day, the vivid impressions of the dream lingered, and Elise became certain it was a portent of their unhappy future. In the following days she launched an all-out campaign to convince Peter to let her continue in her quest, and as she had always done, she managed to talk him into it.

She didn't want a surrogate (too complicated, especially with all those cases of surrogate mothers giving birth and deciding they wanted the baby themselves), and adoption would have deprived her of the sort of painful martyrdom she had always imagined came with giving birth. If the baby lacked her genes, at the very least she could grow and carry it for nine months.

At this point their sex life began to suffer. Or was it before, when Elise became depressed about the news from the fertility experts? She couldn't remember, exactly, but once it became apparent his efforts in that department would lead nowhere, Peter seemed to lose interest and grow more introverted. Trying to talk to him about it only made the situation worse. He insisted that the stress of his dissertation made him too tired at night, but now their couplings were so infrequent that she felt lucky if even once a month he turned to her in the night, seeking the warmth of her body. Often this happened after an argument, which made her want to provoke him even more frequently. Dr. Geiger had pointed out that this was counterproductive, but somehow she couldn't help herself. Any reaction was better than no reaction.

She sighed, feeling his grip on her hand loosen as he drifted into sleep, and vowed to be better to him tomorrow.

* * *

The next morning's run did not go well. The entire night, Peter could feel Elise tossing in the bed next to him, and in the morning she was up before him, which completely disrupted his equilibrium. He liked to be the one to get up first, to glance over at her in the bed, still sleeping, and imagine he was getting a head start on his day before she awoke. When she slept he was still moved by her beauty, by the delicate crescent slope of her eyebrows and downward sweep of eyelashes, her legs, muscular from yoga, wrapped around a pillow the way she used to cling to a life-size Corduroy bear as a child. Sleeping, she was at her best. In the innocence of sleep she was incapable of plotting against him.

She was drinking coffee and sitting at the table when he got up. He glanced at her, and her eyes meeting his were a challenge. He wished now he'd accepted her tentative offer of sex the night before, had turned into the arms that held him rather than giving her his back. It might have made the day go better. Again he decided not to come back after his run, and he was glad he'd had the foresight to place another change of clothes in his locker. He offered his wife a forced smile before walking out the door.

On the wooded path between the apartment complex and the main road he was startled by a rustling sound next to him. A deer bounded across the path, its white haunches disappearing into the dull fall landscape. Deer in Princeton had become as common as rats, and the previous year a grad student in Peter's department had swerved off the road to avoid one of them, his Nissan sports car hitting a telephone pole. Ali had enjoyed a reputation for being both a ladies' man and a brilliant scholar, a Palestinian exile who wrote about issues like the war on terror and suicide bombers with such aplomb that he'd already been published not only in scholarly journals but also in Harper's. At the D-bar, the grad student bar where Peter and his colleagues sometimes met for drinks, the handsome Ali inevitably left with the best looking woman there, and seldom with the same woman more than once. After the accident, he was unable to return to school, lost his student visa, and moved back to Jordan, where it was rumored a full-time nurse took care of him in his parents' house.

One night at the D-bar, his consumption of an uncharacteristic amount of beer (Elise was out of town) led Peter to ask Ali how he did it.

"How I do what?"

"Everything," Peter said. "You make academic work seem relevant to the world, you have your pick of the women, and you never seem phased by any of it. Tell me how you do it."

"I wish I could tell you that the whole enterprise leaves me feeling very empty," Ali answered, shouting at Peter over the thumping techno music. "But I'm actually quite content. I don't let anyone hold me back. You will never find me with one woman."

"But how do you do it? Not the women—I'm married, so I can't think about that. I mean what you write."

"You must be open to the world and all the lessons it offers," Ali explained, in his British boarding school accent. "We are all so obsessed with texts, but we must not be satisfied with merely translating and cataloguing the events of the past. It is best to take your lessons from the living. Find out what people want to kill or die for. Look at it in a way nobody has thought to look at it. Then make it relevant."

For Ali, an accident had ended all of that, while Peter was still plugging away, struggling to find the relevance of his own work, the gem that would lead him to a brilliant dissertation that became a book everyone would read. He wanted to write something that connected the past with the present and reminded people why history, for those who did not read it, was doomed to repeat itself. He thought often about that conversation with Ali, even more now that Ali was gone and would probably never write another word. Ali could have performed alchemy with the ancient, crumbling texts Peter was studying. To find a lesson for the present in the past, that was what Ali managed to do. Of course it also helped that he was a minority; people were more willing to listen to you if you spoke from the point of view of the disenfranchised. What he wouldn't give, sometimes, to shake off his own privileged background.

Peter dreamed of writing something about Islam that showed its softer side. He was enamored with Sufism, the mystical branch of Islam concerned with the soul's longing to return to the divine, and the expression of that longing through poetry, song, and dance. Sufis, from the beginnings of the religion up to the present-day, did not commit violent acts, nor did they concern themselves with the world of politics. In the basement of the library, Peter dedicated his days to understanding them better. They wrote poems describing a longing for union with God so profound that it became almost sexual. Expressions of love and drunkenness were vehicles for the soul's desire, and although the subject was always ostensibly divine, the reader sometimes wondered if the Sufis had not also experienced an earthly form of these pleasures as well.

He still needed an angle, a hook, something he could write about that had not been explored in great detail before. His latest idea was to recreate the world of medieval travel, to report what travelers had to say when they encountered Sufis, and also to show that when Christian travelers met Muslim ones, there was a time they met without rancor, fear or crusading intentions. Nineteenth and twentieth century Orientalist scholars had constructed that history of animosity later, as if to show that *those people* had always been animals in need of the tranquilizer of Western colonization. Perhaps the kernel for cultural understanding was buried deep in these ancient travel texts, since the history of encounters between East and West was a long one. If he could only write something that would make this relevant to the twenty-first century, he would be content.

Despite a rough start, by eight-thirty Peter was in the library. During the run he had felt winded and sluggish. He continued to turn over the conversations of the previous night, first with Celia and Elise, then with Celia, then with Elise, all of them so intense they began to blur together in his mind, almost making it difficult to remember who had said what. But after a shower and some coffee, he managed to clear his head of its desire to dwell on the complexities of human relationships. His mind became a blank slate that needed to be filled only with scholarship. He descended the stairs of the Firestone Library and unlocked the metal door of his quiet carrel.

The coffee improved his mood, making him feel like anything was possible. He could write relevant and provocative articles with the lost brilliance of Ali; he had only to focus. Concentrate. He decided not to start the day with sea exploration in the fifteenth century, the topic that had occupied several hours of his afternoon the day before. Instead, he picked up a book of poems by the Sufi poet Rumi, translated by a scholar in Georgia, Coleman Barks.

> *You are granite.*
> *I am an empty wineglass.*
> *You know what happens when we touch!*
> *You laugh like the sun coming up laughs*

at a star that disappears into it.

On the rooftop of a hotel in Istanbul a few years before, he had read this poem to Elise and felt a rare moment of being overwhelmed by happiness, outside of time, having succeeded in drawing them both out of the fabric of everyday life and into the city and its infinite, stunning history. Elise listened to him, her profile flaming up in the sunset that surrounded her. High from watching the Mevlevi dervishes perform their spinning dance, their red fezzes like spinning tops, feet pivoting on soft leather slippers, white skirts ballooning like sails around them, he had dropped his book and pulled Elise to her feet, drawing her close to him. Istanbul spread out around them, the domed mosques with their spindly minarets, the giant ferries tacking back and forth on the Bosphorus. As he released her and she spun away, he felt the tugging fear that she might leave him.

His first meeting with Elise had been at a book party for one of Elise's authors. A Nigerian exile, Eric Efemena Babu had written a novel that reversed the themes of Joseph Conrad's Heart of Darkness, following the adventures of an African on an exploratory mission to an unnamed North American city, after the decline and near-disappearance of this North American civilization. Peter had read Babu's other works, searing fictional critiques of colonialism, diatribes that contained no mercy either for Third World corruption or Western exploitation, and he hoped to meet the author, but he needed an introduction. One of his colleagues pointed him in the direction of Elise.

He wished he could go back to that one blank, promising moment, walking toward her again without the knowledge that she was to be his future. She wore a short black dress with cap sleeves that showed off her slender, pale arms and the elegant span of her collarbone. In her hand she held a glass of champagne. Had he been able to see the course of their relationship, what might he have done differently? What if he'd never read his first Eric Babu novel, and never been impelled to approach her?

At the time, she wore her hair shoulder-length, in its natural, light brown color, and he remembered being stunned by the energy and depth of her blue eyes. Engaged in a conversation with someone else, she did not notice him at first.

"So, I came over here to ask you, what's it like to work with Babu?" he started, during a lull in her conversation. They exchanged names, began the talk that, with Americans, so often starts with work. She listened to him drop bits and pieces of his work history: the consulting stint, the Internet start-up, then the travel literature department at Smyth & Copperfield. But then he began to talk about the Peace Corps, and about how two years of living in Morocco had given him the necessary tools to appreciate the ravages of colonialism Babu detailed with such immediacy. Something in Elise switched on at this moment, as if in response to his passion, either about Morocco or Babu, he never knew. With quiet self-assurance she agreed to introduce him to Babu, a tall, striking man with dreadlocks and an enormous presence who stood in one place for the entire party, constantly drawing a small crowd into his orbit. They moved with the flow of people circling around him until finally they were close enough that the writer became aware of their presence. Her easy, affectionate manner with Babu stood in stark contrast to her diffidence with Peter, and he admired her familiarity with this great man. After Peter stammered out some praise of the author's last novel, the handsome Nigerian nodded coolly and said,

"I'm glad you liked it, brother."

Brother. The Booker-prize winning novelist had called him "brother." He hardly merited such an inclusive term, particularly since it had been his ancestors who were responsible for repressing Babu's—chaining them to the decks of boats bound for America, destroying their livelihoods back home, and later forcing African nations to take out huge loans from American banks. So caught up was Peter in the momentousness of Babu's offhand use of "brother" that he could think of nothing else to say. The author's radiant presence next to his luminous, distant editor silenced him, so unattainable was everything they represented: power, success, beauty, and for Babu, the righteousness of being born of a disenfranchised people.

And then he found himself with Elise, spinning away from Eric Babu as others jostled for positions around him. Elise talked to him for a few minutes more, but he was flustered, unable to come up with even the slightest profundity. Eventually, using the excuse of another drink, she walked away.

Before Elise, Peter had dated a number of women, breaking up with all of them at the moment in the relationship when he began wishing he were somewhere else. Not with someone else, but somewhere else. In a restaurant, for instance, he might find himself desiring to be seated at another table, where other people seemed to be having more fun, the very fact that those people were unknown to him enhancing their promise. Whenever the signs appeared he ended his current relationship, ideally before it got so serious that he would have caused lasting hurt. Before meeting Elise, there were only two women he had actually loved, the first a girlfriend of two years whom he broke up with before entering the Peace Corps. And then, in Morocco, he had met Leila, a divorced woman in her early thirties who often brought her elderly father to the clinic where Peter worked, but that had been doomed from the very start.

By the time he met Elise, he was twenty-nine years old and still had no idea what he wanted to do with his life. For several months he worked up his nerve to ask her out, dating no other women but pining away for her much as the Sufis did for their displaced souls. He learned more about her from colleagues: she was considered a brilliant editor, a passionate advocate for her authors, and a bit headstrong. Her writers thanked her profusely and at great lengths in their acknowledgments. In what little spare time she had (since she was in the office every day until late), she threw together elaborate dinners for her friends and volunteered at a rape crisis center. He read all of Babu's novels a second time, finally working up the nerve to stop at her desk and start up a conversation about the most recent novel. Then he invited her to join him in an Indian cooking class he'd signed them up for, followed by a poetry reading at an art gallery. As he fumbled over a cutting board stacked with knobby pieces of ginger, she teased him about his complete inability to wield a knife, despite being a doctor's son. He was delighted to find this relaxed and joking Elise, normally so serious at work. Peter carefully planned the date for weeks, agonizing over what she might enjoy, but that night, in bed together (because after that things seemed to happen with lightning swiftness) she told him she had never been out with anyone so thoughtful. She had liked him from the moment she met him at Babu's book party, she said, and would have gone out with him then.

"What took you so long?" he remembered her saying, her face inches away from him as they lay facing each other in her bed, her eyes already filled with something that looked like love. It was a hot June evening, their bodies tangled in damp sheets, the sounds of the neighbors' *reggaeton* music from the open window a staccato, thumping soundtrack to their lovemaking. He missed those heady first moments when they couldn't bear to be apart from one another. Two years later they married during the spring of his first year of graduate school. He could never remember exactly how many years they'd been together—was it six? Seven, yes, because he was now thirty-six, and even a little on the older side for a graduate student.

In truth he didn't mind if she stopped working, or if they both lived off his money. He was self-conscious about having money, but she was right to tell him not to care what others thought about how they supported themselves. What bothered him was how easily she dismissed a principle she once claimed was so important: namely, that a woman must never let a man support her. If she could so easily abandon her core values, what did this say about her? The Elise he had known for the first several years of their relationship had always been consumed with her work, and she devoted herself to her job with an intensity he wished he possessed. She was a rarity in her profession: an editor who stayed in one place, known for her dedication to writers and to her consistency. Until recently. Her attachment to her career had given him something safe to be jealous of, something that preoccupied her, made her slightly more unattainable. He liked the cerebral, quick-witted, feminist Elise. This new baby-obsessed woman did not seem like the same person. Her single-minded pursuit of conception had left him feeling superfluous, as if her mission to have a baby had become more important than their relationship as a couple.

Ahh, Jelaladdin Rumi... what did you know about the obscure object of your desire, that being you could never truly attain? Peter longed for a world uncomplicated by the confusion provoked by human relationships or intellectual pursuits, a world where he might concentrate on love in the abstract, not on the fleeting and fickle emotions of others. He picked up the Rumi book again and began to read.

> *We've come again to that knee of seacoast*
> *no ocean can reach.*
> *Tie together all human intellects.*
> *They won't stretch to here.*

Rumi might have been talking about Sidi Maarif, Peter's crumbling seaside town where so long ago the world had been filled with so much promise and simplicity. Glancing at the neat stacks of photocopies around him, Peter took a deep breath and began to type.

CHAPTER FOUR

Although New York was just an hour away from Princeton by train, Celia had only been there once, on an organized excursion to Rockefeller Center for ice-skating, just after the Thanksgiving break of her freshman year. Now, facing the task of visiting the psychologist who would determine her mental fitness as an egg donor, she was navigating the trip on her own. Her heart pounded as she boarded the archaic, single train car that shuttled members of the university community to the Princeton Junction station. The other students slouched casually on the brown plastic seats, as if going to New York were an everyday event. Celia was startled to see Nicole Sumner in the back of the car, not dressed in the usual pearls and cableknits but wearing all black, her eyes outlined with a heavy, dark pencil, reading something intently. When they disembarked, Celia lingered at the door to see if Nicole might recognize her, but Nicole looked straight ahead as she filed past her, just slowly enough that Celia glimpsed the spine of the book she was reading. Of course, she'd be reading something serious like Proust, someone Celia had still not read.

Celia followed Nicole under the tracks and over to the other side, where Nicole walked all the way down to the end of the platform. Celia turned around, uncertain, then noticed others filing into the station and remembered she still needed to buy her ticket. She stood in line, pretending she'd done this a million times, even though she had failed to return to the city after her freshman year.

The skating trip, organized by Student Life, had not been expensive, and she signed up with two acquaintances from her first year dorm. Celia had never been skating and was not particularly interested in learning how, but she wanted to see the city at Christmas and did not want to admit that she was afraid to go to the city on her own. The school trip was a good excuse. After trying and failing to stay on her skates for very long, she excused herself to her two friends, both of whom were much more skilled than they claimed. One was particularly talented, her skates scissoring a figure eight into the icy surface as she turned and waved goodbye to Celia.

The bus back to Princeton was not due to leave for several hours, and Celia had started off down Fifth Avenue, amazed at the size of the crowds. Tourists clustered around the Christmas displays in the tall department store windows, the mannequins in their winter furs floating on clouds of cotton snow as they gazed imperiously at the hordes below. In one department store she lifted the sleeve of a gauzy black dress to find a $4,000 price tag. The price tag seemed to emphasize the fact that the store, in fact the entire city, was out of her league.

Her father had been to New York a few times, on business trips and once with her mother, before she was born. She looked up at the skyscrapers, imagining her father at a boardroom table in a lush, carpeted office, discussing a new line of Anayo Mills towels with stockholders.

"Walk down Fifth Avenue," Daniel had told her when she mentioned the school trip. "Maybe you could bring me back a souvenir, a little Christmas present from one of the shops there. And then go up to 59th street, which is right across from Central Park. You might take a carriage ride with your friends. At the very least you should go to the Plaza and see where your mother and I had tea. It was her lifelong dream to go to Tiffany's and then have tea at the Plaza, which we did before you were born."

Celia wondered what other lifelong dreams her mother had had, cut short before she could live long enough to realize any grander ambitions. Linda must have been around Elise's age when she died. Elise did not seem particularly old or maternal, whereas in Celia's memories of her mother, Linda was a presence both ancient and larger than life, a pillowy lap for Celia to climb into, smelling of lavender soap and Chanel Number Five. Her smell was all Celia could recall, since for years her father could not bring himself to part with her clothes. Linda's dresses hung untouched in their closet, the lavender scent gradually fading until Daniel finally carted the clothes off to the Salvation Army.

Playing dress-up as a child, Celia's favorite outfit of her mother's was a white linen sundress streaked with pale green flowers, belted with a thin green ribbon. Staring at the reflection of the dark-haired girl in the voluminous white dress in her parents' bedroom mirror, Celia wondered if she might someday be transformed into the image of her mother, or if her mother's latent blonde genetics might surface years later in her own appearance. Her resemblance to her father further damaged her efforts to conjure up her mother's presence, and she could not picture a woman in this dress checking her reflection before a summer barbecue at a neighbor's house, such events a normal part of the landscape of other family's lives. Linda had been her father's reason for sociability, and after she died he made no effort to maintain more than a cordial relationship with his neighbors or with the other schoolteachers who had been Linda's closest friends.

The day of the skating trip, Celia had traced her parents' footsteps: first to Tiffany's, where she asked the price of what she thought might be the simplest item in the store: a set of gold cufflinks.

Upon learning how expensive they were, she left, comforting herself that Daniel might interpret the present as a taunt, a symbol of his lost white collar status. Disheartened, she wandered back down Fifth Avenue, afraid to stray too far from the skating rink. Finally she bought a wool scarf for her father from a street vendor.

With several hours still remaining, she decided to be a little more adventurous. Walking all the way up to the Met, she paid the student admission price and threaded her way through the crowds staring at paintings, wondering what she was supposed to feel as she looked at each one. In the museum restaurant she ordered the item that sounded the most unusual: a grilled eggplant sandwich with roasted red peppers and feta. The eggplants tasted smoky and mysterious, perfectly crisp on the outside, but with a soft center that collapsed into the flavors of the accompanying roasted red peppers and salty cheese. Returning to Princeton on the bus later that day, she felt pleased with her bravery. She had been to New York, almost by herself. Further excursions now seemed manageable, even imminent.

Caught up in her studies and her work-study job for the rest of the year, however, she never made a second visit. Until now. It was eleven o'clock, and she had no afternoon classes. Her appointment with the psychologist was not until three, but she wanted to allow herself plenty of time.

"I wish I could send you to my shrink," Elise had said casually, as if they were discussing a favorite hairdresser. "But it would be unethical. So instead you'll meet with his partner."

Boarding the train, Celia looked for Nicole again, imagining them riding together, discussing poetry. But she never would have had the nerve to approach her. She watched the landscape as the train sped up, moving through forests whose fall colors had faded from brilliant reds and oranges to a solid shade of brown, the leaves beginning their final descent to the ground. In countless towns along the way, Celia caught split-second glimpses of stop-and-shops, ramshackle apartment complexes, and abandoned factories whose shattered windows reminded her of the battered, x-ed out eyes of comic strip boxers, knocked out after a fight. Compared with the mostly rural surroundings of Deer Bluff, the route to New York was unlike anything she had seen before, an industrial wasteland where so far her experience of the Northeast was limited to Princeton and its calculated, stately elegance. As the train pulled out of the Newark station, the city curved toward her, its skyline rising up in successive waves from midtown to the financial district. Then the train plunged into a tunnel, and she realized with disappointment that she would not get to witness its approach.

The other passengers occupied themselves with newspapers and magazines, oblivious to the staggering immensity of what it meant to enter this city. She remembered now that she had overheard Nicole Sumner remarking to another student in the class that she spent most of her weekends in the city. Celia was determined to find a way to achieve that offhanded casualness, until coming to the city became a taken-for-granted part of her, as organic and integral as one of her own limbs.

In Penn Station she navigated the signs on the subway, finding the A-train with some difficulty. Hanging from a rail strap as if she did this every day, she gazed out at the sea of multihued faces swaying with the motion of the car. At Fourteenth Street she exited the subway, heading up the stairs and toward the psychologist who would query her about her past, her motives, and her psychological fitness for becoming an egg donor.

The office was located in a red brownstone, its identity as a doctor's office only apparent from a discreet plaque at the top of the stairs proclaiming that at this address Doctors Geiger and Schwartz practiced their trade. She still had almost two hours until her appointment, so she took out the list of places Elise had scrawled on a piece of paper.

"You've only been to the city once! What a shame," Elise had said, as Celia colored with embarrassment. Since their dinner, they had exchanged several emails and met once for lunch, but Peter showed no interest in getting to know her further. One day she spotted him in the student center, holding a plastic box of sushi and a bottled smoothie. Absorbed in conversation with another graduate student, he did not notice Celia studying him nearby. With a pale blue wool scarf peering above his brown suede jacket, he looked rather exotic, almost French. His friend, a curly-haired woman in a green crushed velour dress, must have said something amusing.

"Yasemin, you are too much," he laughed, playfully tapping her with his drink. "But I'll catch you later. I've got to get back to work."

Celia had done as much Internet research about them as she could. Typing Peter's name into Google, she came up with a series of genealogy websites, a link to a club for motorcycle aficionados, and a few running sites containing statistics from road races he must have run, mostly in New Jersey and Massachusetts. He also appeared on a website for former Peace Corps volunteers, but it yielded little other than his name and the years he'd served in Morocco. When Celia added "Middle East" and "Near East" to the search terms, she got more hits. At a conference for the Middle East Studies Association, he'd given a paper entitled, "Poetry of the Disenfranchised: Oral

Narrative Traditions of the *Haratin* of North Africa." Another search revealed that "*haratin*" meant "slaves." Other conferences also bore the romantic stamp of obscure paper titles and a fondness for colons: "Lost in Translation: Traces of the Beni Hillal Epic in Precolonial Tunisia," and "Trafficking with Desire: The Rise of Fertility Cults in Moroccan Saint Worship." The last paper title, from an anthropology conference, caught her eye. Fertility cults. She wondered if his academic interests had crept over into real life.

A search for information on Elise drew more hits. She had edited so many books that her name must have been on a thousand websites, most of them referencing authors. Most of the names Celia did not recognize. But she knew one author, Eric Efemena Babu, from a class she was taking in postcolonial literature. Magnificently dreadlocked, Babu had Canadian citizenship but came from somewhere in Africa. His work was dense and allegorical, and Celia had presumed it to be too sophisticated for her tastes. She made a mental note to read another one of his books, or maybe even to choose his work for a paper topic, so that she could mention it to Elise. It would give them something to talk about, and perhaps Elise could clue her in on what it was like to work with great writers. Were real writers struck by inspiration at inconvenient moments, such that they had to duck into a restaurant and grab a napkin to jot down their ideas? Was it necessary to cultivate an eccentricity—a preference for writing standing up, perhaps, or a fondness for a particular kind of liqueur? At home the only bottle in the liquor cabinet that never got emptied was Chambord, a gift from some long-ago business associate. She tried to picture the writer with the dreadlocks opening the globe-shaped bottle and pouring it into tiny cups, sipping the raspberry liqueur slowly as he scrawled on a yellow pad with an old-fashioned ink pen. She imagined Elise sitting with him, going over an inked-up copy of a manuscript.

The part of New York Celia was walking through now was nothing like the Fifth Avenue holiday scene she'd witnessed the year before. This New York felt more casual and less flashy, although despite the modest exteriors of the brownstones, it was still the type of neighborhood where paparazzi captured movie stars as they stepped out to walk their dogs or grab a latté. The neighborhood of the psychologist's office gave way to gourmet supermarkets and then, back at Union Square, chain stores whose hulking presences dwarfed the smaller places interspersed among them. One café whose address Elise had given her was just off the square, but when Celia saw that the least expensive item on the menu was more than her father made in one hour in his new job with the landscaping company, she walked away. The Strand bookstore proved more affordable. With ramshackle bookshelves that looked as if they had been made by hand, uneven heating, and piles upon piles of books that seemed to be crying out for a new home, it was the first place in New York where Celia felt comfortable. She left with several books whose combined price would have purchased her lunch at the café Elise had suggested. Instead she bought a tuna sandwich from a small, nondescript deli and ate it in the middle of the square, watching a group of street performers pounding drums made from paint buckets as they negotiated a bent-kneed, cartwheeling dance.

"Capoeira," she overheard. She leaned over and asked someone what that meant. "It's like Brazilian karate," the person replied. Workers on their lunch breaks streamed around her, oblivious to the dancers, who were an obstacle in the beeline they were making to their offices, toward the next caffeine fix, toward whatever held them here in the center of the world.

Celia remembered one of Nicole's poems, whose sentiment she suddenly understood. "After Paul Auster" she had titled it. (Celia had to look him up after class): "My body," Nicole had written, "transcribes a path/on the city/merging slipstream on Seventh ave/disappearing inside myself."

The waiting room at the psychologist's office was stark, completely incongruous with the warm outer façade of the brownstone that contained it. Celia waited on a spindly metal-and-plastic chair that resembled the carapace of some postmodern arthropod. From under her intellectual, horn-rimmed glasses, the receptionist looked her over with skepticism, her severe black dress completing the intimidating effect. The waiting room hardly seemed conducive to comforting the troubled minds that must come here to be sorted out.

But the office of Dr. Schwartz, with oversized, red leather chairs and a colorful Tibetan rug, was emotionally a few degrees warmer. Rather than the Germanic, beard-stroking figure Celia was expecting, Dr. Schwartz was an energetic woman in her early forties with a frothy mass of curls, a chic, gray silk turtleneck, and black wool pants that flared out at the bottom over sleek, high-heeled boots.

"Sit down, Celia, it's nice to meet you. I'm sorry you couldn't see Dr. Geiger, but he and Elise talked this over and decided ethically it would be better if I met you instead."

"That's fine," Celia said, taking a seat in the smaller of two red leather chairs.

"Tell me a little bit more about yourself," Dr. Schwartz said. Celia told her the abbreviated version of the main events that had punctuated her life—her mother's death, her success in school, the small town in which she'd grown up, her father's job loss.

"And how has Princeton been for you? I assume with your father's work situation that you have a scholarship?"

"Yes," Celia answered. "A full scholarship, plus a fifteen-hour-a-week work study job that I've stopped going to."

"And why did you stop going to your job?"

"Well, the professor I was working for got sick. Then I heard about the opportunity with Elise, so I decided not to take another one."

Dr. Schwartz nodded, writing something down on her tablet. "How have you liked it so far? Princeton, I mean."

"It's been great. I'm learning a lot. I like my classes." Her answers sounded, even to her own ears, staccato and youthful.

"What about the transition, coming all the way from a small town in South Carolina? Has that been hard for you?"

Celia wondered if her accent always gave people this impression. Country mouse hopelessly out of place in the city.

"Probably no more than it is for students who come from other parts of America that are not New York or California." Dr. Schwartz raised her eyebrows slightly, as if sensing her defensiveness.

"I mean," she continued. "I didn't have a conventional upbringing. I didn't have a mom, and our family was small, so I always felt a little like an outsider, even in Deer Bluff. I had friends, but I didn't really belong there. So Princeton is not that different for me. I'm used to being an observer."

"You felt like an outsider?" Dr. Schwartz pounced on the word, and Celia cringed, sensing herself being categorized. "How so?"

"In the South there are a lot of big families. But none of my grandparents are living, and my father was an only child, so I never had hundreds of cousins to play with, like a lot of Southerners do. When my mother died my father didn't have time for much except work and taking care of me. He always told me I was going to leave the South for college. I think he was disappointed with the way his life had turned out. He went to the state university, married his college sweetheart, then came back and got a job that was supposed to be for life. But the sweetheart died and the job went away too, and he didn't have any other map to follow. I never wanted to let him down."

"Hmm," Dr. Schwartz murmured sympathetically. "Was this a lot of pressure for you, to be all that he had in life?"

"No, because he loved his work, too. Until recently. And I loved school—I couldn't get enough of it. It was too easy, almost. He always told me if I were the best, my future would be so far beyond my wildest imaginings that I could go anywhere, and I wouldn't be stuck in Deer Bluff, like he was."

"Like he was," the doctor echoed, writing furiously. "Have you told him about your plans to donate?"

"No. He wouldn't get it."

Dr. Schwartz raised her eyebrows. "So you don't plan to talk to him about it? We usually recommend prospective donors talk it over with close family members first."

"He's old fashioned. He's a smart guy, but it would probably upset him.

"And what do you want to do with your life, once you finish Princeton?"

"I want to be a writer," she replied.

"Good for you!" Dr. Schwartz said encouragingly. "Some of my favorite writers are southerners. Flannery O'Connor, Faulkner, Dickey."

Celia nodded.

"Why did you decide to become an egg donor?"

She had been expecting this question. Everything she'd read, from the blogs to the literature from the fertility clinic, emphasized that the donor's primary motive should be altruism. Some donors even insisted that they would be willing to donate without receiving any money at all. Compensation was secondary, a gift for the time and trouble involved and not, it was emphasized, for the eggs. Although altruism was somewhat low on Celia's list of motives, she decided not to tell this to Dr. Schwartz.

"I thought that helping someone to have a family would be very rewarding." The lie sounded hollow. "I was also motivated by curiosity," she added to inject some truth into the story.

"Curiosity? Tell me more about that."

"I thought I might be a good candidate. The ad was very carefully worded, and it seemed like it was written to me. Elise told me later she was looking for someone with a love of words. That really came through in her ad. She's an editor, which is perfect."

"Have you asked her to help you at all aside from the donation? With your writing?"

"Oh, no," she answered quickly. "I just mean that I think she's hoping to preserve her love of words somehow in her future child. If that's genetic, maybe I can help with that."

"And if the procedure is a success? Will it be strange for you to know that a child exists who is biologically yours?"

"Not at all, and this is what seems so strange," Celia said. "Does anybody grill a sperm donor? Does a sperm donor have to talk to a psychologist? The outcome is the same. Sperm and egg donors both have kids running around that they don't know."

"You're right," Dr. Schwartz agreed. "We do tend to place more value on a woman's contribution to the reproductive process, in some ways. But there are considerable risks involved with ova donation that don't exist with sperm donors. I'm sure the doctor at the clinic will talk to you more about these risks. Very few studies have been done about the effects of some of the hormones, not only what they do to you but to your own reproductive capabilities later."

"I know about that."

"And you're not concerned?"

"Not particularly." Her own reproductive future seemed so far away. And there was so much she could do with the seven thousand dollars. She could avoid work-study for the rest of her Princeton career. Or she could move to the city the next summer and get a job.

"So it won't bother you to think that you have a child?"

"I wouldn't think of it as my child. I won't be involved with them after we finish this."

"Good," Dr. Schwartz said, continuing to write. "These are usually done anonymously. Only about 20% of donor recipients know their donor, and I did have some concerns about Elise's desire to get to know you. But it sounds like you've been able to handle it. Do you have any history in your family of mental illness?

"No."

"Have you yourself ever experienced depression?"

"No. I'm pretty even keeled."

"What about sex? I apologize for asking such intimate questions. It's sort of part of the process." Dr. Schwartz ran her hands through her curls, which sprang up as if electrified. "Have you ever had sex?"

"What does that have to do with anything?" Celia asked.

"Well…" The doctor seemed reluctant to explain her question. "There's some thinking that women are attracted to egg donation because of their own sexual or reproductive issues. Like they've been abused, or they've had problematic sexual histories in some other way."

"I've only had one partner, back in high school. I think he might have been gay, but I don't know if that means I've had a problematic sexual history."

"You haven't been involved with anyone since you started college?"

"No."

"And did you enjoy your past sexual experiences?"

The question seemed voyeuristic, but Celia answered anyway.

"I enjoyed it as much as I could have considering the threat of pregnancy and AIDS, and the fact that we were both afraid of getting caught. We only did it a couple of times." *Did it.* She must seem so young and naïve to this woman.

"Most parents would be relieved to have a daughter like you," Dr. Schwartz said. "Intelligent, sure of herself, not interested in typical teenage distractions. I'm taking you at your word here. You seem very stable."

Dr. Schwartz stood up. The interrogation over, the psychologist reached out to shake her hand.

"I should mention that if you ever do need someone to talk to, I'm here."

"Thanks," Celia said. "But I doubt I could afford your services."

"I have a sliding scale."

"I appreciate it, but I hope I won't need to come back."

"You never know."

* * *

I hatch from the seeds of the acacia tree. My father was wind, my mother despair. I am not like other men.

The luck of other foals—shod in horseshoes, eyes strapped with blinders—is not mine. I bear witness. My feet graze the dirt of the birthing hut, the stones of the path to the cities, where the others are shaped into mimic men. Their legs are brown branches clad in khaki, the occupier's clothes an ill-fitting costume, but his violence we take as if it were our birthright.

Not for me, the teller of tales. I inherit only dust and sadness. I seek the gathered voices of the elders, repeating history turned myth beside fires that never compete with the brilliance of the sky. Only their embers remain in the ruins of our villages, Babel towers staked on the graves of our grandfathers.

Celia was reading aloud from the opening page of Eric Babu's Booker-prize winning novel, *Lagos Burning.* The cover had been removed from the hardback edition, so that Elise did not recognize it on first sight, as she might have if she had seen the cover art, a Nigerian artist's almost abstract rendering of a woman with snakes for hair, fishes swirling around in the fire behind her head. Babu was a master at combining Greek and Christian mythology with his country's own traditions, his aim to show that all civilizations are founded on stories, the monotheistic religions merely the most current incarnation of the myths that some use to justify their power and domination over others.

Elise and Celia were sitting in the Annex, a basement bar with dingy red walls and a dining room that served what Elise considered disdainfully as down home American fare—chicken and gravy, spaghetti, broiled flounder with potatoes. Probably the kind of food Celia was used to back home. While the girl read aloud, Elise sipped a whiskey sour and closed her eyes, letting Babu's power as a storyteller jolt her back into another world far removed from this one.

She and Celia were meeting regularly now, and under normal circumstances Elise would have begun to think of her as a friend, or maybe a little sister. Celia's love of words was delightful, intelligent yet naïvely refreshing, untrammeled by the blinders of literary criticism she might pick up if she spent too much time in the comparative literature department. Under Elise's influence she had declared English as her major and confessed that her most ardent ambition was to become a writer, though she was still shy about sharing any of her work. Although Elise had not decided when she might go back into publishing, with Celia she spoke of her absence from that world as temporary. It was easy to recall her former passion for her work, particularly as Celia seemed hungry for details.

Celia closed *Lagos Burning* and placed it on the table. "This book was kind of tough for me," she confessed "I know as readers we're not supposed to try to relate our own lives to everything, but some of this was just beyond me. I was impressed when I noticed that you were mentioned in the acknowledgments, though. I was hoping you could explain to me what I was missing."

What she was missing. What anyone was missing who could not immerse themselves in Babu's world. Elise wondered how much to tell her.

"Tell me what you got out of reading it," Elise asked.

"Okay, well, our professor told us that the story of this one person is an allegory for the entire nation. I think that's Frederic Jameson's theory. But I couldn't understand the main character's motives, or why he was so passive. Christian grows up with Ibrahim, who becomes very powerful in the government and offers him a position in his cabinet, but Christian refuses. And not only does he refuse, he lets his enemies frame him so it looks like he's against Ibrahim and the country too. Then there's the long prison sequence, which was disturbing. So much torture. And I also didn't get his relationship with his wife. He thinks she's cheating on him, so he kills her? He's been a pacifist the entire book, so why would the one act of violence he commits be against a woman? And then he ends up in prison again and that's the end of it."

"His wife's imagined betrayal is a reference to Othello," Elise said.

"Of course—well, this was pointed out to me, but it still doesn't explain why he suddenly wanted to kill her, of all people. The misogynist bells went off in my head."

Elise laughed. "Eric Babu is no misogynist. It's a symbolic act—the wrong people are always paying for crimes they did not commit. But overall, he wants to show that the corruption of Third World nations results from the destruction of traditional society. His characters are people who have lost their moorings. Christian is passive like most citizens, who are pawns in a game that they are excluded from playing." She paused, letting her words sink in.

"Wow," Celia said. "I like that. 'Pawns in a game that they are excluded from playing.'"

"There's no way he can escape the corruption," Elise continued. "Those who resist are doomed. But Babu's brilliance lies in the fact that he blames everyone, not just the British colonizers. Even the Nigerian people themselves. No one escapes unscathed." She took the book from the table and flipped through its pages with reverence.

"I guess that's what disturbed me the most," Celia said. "If you have three parties in this situation: the colonizers, the corrupt officials, and the people, and only two of those three parties have power, isn't the third an innocent victim?"

"Nobody is innocent," Elise sighed. Editing Eric Babu's work had been the major coup of her career. Nobody could have foreseen that *Lagos Burning* would win the Booker Prize, but Elise had faithfully worked on his two previous novels and realized that she was in the presence of genius. Despite his Canadian citizenship and his family in Toronto, Babu was an exile. *Exile*. The word conjured up visions of deposed royalty and refugees, romantic figures doomed to wander the earth in eternal estrangement from their homelands. Babu had angered nearly everyone in Nigeria, although the prize had gone a long way toward restoring official pride in his work. In recent years he had become a part of the fashionable tendency of oppressive regimes to tolerate a token opposition, a strategy designed to give the false impression to the West that dissent equals democracy.

Ironically, the novels of Eric Babu had brought Elise and Peter together. Peter was forever trying to atone for his misplaced guilt about being born white and upper class. His inability to get over his years in the Peace Corps testified to that particular complex. Living in a small beach town near the Sahara desert, surrounded by landscapes dotted with tiny, drought-stricken villages and lush palm oases, Peter had witnessed firsthand the types of hopeless corruption and human resilience Babu described in his books. There he had felt, he told Elise, as if he were somehow a part of the suffering of others. But rather than leading to a career of humanitarian work, the two-year Peace Corps stint seemed to paralyze him, his years of dabbling in various unrelated careers and the academic world further evidence that he'd never quite recovered from Sidi Maarif.

"So, do you think I should reread *Lagos Burning* in a few years?" Celia was asking. "Is it the kind of book you understand better after you've had more life experiences?"

Elise sighed. Celia's observations were normally so astute. Comments like these reminded her that Celia was only a college sophomore.

"You might go abroad," Elise suggested, thinking of Peter. "Spend a semester in a developing country, if you have the opportunity. Then when you've met characters like the ones in this book, you'll have a better idea what he's talking about."

"Have you spent much time overseas?" A waitress arrived with a plate of jalapeño poppers; they would be Elise's only dinner. She picked up one of the peppers, dropping it quickly when she found it too hot to touch.

"I've never been to Nigeria. I went to Morocco once, with Peter. I've been to Turkey and Thailand, in addition to Europe, of course." She did not add that she had never stayed long enough to witness any corruption, aside from the occasional taxi driver rip-offs or insignificant acts of bribery. In all these places she had traveled on a level well beyond the financial abilities of most locals.

"Peter was in the Peace Corps, right?"

"Yes, and I'm sure he'd be more than happy to tell you about it, ad nauseam."

Celia picked up a jalapeño popper. "I would like to travel. I've never been outside the United States, though. I don't know where I'd start."

"You could always use some of the money you're getting for this to go abroad." Elise gestured at her own belly as if to imply the baby's inevitability.

"That's true, I could." Celia sipped her Coke.

In some ways Celia reminded Elise of herself when she was younger, only without the same propensity for despair. Like Celia, she'd been raised in a single parent household, her father registering mostly as a distant financial presence who paid for camps, dance and piano lessons, and her college education, in addition to sending the occasional gift to show he had not forgotten his daughter from his first marriage. Her mother refused her father's offer of an expensive prep school, insisting that Elise attend the public schools in the Baltimore suburb where they lived. In high school Elise was a good student, neither popular nor an outcast. As the editor of the school literary magazine, she aligned herself with the artistic crowd, with students who bought their mostly black wardrobes from the Salvation Army, listened to androgynous, melancholy British bands and smoked pot in their cars before coming into school each morning. On the weekends Elise participated in these rituals as well, just enough to gain membership in this group while still maintaining her good grades.

Even then she knew that this world was temporary, and that she would transform herself, just as her father had, in the city that was the apex of reinvention. Columbia rejected her, but she was admitted to New York University, and despite her mother's urging that she choose a small liberal arts college where she could be nurtured, she packed up her thrift store wardrobe and moved to the city.

The transition was a difficult one. Intimidated by her self-assured classmates, some of whom seemed light-years ahead in terms of sophistication, she developed anorexia. The disorder was made worse by the fact that her attempts to forge a stronger relationship with her father were failing miserably. He rarely returned her calls but instead had his secretary phone her occasionally, just to ensure that his tuition checks were arriving on time. Infuriated, she started to ask the secretary for more spending money, which was deposited into her bank account without question. As her weight dropped, she took note of what the other students were wearing, began reading *Vogue* and spending inordinate amounts of money on clothes. Bearing a first semester's report card full of C's, Elise returned to Baltimore for winter break in a five hundred dollar pair of size zero jeans that barely clung to her prominent hipbones. Her mother marched her protesting to the bathroom scale, where she asked if she could first take off her jeans and shoes, just to make sure she got an accurate reading. When the scale read ninety pounds, clothes and all, her mother checked her into an expensive rehabilitation clinic. She cried to see Helen's shame at having to ask her father for money, but from her father she heard not one word about the whole affair.

She remained under Helen's care after being discharged from the clinic and did not return to school until the following fall, this time with the stipulation that she bring home a report card with no C's. In the interim, as part of a plan her mother had devised, she worked at a bookstore in Baltimore, visited her first psychologist, and spent fifteen hours each week volunteering at an inner city hospital where drug overdoses and gunshot victims were as common as indigestion. Volunteering in that environment was shock therapy, designed to make Elise realize how lucky she was, and it had worked. She did everything she could to convince her mother she was ready to go back to school, away from the trauma of those lives, violently lived, that she had seen sapped away on gurneys in the emergency room. For the remainder of her time at NYU, she maintained a high GPA and let her transformation into a New Yorker happen at a more measured pace. There were still minor instances of self-destructive behavior that she dealt with in therapy, but for the most part Elise felt that she had her life under control.

"You don't have to go abroad to see the kind of suffering Babu describes," Elise said. "It's all around us. I grew up in Baltimore, but even though there were certain neighborhoods we never entered, I didn't know how bad things were until I spent five months volunteering in a city hospital. It really opened my eyes."

"Did you do that as part of a service requirement in high school?" Celia asked.

"No. I took some time off from college when I got sick. My mother wanted me to see all that I had to be grateful for, and she thought that volunteering in a hospital might help. I'm glad she made me do it, even though she was wrong about it fixing the anorexia. I didn't get sick because I was ungrateful. It was more complicated than that. I'm still trying to work it out."

"Still, it's always seemed strange to me that most people who develop eating disorders are young women."

"All suffering is profound, even if it's self-induced," Elise replied. She drained the whiskey sour and wondered if she should order another one. The ostensible purpose of this meeting had been to inform Celia about the schedule Elise had made out for her, which would culminate in an early February donation, just before the start of the second semester. Now that Dr. Schwartz had pronounced Celia to be sound of mental health, an ultrasound and complete physical were the first events on the schedule. But she hated to change the subject back to business. Talking about suffering was so much more interesting.

Elise waved the waitress over and ordered another whiskey sour.

"Another coke?" she asked Celia. "Some more appetizers?"

"Just a glass of water," Celia said.

"Water's good," Elise replied. "I'm glad you're so healthy. You know, you remind me of myself when I was your age. Minus your healthy outlook, of course."

"How's that? I can't imagine a time when you were ever anything like me." Elise looked at her, waiting for the insult. "You just seem so... worldly."

Elise smiled at the compliment.

"It's just an image." She was aware that once she gave away all her secrets the magic would be lost, and Celia would realize she was like anybody else. "Anyone can do it. But we have a lot in common. I was ambitious, too. I just wanted to get out of Baltimore. But I was also more insecure than you are. I think you could go far in life. You know, when you graduate, if you want to work in the publishing world, I could probably help you get an internship or something."

"You would do that for me?"

"Of course." The second whiskey sour arrived.

"Here, try a sip of this. They do a great whiskey sour here; you can hardly tell it's got alcohol in it." Celia dutifully reached over and took the glass from Elise's outstretched hand. She sipped it, her mouth puckering with distaste.

"Forget about your father for a minute," Elise said. "I know that's what you're afraid of. But just give it a chance. It's not going to send you on a long descent into the bottle. Alcoholism is part heredity, part circumstance." Celia took a longer drink.

"It's good," she admitted. "I still want to hear more about Eric Babu. Is he nice?"

"He's a bit of a rogue. Married, has two kids, but still hits on anything in a skirt."

"But you said he was no misogynist."

"Oh, you can still have respect for women but be irresistibly drawn to more than one at once." Celia looked doubtful. "And I can't say I was entirely immune to his charm." She tried to sound nonchalant.

Elise suddenly felt sad. She missed that world, and her role in it. It had been two years since Babu's last book, and he would be due for a new one soon. If she never worked for Smyth & Copperfield again, her final remaining connection with Babu would be lost.

"You know he's giving a reading here in a couple weeks," Celia said.

"What?" The news so startled her that she wasn't sure she could process it.

"I thought you would have known that. So you're not in touch with him anymore?"

"Um, no, it's not that, I think that he told me, I just forgot about it," Elise said. The news had caused her to lose her composure, but she made her voice sound calm, offhand. "I had other plans that weekend so I don't have it on my calendar."

"I don't think he's reading on a weekend. It's on a Thursday."

"I'll be out of town," Elise insisted. She was not ready to see Eric, let alone on her own turf. Her old life intruding into the new one would just be too weird. "You'll have to go and let me know how he is. I haven't seen him in awhile." She shifted nervously. "Plus Peter's a little jealous of Eric. It's irrational, I know, but there was still some tension about my closeness with him after we got together."

"So, what was it like when you met Peter?" Celia asked. Elise was relieved she'd changed topics. "Did you know he was the one?"

"Not at first, no, I didn't," Elise said. "But I started noticing him around more after that party, and I knew he was a nice guy. I decided I'd had enough of losers at that point."

"When did he first ask you out?"

"A few months later. He said he'd been working up his nerve to approach me, but he was probably busy dating other girls. We went to a cooking class together. His idea. He used to come up with all these really fun plans for things we could do together-- he would find something in the city we'd never done before, like going to a dominoes tournament up in Washington Heights, and watching old Dominican men competing on a street corner while drinking rum out of little paper cups. One time he got us U.S. Open tickets and then found some obscure Indian restaurant in Queens where we ate afterward, a place where there were only Indian families and the food was just amazing. I think that's why I fell for him, because he made it seem like life was going to be filled with these tiny adventures."

Elise put down her glass. "I hate to change the subject, but I have this schedule to give you," she said. "Peter's going to be expecting me at home soon." From her bag she retrieved the schedule, which started with a round of doctors' visits for Celia the following week. "I can drive you to the doctor's office next week, since you don't have a car. If all goes well, we could hopefully schedule the harvesting for February."

"Can we not use that word, harvesting?" Celia asked. "It makes me feel like a farm."

"Okay, then. How about 'retrieval?'"

"I guess it's better than saying 'harvesting of the eggs.' I am neither a farm nor a chicken coop."

"And I am neither Old McDonald nor the little red hen," Elise said. Celia smiled.

"I have a request, too," she said suddenly. "It might be nice if Peter came to meet us sometime."

"Why is that?"

"Well, this whole transaction sometimes feels like it's between the two of us. I wonder if he feels left out."

"I'll ask him," Elise said, knowing that she probably wouldn't.

That night, waiting for Peter to come home, Elise sat in front of her computer, looking through old emails for Eric Babu's address. Celia's strong reaction to his work (even if she hadn't fully understood it) and the reverential way she asked for information about him made Elise long for contact with that world that had sustained her for so many years. With a twinge she remembered the days when she was single, living in a small studio apartment in Chelsea. Each day she exited the corner deli with a cup of coffee in her hand, enjoying the way people looked her over in her professional clothes as if she might be someone important, someone worth knowing. She missed working with the writers, before she'd demoted herself, missed meeting Babu for coffee in his expansive loft, drinking cup after cup of strong espresso from the thousand dollar machine he owned while they put his work to ruthless scrutiny, deciding what to cut, what to keep. Giving up her job had not disturbed her until now.

Dear Eric,
It's been a long time since I've heard news of you. I am freelancing from Princeton but am considering returning to the city to work full time.

Elise paused for a minute. This was dishonest; she had no intention of leaving Princeton. She kept typing.

I hear you're coming here - remind me of the date again? Will you be reading something new? I was curious to hear what you were working on lately. I'm taking a temporary leave of absence from Smyth & Copperfield, but I would certainly be able come back to help with your latest book. Let me know if you're still interested, and I'd be happy to talk to Diana Berg to make sure I'm lined up to receive it.
Best,
Elise

* * *

On Wednesdays from three to five, Peter held court with his students in the graduate student lounge. The lounge in the Department of Near East Studies looked more like a neglected library, with bookshelves lining one wall and a table in the center of the room containing an array of newspapers from the Middle East. The shelves held ancient, yellowed journals and books with titles like *Out From Samarkand* or *Customs of a Levantine Merchant*, and the Arabic and Hebrew newspapers scattered across the table were usually a week or so out of date. Other graduate students sometimes ate their lunch there or came to read the newspapers on breaks between classes. As a teaching assistant, Peter used the room for his office hours. Usually only one or two students stopped by to ask questions about their homework, which was something of a relief.

But this Wednesday it was his advisor, Youssef Kronenberg, who stopped by to see him. Youssef was the de facto chair of the department, since the actual chair, Mortimer Hayes-Blair, an Ottoman historian in his early seventies notorious for his denials of the Armenian genocide, had recently suffered a stroke, and nobody had the heart to admit that he might not be able to return to fulfill his duties. Kronenberg was a Sufi convert, a member of a sect that met in the city twice a month to chant from the Qur'an and to dance in the spinning style of the Turkish Mevlevi order of dervishes. Although he made no secret of his religious sympathies and was well aware of Peter's academic interest in Sufism, Kronenberg had never once invited him to attend one of the New York sessions, as if these activities might bring too personal an element into their professional relationship.

"Mind if I take a seat?" Youssef asked. Over his jeans Youssef wore a white linen tunic with blue embroidery circling the neckline. With his dark, thinning hair and beard, he would have blended in anywhere in the Middle East. His accent, however, was pure Brooklyn.

"Please." Peter closed the lesson he was working on for his next class.

"So, how's it going with that dissertation? Made any progress since we last talked?"

"Yes, I'm narrowing my focus on encounters between Arab explorers and Sufis. Specifically in Morocco."

"You been able to find much written on that?"

"There are some archives in Cairo that I hope to check out next summer."

"You know, you've gotta let the department know in advance what you're planning. We need to line up our teaching assistants for next year. Are you thinking you'll be in Egypt?" Youssef Kronenberg did not mince words. He might circle around the point for a moment before diving in, but he was not one to play games, a refreshing change from some of the other academics of Peter's acquaintance.

"I applied for a dissertation grant for next fall," said Peter. "I know this is my last year on department funding."

"You can always keep teaching," Youssef said, "and make a little money that way. It looks good on your record to have a lot of teaching experience, so you really ought to do more of it. When it comes time to apply for jobs, you want to be able to show that you have good experience."

Peter winced inwardly at the mention of the job market. He associated the Job Market with the basement of the large hotels where academic conferences were held. Unwittingly he had stumbled into the Job Market during the last Middle Eastern Studies Association conference and was dismayed to see hordes of nervous graduate students wandering about, eyeing one another suspiciously and checking bulletin boards for job postings, hoping for that elusive interview. It was no coincidence that the word "job" itself had Biblical connotations, of suffering without relief. Boils, locusts, and despair of epic proportions.

"I'll try to keep teaching," he replied. "I've enjoyed being the teaching assistant for Introductory Arabic this fall."

Kronenberg nodded.

"Oh yeah. And about that. Don't get alarmed, but a student in your class has complained to the department chair about you."

"What was the specific nature of the complaint?" Peter immediately thought back to his conversation with Kevin. Ever since then, Kevin would say nothing in class unless Peter called on him. When he answered, Peter could still read the hostility in his eyes.

"Well, you know about this Internet Watch campaign that keeps a list of professors with pro-Palestinian sympathies? You're on it."

"I'm just a teaching assistant," protested Peter. "And I've never once mentioned anything about Palestine in class. I don't think I've indicated my sympathies one way or another."

"Relax, you've got nothing to worry about. I'm on that list too," Kronenberg chuckled. "Of course, having tenure and being ethnically Jewish gives me a certain amount of immunity. I can speak my mind a little more freely than you can. I'm just warning you to be careful. The student has issued a complaint, and while he doesn't go so far as to say that you're anti-Semitic, he did say that you had graded him harshly on assignments where he expressed a positive viewpoint of the Zionist state."

"That's not what happened at all," Peter said. "They were supposed to write a paper about Middle Eastern culture. The student wrote about how uncivilized Middle Easterners were. He said the only civilized country in the region was Israel. I graded him harshly because he was making value judgments, not describing something cultural about the region."

"Did you save a copy of the paper for evidence?"

Peter shook his head. The word "evidence" implied a trial, accusations against him.

"He said you accused Israel of being a terrorist state."

"I said no such thing! I told him that any state that uses violence against its enemies cannot be considered completely civilized. That could include this country. I'm a pacifist; those would be my views about any state, no matter where in the world it's located."

"I understand." Kronenberg reached up to push aside an invisible lock of hair, a nervous tic he had. "But you gotta be careful. Words can very easily be misconstrued. You don't want to risk discussing politics with your students at all. Lay low for a while, keep the discussion neutral in class. Leave culture and politics out of it. This will blow over. The department is on your side, but don't put us in a difficult position. Some of these kids have very powerful parents."

"Meaning?"

"Meaning just think before you speak."

"I will, Youssef. Thanks for the warning."

"And show me your chapters," Youssef said as he was leaving. "I'll be waiting. Next week some time, maybe? Bring me some writing."

Peter loosened his shirt collar, feeling the anger coloring his face. He was sweating, and the room suddenly felt very hot. Leaving his books on the table, he pushed his chair back from the table and headed toward the door for some fresh air. The stone hallways of the Near Eastern Studies Department were dimly lit, giving the place the feel of a medieval museum. He pushed open the heavy door to the outside, grateful for the wave of cold air hitting him in the face. At times like these he almost wished he were a smoker. Pacing with a small, destructive prop would feel good at this moment.

He breathed in deeply and looked up at the sky. The days were growing shorter, the weak sun already falling behind the bare limbs of the oaks. He needed to run, to do something to expel the flood of nervousness that coursed through him. He imagined going far away just to run, spending hours doing nothing but running. In Princeton getting up in the morning to run became more and more difficult as the temperatures dropped. Then in January, when the ground would be covered with snow and ice, he would have to drive to the gym on the other side of campus and run on the indoor track. Or maybe he and Elise could spend a week or two in Miami over the winter break at her father's condo. The condo was almost always available, since Elise's father worked so much he rarely enjoyed a vacation.

"Peter?" He turned with a jolt, surprised that he had not noticed anyone approaching him. It was Celia, in running clothes and a black windbreaker. She had pulled her hair back in a ponytail, her face scrubbed clean of makeup, making her look even younger than he remembered.

"Oh, hi there," he said, not entirely thrilled to have this reminder of his complicated life standing in front of him.

"I'm just heading over to the tow path." Her cheeks were flushed, and she was a little out of breath. "There's a 10K here in Princeton in a few weeks that I decided to run, before the weather gets too cold. Will you be running it?"

"I hadn't planned to," he told her. "I've been busy."

"Too busy to help the local bank in the Race Against Hunger?" He wondered if she meant to be sarcastic.

"I love it how it's a bank sponsoring a race against hunger, as if hunger were something you could just outrun."

"It'll be fun, though," Celia said. "But I can understand if you're really busy."

"You know how it is. There's a lot of pressure on me to finish my dissertation."

"Pressure how? It looks to me like a pretty good life. As a grad student, I mean. You're not taking any classes, but the university gives you money to spend your days studying something you love. What more could you ask for?"

"It's not that easy," he sighed. "I know it sounds ideal. But you can't imagine what it feels like to have all these expectations surrounding you to conduct significant research. Then you're supposed to produce a three hundred page document that says something new about subjects people who are smarter than you have already written about." He stopped himself; he was saying too much.

"If it's your work and you believe in it, then that's all you need, no?"

"It should be, but it's not. The problem is I don't always believe in it."

"What would you rather be doing? If you don't mind me asking."

"I don't know." Peter tried to think of a way to excuse himself from the conversation, but the prospect of continuing his office hours seemed equally unpleasant. "Hey, if you've just started your run, maybe I could go with you."

"That would be awesome." She looked genuinely happy about the prospect. Was Celia sympathetic? She seemed to be, but then she was already over in Elise's camp. He knew they had been meeting regularly.

She waited for him outside the gym while he changed. The only running clothes he had in his locker were a beat-up pair of sweatpants and an old Brown t-shirt. He fished around, looking for something nicer, then wondered why he was caring how he looked.

They started off, running behind the Near East studies department, where Youssef Kronenberg was unlocking his bicycle from the bike rack. He nodded at both of them, looking from Peter to Celia.

Peter wondered if Youssef knew he was still supposed to be having office hours, or if he was thinking he shouldn't be fraternizing with a student this way.

"Do you mind if I talk?" Celia said. "If you like the quiet, I don't have to."

"No, I don't mind," he said. Usually he loved the solitude, but this was something different. A social run. It had been a long time since he'd gone for one of those. Celia was a bit slower, but not enough that it made a difference. He glanced over at her, surreptitiously studying her features. She had a nice profile. A straight nose, a good chin. He could almost see the Native American features Elise raved about. He tried to picture his child having that profile.

"Elise said you were in the Peace Corps."

"In Morocco," he answered.

"She said it was the happiest time of your life."

"It's really not her place to be telling other people how I feel about my life."

As soon as he said it, he realized how rude he sounded.

"I'm sorry," he apologized. "That came out wrong. I just—well, my adviser back there was giving me a hard time. Do you remember I told you about the student I'd had a conversation with the night you came over for dinner?"

"The one who was challenging you about a grade?"

"Yes, that one. He apparently complained about me to the department. Said I wasn't treating the students fairly, and that I didn't like his paper because I'm against Israel."

"What does Israel have to do with an introductory Arabic class?"

"I didn't want to get into politics at all. But the student just wrote a really crappy paper. And now he's started this whole problem."

"That's not good."

"The department will get over it, I guess." They were running faster now, their words coming out in short bursts. He let Celia lead as they reached the bottom of the bridge, the sandy path stretching out like a ribbon in front of them alongside the sluggish creek.

"My advisor just told me I needed to watch my back." How could he explain that all he wanted was to turn his students into critical thinkers, to make them understand that academic papers weren't based solely on opinion?

"That's a little ominous," Celia said. "What is this, the McCarthy era?"

"Yeah, right," said Peter.

They ran in silence for a moment. The trees were losing their leaves, and the sky was a flat tent of gray hanging over them. In winter

Peter could feel himself closing up inside, bracing against all the darkness. Something about the intimacy of a run, Celia breathing hard beside him, made him want to confess this to her. He wondered if winters hit her as hard, since she came from a warmer place.

"So which class would you recommend to someone who knows nothing about the Middle East?" The question pulled him back from the direction his thoughts were taking him. They spoke easily now about classes, the department, what Celia had studied, what she liked and disliked about Princeton. He suddenly thought about Elise, and what she might have said about him.

"I don't even want to think what Elise has told you about me."

"Very little. I told her the other night that I wished you would meet with us sometime because I felt as if I didn't know you at all. I know plenty about her, though."

"I bet you do," Peter said. "She can get a bit confessional with her friends." By unspoken agreement they had both turned around, and were heading back to campus through one of the leafy side streets dominated by mansions.

"Maybe it is better if this whole thing is just between Elise and me. I only wondered if you felt left out, or not really involved somehow."

His smile grew strained. "No, it's fine, really. I'm happy to let her handle all the arrangements. It's her baby, so to speak." He laughed nervously. Out of breath, his laugh came out as a strangled gasp.

They ran in silence the rest of the way. When the run was over, he thought about asking her to run with him some other time. But the issue with Kevin made him think twice. He had to draw some boundaries where students were concerned.

"My dorm's over there," she said, pointing at the gothic stone building where she lived.

"Okay." Would they shake hands? Celia waved awkwardly and began jogging away from him."

"That was nice," she said. "Maybe I'll see you at the race in a few weeks." He looked down at his watch; it was five o'clock already. Five o'clock: time for a quick shower and at least one more hour in the library before going home. He sighed and found himself wishing again for a cigarette.

83

CHAPTER FIVE

In her third excursion to the city, Celia made the long trip to LaGuardia. She usually flew out of Newark, but this time the cheaper fare to South Carolina left from the city, and for a second time she navigated the New Jersey Transit to Penn Station, then took the A Train up to 125th street, where she climbed on the bus that cut across Harlem, past fried chicken joints and African hair braiding shops and over the water to the rundown chaos of LaGuardia. With her last few hundred dollars of work-study money Celia had bought a plane ticket to return home to Deer Bluff for fall break.

"Fall break?" Elise exclaimed. "You're leaving for a whole week?" Peter had failed to mention the weeklong holiday to his wife. "I wasn't even aware fall break was already here. I guess Peter was just planning to head out each morning at 6:30 as usual. Anything to avoid having to actually pull himself away from the library and take a break."

After the intensity of the past several weeks, leaving Princeton was a relief. The psychologist's visit had been followed by a rigorous physical exam, where she'd undergone every conceivable test, from tuberculosis and STDs to an ultrasound, to make sure everything was in order with her ovaries. Afterward Elise took her out for lunch at an Indian restaurant, where she ordered for both of them: bracingly spicy vegetarian curries, steaming baskets of *naan* bread laced with onions and garlic, and the usual two glasses of white wine for herself.

Elise ate the curries with only a spoonful of rice, leaving the bread largely untouched, but by now Celia was used to her food-related eccentricities. At each meal Elise seemed to make a bargain with the food beforehand: only alcohol, no dinner later in exchange for the reward of deep-fried oysters or jalapeño poppers now. Celia wondered whether Elise would continue to eat and drink this way when pregnant, but she reasoned it was really none of her business.

The clinic literature impressed upon her the need to think in terms of gifts and not compensation, one mother's altruism toward another, but Celia was still unable to view the transaction in this light. Altruism, after all, came without a price. Instead she thought frequently about how her own bank account, which averaged a balance of no more than three hundred dollars, would be full, and what she would do with the money. Her wiser instincts told her she should save the money for an emergency, in case her father stopped working again. But still she allowed herself to fantasize, imagined buying a spur-of-the-moment plane ticket to Thailand or a devastatingly expensive pair of jeans. In the Princeton U-Store and the shops that lined Nassau Street she had seen other students make impulse purchases, handing over credit cards for overpriced sweatshirts or stacks of CD's, their offhanded casualness suggesting that someone somewhere else was taking care of the bill.

Elise also acted as if her wealth sprang from a deep and never-ending well, and while Celia did not want to admit her envy, she could not help but feel thrilled whenever she watched Elise drop money on ephemeral luxuries. At restaurants Elise sometimes ordered without so much as glancing at the prices, as if there were no distinction between a fifteen-dollar order of *moules marinières* and a cup of coffee at Small World. Skillfully prying apart the mussels with a utensil Celia had never seen, Elise regaled her with stories about the publishing world and about her own college experiences in a much wilder time and place.

Elise's professed estrangement from her real estate mogul father indicated that Peter must be the source of the money. From the way Elise talked about him, Peter continued to be an indifferent and slightly mysterious figure, living a disciplined existence that involved daily six to eight mile runs and a punishing schedule in a windowless library carrel. (In characteristic confessional spirit, Elise had hinted at problems in the bedroom as well, which made Celia blush, her mind jolting back suddenly to Peter's breath, heavy and in time with hers, on their chance run together). He worked even on the weekends, and Elise had said more than once that she wished he would make more time for her.

"Just to do those normal couples things, which we used to do," she explained. "Like going to the city for a play, or even just going out to dinner without him looking at his watch every five minutes. Or talking about something other than department politics and my ovaries." The reality of marriage was much bleaker than Celia had imagined. As an outsider it was so easy to perceive the cracks and fissures in other people's relationships, but she reasoned that the inexplicable glue that held them together (perhaps love, perhaps something else) was still not something she fully understood.

She was looking forward to a week away from this new situation. She missed her father and their easy, uncomplicated intimacy, and she worried he could not take care of himself without her. Lately Daniel had sounded better on the telephone, but she needed to see for herself how his new job was suiting him.

"All work," he'd repeated throughout her childhood, usually whenever she expressed surprise at the jobs some people in society had to do, "is honorable." She wondered whether this applied to what she was doing with Elise, if she could call this work.

The plane coasted to a landing in the Columbia airport, still a two-hour drive from Deer Bluff. As soon as the plane thudded to a stop at the gate, seatbelts began to click open. Elise waited her turn to file out of the plane, observing these travelers who were without a doubt South Carolinians. In khakis and polo shirts stretched over generous bellies, the men looked ready for golf, their wives carefully assembled in various shades of pastel. New Yorkers wore black like a uniform, and even in Princeton, the fall and the cold led naturally to dark, muted colors. Celia had worn a black turtleneck and gray, tailored pants, wanting to affirm a careful distance from her home state. Elise had given her the gray wool pants in an offhand manner, claiming they were hand-me-downs, but Celia found a tag in the back with the price still attached, indicating that they cost over a hundred dollars. She did not know what to make of the gift.

Compared to LaGuardia, the airport of South Carolina's capital city, with its wicker rocking chairs and gleaming floors, was staggeringly clean, and nobody seemed to be in a hurry. Her carry-on suitcase trailing behind her, Celia walked toward baggage claim, looking for her father. When she did not spot him immediately, she gathered her luggage from the conveyor belt and sat down with a book to wait.

He arrived almost an hour late. Dressed not in the remembered business suits of her childhood but in carpenter pants and t-shirt, his face tanned a deep reddish brown from the sun, Daniel looked older, and a little weather-beaten. She scolded herself for the initial impulse of embarrassment; this was exactly the effect her father had feared an Ivy League education might have on her. She stood up to hug him, breathing in his familiar soapy smell mixed with something she did not recognize, the scent of gasoline and cut grass.

"Breaks my heart to have you waiting for me this long," her father apologized. "I had to work until three, and I jumped straight in the car to come get you. I didn't bother to change clothes. Let's go get some dinner. My baby girl must be starving."

"It's only five," said Celia. "I'm not hungry yet. Maybe we could just go home."

"Sure we could, June bug, but I'm famished. Let's just stop somewhere real quick on the way home. I never got my lunch break today."

They drove to a chain restaurant whose décor consisted of hokey, would-be Americana, distressed washboards and rusty watering cans hanging from the wall. Her father chose a table next to the bar, beneath a television blaring out Fox News.

"I'll have the mushroom bacon supreme with fries, plus a Jack and Coke," he told the waitress. "Cee, what do you want?"

"I'll have the Asian chicken salad," she said, "and a ginger ale." Her father raised an eyebrow skeptically.

"My June bug is ordering an Asian salad? You always used to like the mushroom burger."

"I'm trying not to eat so much meat," she explained.

"Vegetarianism, eh?" he teased her. "I knew you'd come back from the Ivy League with some crazy ideas. Or else you've started worrying about your weight. But you look terrific. All grown up. I was expecting you in jeans. I hope you haven't gone off to school this year and decided you were fat. I saw something on television the other night about how college girls these days stick their fingers down their throats so they'll be skinny as sticks."

The waitress appeared with their drinks, her father taking a deep sip of his Jack Daniels-laced coke.

"Now, this is a fitting end to a hard day's work," he said. "We did the Pine Bluff golf course just out of town. Can you imagine how long it takes to get over all those hills on a John Deere?" The Pine Bluff Golf Club's five thousand dollar yearly fee ensured an all-white clientele, and Daniel once had a membership there for entertaining visiting Japanese executives.

"Does anybody still belong to that club?" she asked.

"As long as people are getting sick, divorced, or bankrupt, we'll still have doctors, lawyers, and bankers. Any of those careers would be good for you. With a degree from Princeton, you'd be a shoo-in for an MBA or law school."

"I've decided I want to be a writer," she blurted out.

"Well, now," her father said. The Jack-and-Coke might have been water, and Daniel was already signaling to the waitress that he wanted another one. "If you want to be poor like your old Dad, then that's just fine. You can do whatever your heart desires, and I am not saying there's anything wrong with being a writer. No, sir. It's a noble profession. But if that school is giving you all that money to go there, they probably have bigger plans in mind for you."

"I don't think Princeton cares whether I go into law or medicine," said Celia. "They gave me a scholarship because they believed in my promise as a student."

"And you've certainly showed them that you could take whatever they threw at you," her father said proudly. "All A's and one B your freshman year. Anybody would be impressed with that record. You would have no trouble getting into an MBA program if you keep that up."

Celia was silent. Her father's second drink arrived, along with their food: his oversized burger perched on a monstrous roll, her salad with its tiny mandarin orange slices and crunchy wonton sticks. He sipped his drink slowly, apparently more thirsty than he was hungry.

"Asian chicken salad," he said. "Tell me what else you've tried this semester."

Growing up, Celia discussed almost every detail about school with him, but reporting what had happened in chemistry class was different from explaining what she learned in courses with titles like Writing About the Self and Gender and Revolution. Even the most central event in her life at the moment was not something she could share with him. She decided to tell him about her recent trip to New York, omitting the part about the visit to the psychologist.

She described her first solo excursion into the city, wishing he could somehow experience what she'd felt, gazing out into the diverse sea of faces in the subway car. He looked at her intently, nodding between bites of his burger. When she finished, he shook his head in amazement.

"My girl goes to the big city all by herself. Honestly, I am proud of you."

"Maybe you can come up and visit sometime, and I could take you around," she said. "I remember you said you'd been to New York with Mom a long time ago."

"That was another time and another place," he said. "New York used to be pretty dangerous. Your mother was scared, but I told her not to be. I knew my way around. But I don't know this part of town you're talking about. How did you find it?"

"I have a new friend who lived in New York for several years. She gave me a list of places to visit when I went there."

"Why didn't your friend just go with you?"

"I wanted to go by myself. I thought it'd be a good adventure." He would understand this; they were both solitary people. Daniel stared up at the television.

"I'm still torn up that the Braves didn't make the Series this year," he said. Celia excused herself to go to the bathroom.

When she came back she saw another full drink on the table before him. For a few minutes, neither of them spoke, the noise from the bar defeating their efforts to shout at one another across the table.

"Can I drive home?" she asked. "I miss driving."

"Sure, if you can remember how," he said. He reached into his pocket and handed her the keys. "Finish up your Chinese salad first."

The next day Daniel took Celia to the town's only diner for breakfast. Established in 1953, Millie's was a Deer Bluff institution. Celia could picture the way it must have looked when it first opened, with eager soda jerks serving young couples from shiny Hamilton Beach milkshake machines, but now the place was rundown and nondescript, its yellow décor faded and unchanged since the 1970s. Waitresses in pink polyester uniforms slammed plates onto Formica tabletops and barked out orders to the cooks, ignoring Daniel and Celia for as long as possible. Was she imagining the waitress' disdain when she finally came to take their order? Celia recognized several people, including the parents of a girl who'd been her best friend throughout elementary school, but nobody acknowledged them or came over to ask Celia about college. She wondered if people still blamed Daniel for losing the mill, or if they felt vindicated by the obvious change in his circumstances. *Schadenfreude*, that was the new word she'd learned for it, for the way Deer Bluff must be gloating at how Daniel had come down in the world.

Oblivious to the people around him, her father tucked into his food, the runny eggs, pancakes, sausage, and coagulated grits swimming together in a greasy pool. Celia poured gummy syrup on top of her pancakes, but she had little appetite. She was losing her vision for this place; she recognized the blurring of her sight but could do little to bring it back, and the cloying sweetness of the pancake syrup disgusted her. Risotto, curry, sushi, and mussels: Elise was opening her up to new possibilities, refinement, to places that lacked the dead-end atmosphere at Millie's.

"So, what's the latest?" she said.

"Not much to tell, sweetie," her father said, spearing a sausage link and flicking it off onto her plate. "There's talk that BMW might open another plant about forty miles away, smaller than the one in Greenville, but we still don't know."

"How about the mill workers?" asked Celia. "They still mad at you about the mill closing?"

"Oh, no." Her father coughed into a napkin. "People have just about forgotten that by now. I work with a few former employees of mine over at the landscaping company, and they've been nothing but cordial to me."

"That's good to hear." She looked gratefully up at the waitress refilling her coffee cup, the woman offering her a thin-lipped smile in response.

"Your old friend is back in town," he volunteered. "Steven."

"I thought he was away at Chapel Hill," she said.

"He was. I ran into his mother at the supermarket a few weeks ago, and she said he was taking time off from school." Daniel hesitated, and Celia knew he was weighing whether or not to tell her something. "The rumor going around town is that his parents caught him this past summer doing things he shouldn't have been doing, and that they decided to withdraw him for the semester so he could get his head on straight."

"Doing what sort of things?" Celia asked.

"I don't even want to venture to guess exactly, but he was spotted around town with that twitchy choir teacher you used to have back in high school. You know, the one who's as queer as a three dollar bill."

Celia cringed at his expressions but said nothing. But later in the afternoon, after her father was settled in his recliner, nodding off into the muddied waters of his Jack Daniel's, she picked up the phone and dialed Steven's house, hanging up just before pressing the last digit. She realized she had no idea what to say to him.

The next day was Sunday, the last full day she would get to spend with her father before he returned to work. They never went to church, since Daniel had given up religion after her mother died, aside from the obligatory Christmas tree with a few tarnished bulbs and poorly wrapped presents scattered beneath it. In Deer Bluff, their lack of membership in a congregation set them apart, yet another oddity that Celia constantly had to explain to the concerned parents of her childhood playmates.

Elise had asked warily about Celia's religious genealogy, as if she feared that some latent backwoods evangelical tendencies might be transmitted through the genes to her future offspring. Her jaw dropped when Celia informed her that she'd never even been baptized, which apparently shook up Elise's belief that all residents of the Bible Belt were waiting for the rapture.

"My parents were both lapsed Catholics, but all I inherited was the guilt," Elise said. "Peter comes from a family of practicing Episcopalians. He's more of a Sufi himself, though."

"He's converted to Islam?" Celia said.

"No," Elise laughed. "It's just the religious tradition he feels the most kinship with. He loves the stories—all those poets and mystics out in the desert, having visions of God under the night sky."

With Elise Celia tried to play up her father's inattention to religious matters, implying that he consciously rejected God when his wife was taken away from him. In truth she had no real idea what Daniel believed, yet the glib, vaguely scandalized way he informed her of the rumors about Steven made her suspect that he still held the values of the rest of the community.

Her father still asleep, Celia turned the key in the ignition of the battered Ford Taurus and backed the car out of the driveway. On Sunday mornings the majority of the town's fifteen thousand residents descended upon their preferred place of worship, ranging from three varieties of Baptist to a small AME Zion church for the small African-American population. As a child, Celia's experience of religious diversity had been nonexistent: there were no Jewish families in the town and only two Catholic ones. The Patel family, presumably Hindu, owned the Starlite Motel on the outside of town, and at graduation their fifteen-year-old son, Amit, had defeated Celia for the prize of valedictorian.

Deer Bluff's principal drag bore Main Street for its unoriginal moniker, most of its storefronts deserted except for a woman's clothiers (its dusty mannequins still clad in fashions from the Reagan era), a pharmacy advertising ALL TYPES OF DIABETIC SUPPLIED HERE, and a hardware store. A few bushes in brick planters rose from the sidewalk, but a million dollar civic landscaping grant had done nothing to attract new businesses to the area. The arrival of the new Super Wal-Mart on the outskirts of town virtually guaranteed that any vestiges of Main Street's pedestrian life would forever be abandoned.

She drove slowly past the public library, where she had read through every single one of the books in the children's section, and an empty playground with industrial swing sets and sturdy jungle gyms, their colors now faded to a uniform shade of gray. A nondescript row of brick office complexes began just beyond the historic district. As the state road changed from two to four lanes, the fast food restaurants started to appear, and there was no shortage of those, their tall neon signs competing for attention with the billboards demanding passers-by, HAVE YOU BEEN INJURED IN AN ACCIDENT? And PREGNANT? CONFUSED? WE'RE HERE TO HELP. CALL SHEPHERD'S WAY. The Starlite Motel, its ancient art-deco sign unintentionally stylish, was still in business, a white pick-up truck and raffish old Cadillac parked side by side out front, as if trysting with one another. It was there that Celia and Steven had once rented a room, consumed with fear the entire time that their parents might drive out this way and recognize Steven's car.

Past the Starlite Motel, on a street marked only by an overflowing dumpster on the corner, asphalt gave way to macadam, leading back to the old mill. Kudzu crept over the abandoned road, its vines making a path from one side of the road to the other. Her father had told her that kudzu could grow up to three feet a day, a plant originally imported to renew the land that it had instead invaded and consumed. Celia locked the car doors against the dense, impenetrable foliage, a place where bodies might be disposed of and never recovered. Anayo Mills, her father's lost empire, was smaller than she remembered, a lonely brick building with high windows overlooking railroad tracks where trains once stopped twice each day to fill up entire boxcars with stacks of freshly woven cotton towels. A rusted conveyor belt protruded from one side of the building, descending down into overgrown grass before disappearing. The few desolate attempts at graffiti scrawled on the walls reminded her of Newark, but at least there the empty buildings had one another for company and were not so isolated.

Celia sighed and swung the car around. She drove back through town, turning off onto the side road that wound past the First Baptist Church. Of all the churches, this was the most affluent, a formerly modest brick building with a white steeple that had been expanded so that the façade was now a coliseum of tall, multicolored stained glass windows. Pulling into one of the last parking spaces close to the wooded cemetery, she watched undetected as people began to file out of the church. Her father and the crew from King's Landscaping had just been here, and she made sure to admire Daniel's work: the lawn shorn down to a yellow stubble, bare in patches, which could be blamed on nothing but the lack of rain. Finally she saw who she was looking for: Steven in a tie and schoolboy's blue blazer, his once-long hair cropped into a short, almost military cut, steering his mother out of the church. Bunny Addison, a Charleston-born ex debutante for whom Deer Bluff would always be the major comedown of her life, was impeccably dressed in a pale yellow Chanel suit. Mr. Addison was nowhere in sight.

Celia decided against her initial impulse to jump out of the car, intercepting them just as they reached the end of the Oz-like brick walkway leading away from the church. Instead she watched from under her sunglasses until they arrived at their car. Steven opened the door for his mother, holding her hand as she stepped into the car, his face betraying no particular emotion about any misfortune that may have befallen him. Their car fell in line behind the others forming a caravan out of the First Baptist parking lot, Celia waiting a few minutes before she joined in behind them.

Loneliness was an emotion that she was usually able to keep at bay, but at that moment it struck her that Steven, the only person she'd been close to in Deer Bluff aside from her father, was a stranger to her now. She pictured him in ten years, one of those men who testified on talk shows that with the help of the Good Lord, they'd managed to shake off their homosexual tendencies, men you knew were lying, were still sneaking off for furtive encounters in the restrooms of public parks.

At the house her father was sitting at the table drinking coffee, staring morosely out the window.

"Where've you been?" he asked.

"Just driving around," replied Celia. "I wanted to see what was new in town."

"Since you left at the end of the summer? Not very much," he said. Yet Deer Bluff had aged since her last visit.

"I went by the Baptist church," she volunteered. "Lawn looks good."

"You went there just to check out my handiwork?" he said. "Or did you get some religion along with that vegetarianism up at school?"

"No," Celia laughed. "Actually, I wanted to talk to Steven. I saw his family leaving the church, but I couldn't bring myself to say anything."

"You were here all summer," Daniel said. "You didn't seem to give much thought to him then. He was right up the road interning at Starnes & Munn, but y'all never met up."

"I guess I wanted to see if what you said about him was true."

"I don't think you can tell that about a person just from looking at him," Daniel said. "Celia, this town has a mean streak when it comes to gossip. It's a small place, you know that as well as I do. You can't pay too much attention to what people tell you. What they're saying about Steven might not be true. I shouldn't have even repeated it." He got up and opened one of the cabinets, pulling out a loaf of bread. "Do you want a sandwich? I'm going to make some toast."

"No, thanks," Celia said. "But what would be so terrible if what they say is true? There's nothing wrong with being gay."

Daniel placed two slices of bread into the toaster. "What's my daughter doing at Princeton? Well, she's become a gay rights crusader."

"Dad, that's not fair," she said. "But I certainly don't believe that a church can save someone from being gay." From the refrigerator Daniel took out a carton of egg substitute and a stick of butter.

"How about this? A healthy omelet," he said.

"The butter kind of negates that," she muttered.

"I'm only using a little bit. Doctor says I've got to get my cholesterol down. You want one?"

"Dad, you're changing the subject," she said.

"I'm not changing the subject. The conversation has reached its logical end. I've just moved on to other topics."

"Maybe I'm not through," she protested.

"Keep talking then." He disappeared into the pantry. "I'm all ears."

She waited for him to come back into the room. When he reappeared, he was carrying a bottle of vodka and a large plastic bottle of spicy tomato juice.

"Bloody Mary?" he asked. "My morning cocktail." Celia shook her head.

"I was hoping college would make you less of a teetotaler," Daniel said. "It's not nice to let someone drink alone." Celia started. Recently Elise had said something very similar.

"Drinking is about being sociable," Elise said one day at the Annex, pushing a whiskey sour across the table at her. "People don't feel comfortable unburdening themselves when someone sits there sipping at a soda."

Celia looked at her father and nodded. "Fine, but go easy on me. Remember I'm only twenty."

"And the safest place to drink is with your family, although Grandma Hutchinson might not have agreed. Not when Grandpa took out the strap after polishing off a pint of Jim Beam and beat his kids for the bad marks they'd brought home that week in school. My mother certainly got her share of whippings." Long-suffering Great-Grandma Hutchinson was the reason Celia had been allowed to check "Native American" on her scholarship forms. Celia knew her only from black-and-white photos, a stern, thin-lipped woman, dark hair restrained in a bun, her high Cherokee cheekbones and square face her bequest to her great grandchild.

Into two tall glasses filled with ice Daniel poured shots of vodka, followed by the spicy tomato mix. "Now, the real way you make it is with Worcestershire sauce and Tabasco. But I find the Mrs. T's blend to be perfectly adequate." From the refrigerator he removed a few withered celery sticks, using them to stir the drinks. "And I even had celery on hand to make the experience complete. This is a good way to get a daily serving of vegetables."

Daniel placed the Bloody Mary in front of her, the celery sticks drooping out over the top of the glass. She lifted the drink and closed her eyes, pretending it was Elise asking her to try this, Elise introducing her to a sophisticated new drink. A flood of salty, spicy tomato concentrate washed across her taste buds. The smoky aftertaste in the back of her throat must have been the vodka.

"I don't know whether I like it or hate it," she confessed.

"Keep drinking. I'm sure you'll like it. The taste of all alcohol moves from hate to love after the first couple swallows." He turned back toward the counter and began preparing his omelet.

Daniel was right; the drink did grow on her. After the first one she became loquacious, remembering a thousand events that had happened to her that semester that had nothing to do with Elise and Peter.

"Another one?" her father asked, standing up from the kitchen table.

"Why not?" she said. Warmth, a convivial atmosphere, the possibility for meaningful exchange, all could be facilitated by alcohol. The great potential of drink was beginning to dawn on her. With Elise she had held back, partly out of fear that she was not yet twenty-one, although Elise had assured her that certain places could care less about her age. But the other reason for restraining herself was now becoming clear. She was afraid that she would like it.

"I always knew sending you away for college would be a good idea," her father was telling her, midway through her second drink, his third. "I couldn't see you at Carolina. You'd be lost there. I wanted you to get as far away from this place as possible. From this town, this Godforsaken state. You're like your father—always on the outside looking in. I'd rather you be an outsider in a place where you really are an outsider. Not like here, where by rights you ought to belong. Someday you can come back with your Princeton degree and really show these people a thing or two."

"What if I don't want to come back?"

"You'll always come back to your daddy," Daniel said. "Even if you don't stay." He looked slightly forlorn. "Ever since your mom died, you've been my entire life. You know that."

Celia nodded. The thought of returning to live in Deer Bluff after college made her want to crawl in bed and never come out.

"Fifteen years is a long time to mourn someone."

"Your mother deserved it. There was no one else like her. I loved her from the minute I first met her." Celia had heard the story before: the Kappa Sigma dance, her mother the date of one of his fraternity brothers. After that night, they were inseparable. "I lost a friend but gained the love of my life," he was fond of saying. One of the stock narratives her father repeated so many times, it had acquired the patina of myth, revealing little about the woman Celia wanted so desperately to know.

"I wish I could remember her," she said, trying to prompt him. As if on cue, he started reminiscing, but the stories were, as she suspected, all ones she'd heard before.

An hour later he was still talking. Celia stopped listening with all her attention, had refused the third drink and could feel herself sinking back down to earth. The gradual fading of warmth made her feel deceived, the fuzzy sadness left in its wake presumably one that led a person to continue drinking to postpone the moment when it would return in full force, exposing all the uncomfortable gaps and absences in life.

* * *

For fall break Peter had no interest in going anywhere.

"There are no holidays in grad school," he told Elise when she accused him of deliberately failing to mention the break. It was Sunday, the one day Peter usually stayed away from the library, allowing himself to sleep in until at least eight. "The more time you give me to work, the sooner I'll finish the dissertation."

For no reason Elise woke up in a fighting mood. As soon as she opened her eyes that morning, everything seemed slightly off. Even the sight of Peter, standing in front of the kitchen counter, the Sunday New York Times open in front of him, was irritating.

"I know grad students work all the time, but it would have been nice to plan a vacation," she protested.

"We're going to Boston for Thanksgiving." He kept reading.

"We've hardly spent any time doing anything lately. This routine is driving me crazy."

"What routine? You don't seem to live by one. I don't see how quitting your job, finding an egg donor, and developing a bizarre relationship with her is routine."

"I'm talking about your routine," she said. "Spending your entire day in the library. Coming home, never before 6:30."

"People with jobs have to do this too. They leave the house early in the morning and don't come home until late. That's the only way work gets done."

Without work deadlines looming over her head, Elise had to admit she was slightly bored. This week, with Celia visiting her father down South, there was little to occupy her except for the clinic visits to check the effects of the estrogen. This was empty time that would presumably soon be occupied with children, but until then, there were moments she felt she might go insane.

"If you want to be a housewife, why not go back to volunteering at the rape crisis center? You used to love doing that."

"I wouldn't be a good listener these days." Plus, the world of the post-millennial college rape crisis center was vastly different from the one she had volunteered in several years before in New York. Sometimes the phone lines hardly rang at all, and she did not know what to make of this.

"Or maybe you could take some cooking classes. Learn some new techniques in the kitchen."

"That's what you want in a wife? A hot meal on the table every night?"

"I didn't mean it like that. I'm only making a suggestion." He put down his newspaper and got up to refill his coffee. "I don't know why you didn't consider Diana's suggestion to go back to work full time. At least until you're further along in the pregnancy. Pregnancy doesn't have to be a full time job."

"Getting pregnant does. Especially when you're doing it on your own."

Elise lifted the metal carafe out from the coffee maker, annoyed to find it empty.

"You only made enough for yourself?"

"I didn't know how long you would sleep. You always say that after it sits for eighteen minutes you won't drink it. Take my cup."

"You use too much sugar."

Elise took the coffee out of the freezer and began to prepare another pot. Peter turned back to the Travel section, oblivious to her frustration. He was right that she needed to do something, but she didn't want to admit it. There was truth in Diana's accusation that her work had been uneven lately, but now she regretted quitting without so much as a word of protest. Eric Babu still had not answered her email, and she was plagued by the fear that she was easily replaceable, that Diana had found someone else who could do her job equally as well. Elise had always considered editing a special craft, an art form that required not merely the ability to make mechanical corrections but a fine, precise eye and a passion for language. All texts were imperfect, but a good editor understood and shaped a writer's vision, refining the work so that it bore both the author's distinctive voice and the unmistakable hand of the pilot who helped steer the craft to shore.

But her enjoyment of the work had faded. All the novels were beginning to bore her, and a nagging voice inside urged her to quit, to experience the fullness of pregnancy and to see what it was like to become part of that surging tide of middle-upper class women who were abandoning high-powered careers to experience motherhood.

Caitlin, her best friend from college, had done just that. For years they had been inseparable in almost everything they did. As first year college students, both of them were caught off balance by New York (Caitlin was from Michigan), and while Elise worked through issues with her anorexia, Caitlin was in therapy for other college-related issues. When she drank, Caitlin had a tendency to go on autopilot and find herself waking up in places she did not recognize, with people she did not recall meeting. In several instances, this had ended badly. Both girls discovered similar root causes to their distress (absent fathers), became English majors (sharing a fondness for the postwar suburban despair of writers like Richard Yates and John Cheever), and entered the publishing industry after graduation. They remained friends even after Caitlin left publishing for a brief stint in graduate school, later marrying a restaurateur (absent father replaced by absent husband).

Now she lived in Darien, Connecticut with two perfect, blonde children, upon whom she lavished all of her considerable energy and attention. Caitlin was the kind of woman who became more beautiful as she aged, the insecurities of her youth falling away one by one to be replaced by tangible proof of her success: house, wealth, husband, and of course the requisite gifted children. Her situation suited her, and Elise longed for that symmetry that usually marked both their lives. She had not yet told Caitlin that they'd progressed to needing a donor, though she had talked about her problems starting a family. When she left Smyth & Copperfield, her friend assured her she'd done the right thing.

"You'll be glad you did it," Caitlin said. "You'll be pregnant before you know it. Raising kids is, hands down, *the* most rewarding job I've ever done. You get to be there for all those milestones—the first word, the first steps."

Elise's mother was less understanding.

"I'm not sure now is the time to be quitting your job," Helen had said. "What about insurance?"

"Peter has it through the university," she explained. Her mother, a feminist of the old school, sighed.

"Work is a privilege. To be taken seriously in the same careers as men is something that the women of my generation had to fight for. Now you're there; you've arrived without even having to claw your way to the top. I'm not sure you realize what an accomplishment that is."

"I do, Mom," Elise insisted. "I just need to take a break. The work is stagnating."

"If you went back to full-time, that wouldn't be the case," her mother said. Her mother made an effort to read most of the books she edited, as if Elise herself had written them.

"That's not going to happen," Elise said.

"Defying your parents is not an easy thing," Dr. Geiger assured her. "All those years of listening to your mother's lessons in feminism. You're going against her beliefs. But you have to be confident in your choices, certain of what you're doing. Why do we make the choices we make? We have to interrogate those choices, to understand why we do what we do."

Interrogate our choices, Elise repeated like a mantra. *Interrogate our choices*. Interrogation became more like torture, her choices subjected to so much scrutiny and analysis that any hope of comprehension became impossible. It was easy to be stubborn, to select a path in a flush of impulsiveness, but Elise had a problem with fall-out. Peter certainly offered little support, dropping little remarks here and there about her newly unemployed status.

She filled up her mug of coffee and looked over at him, absorbed in the newspaper. Even the New York Times infuriated her, its pages full of reminders that others were making news while she herself had fallen out of the race. She had only appeared in its pages as a subject once, the wedding announcement to Peter indisputable proof of their success as a couple. From time to time she looked at the clipping, her hair dark blonde then, pulled up in a neat chignon that showed off her neck and shoulders, a single pearl tucked in the hollow of her throat. *The bride is keeping her name.* A concession to her mother. *The couple will honeymoon in St. Bart's. They will live in Princeton.* Princeton, the tweedy promise of happily ever after.

"We need to talk," she said, pushing down the front of his newspaper.

"About?"

"About how you're not being very supportive of my decision to stay at home."

"I'm not?" he said. "What makes you think that?"

"You make little jokes. You belittle what I'm doing."

"I'm not doing it on purpose," Peter replied. "I just don't think it's making you happy."

"How would you know what makes me happy? You're never around."

"Elise, can't we just have a quiet morning and enjoy each other's company? I don't feel like fighting."

"It's just that I see you putting up the constant defense of your dissertation, your dissertation, your dissertation. It's the reason you give for everything, for why we hardly ever have sex anymore, for why you have to disappear each morning and spend the entire day buried in the library. But you never show me anything you've written."

"Look, whatever you're upset about, I'm sorry. If I did something, I'm sorry. Is that better?"

"I don't know." She could feel tears pooling in the corners of her eyes. "It's just so much emotional work, trying to have children."

"Well, get over it already! There are worse things in the world that could happen. You're doing the next best thing. You're going to have your baby."

Elise glared at him.

"Oh, so now it's 'your baby.' You're not in this too?"

"Stop twisting my words," Peter said wearily. "I support you. How many more times do I need to say it?"

She had pushed him, perhaps almost to the limit. His face was cold; he might have been talking to a stranger. The words were out, and now she regretted that she'd started the day this way. But she didn't really want his support. She wanted something else: love, anger, whatever was the opposite of indifference. The adoration of the early days, though that might be too much to ask. Walking around to his side of the counter, she laced her arms around his waist.

"Now I'm sorry," she said. "I don't know what's gotten into me." She rested her head on his shoulder, turning her head slightly to kiss his neck. "I woke up on the wrong side of the bed this morning. I think it's the hormones. I know I haven't been myself lately."

"I forgive you," he said. Lifting her face toward his, he kissed her, not in the perfunctory manner of most of his embraces lately, but with actual gentleness and longing. She reached up and touched his hair, moving her body into the narrow space between him and the counter.

"Let's go over to the sofa," she murmured. He said nothing but held her there, bending down to bury his face in her hair. Brushing her lips against his neck, she could feel the warm pulse of his heart. Shoving aside the newspaper, a plate clanging dramatically into the sink, he lifted her up onto the counter, and she wrapped her legs around him.

"Oh Elise," he sighed. "What the hell is wrong with us?"

"Don't talk," she said, unbuckling his belt, sliding her hand into his jeans. And now he was responding, his eyes tightly shut, hands pushing up her nightgown, angling his body up to meet hers. He lurched into her, his arms wrapped tightly around her waist, a small anguished cry escaping his throat. She closed her eyes, not wanting to let go, but she could feel him fading away from her.

"Well, that's more like it," she said. "Why don't we take a shower together and go to the bagel shop? You can get to the library a little late."

"I can't, Elise. I'm working on something, and I want to get back to it. But I promise I'll show it to you soon." He walked back into the bedroom and turned on the shower, closing the door behind him.

"So much for fall break," Elise shouted after him. She took a sip of her coffee but it had grown cold, and the disarray of newspapers suddenly infuriated her. She slammed the coffee mug down on the counter. Finally it had felt like they were connecting again, but Peter still did not want to spend time with her. Tears pierced her eyes, but she took deep breaths and tried to think about how she would spend the day.

Walking back to the spare bedroom they had made into a tiny home office, Elise stared at the walls, the room's neutral space suggesting a project that could conceivably occupy her time. She could get rid of the twin bed and stake out some of the garage sales in the affluent neighborhoods surrounding the university, maybe coming home with a cherry wood crib, or a Shaker rocking chair. Perhaps she could indulge the impulse she often had to pull into the giant Babies-R-Us on Route 1, allowing herself to wander through the displays of tiny infant apparel, imagining the jogging strollers and breast pumps that would soon fill their apartment. But even buying one piece of furniture would be a mistake, might jinx the pregnancy. On the other hand, getting the room ready might indicate her resolve to have a child occupying this room no matter what happened. Should her efforts to get pregnant using Celia's eggs fail, after two or three rounds of IVF, she decided she would be ready to consider adoption.

Elise signed into her email account. A single illuminated envelope indicated that she had a message. She clicked onto the icon, feeling a small thrill at the sight of the name of the sender, Eric Babu, written out to the side.

Elise,

Please forgive the tardy response. I was in London for a writer's conference. Have been working on something I expect will be finished in a few months' time, perhaps we could meet when I'm next in the city in a few weeks' time. As you noted, my Princeton debut is fast approaching, details in the link below. I hope you will be in attendance. I intend to stay in the city for a while, should the atmosphere prove to be hospitable (as I imagine it will). I will be in touch.

Cheers,
Eric

An envoy from another world, Eric Babu instantly reversed the negative course the day was taking. To him she was not a wife, a nag, a distraction from work; he had someone else in his life who filled that role. Elise read the note again, picturing him writing it from his Toronto flat, which she knew from a documentary that had shown Babu at work, his spacious study on the second floor of a duplex, the mahogany desk where he wrote everything out on a sleek silver laptop, surrounded by his bookshelves and Nigerian wood carvings.

Elise had never been to Toronto, where Babu lived much of the year with his wife and three children. His marriage was a traditional one, made years before he achieved fame as a writer, and he intimated that it had been arranged. Although in the West he was the one with fame and prestige, his wife was of higher birth, he said, and in Nigeria he was considered to have married up. The wife provided sustenance, children, and unquestioning support of this profession that brought in so much income and acclaim. She did not read his books. In the documentary the viewer caught a glimpse of her stirring a large iron kettle of peanut stew, a beautiful Nefertiti with downcast eyes and an aquiline nose, resplendent in a red, gold and black traditional Nigerian gown with a matching scarf wrapped around her head. They were a striking couple, his wife's feline beauty complemented by Babu's commanding presence, the heavy, leonine dreadlocks a halo surrounding his fierce, almost Roman features.

At one point, Elise had been jealous of this woman, who would be recorded in history as Babu's wife. While he might thank Elise in his acknowledgments, the world would only know her as his editor. A self-professed lover of women, Babu was the type who needed to compartmentalize, to find a variety of women to share different aspects of his life, unable to consider the possibility that all might exist in a single package.

"Women were like a bouquet," wrote Babu about one of his characters. "Together they completed him, and their combined effect was worth more than a single, stemmed rose, its beauty intoxicating, its prick deadly. To love just one was to risk his own destruction."

Elise knew he kept them all (including her, including his wife) at arm's length. The ultimate unavailability of men like Babu intrigued her. As time passed, Peter had ceased to be an enigma and became more of a resistant object. But Babu remained a challenge. For him she had worked to remain alluring, to play the same game of distance alternating with warmth that she knew would hold his attention. When she first met him, she knew of his reputation and was determined to remain on her guard in case he tried anything. But for the first two years of their professional relationship, nothing happened. This was his genius with a woman, overwhelming her with charisma while making her think all along that it was she who finally asked him to honor her with his affection.

Although she would never have been so presumptuous as to think of herself as a muse, there was one character in his last book that resembled her. Sometimes, when she needed reassurance of her past accomplishments, she took *The Dam-Builder's Apprentice* from the bookshelf in her bedroom. She went first to the acknowledgments page, which contained a veiled reference only she would be able to decipher: "Many thanks to Elise, whose editing skills are as keen as a cup of espresso." Eric claimed espresso was like cocaine, the secret to his stamina on the sleepless nights they spent doing everything but working on his book.

She read the dedication over a few times, finally turning to page thirty-seven, on which he characterized an American woman, an employee of an evil petroleum conglomerate, who dazzled the corrupt Nigerian executives in the boardroom with "hair limpid and yielding as the muddy banks of the rivers of their childhood, eyes the fortunate blue that mothers pin on infants' breasts to ward off the evil eye, those eyes always casting a look that, like the country she represented, promised without ever really delivering." Was it any coincidence that on page one hundred twenty-eight, this character, Alice, seduced the hero, Onuwa, with promises of a visa that disappeared with the taillights of the plane carrying her back to Houston?

Babu was the one secret she had never told Peter. The irony in how they met, at Babu's book party, would be something she kept to herself. Even after she and Peter began seeing each other, there had been a few transgressions, but she cut off the physical relationship with Eric once it became clear that Peter was a more reliable prospect. Despite Babu's professed indifference, she still felt satisfied to have been the one who ended their affair.

His email, his promise to finish working in New York, "should the atmosphere prove to be hospitable," made her wonder what sort of hospitality he was seeking. Was this an offhand remark about his working environment or had he intended to drop these few words as a hint for her to linger over?

"Elise, you're right. I can get to the library by noon. I don't need to rush things."

Peter's voice interrupted her reverie. Closing the email, she swiveled around in the chair. His hair was slick from the shower, his white robe a stark contrast with his dark skin, still tanned from running, giving him a slightly exotic look. He reached out his hand to her, and she let him pull her over to the bed. They lay on the narrow bed in companionable silence, relaxing into the familiar hollows and gaps of each other's bodies. She breathed in his smell of soap and saltiness, which always reminded her of the ocean. She closed her eyes, but it was Eric Babu who appeared as if stamped on the back of her eyelids, sauntering toward her from across his loft with two small, perfect cups of espresso.

* * *

Later, Peter sat in his carrel typing furiously, surrounded by Arabic texts and his beloved stack of photocopies from the colonial archives about Sidi Maarif. From time to time he consulted them, needing support for the argument that was beginning to build on the computer screen in front of him. The hours blurred by as his fingers magically tapped out hundreds of words, as if he were possessed by a *djinn*. Although he did not know where this new chapter was going, he was inspired, for the first time in months. He had opened himself up to the entreaties of the Sufi poets, forever talking about love and the elusive union with the Beloved. And at last, something was happening.

His eyes slid over the fine script, the inky calligraphy swirling up, taking root in his brain so vividly he could picture himself still there, in a town that actually bore no resemblance to the place that travelers had raved about.

"Sidi Maarif is guarded by Barbary pirates, and our approach by land was deterred by mountains so stony and fortified as to seem impenetrable," wrote a British traveler who visited Morocco at the end of the nineteenth century. "To reach its mud-walled casbahs, one walks for three days along mountain footpaths with a native whose feet are guided by such memory that even sudden blindness could not deter them from their course. Many are lost on these mountains, but if one perseveres, Sidi Maarif rewards the visitor with her ample pleasures, possessing potable water, palm trees overflowing with fruit, and inhabitants who are as pleasant and hospitable as the most lavish of desert shaykhs. This is to say nothing about their rugs, which fetch a higher price in the markets of Marrakech than a caravan of gold. Even the famous Dacca gauzes of India pale by comparison."

The rugs! Peter tried to recreate them in his mind, having seen only one true example in an exhibit of textiles at the *Institut du Monde Arabe* in Paris. The actual rug was only a fragment, eaten away by moths, and he squinted at the faded piece of cloth and tried to reconcile it with his research. He read the words of a French explorer, Charles Perrin, dated 1890, well after the start of the Algerian occupation, Morocco's riches still a glimmer in France's eye.

"They are called *zarbeeya*," wrote the Frenchman. "I have seen one or two of these fine rugs, once in a home in Oujda and also in Algiers. The owner of the former, an educated gentleman from one of the old *cherifien* families, a lord of no small renown in his own country, had traveled to this place as a young man and could not be certain of its whereabouts. This gentleman had been involved in the Saharan salt trade, passing through the great cities of the Soudan, from Dakar to Bamako, Dahomey to Marrakech. Once he had come to this town, and said that it was inhabited by nomadic Arabs who practiced an obscure version of Mohammedanism much influenced by the worshiping of spirits and saints."

"Sidi Maarif existed, the man informed me, for no other purpose save making these ethereal fabrics which were not in the least like the rugs made by other tribes. It was said that the inhabitants once cultivated silkworms, and that the rugs were woven of the finest wool, the softest silk, and the most intricate designs. The labor of the women was so valued that they themselves governed the town, and, in fact, the men. Inheritance passed from mother to daughter, and men lived in their wives' houses after marriage. But when pressed to name a location, this gentleman could not be certain, except to say that the village could be found in the first shallows of fine sand which begin one hundred kilometers south of Agadir."

With the help of these travelers, he was recreating a forgotten world, one whose very existence would transform the literature on women in the Muslim world, exploding the stereotypes of their passivity. These women were artists, their matrilineal customs a stark contrast to the completely patriarchal societies surrounding them. To Peter some of the archival material further hinted at a Da Vinci code-like conspiracy surrounding these women, where it was in the mutual interest of both the Moroccan sultan and the colonial French and Spanish officials to obliterate all traces of their existence. In the early twentieth century, certainly, the presence of such heretical customs would require "civilizing" these women to the rule of men. All morning he had been focusing on this untold story.

He took a deep breath and decided to take a break. He checked Facebook, which was a mistake, because now he could see the status updates of his friends from the Near East Studies Department. The mundane but competitive descriptions of what they were up to immediately stifled his desire to write. There were updates of the I'm-here-and-you're-not variety. *Mourad... is in Fes!* The gratuitous updates that begged for more information, from a colleague who often flirted with him. *Yasemin wonders why it has to be this way.* Why what has to be what way? Who cared? Then there were the competitive status updates, which just made him feel anxious. *Edgar is buried in the Widener Library.* Or *Esther... has a brilliant idea for next year's Fulbright!* And from his colleague who was about to finish: *Boris... onward with final corrections! 522 pages of dissertation, ready for submission.* 522 pages... an enviable fact, considering that Peter and Boris had begun graduate school together. His awareness of the whereabouts of everyone in his cohort made it feel like they were all a part of the same military regiment, imposing a psychic discipline upon each other. Those who were not working were in danger of falling behind, while others sped ahead in the acquisition of knowledge that might give them an edge later in the bilious waters of the Job Market. Peter preferred to lurk rather than update, thinking that if he was this annoyed by his colleagues, certainly by updating he would inflict the same suffering on them.

He saw he had a friend request. Celia had friended him. He accepted, browsing to her profile picture, which represented only a fourth of her face, one green disembodied eye looking out at him. The image was that of someone who wants to show off a single facial feature but is uncertain about the sum of its parts. A few friends had posted comments on her wall, but like him, she had no status updates. It was a relief, at least, to see that someone from a supposedly more tech savvy generation who disliked putting herself out there as much as he did. He clicked on his wife's page. *best.morning.ever…* He smiled. At least he'd finally done something to make her happy. Elise usually favored enigmatic posts that he knew were probably intended for him. Some of the older updates were still on her page, a coded journal of her pregnancy aspirations. *Elise is hoping for something positive. Elise is waiting, again… Elise another losing number in the lottery. Elise wonders if there's a cure.*

He cursed himself for thinking Facebook would be a good idea for a break. Academic labor required a delicate environmental balance that was almost maddening in its exactitude. The easiest factors to control were the physical setting, as long as he was out of his apartment. The mental environment was harder to control. The knowledge that Elise was always at home, obsessing over her childlessness, was a major source of consternation. He missed the independent Elise who did not really need him. Her disappearance had been gradual. At first, both of them participated eagerly in the game of making a baby, but when it became apparent that this wasn't something she could conquer with the sheer force of her will, she seemed to unravel.

First there were the visits to fertility specialists, Elise often requiring his presence in the waiting room for moral support while she underwent various tests. These took endless hours away from his work schedule, but at first he did not mind. He could empathize with her humiliation at having to submit her body to the clinical gaze of the doctors. Being frequently invaded by cold metal instruments must have been a turn-off, explaining why she had lost interest in sex with him once the doctor's visits started. As the prognosis became increasingly grim, she seemed at first to descend into herself, growing uncharacteristically silent, confiding only in her therapist and deriving little joy from anything she did. She started working part-time from home, sometimes staying in her pajamas all day, eating even less than usual and falling asleep in front of the television at night. Peter tried to remain supportive. He kept the house clean, did all the laundry, and took over the cooking. Finally she seemed to snap part of the way back into her old self again.

"I have accepted everything," she said one evening when he came home to find her at the stove, her expression bright and manic. She was tossing a multi-hued stir fry in a hissing wok with all the verve of a chef at Benihana's. "I can't have a baby. So what? It's not the end of the world. There's more to life than having children."

"We can adopt," he reassured her. "Or we can try some of the other strategies the doctors suggested. You could hire a surrogate. Why not wait until I'm finished with school, then we'll have more time to consider our options?"

But Elise didn't want to wait. That night, after he pushed away his plate, feeling satisfied and hoping that life was finally back to normal, she told him quietly that she had decided to pursue a donor. She outlined her plan, citing the popularity of the classified ads taken out in college newspapers. Already she had composed a prospective advertisement.

"I worded it carefully. I'll be looking for a creative response, one that shows verbal intelligence. Attractiveness would be nice too, but you know how these Princeton kids are. Money and good breeding make them attractive. I don't see how we can lose."

"Do you think someone with money and good breeding is going to respond to this ad?" he asked, but she ignored him. After they found a donor, she and Elise would begin taking birth control to synchronize their menstrual cycles. Once that happened, the donor would inject hormones into herself to stimulate the production of multiple ova. Finally, ten to fourteen days later, a simple operation would retrieve the eggs from the donor, after which they would be fertilized in a dish with Peter's sperm and finally implanted inside Elise.

"And that's where you come in," Elise said gleefully. "As usual, you'll be on call to deliver the goods."

His own contribution to the operation disturbed him. Entirely absent from the proceedings until the last minute, he would then indirectly plant his genetic load into his wife, thanks to the advances of modern medical science.

"How effective is this?" he asked.

"The clinic claims that forty percent end up as live births." She told him about the potential complications, about the risk for the donor, who might develop a condition called Ovarian Hyper-Stimulation Syndrome, where the body went into overdrive after the extraction of the ova, producing so many eggs that the ovaries went haywire and could potentially become scarred.

"What kind of person would be crazy enough to undergo this?" he wondered. "It could take months of her time, she'll have to give herself shots, endure a painful operation, and then potentially risk her own reproductive future."

"That's why we're offering ample compensation."

"We are?"

"For her time and the risk involved, not for the eggs."

"So you're not buying her eggs, then."

"The eggs are a gift. The money is for her time."

"A gift. Then why can't we find someone who will give them for free? I hear in Europe you can't compensate donors."

"Europe is not America."

"Well, I'm just saying, maybe we should stop talking about it like this woman is really giving a gift if it isn't a true gift, you know?"

"I think it's nice that there's financial incentive," Elise said. "But in some of the blogs I've read, the women who donate the eggs say they would even do it without compensation."

"But organ donors don't get compensated for the time and risk involved."

"Organ donors are usually dead."

"Not kidney donors," he said. "Suppose I wanted to donate a kidney and ask for ten thousand dollars. The money is not for the kidney, but for my time and the risk involved. But yet compensation for organ donation is illegal. How is this different?"

"Eggs are not organs."

"It's still a risk to make someone donate them."

"Not really," Elise deflected his point. "I've done a lot of research, and I think it's the best way to go. This way I can ensure the prenatal environment I create for our child. It can have your genetic material. I can also have the whole experience of pregnancy and delivery, and we don't have to tell anyone in the family that I can't have children."

Against his better instincts, Peter had agreed, although the ethical implications of the whole situation were discomfiting. At first he thought about approaching Celia alone, to make sure she knew of the risks and had not been brainwashed by Elise. No, he knew better than to get involved. His ability to concentrate was already shaky, and getting in the middle of all this could make his mental working environment a living hell. Even his spontaneous run that day with Celia had made him lose focus, had paralyzed his working hours with worries about whether they were exploiting her.

If reproduction could happen so easily without sex, would it someday lose its evolutionary relevance? Americans liked to think they were evolved enough to enjoy sex for the act alone, spending a good fifteen or twenty years of their lives seeking sex but completely divorcing it from its original purpose of procreation. And yet when he and Elise had begun their own attempts to start a family, something like instinct took over. When they made love, it was with the intention to create something, and he found this to be a powerful emotion. In truth he did not know how he felt about children, but he took Elise's word for it that they were a necessary stage in life. The idea of making a new little person who blended both their traits and features into one being became appealing. When they failed, she seemed to push him away, and in turn he found his desire for her dwindling.

Peter looked at his watch. Already an hour had passed without his brain processing a single word. He began to shuffle through his photocopies again, trying to turn his thoughts back to Spanish colonial occupation. The Spanish had destroyed everything, tearing down Sidi Maarif's mud casbahs, replacing them with a movie theater, a library, and even a bullfighting ring. The sea now safely free of pirates, they built a sort of monorail that extended out into the Atlantic, intended to drop goods into the Spanish ships that would receive them. The rugs all but disappeared, and the women were encouraged to make a modified, cheaper version that over time lost all resemblance to the travelers' descriptions, vegetable dyes now replaced by cheap chemicals, wool and silk with synthetic yarn.

By the time Peter arrived, the Spanish were obsolete, their abandoned structures a stage set of ruins. Around the formerly grand center, multiple families now occupied the old villas that had once belonged to colonial administrators, and the new Sidi Maarif was a bustling market town, full of identical boxlike concrete buildings, garages, dry goods shops, bakeries, mosques, and a bus station. In one of these concrete buildings, Peter had rented a small, two-room apartment, each day walking a half-mile to the newly constructed government health clinic on the outskirts of town. The women and their tapestries long gone, Sidi Maarif was a forgotten empire of no interest to anyone, and having left no traces, it had no more reality in the present than memory itself. Remembering his own time there, and remembering Leila (who was perfect because she was unattainable, memory making her more so), Peter recalled the magical quality of those two years after college when the future had seemed filled with so much promise.

CHAPTER SIX

Each morning during the week that Celia was at home, Daniel left the house before she was up for his seven-to-three shift at King's Landscaping. She awoke slowly, coming to gradual consciousness in her four-poster canopy bed, in a setting that now seemed so stereotypically girlish Celia could not believe she had once profoundly identified with this room. On her tenth birthday Daniel decided she had outgrown her twin bed and hand-me-down furniture, and he took her to a furniture outlet in Columbia, telling her to choose anything she wanted. Immediately she gravitated toward the little girl's bedroom set with its white canopy, matching white nightstands, white keepsake chest and bureau. She loved the way he commanded them to deliver the set that very week (her father, prior to the closure of the mill, was a man who thrived on authority), and one day when she came home from school she found her room painted pink, the set perfectly in place.

Daniel had always been more than generous with her, so much so that even after he lost his job, he continued to spend exorbitant amounts of money on her. Their shopping sprees in Columbia did not, as might have been the case with a mother, revolve around clothes, haircuts, and makeovers. Knowing how much she liked to read, he would start at a Barnes & Noble (Deer Bluff possessing no bookstore of its own), announcing, "You have one hour and fifty bucks. Go." Meanwhile he drank coffee and browsed through Civil War or Vietnam history books. At the end of the hour, Celia would present her selections to him, nearly always fiction, Daniel thumbing through the books and nodding with approval.

"Will they make you smarter?" he asked, pretending to weigh the books she'd chosen as if their heaviness was in direct proportion to the amount of information they contained. She nodded.

"Okay, then. We have to get them." From there they drove to Five Points, the university area jammed with restaurants, boutiques, and bars. At her favorite running store he would buy her some new running shoes or other form of running-related apparel for cross-country practice. After an obligatory trip to Stuffy's, a bar famous for its buffalo wings and home fries that he once frequented with her mother, they would drive to a music shop, where he bought classic rock CD's (Steely Dan, Journey, and Led Zeppelin were his favorites) and insisted that she pick out something for herself.

"I keep hearing that god-awful hippity-hop music coming out of your room. Maybe you need a change? Or maybe just more of the same," he'd tease her.

"More of the same," she'd say, selecting an Eminem CD, or something old school, like A Tribe Called Quest or the Beastie Boys. Daniel would groan and roll his eyes, never refusing to buy her anything.

For a while after he lost his job, Celia accepted his assurances that he still had money in savings. A life insurance settlement from her mother's car accident had been largely untouched for years, but within one year it was gone. He did not seem to be able to downsize, to adjust to the reality that there was no income. One day, toward the end of her junior year of high school, Celia opened a bank statement and discovered that the savings account was empty, the checking account showing a balance of only seven hundred dollars. That night at dinner, she brought the matter up with her father.

"What about college?" she asked, terrified that she would not be able to attend at all.

"I'm sure you'll get a scholarship. You're the smartest kid in your class. It's Harvard or Princeton for you, June bug. If you don't get a scholarship, I am one hundred percent certain you can attend in-state with a full ride."

"What's going to happen when this money runs out?" She handed him the bank statement.

"Oh, I have something up my sleeve," he told her, and that something turned out to be the ill-fated Key West venture. That summer she read everything Ernest Hemingway had ever written, and on one of her father's days off, she took him on a tour of the Hemingway house. On an excruciatingly humid July morning, Daniel dutifully trudged behind Celia through each room of the old house, admiring the five-toed cats who padded around the place, the carefully preserved room where Hemingway wrote standing up. "In this heat!" he commented, the guide hearing him and chuckling.

"No, in this heat you probably would have found him in a bar, preferably one with a ceiling fan."

"A man after my own heart," Daniel agreed, and of course after the tour that was where they found themselves. "I might like to read something by Hemingway again," he mused. "I read him way back when in college, but I don't remember much."

She gave him *A Farewell To Arms*, thinking he might like something about a war, but he never read it. Later, she thought of the Hemingway short story about the blind man who shows up every day at the same bar, his faith not in God or family but in the bar itself, and in the alcohol that provided the comfort of nothingness. Drinking had always been a hobby for her father, something Celia associated with him in the same way that she knew he liked to listen to his Led Zeppelin records and watch Atlanta Braves games, but since the Anayo Mills closure, alcohol had taken center stage. Working in a restaurant that summer among customers who displayed the many faces of alcoholism, she began to suspect that her father was one of them.

From her restaurant earnings she managed to set aside enough to pay for her college application fees, for the away meets with the cross-country team, and for other expenses that came up during the course of the school year. Four days each week she worked after school at a video rental store, using the money to keep the refrigerator stocked with fresh groceries. Occasionally Daniel drove to Columbia with a stack of newly printed resumes, his suits already beginning to pinch around the waist. The Columbia trips always ended badly.

"I don't know why I keep hoping," he would say, filling a glass with ice and Jack Daniels even before he loosened his tie. "I might as well be carrying a sign: 'Failed Executive: Early 50's- Will Work For Food.'" Several drinks later, after changing into pajama pants and a faded USC t-shirt and settling into his recliner, he slurred, "You're my hope for the future, Celia. I know you're going to do something to make your old man proud. You'll save us both."

She resolved to prove to him that she could. The arrival of welfare checks in their mailbox one day filled her with shame, but when she told Steven about it, he said,

"Why don't you write about it for your college admissions essay? Write about your father's fall from glory. It'll be therapeutic, not to mention original."

"I couldn't exploit him that way," she protested.

"Exploit him? I don't see it that way. Writers don't exploit, they mine their lives for material."

That night, while Daniel slept in front of the television, she sat down at his old desktop computer and began to write. The home office, with its wood paneled walls, thirty-year old, mottled beige shag carpet, and relics from her father's working life (paperweights, framed plaques, a snow globe from 1987), proved inspiring for the essay she wanted to write. She tried to capture the immediacy of her feelings when she discovered the welfare check. She described the office in ruthless detail, her father slack-jawed and fast asleep on the La-Z-Boy, the sweating glass of bourbon and cola on the television table beside him. Then she found herself writing about their summer in Key West, the promise of starting over, and with the trip to the Hemingway

House, her realization that things were never going to be the way they were.

Timidly, although she had a sense she'd written something good, she showed the essay to Steven. He praised it effusively, corrected it in a few places, and then suggested she show it to their English teacher.

"Celia, this is terrific," Michael Lenhart told her after class a few days later. One of those rare teachers with the charisma to incite students' interest in subjects that, in the hands of a lesser person, might have bored them to tears, Mr. Lenhart was her favorite teacher at Deer Bluff High. A former hippie with slightly unkempt dark hair and a beard, he had introduced her to Walt Whitman, the Beats, and Raymond Carver. He stunned the class when he told them you could treat rock music as a text, playing some lyrics by the Doors as an example. The advisor of the school literary magazine, he sometimes brought his own poems to their meetings for critiques from the students. What she liked most about him was that he took his students seriously, did not mince words as a critic, but nevertheless gave praise where it was due.

"You really think it's good?" she asked.

"Absolutely," he said. "I suggested a few revisions, but this is excellent. I've been to the Hemingway house in Key West. It looks just like this. And I love this line: '…the emerald flash of the sun at the moment it sets beyond the pier, Gatsby's elusive green light transported to the bottom of the continent for my father's benefit.' That's brilliant. Your father as a victim of the American Dream."

She was relieved that Mr. Lenhart did not dwell on the alcoholism, which would have been the first thing another teacher might have zeroed in on, interrogating her with smothering concern about her home life.

"You don't think it's too much of a sob story? I don't want the admissions counselors to think I'm trying to manipulate their emotions."

"No, you don't go in for sentimentality, which is what makes it so strong. You're not asking the reader to feel anything, but the reader will. This does exactly what I taught you. Show, don't tell."

"I'm glad you liked it," she said.

"I loved it," he replied. "Celia, you have real talent. No matter what you decide for your major in college, promise me you'll keep writing. And don't ever be afraid of the experiences life throws in your path. By embracing them, you'll deepen as a human being, and your writing will deepen as well. This essay proves that."

At Princeton Celia had taken several writing classes, but nothing her classmates or professors said ever meant as much to her as that conversation with Mr. Lenhart. Getting her teachers' attention in college was not as easy, and she suspected this had something to do with Mr. Lenhart's advice. She had run out of experiences, and the typical diversions college provided held little interest for her. Casual sex and excessive drinking were presumably some of the college experiences to be had, yet they seemed prosaic, unlikely to stimulate literary reflection. On the other hand, Celia was skeptical; shouldn't imagination be enough? Presumably Jane Austen's life was not full of sordid experiences, yet she managed to write rich portrayals of the society she lived in. Romantic and confessional poets had fallen into the trap of thinking that only with experience, preferably painful, could one find fodder for self-expression. Her time at Princeton so far had been less Rimbaud and more Henry James, limited in ecstatic highs or lows but far reaching in the opportunities to observe differences of social class or regional orientation. Elise's classified ad in the *Princetonian* was the first unusual experience, and this had motivated her almost as much as the money.

 On the third day of waking up alone in her childhood room, faced with the prospect of another eight hours at home, Celia decided to visit Mr. Lenhart over at the high school. All her homework for the following week had been completed, and she'd even snuck into her father's bank statements to make sure he was not in desperate financial shape. In his files, most of the receipts she found were from the Piggly Wiggly supermarket and the ABC liquor store, with nothing to indicate he was still living beyond his means.

 Daniel had taken the car to work, so she decided to run to the high school. After breakfast, she put on a clean t-shirt and pair of shorts, enjoying the last of the warm weather before she returned to New Jersey. Her running shoes were frayed and worn out on the bottom, but the kind she liked cost over a hundred dollars, a sum of money she did not have at the moment.

 She locked the door and began walking down their street, a cul-de-sac of 1950s ranch houses in shades of brown, gray, and white. The neighborhood had emptied out for work and school, with only a few retired residents tucked away out of sight of the world, apparently uninterested in taking a walk beneath the sky that was a crisp, unpolluted blue, in air warm enough to be enjoyed without a jacket. In South Carolina people experienced only a taste of winter, not enough to feel the urgency she had that these days would soon be gone for what would seem like forever. Celia imagined she had developed the mentality of a northerner, savoring the last gasps of fall before the bitterness of winter set in, a winter that threatened to sink everyone into a depression induced by cold and the absence of light.

She began to run, winding her way through the other streets of her neighborhood, all of them more or less identical. The value of these houses would never shoot up for any real estate boom; they would never become anything more than they were now: mere places to live, sunken into the landscape and resigned to complacency, their lawns yellowed and dormant in the fall. From here it was only a short distance to Main Street, but rather than heading toward the commercial district she turned right, the sidewalk tapering out after a half a mile so that she had to run on the shoulder. Only a few vehicles passed her as she ran, most of them without incident, except for a slow-moving, decrepit Lincoln Continental that veered dangerously close to her on the shoulder, and a single catcall from a black truck raised up on wheels inflated to steroidal proportions.

Her timing as she veered off the main road into the Deer Bluff High School parking lot was perfect; students were changing classes or heading to lunch, and in the commotion, she could avoid detection by her former teachers. Mr. Lenhart was the only one she wanted to see. Locating the classroom where he always taught English, she peered through the square of glass, expecting to see her former teacher's head bent over his papers, or in conversation with another student. A teacher she didn't recognize sat at his desk. She knocked tentatively, and the woman, who might not have been much older than Celia herself, motioned for her to enter.

"Mr. Lenhart? I don't think he teaches here anymore," the woman said, without the Southern accent Celia had been expecting. "I'm new this year, but I don't know him. You might ask at the principal's office. I can go with you if you'd like." The teacher must be new; she was still striving to be bright and hopeful, perhaps she'd even been sent there by Teach For America to perform her two years of service in America's version of the developing world.

Dismayed, Celia wove her way through the crowded hallway, past boys shoving each other roughly, girls arranging themselves in haughty cliques and casting disparaging glances over their shoulders at rival factions. The air was electric, hostile, smelling of sandwiches left too long in lockers, of strong, cheap perfumes mingled with sweat. Somehow Celia had never noticed how intimidating this environment was. She had survived high school by floating dreamily through it, surrounding herself with books and a few friends, always certain of the situation's temporality. This, too, shall pass. Her father always assured her of this, virtually engineering her escape from Deer Bluff by withdrawing them both from this world.

"People are always going to talk," he told her once in the tenth grade when another student made fun of her for reading Shakespeare in class with too much enthusiasm in her voice. "Ignore them. They're jealous. If you let it get to you, then their strategy worked. Act like they aren't there at all. They'll find someone else to pick on. Aren't you the top student in your grade, except for Amit Patel? Just remember that. You'll go places they never dreamed of. Let what they say slide off of you. Like water off a duck's back." She had insulated herself from the painful jostling she saw now in the hallways of the high school. But this blindness, her refusal to get involved, her immunity to the pain of social slights, would not serve her well as a writer.

Miss Sally, the school secretary and unofficial first line of defense at the principal's office, was ageless, a stout woman with a meringue-topped helmet of hair from an era no one could ever quite identify. She looked Celia over, apparently not recognizing her.

"I'm looking for Michael Lenhart," Celia said.

"Mr. Lenhart is no longer with us," Miss Sally informed her, her singsong voice rising officiously at the end of her sentence, making it clear that she would reveal no secrets to this anonymous upstart.

"Do you know where I could find him?"

"No, I do-on't," Miss Sally said.

"Can I see Principal Gaston?"

"He's not available right now. And you are?"

"I'm Celia. I graduated two years ago."

"Well, Celia. Currently un-enrolled students are not to be on the school grounds without first visiting the secretary to announce the purpose of their visit."

"I'm doing that, aren't I?" Her attempt at Northeastern directness was clearly perceived as smart-ass talk. Miss Sally gave Celia a cold stare.

"Mr. Lenhart is no longer employed by the school district. For more information, you can contact the Superintendent of Schools, Rick Hopkins. His number is in the phone book under county offices." She picked up the phone and started dialing. Celia stood there for a minute, but when it became clear Miss Sally had moved on to another matter entirely, she gave up and walked out of the office.

"Celia!" a voice called out as she was leaving the building. "Divine Celia of the sultry alto!" Too vivid for this environment, Pendleton Simpson, the choir teacher, wore an iridescent red dress shirt, a yellow tie dotted with hot air balloons, pale yellow slacks, and pointy-toed calfskin dress shoes. An attractive man in his mid-thirties with a tousled head of blonde hair, he was the town's sole uncloseted homosexual. Deer Bluff tolerated his presence grudgingly, probably because he came from a prominent Columbia family whose sizeable tobacco farms employed numerous Deer Bluff residents.

"Hi, Mr. Simpson," she smiled. "Not sure how sultry my alto is, but it's good to see you." He hugged her.

"Look at you," he drawled, casting his eyes over her running clothes. "Didn't make much of a fuss for Deer Bluff today, did you."

"I was hoping to escape undetected. Maybe blend in with the other students."

"Without shellacking your face in make-up? No way. To what do we owe the pleasure of your visit?"

"I'm home for fall break. I was trying to find Mr. Lenhart; do you have any idea what happened to him? Nobody seems to want to tell me."

"Honey, Michael Lenhart crashed and burned. He is no longer teaching here."

"What do you mean?" Mr. Simpson drew her to the side to let a group of students pass. In a low voice, he whispered,

"Nervous breakdown. His wife left him to join the circus."

Celia raised her eyebrows.

"That can't be true."

"But it is. I don't mean just any circus. I mean Debbie Lenhart missed her groupie days on the road, sharing the bed of whichever Allman Brother was drunk enough, or sober enough, shall we say, to rise to the occasion. Debbie Lenhart left her husband to follow the Greg Davenport Experience, a re-formed, second-rate Southern rock outfit from the 1970s. Picture the movie Spinal Tap, if you will, and that's the nightmare Mr. Lenhart's life has become."

Michael Lenhart's wife was a pale, willowy blonde who wore Indian sundresses with beads and tiny, shimmering mirrors. To Celia the Lenharts had been an ideal couple, perfectly unconventional in Deer Bluff, the type who might spend their Saturday nights fixing tofu curries and burning incense.

Celia asked if he had any idea where Mr. Lenhart was now.

"Are you old enough to drink? If so, you might find him around happy hour at The Diamond. If not, your best bet would be to call him at home."

"There's something else I wanted to ask you…" She trailed off, thinking of Steven but wondering if the choir teacher's let-it-all-hang-out demeanor extended to confirming rumors about his own life.

"Ask away, *chéri*."

"I heard Steven Addison dropped out of Chapel Hill."

Mr. Simpson touched her arm, assuming a confidential pose.

"Honey, don't believe the rumors. Steve will be back at UNC in the spring."

"This might be crossing a line, but were you and he..." She tapered off, unable to do more than allude to what she could not ask directly.

"No, no, no!" he protested. "Don't believe it. We're friends, it's true, but I would never, ever date a student, even a former one."

"So is it true that his parents pulled him out of school to try to brainwash him... away from his, um, orientation?"

"Steve," Mr. Simpson sighed, "is working through some issues right now. It's more complicated than what you've heard. You should know better than to believe what anyone says in this place."

"I know," replied Celia. "I just wasn't expecting things to change so much. First Steven, now Mr. Lenhart."

"If I were you, I wouldn't worry about Steve—his grades were fine his first year at Chapel Hill, and he most certainly will not be a drop-out, but there are some family issues... his mother's a little loopy, you know, a little too inclined in recent years to believe in the power of the Word to solve what she can't control. So Steve agreed to take a semester off from school so she could see with her own eyes that he's fine. I am quite convinced he will go on to medical school exactly as they've planned for him... maybe not bringing home the belle of Charleston for his wife, but they will learn to accept that."

"And Mr. Lenhart?"

"Now that one is deserving of your concern. I would definitely recommend you try to see him. Remember: The Diamond, 'round about happy hour time, you should find him there."

Back at home, Celia took a shower and fixed herself a peanut butter sandwich on the horrible white bread her father kept in the refrigerator. At three thirty, Daniel came home from work, his t-shirt stained with grass and mud, his face ruddy from working outside.

"How do you like your father as a blue collar worker?" he smiled, reaching into the refrigerator for a beer.

"You look good—you're keeping your weight down," Celia remarked. "But what matters is whether you like your work, not what I think."

"It'll do," he said. He sat down at the kitchen table, Celia closing the book she was reading. "I'm resigned to my fate. I've learned that having somewhere to go each day does wonders for my state of mind. Helps me function better in life."

"You always told me that all work is honorable. I'm just relieved that you're off welfare."

"Don't use that word. Say 'unemployment.'"

"Unemployment."

"Good girl." He tilted his head back and took a long swallow of beer. "Nothing like a cold beer after a hard day's work. Maybe I'll take up listening to country music."

"Dad, where did you see Mr. Lenhart a few weeks back when you told me he asked about me?"

"Mike Lenhart? Let me think. Did I see him at the grocery store? No, I think it was out somewhere. Maybe at The Diamond."

"I went by the school today and they told me he wasn't teaching anymore."

"He didn't mention that to me." Her father looked thoughtful. "But then again, I never used to see him at The Diamond until recently. We can drive over there later, after I take my shower. Try not to dress so much like a sophisticated Yankee. You'll look out of place. Wear jeans. You could even tease your hair up a little bit and I'll play you a round of pool." Daniel's eyes twinkled.

Along with Millie's Diner, The Diamond Bar & Grill was one of the few Deer Bluff restaurants not part of a chain. But while Millie's was a place for families and churchgoing couples, The Diamond's main clientele consisted of men in their forties and fifties, habitual drinkers or those with problem marriages. Food was secondary: wings, chicken fingers, and for the truly intoxicated, pickled pigs' feet suspended in a gigantic jar next to the bar cash register. The Diamond offered a limited selection of domestic beer and liquor. Located in a windowless aluminum building that would have been the first structure in the town to blow away in a tornado, the dark interior always stank of stale cigarette smoke. She entered with her father, allowing her eyes to adjust gradually to the darkness.

Celia had been inside The Diamond only once before during high school, when the bartender called their house in the middle of the night to ask her to collect her father, who had fallen asleep in one of the booths. Because Daniel had taken the car, she'd been forced to call Steven, waking up his irritated parents. Steven came over right away, tactful enough never to refer later to that night, or to the condition they found her father in, sprawled not in a booth but on the sawdust-covered floor beneath a table, his face bleeding from a cut that he did not remember receiving. They roused him to consciousness, coaxing him out of the bar and into the backseat of his own car, which Celia would drive home.

The bartender, a tough old man with a handlebar mustache and a Harley t-shirt, stood with his muscular, Popeye arms folded across his barrel chest. "You're lucky I didn't carry him outside and leave him in the parking lot. I don't want to see him back here for the next year. He's banned from The Diamond." Celia left Daniel in the backseat of the car that night, taking the keys inside the house and placing them in a drawer. When he woke up the next day he was mortified, enough so that even after the year passed, he rarely frequented The Diamond more than once a month.

In the center of the bar a woman with frizzy blonde hair and tight, acid washed jeans bent over one of the two pool tables, lining up her shot as her companion, equally trapped in the eighties with a mullet haircut and mustache, looked on. Illuminated beer signs appeared to be the only source of light, and Celia looked over at the bartender, whose face glowed beneath a large, blinking advertisement for Stroh's behind the bartender's head. With relief she noted that he was not the same man who had banned her father from the premises a few years earlier. Lynrd Skynrd blared from two large speakers on either side of the bar, where two old men sat as motionless as figures in an Edward Hopper painting.

This was not the kind of place Celia would have imagined finding her former teacher, but there he was, sitting in the very last booth in a corner. He waved and stood up, Daniel pushing her gently in the direction of the booth.

"I'll be at the bar. Give y'all a chance to catch up."

"Celia! My favorite student. I'm so glad to see you," he said. They hugged awkwardly and she slid into the booth across from him. A bottle of Budweiser sat in front of him, his notebook on the table filled with writing.

"Are you twenty-one yet? What can I get you to drink?" he asked.

"Just a coke," she said. "I'm still not legal." He left the table for a moment, returning with her drink.

"I see you brought your old man," he said. "Should we invite him over?"

"We don't have to. I told him we'd be talking about literature and stuff." Michael Lenhart looked the same as always, perhaps a little thinner, but his dark eyes still emanated warmth. He might have been Italian or Spanish, but she remembered from a conversation they once had that his ancestors were Scottish. He resembled Peter, she realized suddenly. Something had been familiar about him.

Celia realized she was staring at him just a bit too long.

"I've decided to major in English," she volunteered. "I'm going to try for a certificate in creative writing, too."

"Oh, that's terrific. Have you studied with Joyce Carol Oates yet?"

"No, but I've had some other semi-famous professors," she said. "Right now I'm in a class with Carla Lopez-Ibarrez, although I can't say

I've managed to make much of an impression on her. I've also made friends with a woman who works in publishing. She's an editor at Smyth & Copperfield."

"Carla Lopez-Ibarrez… The lady who wrote *Mama Con Leche*? Wow. And you've got a New York editor friend. That's great, Celia, you're networking. You're in such a good place. I knew you'd be able make contacts who would help you get into that world." He smiled proudly.

"My father's disappointed I'm not interested in law school or an MBA, but I know him. He won't put up too much resistance."

"No, I don't think he will. He trusts your judgment. He knows how lucky he is to have such a level-headed daughter." Michael Lenhart had no children of his own. "My students are my children," he often told them at literary magazine meetings. What would he do now that wife and students had all but deserted him?

"What's that you're working on?" she asked, pointing at the notebook.

"A novel." He picked up the notebook reverentially. "I'm writing a novel about Deer Bluff. You know, I've been here for ten years now, but I still feel like I don't belong. That outsider's distance helps me to really see this place for what it is. That's why the novel is set here, and not back in Atlanta, where I grew up."

"I was shocked when I heard you weren't teaching anymore."

He lowered his eyes. "Thank you. It means a lot to hear that from a student."

"I'm serious," said Celia. "I've had good teachers at Princeton but never someone who inspired me as much as you did."

"No, I've decided to move on from teaching," he said. "You may have heard this through the grapevine, but Amy and I split up. Came as a surprise, but it gave me the chance to reevaluate my life, and I really wasn't happy with the direction it was taking. Sometimes even when you love your work, you start to feel like everything is stagnating. Especially if your marriage is on the rocks."

"But why did you decide to do your writing here? In The Diamond?"

"Well, it isn't Prague or Paris. But you don't have to go somewhere far away to be in the center of the world, you're already in it. You remember what Thomas Wolfe says in *Look Homeward, Angel*. You are your world, Celia. Anyway, bars are great places to write. It's like a glimpse at the human condition writ large. 'Ahh, the humanity.' I see people here who've lost more than I have. Iraq to Vietnam. Your father and his people at the mill. It's a reality check for me. A marriage isn't that much to lose, in the scheme of things. Trying to write about it without sounding maudlin, that's my goal. Part of my novel is set in this very bar."

"I'd like to read it sometime," she offered.

"Maybe I'll send it to you someday. But tell me more about you, Celia. More than just what classes you're taking and the professors you've studied with. What's Princeton really like?"

She understood he meant not classes, not particular professors, but life in general.

"I keep thinking back to a conversation we had once. You told me never to be afraid of experience. But I've had a hard time breaking out of the role of being the good girl. I don't know which experiences, exactly, I should be looking for."

"I never meant to give the impression that only experience makes a good writer," he said. "But you were always just watching things. It never seemed like you jumped into life like you should. I understand your urge for self-protection-- you never had a mom, and then your father, nice man that he is, let you down, even though you'd never admit it. You're a very likeable person, Celia, people would love to be friends with you if you would only let them. Don't be afraid to embrace life." He took a long swallow of his beer, nearly draining it. "Any boyfriends?"

"No." She was grateful that in the darkness he wouldn't see her blushing. "But I am doing something kind of crazy."

"Tell me." Perhaps confessing this was going too far, but the urge to share Peter and Elise with someone was overwhelming.

"I saw an ad in the student newspaper for a couple who were looking for an egg donor." She waited for his reaction. He nodded.

"Go on."

"So I'm doing it. The wife is the one who works in publishing; she can't have children. Her husband is a graduate student. He studies Islamic history. They're an interesting couple, both in their mid thirties. Independently wealthy, a little neurotic. Elise has become very attached to me. I think she's trying to mentor me, the whole Eliza Doolittle thing with the southern girl. She's always making me embarrassed about my accent. But she spends a lot of time talking about the literary world like it's this exclusive club. I guess it is, but she just makes me want it more. But she also tells me she made a lot of mistakes in college and that she wants to keep me from doing the same things."

Mr. Lenhart rubbed his beard thoughtfully.

"We can never make someone else's mistakes, only our own," he said.

"Are you saying I'm making a mistake? Maybe this is just too bizarre."

"Nothing is too bizarre," he said. "On the contrary, I envy you. A glimpse into an unfamiliar world. Islamic history, eh? That's a subject I know zero about."

"I don't know the husband as well," Celia said. "Peter's a nice guy, but kind of reserved. He seems a bit suspicious of the whole deal. I haven't figured him out yet."

"Let me give you some advice," he urged her. "Study these people. Observe them. Get inside their heads, find out what makes them different from you. You needed to leave the South, to see people who are not like you. That whole idea that people are the same everywhere is far from true. There is no common humanity. We like to say that underneath the skin all people are alike, but we're not. And do you want to know what separates us? Money. Power. How is it that these people are in a position to offer you money to donate your eggs? And why are you accepting? Would you accept if your father were still CEO at the mill and gave you a thousand dollars each month for spending money?"

She laughed. "I don't think he ever had that kind of money. Being the CEO of a company in Deer Bluff is light years away from, say, being the CEO of Microsoft."

"If your father were still working," he said, leaning forward, "you wouldn't be at Princeton now. A family bringing in sixty, eighty thousand each year can't get financial aid. You have to sink to the bottom, to taste what it's like to be dirt poor, before those schools will give you money. Then you can be one of their charity cases. Believe me, the closing of Anayo Mills was a blessing in disguise. One person's misfortune becomes another's good luck. Your father's big sacrifice for his daughter's future."

An edge had crept into his voice. He put his empty glass down for emphasis and got up.

"Excuse me, Celia. I'll be back in a minute." He walked over to the bar, giving her time to think about what she would say when he came back. In a moment he returned with a tumbler of whiskey.

"You make it all sound so calculating," she said.

"I'm not saying you aren't smart and talented. You are. But you also come from a community with a per capita income comparable to a Third World country. On paper, you're lower class, even if you didn't grow up that way. Just be careful."

"Be careful of what?" She felt distressed. She wanted him to like her idea.

"About these people you've met, the editor and her husband." He shook the ice in his glass, taking a long drink. "I just don't want them to take advantage of you. I know they make you feel like an equal, but you're really not. They might not even be conscious of it themselves. I'm not saying you shouldn't do what you're doing. But consider this. I saw this show about rich people who fly down to Brazil and pay huge sums of money to get kidneys from people in shantytowns. What do you think happens when the poor guy in the Brazilian shantytown needs a kidney transplant?"

"Egg donation isn't as big a deal as giving up a kidney."

"All I'm saying is, don't let yourself get screwed in this deal. If you give something, be sure what you take is of equal value. Anytime you turn your body into a commodity, the ethics get a little fuzzy."

"I'm not a commodity," she protested.

Mr. Lenhart held up his hand for her to be silent.

"We're all selling ourselves in some way or other. Whether it's for our labor or our bodies, we're always getting screwed. All that nonsense about our common humanity is a lie made up by the rich and powerful. It just hides the extent they're exploiting the rest of the world. The secret, I've learned, is to find a way to screw the other guy right back."

"I never had you pegged as a Marxist," Celia joked. This was not the Michael Lenhart she remembered from her AP English class, the gentle poet who wrote about canoeing in the Pacific Northwest, or falling asleep on a hill at a Grateful Dead concert. As if he could read her mind, he said,

"What can I say? I've become bitter. 'All that is solid melts into air,' to quote the guy you just mentioned."

He told her about his wife, stating only that she left him for another man. His version of events was pared down to the bare essentials, and not so florid as Mr. Simpson's. Michael Lenhart did not mention Spinal Tap, or the Greg Davenport Experience.

"When you've experienced true betrayal, for the first time in your life... Some of us don't handle it so well. But I got my revenge. My ex-wife had a lot of family money she'd inherited. I sued for alimony, got a shrink from Columbia to declare me unfit to work. A convenient nervous breakdown, so I had to quit teaching. So this," he said, lifting the notebook, "is my blessing in disguise. I'm taking a little sabbatical."

Celia wondered if his nervous breakdown really was a fiction. The cynicism was new. Perhaps it had always been deeply buried, needing only a betrayal to surface. Or maybe he was finally talking to her as an adult. Suddenly Celia wanted to go home, not to her father's house but back to her dorm room in Princeton, to lie in her bed under her ceiling of stars where she could go back to the fantasy that she had finally arrived, that all she needed to do was to be at Princeton for her aspirations to be realized.

    Offering her excuses to Mr. Lenhart ("Call me Michael," he said in parting, giving her a hug that lasted just a few seconds longer than was appropriate), she went to the bar to collect her father, taking the keys from him wordlessly. They stepped out into the cool night air, the sounds from the bar growing muffled as the door closed behind them. Under a bright moon, the parking lot was a graveyard of pick-up trucks. Daniel asked her nothing about her extended conversation with her teacher, but he put his arm around her as they walked to the car, the gravel crunching beneath their feet.

CHAPTER SEVEN

In yoga class Elise had been trying to mentally prepare a space for the baby, sending positive messages to her womb to be hospitable. If she were more religious, she might have called what she was doing prayer, but she hated the thought that in the popular imagination, prayers were directed at a man in the sky. Yoga was more neutral, just another way among many possible paths for sending positive energy out into the universe. Sometimes she felt as if the clinic had taken control of her body for some ill-conceived science experiment. Lately the doctors had been injecting her with hormones to determine which specific combination of meds would create the least hostile environment in her womb. Yoga was the perfect antidote to all those synthetic hormones. She was trying to eat better, too, cooking more dinners for her and Peter and abandoning some of what Doctor Geiger called "her unhealthy bargains with food."

How ironic that earlier in her life, pregnancy had come unasked, but now that she desired it, her body refused to comply.

"One single abortion probably wouldn't be the cause of your fertility difficulties, unless there were complications," her doctor had assured her. "Sometimes we see issues with women who've had multiple abortions."

There had been only one. And it wasn't a confirmed abortion, really. The details grew hazier with time: sophomore year, an Around-The-World party (which involved moving from dorm room to dorm room, taking a different liquor shot in each room), Elise stumbling back to her room with a man in tow, her roommate Caitlin still at the party. She could no longer remember his face, but he seemed harmless enough: a wiry, artsy guy in corduroys and a Phish t-shirt, a few piercings winding up one ear. The party was safely down the hall, and Caitlin would be back in a few minutes. Or so she thought. She hadn't intended to sleep with him, had thought they might make out until Caitlin stumbled back into the room, when he would have to be on his way. She remembered him kicking his shoes onto the ground and lunging in on her like a wolf, pressing her back down on her bed. Then she'd had the weirdest sensation of going absolutely blank, as if the lights had been switched off in her head and everything went black. When she woke up the next morning, Caitlin was asleep in the other bed, but the guy was gone and she knew from the slight ache between her legs that she had slept with him.

Not knowing what had happened was the worst punishment of all, losing the awareness and control over her body that she fought for so ferociously at all other times. For this there was nobody she could blame but herself. She was the one who had invited him back to her room.

"It's okay, you just had a blackout," Caitlin tried to assure her, but Elise knew she was not prone to blackouts. She remembered now that in the last room of the party he had insisted on getting her a drink, and that she'd lost sight of him for a few minutes in the crowded room, until he magically appeared again with two punch-filled Dixie cups.

"I think he drugged me," she told Caitlin. "I mean, I was just gone. It was like I was there, and then I wasn't anymore. What if he had AIDS or something?"

"That's what black outs feel like," Caitlin said. "You can get tested for STD's later, God forbid, but what if you're pregnant? That entire day was a nightmare, both of them hung over, waiting at a clinic to see a doctor and obtain the necessary prescription. At that time the morning after pill was not available, but taking a large dosage of birth control pills to flush out anything that might have been conceived was a well-known secret. Elise took the pills, her hangover blurring into a feverish purgatory of illness, the pills sending her shuddering to her bed with horrible cramps, bleeding, and nausea.

Did the after-effects mean she was pregnant? There was no way of knowing that early; the pills were just a precaution. But she had felt something, a deep and stirring sense that she'd conceived. She knew women who claimed they could sense the moment of their child's conception, as if that instant of sperm meeting egg was so volatile and profound that the body possessed the instinctive, almost psychic knowledge that it cradled new life. As soon as Caitlin had said those words, "What if you're pregnant?" Elise believed that she was. It had given her something else to think about besides what had actually happened. Later she realized that she'd done everything wrong. The first thing she should have done was to go to her RA, or the police, to have them do a rape kit on her. She should have reported the guy, describing him to the best of her abilities. But that day, all she could think about was how miserable the pills were making her feel, her stomach turning inside out until she was completely hollow, an empty gourd with only dried-up seeds rattling around inside.

Lately in her sessions with Dr. Geiger, she found herself going over this incident again, convinced that her infertility some sort of karmic punishment for her misdeeds.

"You never saw the guy again?" he asked.

"No. I couldn't even remember what he looked like." Elise had been crying; the one place she was able to do it well and often was in front of Dr. Geiger. "I can see his pointy little teeth, and that stupid Phish t-shirt. I've forbidden Peter from ever playing Phish around me. But I can't picture his face. Even right after it happened, he was just a collection of distorted features that didn't fit together."

"Like a Picasso painting," Dr. Geiger mused. "And later you began volunteering at a rape crisis center, but you never wanted to admit you'd been raped."

"It just sounds so harsh to say those words." Elise had a hard time bringing herself to say that she was 'raped.' After all, she heard so many worse stories from other women. Those stories were like her mother's shock therapy sessions with the gunshot victims of Baltimore; they made her realize her own experience had been relatively benign. "And I never wanted to be a victim. After all, I was the one that let him come back to the room."

"But you're a smart woman, Elise. You know it wasn't your fault."

"But I don't even know what 'it' was. I wasn't present. I wasn't there to know what happened to me. That's the worst of it. Just like I don't really know whether I was pregnant or not, I just felt it."

"What about after him? Did it affect your relations with men?"

"Not that I know of, except that I made a rule. From then on, no one-night stands, only boyfriends. Or dates, but none that ended with sex, unless it became clear that the guy wanted to see me on a regular basis. I tried to stay out of anything that might get complicated."

"And Eric Babu, what was he to you?"

"Oh." Elise crossed her legs and pressed her face into a tissue. "Not a one-night stand, but not a boyfriend either."

"Uncategorizable."

"Exactly." Elise read a look of awareness in Dr. Geiger's sharp blue eyes. He was a gray-haired Buddha, radiating serenity and knowledge about her that he would reveal in due time. At moments like this she believed in his complete and total comprehension of her existence.

"So why do you continue to punish yourself for this incident, more than fifteen years later?"

"I'm convinced I did something to damage my own fertility."

"But the doctor you're seeing now told you this was unlikely. You even told the doctor you'd had an actual abortion."

"I feel it, though. I think I wounded myself somehow."

"It's funny," Dr. Geiger mused. "You struggled with anorexia for many years. Your behavior still exhibits signs of disordered eating: skipping meals, substituting alcohol for food, an obsessive concern with controlling what goes into your body, alternated with minor binges on food that's not good for you. All of this could have damaged your body over time, yet you keep returning to this one experience."

Working on her eating habits with Dr. Geiger was an ongoing project.

"Maybe in punishing myself, I sent psychological messages to my body to stop functioning properly."

"I think it's significant you internalized this incident to the degree you did," he said. "You describe it as losing control of a situation—others would certainly call this date rape. Yet you want to rush through the story and get to the abortion part, and how your fertility problems now are your fault. What does Peter say about it all?"

"Peter doesn't know." Dr. Geiger raised his eyebrows.

"So you never told him."

"I told him in college I hooked up with somebody and had to get a morning after pill. He knows I wonder if it caused my problems now. But he's uncomfortable talking about it. He doesn't like to hash out past sexual encounters with me."

It had been easier, with Peter, to be breezy about the whole thing, even though she knew she was making herself sound promiscuous. She still blamed herself for her stupidity in allowing that situation to even take place, and for the clumsy, stumbling way she'd come into knowledge of sex. In college she wanted it to be casual, wanted to enjoy it as men supposedly did, but desiring this could not make it happen, could not throw off the weight of society and its judgments. Sex was never simple, never an experience that came without baggage. From the women's studies classes she'd taken, she believed that the guilt and shame women felt about their behavior were vestigial traces of patriarchy, a relic of the days when a woman's sexuality was the property of a man.

"We lived through the sexual revolution so that the world could be different for you," her mother had told her. Trying to intellectualize the body, however, failed miserably.

The fertility quest brought these issues into sharp relief. Submitting herself (or not herself, really, because the self was elsewhere, separated from the body that always betrayed it) to the hands, instruments, and medicines of doctors, Elise felt even more out of control than usual. After the clinic visits, she often spent the rest of the day trying to recover mentally from the latest invasive procedures. She suspected she might be sensitive to the effects of the different hormonal combinations the doctor was giving her these days, some of them vaulting her to emotional highs or sending her to the gloomy depths of her memories, where she agonized over every transgression of the body, wondering whether she had damaged herself beyond repair.

To make matters worse, since her return from South Carolina, Celia had been distant. Over the break, Elise had sent her several emails, all of which went unanswered until Sunday night when Celia got back. Then her reply was brief, verging on curt. There had been no Internet access at her father's house, the trip was trying, and she was exhausted and would get back to Elise later. As of Wednesday, Elise had still heard nothing. A slight panic set in; she worried Celia might have had second thoughts while she was at home. She needed Celia to return to the clinic for more tests, but the clinic reported she was not returning their calls. At the end of the week Celia finally responded to her invitation to meet the next afternoon at the Annex.

Elise arrived early to their meeting, sitting at a table and ordering her usual glass of *pinot grigio*. A trio of male graduate students sat at the bar, strapping, overgrown boys speaking loudly in some Slavic language. They noticed her immediately, their voices falling silent as they turned one by one to look her over. She enjoyed male attention, always taking extra care in her appearance to make sure she received it. That day she'd worn a Hermès scarf with a short black dress, one that emphasized her long legs. It was a dress that turned heads in New York, especially when she wore heels. Now that Peter hardly seemed to look at her, an approving glance from a stranger (or in this case, three) could make her day.

Sensing something had chilled in her dynamic with Celia, she had decided to buy her a present. Trying to think of something she would like, she asked Peter the night before what she should get her. At first he was exasperated; did she really need to give Celia a gift?

"Think about what she's giving us," Elise said. "I'm just trying to be thoughtful." She was relieved that Peter could not read her fear that Celia would change her mind.

"Get her something from the running store," he said. "I noticed when I saw her running last week that her shoes were in pretty bad shape. A hundred dollars would get her a good pair."

When Celia entered the bar, Elise detected a change in her. Her smile stopped at the lips, not taking over her entire face, as it often did when she was excited about something. She wore her long hair twisted into a knot, secured with chopsticks, emphasizing her high cheekbones (that Cherokee blood, Elise thought again excitedly, that her child would have) and tanned skin. Elise complimented her on her color.

"South Carolina must have agreed with you."

"It never agrees with me," Celia said, "but I had a nice time with my dad." The waitress came over to take her order, Celia asking for orange juice.

"So tell me about it," Elise said. "Actually, before you start, I have something for you." She handed her a bag from Micawber Books, containing a hardback copy of Eric Babu's last novel. Celia took the novel out of the bag.

"Thank you," she said. "I haven't read this one yet. Maybe I'll get him to sign it when he comes here."

"One of the characters is loosely based on me," Elise announced. "The corrupt oil executive." Celia opened the book appreciatively, running her hand across the thick, cream-colored paper.

"Can you imagine what it would be like to know that this was your novel?" Celia said. "You must feel that yourself sometimes when you look at a book you edited."

She agreed that she did. "But I know what you mean. Writing a novel would be a real accomplishment. I never seriously had that ambition."

"One of my former teachers in Deer Bluff is working on a novel. He's writing it out by hand, in Deer Bluff's only bar. His wife pays him alimony, so he quit his job and declared himself on a writing fellowship."

"That's risky," Elise said. "He doesn't want the institutional association a real fellowship could give him? Like a grant to a writer's colony?"

"Money is money. What better patron than your ex-wife, who's just abandoned you to become a groupie for a second-rate 1970s southern rock outfit called the Greg Davenport Experience?"

Elise laughed. "That's colorful. I still think it's risky. What will he have to show for it, if the novel's no good? No job, no wife, no novel."

"For most people, life is a series of risks and rejections." Celia looked up at the waitress, bearing a tray with her orange juice and a salad for Elise.

"Open the front of the book. There's more." She turned to the first page of the book, a one hundred dollar gift certificate to the Princeton running store falling out of it.

"This is incredibly generous of you. How did you know I needed new shoes? You must be psychic… But I'm not sure I can accept this."

"Of course you can." Elise studied Celia's dazed expression as she held up the gift certificate, torn between wanting the running shoes and refusing. Observing her hesitation Elise had a sudden hunch about the source of her reserve. "You're giving us something no one could even put a price on. I could give you a thousand material objects and none would mean as much as what you're doing for me."

"I was thinking about it over the break," Celia began. "I began to think about what it all means, this gift. I don't think it's the kind of gift that can ever really be compensated."

"Oh, no," Elise agreed. "I'm fully aware that we're asking for something that has no monetary value. The money is just to compensate you for your time. It's for any emotional or physical pain you have to endure. When we sign the contract, there will also be a clause in there for ten sessions with a therapist, if you decide you want to avail yourself of that."

"Seven thousand dollars," she said thoughtfully. "My dad always says bad luck comes in sevens. I'm not usually a superstitious person, but going back home made me think twice about what I'm doing."

"Did you tell your father you were going to donate?" Elise was alarmed; Celia was dancing around the issue, the way men did before a break-up, trying to let you down slowly but actually prolonging the agony. Was she planning to back out?

"No, I didn't say anything to him. But there were some things that happened while I was home that gave me pause."

"Tell me," said Elise. "You know you can confide in me. I'm your friend."

"For now, you are," Celia said, and Elise was hurt by the sharpness with which she said it. Her expression was completely neutral, unreadable. "But after your child is born, we won't have contact anymore. I'm not asking to have any role in the child's life—I don't care about that, honestly. But when I was away last week, I thought about it and realized that our friendship is completely about this experience. We wouldn't have met otherwise. I have a difficult time getting close to people. So it surprised me how our relationship is taking center stage in my own life. I'm only afraid of what's going to happen when this whole process is through."

"Well." Elise had no idea how to respond. "I guess that's what the therapy sessions are for."

"I'll be honest with you; I come from a different world. You've dangled this exciting existence in front of me. You're always alluding to the people you know, the writers you've worked with, the experiences you've had. I really want a life like that, but I have no idea how to obtain it."

"What is it, exactly, that you want?" As if sensing Elise's distress, the waitress appeared at that exact moment, silently removing her empty glass of wine and replacing it with a second.

"I want that kind of assurance you have. To take my place in the world for granted. To feel at home in New York. To have an amazing job and a successful spouse."

"I don't take anything for granted," Elise said. She wished Celia could see her with Dr. Geiger, curled up on the sofa with tears rolling down her face. "You have no idea how much self doubt I have." The three graduate students at the bar had angled their chairs in their direction and were now openly eyeing both women. Elise felt irritated; couldn't they see a serious conversation was taking place?

"What I'm afraid of is finishing Princeton and then going back home again to nothing."

"Why would you have to do that? You'll be able to get any job you want with a Princeton degree. You don't have to go back to South Carolina."

"I don't want to," she said. "I've never felt at home there, or here, for that matter. I just want to feel like I belong. I want to be at home in the world, and not to feel like an interloper. I want to know how you do it."

"It's an act," Elise said. "Do you think I fit in here in Princeton as the wife of a graduate student? I've got no identity here. If you think about it too much, you'll never feel like you belong anywhere. You already have that poise, whether you're aware of it or not. What matters is that you seem confident to others, not how you actually feel. You just decide to reinvent yourself, and you do it."

One of the three graduate students put an imaginary phone to his ear and pointed at Celia. She slowly lifted her middle finger and glared at them. Chastened, they turned away.

"Wow, that was ballsy." Elise was wide eyed.

"I should go," Celia said.

"Don't," Elise said, putting her hand on Celia's. "Please, I wouldn't have chosen you if I didn't think you had enormous potential. I can help you, too, if that's what you're asking. I can get you an internship in New York for next summer. It won't be much money starting out, but it will help you get your foot in the door. You can use the money you're getting for the donation to pay your rent over the summer. There are always shares available in the city for a few months. If you want to live in New York, just do it. Half of the game of fitting in there is just having the chutzpah to declare that you do."

"Bad luck always comes in sevens," Celia said again, cryptically.

"I thought it was threes."

"Maybe I'm more superstitious than I thought. Maybe seven thousand isn't the right amount. It's inauspicious."

"How do you feel about eight thousand, then?" Elise was feeling increasingly desperate.

"And you'll help me get an internship?" Elise nodded. "You'll have to excuse me for sounding mercenary, but I have to think of my own interests here. I need to get this in writing. It's fine to put in there that we won't see each other any more after the pregnancy is successful. But I need the certainty of a contract. As much as I like you, I have to keep reminding myself that this is still essentially a business transaction."

Elise nodded silently. Shouldn't Celia's trip back to the South have reawakened her genteel politeness and passivity? Or was this the new Celia, steel magnolia? Before, she had seemed indifferent to the compensation, more interested in simply spending time with Elise, seeing where it led them. But who could blame her for her insecurity in this situation? Getting her the internship would be simple, and the sum of eight thousand dollars was not beyond the realm of possibility. Peter would not like it at first, but when she explained how they were in danger of losing the gift of her eggs, he would understand.

* * *

Peter stood at the front of the classroom, a piece of chalk in his hand. On the blackboard, he'd written the Arabic future tense, composed simply by adding "sowfa" or the abbreviated "sa" to the present tense of the verb.

"Why can't there be a new word?" asked Christine, who could always be counted on to ask the stupidest question. Although teachers were supposed to believe that there were no stupid questions, he often found himself astounded at some of the questions students asked. "In French the future tense becomes a new word entirely. This seems almost too simple. What's the trick?"

"There is no trick," he explained. "It's just like English. I will run a race this Saturday. I will buy ice cream for my students if they're good." The students laughed.

"I will promise not to say anything about politics for the remainder of the semester," Kevin spoke up suddenly.

Peter ignored him. Since their run-in and his subsequent conversation with Kronenberg, he had done his utmost to avoid offending Kevin.

"When we're with Dr. Khoury, we always spend the last fifteen minutes talking about current events," Kevin continued. "Why can't we do that in here?"

"Because if I don't cover the requisite amount of material, we won't get to where we need to be by the end of the semester. We're different teachers; we have different teaching styles."

"Yeah, let's talk about current events!" said Haley. "Like the bombing in Iraq this week."

"Or terrorism," said Kevin. He looked around at his classmates. "Our professor here doesn't believe in the War on Terror."

"Why not?" Christine asked. "How can you not believe in the War on Terror?"

Peter bit his lip. Kevin was trying to bait him. He often did, but Peter refused to rise to the challenge.

"That's not exactly true, Kevin. I never said I didn't believe in the war on terrorism. But let's get back to conjugations."

"He doesn't believe in it because it's completely ill-conceived," Haley responded. She was the political one in the class. "It's just an excuse to extend American imperialism over a larger area. The end result is that a lot of people die over oil."

"American imperialism? How can we help it if there's a demand for American products overseas? Particularly in the Middle East. And those products need a peaceful environment to flourish," Kevin said with certainty.

"Yeah, but we're not winning any friends when we bomb villages accidentally," Haley said. "Or break into people's homes at night to cart away the men."

"It's all in the name of security," Kevin said. "They claim they want to live in the time of the Prophet, then they behead our citizens and broadcast it all on the Internet. And we should sit back and do nothing?" The other students looked at each other uncertainly. Peter could feel the class slipping out of his hands.

"Kevin, I will remind you that 'they' are not a monolithic entity. 'They' are a diverse collection of nationalities, religious persuasions, cultures, and social classes. 'They' are not all united against us, but if they met you as a representative of American-ness, I'm sure they would be." The other students laughed. "Now, if we don't go back to conjugation right now, you're all getting F's for class participation today."

"How come you won't take a stand on the War on Terror?" Haley said.

"What if we try to discuss the issues in Arabic?" said Christine. "Would you let us talk about something besides grammar then? All we do in this class is grammar."

"You can discuss the issues with Dr. Khoury. She has entrusted me with the task of teaching you grammar."

"But what's the point?" Haley asked. "Why should we be expected only to focus on grammar? We need to understand the cultural factors behind this language as well."

"The cultural factors that lead them to resent us for everything that we enjoy over here," said Kevin. "Our democratically elected governments. Our freedom. Our thriving economy."

Haley snorted. "What thriving economy? What planet do you live on?"

Peter had tried to remain silent, but he could not resist weighing in on the debate.

"Haley, you're correct that we need to expose ourselves to the culture as well," he said. "But you can do this in your spare time. There's an excellent film series this semester of Middle Eastern films. That would be a good way to start. From films you'll see that 'they' are Moroccans, Syrians, Iraqis, Libyans, and Algerians, as different from each other as we are from Canadians and Mexicans. I would love it if we could keep politics out of the discussion for just one day."

"What about the ones who do hate us?" Christine said. "What are we supposed to do when we meet them?" The other students burst out laughing.

"Just hope you don't meet them when they're about to blow up your plane," Kevin said.

Peter was suddenly angry. "They don't all want to blow us up, and as long as people like you continue perceiving all Middle Easterners as evil, there is no hope in this world for peace or cultural understanding."

"People like me? What's that supposed to mean?" Kevin looked at him, waiting to pounce.

"People who are convinced that their vision of the world is correct and absolute. What's the point of college if you come with your opinions already set in stone? College is supposed to be a place for you to consider other points of view."

"Oh, I consider other points of view," Kevin said. "Consider them ill-informed and not based in reality, maybe. People who spend their lives buried in the library can hardly be expected to understand politics."

Peter sighed, looking desperately up at the clock.

"Then if I am included in that category… as someone who spends his life buried in the library and can hardly be expected to understand politics, you'll understand why we must not approach the subject in class." There were five minutes left in class. He looked at one of the students who had been quiet so far.

"Jacob—translate this for me: 'I will eat lamb kebabs for dinner.'"

"But I'm a vegetarian," Jacob protested.

"Just pretend."

"*Sawfa akul kebab al-kebsh li al-asha.*"

After class, Haley lingered for a moment until all the other students are gone.

"I wish you'd just tell him off sometime," she said. "He's trying to undermine you."

"I know that," Peter said, closing up his books. "The problem is that there are too many divergent opinions in the class. I have to try to steer things away from these volatile topics. We're here to learn Arabic, whatever our reasons."

"But Kevin is a bully. He's the only one who ever manages to speak his opinion, and he dominates the other students. You never weigh in on the debates, so the other students think he's right."

"They do?"

"I think so." She looked uncertain.

"You do a pretty good job standing your ground with him. Teachers aren't supposed to fight with…" He almost said "bullies," catching himself just in time. "With students. Argue with each other sometime. Try to do it in Arabic, that would be a good exercise. Come to the Tuesday night Arabic table. That's a good place to practice over a free dinner."

Haley looked disappointed, but Peter was pleased that he had been able to restrain himself. It would be such a relief if you could tell your students how you really felt. For instance, if he could have said to Haley, "That kid's a real asshole." Or if he could have looked Kevin in the eye and said, "You disrespectful son of a bitch." He was tired of the hierarchy that required him to stand in front of them, giving orders. Trying to keep order. He imagined snapping one day, saying it in front of the entire class, grabbing Kevin by the throat and throttling him. Kevin had pushed him up against the wall, leading Peter to assign only innocuous homework that was a bore to grade. Trying to keep the upper hand had made him look weak in front of the other students.

The class was leading him to serious doubts about his choice of profession. The dream of the small New England liberal arts college was taking a hit from the realities of the classroom. Now he was beginning to realize that no matter where he was hired, his primary duty would be teaching Arabic to students who hoped to work for the CIA. Putting out fires would be a constant demand of his job. Arabic was becoming important, but not for the reasons of scholarly curiosity that had led him to pursue it.

By approaching the Middle East as a scholar, he hoped to uncover clues that would explain these unfamiliar civilizations, and by extension, himself. It was an Orientalist desire, he knew, but he couldn't help himself. The Orientalists were the white male scholars of the past, who projected their buttoned-up Victorian desires onto what they imagined was a lascivious world of harems and hookahs. But there was something in the impenetrability of the past, and of the Middle East and North Africa, that he found irresistible. The closest he came to understanding was in the Sufi literature, with its emphasis on desires that could never be satisfied, and on the soul's longing to return to a forgotten source, divine yet described in earthly terms: love, intoxication, ecstasy.

Trying to have children with Elise had conjured up memories of Leila. For years, although he was fond of recounting Peace Corps stories to anyone who would listen, he kept his stories of Leila to himself, allowing himself to think about her only occasionally. Elise knew only the briefest details of their relationship, namely that there had been a woman in Sidi Maarif whom he was fond of but for numerous reasons could not be with, and she never bothered to inquire further. It was like her not to care, to ignore this crucial episode in his life.

Leila came to the clinic one day holding the hand of her elderly father, a diminutive, wizened man in white robes whose rheumy eyes were focused on distant, invisible places. The old man wandered off in the middle of the night, Leila said, in search of her mother, who had died twenty years before. Sometimes he seemed to have no idea where he was, calling out instructions to members of his World War II battalion in French, a language she did not know he spoke, though he had been a *goumier*, a Moroccan soldier who once fought in French wars.

Dr. Berrada, Peter's supervisor, was dismissive. He had very little patience for these uneducated townspeople, and whenever possible he handed off their problems to Peter, frequently leaving his post for days on end to return to his family's villa in Casablanca. "This is a psychological matter. I'm not a psychologist," Hassan Berrada had said, leaving Peter in the room with Leila and her father.

With almond-shaped eyes, skin the color of milky coffee, and a proud, erect carriage, Leila's beauty reminded him of an East African fashion model, but most of the Moroccans he spoke with did not agree, favoring instead lighter skin and more Arab-looking features. She was Sahrawi, from an ethnic group with ties to the desert, whose women wore brightly colored batik robes and matching headscarves. In his limited Arabic Peter told her that her father suffered from dementia, and that there was very little they could do for him. Upon seeing her dejected expression, he remembered a stock of homeopathic pills someone had given him, pills that were supposed to improve memory function. The medicine was at his apartment, he told her, and if she would give him her address, he would deliver them personally.

"Let me come to you," she said, explaining that a visit from a *gaowri* doctor might confuse her father, particularly considering his French army delusions. Leila appeared at his door that evening, wearing a cotton tunic patterned with colorful blue swirls over matching pants, a garment that seemed to Peter to be both quintessentially African and very exotic. Entering his apartment, she removed her headscarf and sat down at the kitchen table, asking for a glass of water. He was impressed that she unveiled so easily in front of him, her thick black hair pulled into a knot at the nape of her neck. He poured her a glass of water, wishing he had something more to offer, but his small refrigerator was empty except for a few stray vegetables and a bundle of mint a patient had given him the day before, and he had no tea.

She drank the water, accepted the medicine for her father, and thanked him profusely as she left. Peter assumed he would not see her again, but the next week she knocked on his door again and entered, pushing her scarf off her head, asking for water, this time accepting a glass of Fanta as well. She reported that her father's medicine was working well (Peter, who had doubts about the effectiveness of homeopathy, was skeptical), and he learned that she was her father's sole caretaker, her four brothers and sisters occupied with their own families or living elsewhere.

Their friendship developed slowly, always with the same rituals: Leila stopping by his apartment one or two nights each week, taking off her scarf, asking for water. Intending to prepare tea for her one night, he bought a box of black Chinese gunpowder tea and a handful of fresh mint, but when she watched him fumbling with the mint, tearing off leaves and dropping them in the teapot, she laughed and pushed him out of the way to prepare it for both of them. Usually her visits lasted no more than thirty minutes, just long enough for them to exchange a little more information about their lives.

His relationship with Leila was his only significant contact with women during the entire time he was in the Peace Corps. In the urban areas of the north women were considerably freer, but the south was still traditional, and an unrelated man and woman alone together were assumed to be engaging in illicit activities. Sidi Maarif was a small town, and although Leila asked him to leave his door open while they talked, he knew the neighbors assumed they were up to no good. He wondered what social costs she incurred by maintaining their friendship.

He could not remember when he began falling in love with her. He found himself thinking of the way she moved, her hands dramatic props to the theater of her mellifluous, sing-song speech, her elegant, henna-stained fingers pushing the headscarf back off her head, the meditative look that passed over her lowered eyes as she poured tea into their glasses, moving the pot further and further away from the glass as the amber liquid cascaded down from a great height. He was impressed by her curiosity, her desire to know as much about the world as possible despite her limited education (she had stopped going to school when she was thirteen and her mother died). She followed the news avidly, keeping up with current events, and her knowledge of the history and lore of Sidi Maarif was impressive. The Spanish had departed when she was a child, and through stories she recreated their presence for him, recalling a few colorful figures who still lived in the town as she was growing up: Elena, a former beauty who promenaded about town with a parrot on her shoulder and a red scarf draped around her neck, and a retired Spanish colonel who sat all day in a chair in front of the ocean, giving away candies to the small children who approached him. Under different circumstances, he imagined, she might have put her intelligence to great use; even in Morocco, women were now university professors, doctors, and engineers, so why not Leila?

Leila wove carpets, although the ones women produced now looked nothing like the fine silk carpets the colonial travelers had described in Peter's archives. In her father's house, which he never saw, was a loom where Leila would sit for months working on a large rug that might bring them the equivalent of two hundred dollars. Later that same rug would be sold for five times as much to a tourist in Marrakech. One day she gave him a present, a small red *kilim* shot through with silver and black threads, their designs a kind of alphabet that might help him divine Leila's true thoughts if only he could decipher it. Knowing she could use the money, he tried to pay her for the rug, but she refused to accept anything.

The incongruous details of her life gradually began to make sense. She had the freedom to come and go as a man might because she was divorced, and because the sole person who had the right to assert any control over her movements, her father, was senile. At twenty she had married, but after four years of marriage her husband's family forced him to divorce her when their union produced no heirs.

"There was a great love between us," she told Peter, but her controlling mother-in-law had needled away at her son until he finally agreed to divorce Leila. She suspected the infertility might have been her husband's fault, and he even promised that if his new wife did not give birth, he would divorce her and return to Leila, but he had moved to another city for work and she had no idea what had become of the marriage.

"No one will marry me now," she said. "I could always marry an old man, a widower who wants to remarry, but why would I do that? I have already one old man to care for."

Her words fixed in his mind, he began to fantasize about marrying her. At thirty Leila was a good seven years older than he, and marriages between younger men and older women were unheard of in Morocco, except where the older woman was foreign and held out the promise of a visa. His plan for his own life did not include marriage until he was at least thirty, but these were unusual circumstances, and he knew that if he did not do something by the time his Peace Corps stint was up, he might never see her again. The thought of a life without her weekly visits was almost too much to bear.

There were a few obstacles. Islamic law stated that a non-Muslim man had to convert in order to marry a Muslim woman. At the thought of converting, Peter felt sanguine; the religion's fairly straightforward list of requirements, particularly the call to perform five prayers a day, would bring an appealing sense of order and discipline to his life. He could already picture himself bending down to press his forehead to a sumptuous Persian carpet inside a cool, domed mosque.

Leila spoke no English, but he imagined teaching her himself, or enrolling her in an ESL program when they moved back to the States. They would live in Washington, where he would work in the nonprofit field, perhaps offering his opinion on how to implement AIDS-education programs in developing countries. Maybe he would get a degree in public health. Eventually she might work too, and once she became fluent in English, she could even go to college. They could start an import business selling the Sidi Maarif rugs to interior designers and furniture shops, and she would travel back and forth to Morocco to bring merchandise. She would still wear the swirling, colorful fabrics of the Sahara, and his friends would remark on her beauty as she poured tea or prepared rich, spicy stews.

Just as it would later take him months to ask out Elise, Peter waited until the last possible minute to present his plan to Leila. With only one month left in his Peace Corps service, he needed to begin the paperwork for converting, marriage, and visas. This might take longer than a month, he reasoned, but even if his service ended, he could stay on for as long as necessary.

He asked if they might go for a walk rather than talking in his kitchen, as they normally did.

"In a month I will leave," he said to her in Arabic. "There's something important I must discuss with you." At first Leila seemed uncertain, but when he pressed her she agreed to go along. Any costs to her reputation, he decided, would be mitigated by the fact that he was planning to marry her and make their relationship legitimate. She drew up her headscarf and they set out, heading in the direction of the old Plaza Mayor, where, gazing out onto the dark expanse of the Atlantic before them, he would propose.

Outside the safe confines of his apartment, she was silent and nervous, her eyes lowered as they passed other Maarifians on the way to the old Spanish district. Peter had never been so aware of his outsider status as he was now, when the hostile glances of nearly everyone they passed indicated that he had clearly transgressed some invisible boundary. But he was thrilled to finally be outside with her, as if they were announcing their relationship status to the entire community. They passed the dilapidated bullfighting ring where teenage boys skulked in the dusty bleachers smoking hashish. He looked out over the water, imagining them together on a plane crossing the Atlantic. The sea was a dull, unbroken line, except for the abandoned monorail, a rusted sentry guarding the town's crumbling art deco architecture. A ring of fat date palms crowned the cracked and faded squares of the Plaza Mayor. Glue-sniffing adolescents, runaways from other cities, squatted in the doorway of the vacant church nearby. At sunset all the buildings took on an eerie, pink glow.

In the Plaza, a man in a heavy leather jacket, his face riddled with scars, stared at them, his eyes narrowing as he drew in smoke from his cigarette. The man spat on the ground before them as they walked past.

"*Qahba*," the man said. Then, Spanish. "*Puta.*"

Leila stared straight ahead, but she was visibly shaken.

"Should I go back and say something?" he asked, wondering if he should defend her honor. She shook her head.

"I must go," she apologized, turning around just before they reached the old railed promenade that extended along the waterfront. He pleaded with her to wait, grabbing her arm as she twisted away from him, but his Arabic failed him, and the only words he could get out were,

"*Bgheet--*" I want-- the words falling off in mid-air as she hurried away from him. But she had already slipped into the night.

He did not see her the next week, or the one following, and although he knew the address of her house he was afraid a visit from him might damage her reputation even further. Being seen with him must have branded her, marked her forever as a whore, as the man with the scars had called her. Finally he turned to his friend Ibrahim, a tour guide, who had once lived in Spain and could always be counted on for his reasonable yet worldly advice.

"She probably knew that you wanted to make a proposal," Ibrahim said. "If she doesn't come back to visit you, you shouldn't press the matter any further. She has her father to think of, after all. I don't think she would leave him."

Intending to follow Ibrahim's advice, Peter waited for her each evening, keeping the tea and mint ready for her visits, but she never came. Eating was difficult, and sleep came very late, if at all. He was torn whether to leave or to postpone his departure until he figured out what to do. At work he was listless.

"This place gets to you, doesn't it," Dr. Berrada said, sensing his depression. "At least you're leaving soon. I am stuck here for another year." They were alone in the clinic together, Peter slumped in a chair while Berrada sterilized his instruments.

"It's not this place. It's a woman," he responded. He was beyond caring whether Hassan Berrada knew the details of his personal life. He would never see this man again.

"A woman?" Hassan replied, suddenly interested. "Which woman?"

"Leila," he said. "She came to the clinic a year ago about her father, the old *goumier* who lost his mind. We've been seeing each other ever since. I wanted to ask her to marry me, but she left town."

Hassan broke out into laughter, slapping his knee as if he found this uproariously funny. "Marriage? That woman? But she's a known prostitute, my brother."

Peter looked at him, trying to determine whether he was telling the truth, or whether the comment merely reflected Hassan's overall scorn for the townspeople.

"How would you know?" he asked coldly, but he realized that Hassan, who spent many of his nights drinking whiskey with the town alcoholics, would be likely to possess this type of information.

"Everyone knows."

"But she lives with her father. She supports them by weaving rugs."

"And by other activities."

Peter did not want to believe him. Without a word he got up and left the clinic, walking back through town toward the Hotel España, where Ibrahim spent his days waiting for tourists. Ibrahim would tell him the truth.

But it turned out that reality was slightly more complicated than Hassan had made it sound.

"She was married then divorced," Ibrahim said. "A few years after her marriage, she grew big, and then she left Sidi Maarif. Someone from my village saw her in Agadir, begging on the street with a baby at her breast."

"But that doesn't make sense," Peter said. "She told me she couldn't have children."

"Perhaps her husband just wasn't a man," Ibrahim shrugged. "Do you think she would tell you this history? It is bad enough she was divorced."

"What happened to the baby?"

"What happens to most of the babies; they end up in the orphanage run by the Sisters. When Leila returned to Sidi Maarif nothing was said of it."

"So now she works as a prostitute? Why didn't you tell me?" Peter could not bring together the disparate threads of the story into something that made sense.

"You are leaving in a week anyway," Ibrahim said. "Is it better to leave with a broken heart or with a heart that has been both broken and betrayed?"

Peter spent his last week in Sidi Maarif packing up his apartment, training the new Peace Corps worker who'd come to take his place, and trying not to show Hassan, Ibrahim or anyone else who knew him the extent of his devastation. He could not take his mind off Leila, though with each passing day his heartbreak began to be displaced by a sense that she had deceived him. What if she had said yes, and he married her, going back to America with his new bride without knowing about her sordid past? What would the other Moroccans in Sidi Maarif have thought of him?

One night, while he busied himself making neat piles of his clothes, which he would leave for Ibrahim to distribute to his family, there came a knock at his door. He looked through the peephole and saw a familiar bright purple scarf, her head a distorted projection through the convex peephole. He stood very still, pondering what to do. Again she knocked. Could he simply open the door, take out his teapot, and rummage around for some fresh mint and the small box of gunpowder tea, as if nothing had ever happened? He had spent some of his best times in Sidi Maarif with this woman, imagining that a chaste courtship was developing between them. Now he knew he'd been completely wrong. But that did not stop his heart from sinking when she turned and walked away, her heels clicking on the steps of his apartment building as her footsteps gradually receded, until all traces of her presence vanished from his life.

In the years since, he analyzed those moments with her endlessly. If Leila had nothing to lose, why had she run away from him that day on the Corniche? He played out numerous scenarios of what might have happened if he'd answered the door that final time. As the years passed, the idea of Leila being a prostitute ceased to shock him. His twenty-three year-old self deserved to be scolded for his passivity, for running away, as if being a prostitute somehow made her less of a human being. He had blamed Leila and not her circumstances. Since single mothers were completely ostracized and could even go to jail for adultery, very few of them were able to keep their babies. Peter imagined Leila, motherless, abandoned by her husband, thinking she was infertile and discovering her swelling belly. Then he tried to picture her on a street corner in Agadir, cradling a baby in her lap, her palm outstretched to receive the pity and the *dirhams* of passersby. This was the bind she must have found herself in-- return to take care of your sick father and risk humiliating your family's honor, or leave behind the child nobody knows you have. Moroccan orphanages could be grim places, the walls lined with cribs in which babies comforted each other and waited for hours for someone to pick them up. Adoption in the American sense was simply not done. Nobody wanted to raise a bastard. The girls ended up as maids, abused by their employers. The boys often became criminals. The more Peter had learned in the years since leaving Morocco, the more he realized he'd made a terrible mistake by leaving, by not going after her.

But that was all hindsight, speculation. The twenty-three year old Peter reflected on none of these things. Instead, he made order of the tiny household he'd kept in Sidi Maarif. After his clothes had been endlessly sorted, categorized, and given away, he cleaned his kitchen, arranging his kitchen utensils, plates, and two cooking pots, as well as the silver teapot in which Leila had prepared tea, trying not to think again of her, of the flash of white teeth against her dark face when she smiled. His bags waited by the door. In a decision he would regret for the rest of his life, he took the small red carpet she had given him out of his suitcase, leaving it neatly rolled up in the corner of his bedroom. Then he went downstairs to give the key to his landlady, walking toward the bus station that would take him away from Sidi Maarif forever.

CHAPTER EIGHT

The starting line for the 10K Fidelity Bank Race Against Hunger was at the edge of the campus. A small crowd of spectators and runners had gathered there, and although Celia did not know any of them, she felt a profound sense of community, and of being a part of something larger than herself. She tried to breathe slowly to control the flow of adrenaline, filled with that sense of anticipation she always felt before cross country meets in high school. The beauty of the new shoes she had purchased with Elise's gift certificate compounded her anticipation. They were shoes that promised to do almost everything save launch the runner into space. She had agonized over the purchase, wanting them but remembering her anthropology teacher's warning that the brand was notorious for sweatshop labor. Thinking of Anayo Mills, which had closed its operations in Deer Bluff only to open a new factory in Taiwan, made her feel slightly guilty as she warmed up, placing her hands on the ground and stretching her calves and hamstrings.

But the gift had swayed her, along with the easy way Elise had yielded to her extra demands. She had gone into the Annex that day intending either to cancel the whole deal or to display just enough hesitancy that Elise might offer her something more in exchange. Instead she found herself acting with the steely reserve of a hostage negotiator. Asking for the extra money was an afterthought, but when Elise upped the price almost without blinking Celia felt a thrill that must have been akin to gambling, pushing one's luck just a bit further than was prudent. Seeing Michael Lenhart at The Diamond had caused her to think, not only about the inequality of her position in the situation with Elise and Peter but also about her own life. Did she want to end up in Deer Bluff, ruined by people who had taken advantage of her innocence? He was right: she should use her connections to secure her own future. Elise and Peter were not allies but business partners who held an unequal share of the resources.

Over a microphone a man's voice was announcing the start of the race. Celia breathed into her hands, the air cold but bracing. Once she started running she would begin to warm up, and then the weather would be perfect. People began to cluster together at the starting line, the faster runners jostling one another in the front, men with thin, streamlined bodies in tight jackets and running tights, women in fuzzy terrycloth sweatsuits, high school kids tossing their team track jackets to their mothers on the sidelines. Celia spotted a group of overweight women wearing matching sweatshirts that announced they were part of a weight loss team. People ran for different reasons; Celia in particular enjoyed the solitariness of the sport, the fact that no matter how much she trained or how fast she was, there would always be better runners, so that ultimately she was only in competition with herself.

In front of her she saw a familiar head of dark hair. Recognizing Peter, she thought about pushing her way up to him and tapping him on the shoulder but decided against it. He might feel obliged to slow to her pace, to converse awkwardly as they ran. She kept him in her line of sight as the gun went off and the cluster of runners began to separate out. He ran with a fast but graceful, almost loping pace. Other runners seemed to pound the asphalt, their legs pistons releasing enormous amounts of energy with each step, but the way he ran was almost effortless.

For the first two miles the only sound was the slap of feet on asphalt and heavy breathing as the runners wound their way through stately, tree-lined neighborhoods, past the Institute for Advanced Study where Einstein once lived, and out toward the Princeton Battlefield. Along the way volunteers offered plastic cups of water with outstretched arms, but she accepted nothing, not wanting to slow down. After awhile Peter sped away and she lost sight of him, so she picked others to watch, trying to match her pace with theirs and sometimes overtaking them. There were only a few people waiting at the finish line, probably family, and Celia imagined her father there, cheering for her. When she crossed over the line she looked up at the clock; her time was a good one and she was pleased.

She kept walking until her heart rate slowed, accepting a cup of water and a banana. Her feet had blistered from the new shoes, and she could feel them throbbing, but the slight pain was negated by the elation of finishing a good run. Further ahead a few school buses sat idle, waiting to return runners to the starting line. Around her a few men chatted competitively about their times, sizing each other up. At the finish line she watched as one man cheered for his wife, embracing her as she ran over to him, not seeming to mind the sweat that poured down her face.

A voice hesitantly called out her name, and she turned around to face Peter. His smile was wider and more open than usual, as if the weather and the crowd and the fact of their shared exertion had temporarily united them.

"I saw your time as you crossed," he said. "Good job." She thanked him, noting his faded Brown sweatshirt and frayed running shorts, a change from the pressed khakis and professional briefcase she always saw him with. He looked younger, and happier, than usual.

Observe them, Mr. Lenhart had said. *Find out what makes them different from you.*

Riding the bus back into Princeton, they exchanged small talk about running, and Celia was impressed to hear that he had run the Boston marathon. From time to time he glanced down at her shoes, and she wondered if he knew about the gift certificate. As she was about to excuse herself to walk back to her dorm, he suddenly asked,

"Do you want to have breakfast together? I could go for some pancakes at PJ's."

"Is Elise meeting you there?"

He laughed. "She's probably still asleep."

Amid pricey jewelry shops, French restaurants, a trendy brewing company, and stores selling overpriced preppy apparel, PJ's was one of the few places in Princeton that had a down-home, down-at-the-heels feel. Although it was still early, the restaurant was almost full, and Peter and Celia slid into one of the last booths. An older woman with a beehive hairdo and the leathery face of a smoker slapped menus down in front of them and filled up their coffee cups in a single, practiced gesture. The waitresses might have been from Deer Bluff, imported from elsewhere into the rarefied Princeton environment.

"I like this place," Peter announced. "It reminds me of a restaurant in south Boston where I used to go when I was growing up. It was a bit of a drive from where we lived but my father always took us there because they had scrapple."

"What's that?" she asked.

"Scrapple? You don't know what scrapple is? We have to order it," he said excitedly. "Scrapple is to Pennsylvanians what grits are to Southerners."

"Is it like grits?"

"No, it's something else. Made out of mystery meat. One of Pennsylvania's native culinary treasures. My father grew up there, and every trip to visit my grandparents always involved eating large quantities of scrapple."

"You don't seem the kind of person who would eat mystery meat. I thought you were Mr. Health-conscious."

"I am," he said. "But we all have our occasional indulgences." The waitress returned to take their order, Peter ordering pancakes and scrapple, Celia asking for eggs and toast. "At least you'll have to try mine," he told her.

He asked about her fall break, and Celia gave him the basic version of events she'd told Elise. She tried to make Deer Bluff come alive for him, describing the abandoned mill, Main Street, and meeting her former teacher at The Diamond.

"You don't have a group of friends you still go back to see?"

"Everyone I went to school with is off at college. I lost touch with most of my high school acquaintances. I kept in touch with my ex-boyfriend for awhile, but not anymore."

"It can be difficult to stay friends with exes," he agreed. "Especially when you start to see other people."

"I'm not seeing anyone. I'm pretty sure my ex-boyfriend is gay, but he doesn't want me to know yet. His parents took him out of college to be 'reconditioned' as straight, so he was home, but I avoided him while I was there." It felt good to relay this detail to Peter, to show him that she had her own complicated past, however nascent.

"Wow, that's bizarre," he said. She decided to embellish.

"I think the reconditioning involves lots of counseling from the Baptist preacher. Lectures on Sodom and Gomorrah. Maybe even shock therapy. Who knows which is worse to endure."

"It must have been weird to see your former English teacher reduced to sitting in a bar and scrawling his novel in a notebook all day. God forbid I end up that way."

"It was and it wasn't," Celia said. "He's one of those people I'm still learning from. Only now the lessons are more about what I don't want to do with my life."

"Losing your job, spending your days in a bar, losing your wife," he said. "Those are cautionary tales, alright."

"Especially losing my wife," she said. "That would be the worst." Peter smiled.

"Maybe he'll write the Great American Novel and surprise everyone. Sometimes people just need to be stripped of everything meaningful so they can write out of despair. I could use that kind of extra push to help me finish my dissertation."

"You don't mean that."

"I do and I don't," he said. The waitress arrived with their breakfast. Celia was starving. She looked over at the small plate bearing a flat, gray hunk of meat. He immediately cut into the scrapple, placing a piece of it on her plate. "Just try it. You don't have to like it. For me it's a taste of nostalgia."

Celia bit into the scrapple, a salty, unfamiliar texture sliding across her palate. It did not seem the type of food that Peter would like.

"It has an intriguing rubberiness," she said. "With your wife I've tried mussels and veggie curries. Now I can add scrapple to the ways you've both broadened my horizons." A look of amusement flashed over his features.

"I might take a class in your department next semester," she said. "It's called 'Mystics, Travelers, and Assassins,' taught by Dr. Kronenberg?"

"That's my advisor," Peter said. "He's also a Sufi, so he knows something about the mystics bit. I would give anything to teach that class. But I'd never get to do it here, unless he went on sabbatical. Right now it looks like I'm stuck teaching elementary Arabic."

"Elise mentioned Dr. Kronenberg before. Why did he become Muslim?"

"There are more converts to Islam in the West than you would think. Sufism is like *kabbala*, only not as trendy. In the city there are some very active sects, made up of Americans who get together to chant or dance. Basically it's about finding new ways to achieve oneness with God." He spoke knowledgeably, as if he himself might be familiar with how you did this.

"So you're a believer, then," Celia asked. It was a personal question, but he didn't seem offended.

"I don't know what I am," he said. He had a strange look on his face that she couldn't interpret. Celia spread jam on her wheat toast, relishing its sweetness after the scrapple and trying to think of a way to change the subject.

"What happened with that student in your class? The one who was trying to get you in trouble."

"He's still trying. We almost got into an argument yesterday, but I restrained myself. He tries to catch me, to make me incriminate myself, but I refuse to do it."

"You make teaching sound like a battle."

"Like everything else, it's never what you expect," he said. "Maybe it'll get better once I finish school and I'm no longer just someone's teaching assistant."

"Why did you get into teaching, then? Or did you just want to be a scholar?"

Pausing for a moment, he took a bite of his pancake, considering his words carefully. Unlike Elise, she noticed that Peter did not think out loud.

"I went to the Peace Corps and thought I could change the world. Figured teaching was the way to do that. Also, I wanted other people to get interested in the Muslim world. Maybe if people understood it better, we could have a more peaceful world. I hoped through teaching, I could influence people. But I don't think I'm very good at it."

"Don't underestimate yourself," she replied. "I bet your students like you more than you know. Probably a lot of them don't know what to think about the Middle East. You could win them by showing them the humanity of the people there."

"They don't have to share my point of view. It's not that I want them to think what I think. But for them to understand what made me interested in the region… they would have to experience it for themselves, not in a classroom, but by traveling there, by living with the people."

"Why didn't you become an anthropologist, then?" Celia tried to eat slowly, to drag out the breakfast so she would not have to go back to her room and face the rest of the day alone with her studies. Real life, the dynamics of human interaction and motivation: this was what she needed to be studying.

"Good question," Peter said. "I respect anthropologists. But I wanted to read as much as possible, to find answers in what other people had written, not what I created myself through some fieldwork encounter. I wouldn't know how to analyze the messiness of people's interactions."

"Still, your best source of information so far has been experiential," she said. He took a drink of water, a hazy look in his eyes, and began to tell her about the Saharan beach town where he'd served in the Peace Corps. More animated now, he talked about his colleague, the corrupt doctor who used money designated for medical supplies to buy alcohol, and the people who came to the clinic with problems that were sometimes easily solvable, other times hopeless. He mentioned a woman he had been fond of, and a look of pain flashed across his face.

"And here we are, sitting in Princeton with our new Fidelity Bank Race Against Hunger t-shirts," he finished.

"You've never gone back there?"

"No. I prefer to keep Sidi Maarif the way it is in my mind. I don't like to be disappointed."

"I would visit a place like that in a heartbeat," she said. "You make it sound amazing. So you never thought of taking Elise?"

"We went to Morocco, but not down to the south. She never wanted to see where I did my Peace Corps service. I don't think she could handle the conditions. There are no five-star hotels in Sidi Maarif."

"Why don't you find a way to write about it?" she said.

"I'm working on something right now. I had writer's block for awhile but now I'm onto something."

"Sidi Maarif would be a great setting for a story. Maybe that would help get it out of your mind, so you would at least feel like you could move on."

"I don't have that kind of imagination. I have trouble getting the words down on paper, or, as I said, figuring out what to make of the messiness of human interaction." He looked at her significantly. "I guess that's what you want to do?"

"As a writer? I'd like to. I have a long way to go. But that phrase you just used, 'the messiness of human interaction'? I need more of that to write about." She told him about her creative writing class and the one piece she'd turned in for a workshop that had met with less than enthusiastic reviews.

"I was writing about running, actually," she said. "I wanted the race to be a metaphor for the larger competitiveness of life, but it came across as pretty heavy handed. There's one girl in the class who's an incredible writer, and I realized all I wanted to do was to impress her the way her work has impressed me. But she was just sitting there texting on her cell phone. So I knew it was bad. My teacher kept telling me to write about something I'm passionate about."

"Easier said than done," he said. He put his fork down, wiping his face with a napkin. "You know how they say that some people's finest years were their high school days? For me, it was that time in the Peace Corps. Nothing since then has really measured up."

"Does Elise know this?"

"She gives me a hard time about it sometimes, but I don't think she really gets how important it was to me. I can't fault her. It's hard to step back and really see the people who are closest to us."

Peter's frankness, the intimacy of their conversation, stunned her. This was a true conversation, the opening steps of a friendship, not a performance, which she sometimes felt she was witnessing with Elise. What she was beginning to know of him did not fit Elise's portrayal, which was, she had to acknowledge, almost entirely focused on how Peter responded (or didn't respond) to her. She wondered if Peter knew about their most recent meeting, or that she had altered the terms of their agreement. As if reading her mind, he asked,

"So I noticed you got some new running shoes."

"Did Elise tell you? I don't know how she knew I needed them."

"I told her."

Celia was momentarily embarrassed that he'd noticed the shabby condition of her old shoes. "You're pretty perceptive."

But he did not ask how far along she and Elise were in the medical treatments. He had wanted her to know that he was the source of the gift, but otherwise Elise's name did not come up again.

Peter offered to walk her back to her dorm, but she refused, thanking him for the breakfast and taking the long route back to her room. His comment that nothing in his life had managed to measure up to those two years in the Peace Corps made her sad. She wondered if he had been aware of this while he was experiencing it, or if happiness was something that you only realized after the fact, knowing that it was gone forever.

Hovering on the edge of winter, Princeton was cast in hues of gray, the gray of the gothic stone buildings matching the trees denuded of their leaves and the dull, cloudy sky. An unnamable dissatisfaction had begun to plague her since her return to Deer Bluff, a sense that despite her accomplishments, she was never far from her origins and was always in danger of failing in the same way that others around her had failed. Unconsciously she imitated her father's reserve, letting few people get close to her, but this aloofness was stunting her somehow, inhibiting her potential to learn about character, and about human nature. Engaging with Elise had given her a taste of what it might be like to be around people who were a part of the literary world, yet when they were together things always felt a little strained. Her two interactions with Peter had already been both more fun and more meaningful than all the time she'd spent with Elise.

Celia liked being around people who were older, people living their lives already rather than just in training for them, which was what college was about. This was a prejudice; she realized this now and would have to get over it. But how? On campus she shared her meals with a few people she called friends despite doing little with them socially. Occasionally she accepted invitations to a movie or to a shopping mall, where they wandered aimlessly about for a few hours before going home. Usually her friends were scholarship students like herself, and though they might spend a few dollars for a hot pretzel or a t-shirt at Old Navy, they usually left the mall empty handed, as if by mutual agreement that the mall was a museum of consumption, a place to observe without touching.

Although Celia was skilled in the art of politeness (one of the virtues of growing up Southern), she made little effort at trying to win over her friends with charm. Thus the type of people she attracted were those who merely sought companionship for the brief periods they were forced to be with others in a public space. Like small children engaged in parallel play, they occupied the same spaces but did not interact in any profound manner. It was a stage, Celia decided, that she needed to grow out of.

* * *

Elise was lying face down on the floor in her pajamas, knees tucked beneath her, stomach and breasts pressed against the carpet, practicing the Child's Pose from her yoga class. The Child's Pose was the easiest way to calm down, to retreat into yourself for a moment before facing the day ahead. The position was almost like that of the Muslim prayer, in fact even the word "Islam" meant submission, which this pose seemed to offer. Submission to what you couldn't control, to the forces of the earth that gave life and took it away. Elise was not usually prone to philosophical musings, but she did believe that embodying a gesture that resembled prayer might someday lead to the ability to commune with a higher power.

She would not have called herself religious by any traditional measuring stick. Why believe in prophets, creation myths, and commandments, when each religion asserted that its way was the only one? It was good to live in an era where religious observance was not compulsory, thus leaving her free to pick and choose among a few scattered beliefs. Therapy, in fact, was a kind of religion.

Beneath her stated position on religion was another conflicting layer, enforced by occasional trips to Mass during childhood and two years spent in a Catholic school for girls, but for the moment Elise had submerged this layer so effectively that it only came out in a vague sense of guilt at even thinking thoughts that violated what was basically a Judeo-Christian morality system. Striking the Child's Pose was designed to combat the anxiety she was currently feeling about her plans to go into the city to see Eric Babu.

She got up from the floor, her breathing sufficiently slowed to allow a controlled flow of energy in and out of her body. After a shower, a bowl of yogurt and organic muesli, a glass of organic orange juice and five different vitamin and mineral supplements, Elise chose her outfit for the day. It needed to be conservative yet sexy, something that spoke the message that she was simultaneously alluring yet unavailable. Her clothes should also project power, should imply that she was still at the top of her game, editor to many prize-winning authors. There was still some question about whether Diana would let her work on Babu's novel, so she had to find a way to indicate what her situation was without giving away all this business about the baby. A leave of absence, she would tell him, to work out some personal issues. No, that made it sound as if she were having a nervous breakdown. She would tell him she was taking time off to work on some personal projects. What those projects were she would improvise when the moment came. Elise believed in her ability to speak spontaneously and had the utmost confidence that whatever came out of her mouth was the right thing to say.

Dodging her first impulse, she decided against wearing black. She had worn her favorite little black dress to meet with Celia at the Annex the week before, and look where it had gotten her. A thousand dollars poorer, to Peter's distress, plus she would have to call in some favors at the office to find Celia an internship. If that had been her first meeting with Celia she would have walked away. Celia might have been a believer in the unluckiness of certain numbers, but Elise's particular superstition was the unluckiness of clothes. A bad day in one inauspicious garment might be an indicator that future wearings would bring even worse luck. She kept one whole section of her closet devoted to clothes that were harbingers for potential distress, taking them to consignment shops or giving them away as soon as it became apparent she could not wear them again.

She finally decided on a neutral gray wool skirt with a fitted, off-the-shoulder burgundy shirt just tight enough to give Babu a glimpse of what was no longer his for the taking. In the unflattering fluorescent glow of the bathroom light, she examined her face in the mirror for traces of age, detecting a few new wrinkles, on which she immediately applied a French sunscreen that she ordered from Canada for its reputed success in defending the wearer against atmospheric cellular damage. After age thirty everything went rapidly downhill unless people took immediate and drastic measures to stop aging in its tracks. Fortunately she had not yet progressed to the need for Botox. Elise applied eyeliner and lipstick, shaking her short hair in the mirror, unsure of what Babu would think, since he had last seen her when her hair was long. Long hair made her look younger but also less sophisticated, a crucial element she needed to project in dealing with cosmopolitan men like Eric Babu.

She looked forward to their meeting, which would provide a good distraction from Princeton, Celia's newfound reticence and her husband's continued absorption with his work. Sometimes when Peter did not come home until late she called Caitlin, who could be counted on to commiserate with her about the tendency of husbands to absent themselves from the conjugal domain. Caitlin's husband Martin owned two successful restaurants and a nightclub, all in Manhattan, allowing them to live in an enviably large house but also requiring that he work long and irregular hours, occasionally in the company of models and starlets whose presence was necessary for publicity purposes. In consultation with renowned chefs, Martin designed restaurant concepts, securing the necessary funding, executing the concept, and eventually selling the restaurants for astronomical sums of money.

Talking with Caitlin always reassured her that her situation with Peter was not as dire as she suspected. Martin was probably more like Elise's father, an ambitious real estate mogul. Peter, by contrast, lacked that drive. He was consistent, capable of weathering the storm of her emotions and putting up with a fair amount of erratic behavior. Lately, though, she had begun to feel that his patience was waning, which made it even more crucial that she and Celia get down to business with the ova donation. Once they had firmly established that a baby was on the way, Peter would become more attentive, the baby stabilizing them as a couple, bringing a necessary permanence to their relationship.

Intermittent rain pricked the windows of the train, the heavy sky making the faces of the passengers appear even wearier than usual. Her eyes trained on the landscape as it sped by, Elise tried to determine what she wanted to achieve in her meeting with Babu. The situation was complicated, tied up as it was in her uncertain feelings about her career and the role it should play in her life. She was unsure whether her snap decision to email Eric Babu related more to her desire to cling to the influence she had once had in her work or to her need for male attention. She decided not to think about it, having scheduled her day so that lunch with Eric would be followed by an appointment with Dr. Geiger. This would curtail any impulse at lingering with Babu over dessert, forcing her to engage in the necessary work of understanding the self.

A little after noon, Elise entered the doors of Café Moderne, a small French bistro several blocks from Babu's apartment. On the way from the subway she had stepped in a puddle. She cursed as the wetness seeped through her shoes, the incident nearly destroying her composure. She had hoped to choose a location further away from his flat, to avoid any temptation to accompany him there to see what he was working on, but in their email exchanges he insisted on this particular cafe.

Growing accustomed to the dim lighting of the restaurant (a plus, considering the newly discovered wrinkles), her eyes scanned the restaurant, but he had yet to arrive. The hostess seated her at a table near the window, Elise discreetly checking her make-up in a compact one more time, only to be caught in the act by Eric, who suddenly materialized before her, a wry smile spreading across his features.

"I didn't see you," she apologized. Eric Babu towered above her, the restaurant lights a glowing corona behind his substantial dreadlocks. In the photos on his book jacket covers he never smiled, always staring at the camera ironically, head turned slightly to the side, the hair adding gravity to his already sharp, distinguished features. Experience had given him the right to take himself so seriously. At the age of eleven he'd lost both of his parents, members of an Igbo tribe killed in the Biafran civil war. A gifted student, Babu was educated in the capital of Lagos courtesy of a wealthy uncle who took him in and raised him as his own. After university, he received a scholarship to read for an M.Phil at Cambridge, and it was there that he'd written his first novel at the age of twenty-four. In his forties now, Babu was one of the premier authors of his country, several international literary prizes under his belt and his eye on a Nobel.

"You look stunning as always," Eric murmured, looking her over. "The short hair becomes you." When he spoke, it was in a deep, mellifluous baritone, his words coming out in an erudite British accent. Her face warmed, the very tenor of his voice seeming to allude to the intimacy they once shared.

"As do you," she said. "How long has it been?"

"A few years at least. You had just gotten married." This wasn't exactly true, as she and Peter had been married for a few years already when she last edited one of Babu's novels, strictly platonically that time. "Before we get too settled, I wanted to propose an alternative venue." Her heart sank, thinking he would mention his apartment, and she would have to deal with her discomfort in refusing him.

"I don't have a lot of time," she said. "I've got to be somewhere else at three."

"I have arranged a driver," he said. "You shall be back at your next destination on time and perhaps earlier."

"What about your work? You said you needed to be close to your apartment."

"Something else has inspired me," he said.

Then they were in the back of a Lincoln Towncar heading toward Brooklyn, Elise conscious of his proximity, of his long, elegant hands resting on his jeans, the smell of his cologne. Cologne was something Elise normally detested, though she liked it on him. She did not recognize the neighborhoods they were passing through, the dilapidated architecture in sections of Brooklyn she normally avoided.

"Here they have not yet caught the disease," he said cryptically. "The creeping stealth of gentrification. I find these places to be at their purest."

Finally the driver stopped outside a storefront bearing the painted lettering FAST CHICKEN and AFRICA CALLING – CARDS SOLD HERE. Elise followed Eric into the restaurant, which was no more than an unfinished, concrete floor, basic tables and folding chairs where a few old men sat, staring at her wide-eyed as if she were an apparition. The smell of slow-cooked onions made her mouth water. Through a rectangular window the kitchen was visible, an enormous black woman hard at work kneading dough. The woman wiped her hands on a towel and came around to the front, greeting Eric in a language Elise could not identify. He said a few words in response, and the woman returned to the kitchen, motioning for them to take a seat.

She had never felt more out of her element, with her whiteness and her slick city clothes, Eric clearly delighting in the way he had thrown her off balance. The chicken was, as promised, fast, the woman returning with two steaming plates of chicken smothered in onions and another dish of rice tinted red from tomatoes and flecked with bits of meat. The doughy substance she had been kneading in the kitchen, uncooked, was apparently part of the meal, and Elise watched as Eric pinched off a handful of dough and ate it slowly.

"This," he said, "is the setting for my next novel. I come here twice a week for research. I converse. There is a small West African enclave in this neighborhood that intrigues me, since it remains rather untouched, not nearly so commercial as Harlem. Do you like the food?"

"It's wonderful," said Elise, who found herself eating with relish. He had never shared his culture with her before. She brought a tangle of lemony onions to her mouth, savoring their contrast with the salty chicken.

"I'm glad to see you're not so picky as you once were," he said. Eric Babu was not the kind of person to whom one announced eating disorders or other American neuroses, but in the past he had observed her restraint concerning matters of food. "You would look much better if you were a little plumper," he added. "The time for girlish skinniness has ended. You do not yet have children, I take it?"

"No," she said, eager to change the subject. "What's this dish called?"

"*Poulet Yassa*," Eric said. "It's a Senegalese dish."

"Hopefully the food will make an appearance in your novel," she said. "I'll look forward to reliving it through your descriptions."

"This place," he said, gesturing around him, "is the site of much of the scheming my characters are involved in. Over steaming bowls of *jollof* rice they meet in this nondescript setting and pine away for the homeland. A few of them are Islamic fundamentalists, while others are looking for ways to oppose the encroaching gentrification that threatens to push them further out of the city. The book is about the conflict between the two in this neighborhood, and the overall sickness of our globalized world."

"Brilliant," Elise said. "And timely. Are you close to finishing a draft?"

He paused for a moment and looked around, as if to see if anyone were listening. "That is why I came to New York. I needed a stronger sense of place, and the sterility of my surroundings in Toronto was blocking me. So I'm here now."

It was an answer that was not an answer, giving no indication of where he was in the novel's progress. Babu was not the type of writer who experienced true writer's block, and he assuredly turned out a novel every two years along with a spattering of densely allegorical short stories that would appear in the *New Yorker* or the *Paris Review*. Alluding to writing difficulties was a strategy, something he did to ward off the evil eye. To speak too confidently of his good fortune or prolific nature, even when apparent to all who knew him, might attract misfortune. All of his leading male characters had a fear of this. Superstition and rationality coexisted comfortably in Babu's persona.

She had noticed that he responded well to talk that did not convey information but rather suggested secrecy and intrigue. And so when he asked her why she was not working at Smyth & Copperfield full time, she offered her own evasive response.

"I'm working on something myself," she said. "Something requiring my full attention, a long period of gestation. I can't say much about it other than that. Things are still very much in their nascent stages."

"The language of birth," Babu mused. "An overused metaphor, perhaps, but what lies behind it? You can always confide in me."

Elise smiled, seeing that her language had had the desired effect. What he did not realize was that she was being perfectly transparent. Pregnancy and birth were not subjects that interested Babu outside the pages of his novels. His wife fulfilled that need, and he took his own children for granted, accepting them as an obligatory part of the life process. Mundane but necessary, his wife and children were tangential to his own fame and the momentous task of conceiving difficult works of fiction. Elise knew her own appeal lay in her professionalism, insofar as he associated her with that world. As an editor, her job was to be the midwife to Babu's literary creations.

For the rest of lunch, the conversation was not so personal. They spoke of mutual acquaintances in the writing world, current scandals, and recent novels that had met with great acclaim. While he pretended to be charitable, Babu cast a competitive eye on the work of other writers. As Elise dropped the names of writers whose work she had edited (none in the very recent past, although she tried to be vague), she could sense which authors he found threatening by the way he shifted from side to side in his seat, the great, serene stillness of his body displaying the slightest agitation at the mention of another author's success. This was also a game that seemed to enhance his interest in her, which she could feel deepening as she talked. Finding herself in this unexpected venue, her face flushed from the heat of the restaurant and the excellent food, animated her, this contact with her old life making her happier than she had felt in months.

Later, after Eric's limousine deposited her in the middle of a tree-lined street of brownstones (she had alluded cagily to a further *rendezvous* and asked to be dropped off a few blocks from Dr. Geiger's office), she tried to transform the lunch experience into a narrative form from the safe retreat of her psychiatrist's office. She could still feel the pressure of his hand on hers as she got out of the car, his eyes hopeful when he asked if he would be meeting her in Princeton in a few weeks' time.

"This just happened; maybe it's too soon to be talking about it," she said. "I'm incoherent, aren't I? I'm not sure what to make of it yet."

"How do you feel?" he asked, his blue eyes glimmering. "In the moment. Right now. Tell me what you're feeling."

"I feel great," she said. "I feel like a cloud has temporarily lifted. I didn't have anything to drink, but I feel amazingly good."

"I'm interested in something you said a few minutes ago," Dr. Geiger said, looking down at his legal pad. "You said, 'Talking with Eric is like a game, and I miss the challenge of responding to someone like him.' What do you mean by that?"

"I mean that I have to work hard to be clever," Elise said. "I have to create a sense of artifice. I can judge my success by the way he responds to me—I can tell when his mind is elsewhere even when I don't know what he's thinking. But if he finds me intriguing, he listens, and the more I say without really revealing anything, the more I have his attention."

"This is a contrast, I think, from the way you are with others."

"Yes, I usually think of myself as more direct. I say what I'm thinking, and I tend to be more confessional. But that doesn't work with him."

"So when you're with him you create an alternative persona."

"Something like that."

"Did you think about sleeping with him?"

"I thought about what I'd do if he hit on me." She could feel herself blushing. "But I decided beforehand that I was going to try to concentrate on that sense of innuendo that you can only have when sex is something that's nearly out of reach. Like when it's still a possibility that could go either way. It's not something you feel once you're married and sex is a given. I miss it, in fact."

"Elise," Dr. Geiger closed his notepad and looked at her with an expression that was almost grave. "It would be irresponsible of me to tell you how happy you seem, but still I will say it, followed by a caveat. I don't think we've figured out the real reason why this meeting with Eric Babu was so meaningful to you. The facile, and wrong explanation would be to say there's a Madame Bovary syndrome going on here, and that you're a bored housewife remembering the drama of your previous life." He paused, and she smiled at the literary reference. "I knew you then, too, and even in the midst of your affair with Babu you were profoundly unhappy. And so I have a homework assignment for you."

"Tell me."

"Before I see you next week, I want you to think about your marriage to Peter and write down what you love about him. Don't try to be clever with words, just write down ideas that are real and concrete. I want you to try to remember why you got married in the first place. And then, I want you to write down all the reasons why you want to have a baby with Peter. Finally, I'm not sure it's such a good idea to see Eric Babu too much right now."

"Why?" Her heart sank; her disappointment at feeling the displeasure of the father was almost a cliché. Was Dr. Geiger being moralistic? Was he trying to protect her marriage? She wanted simultaneously to please and defy him.

"It's just not a good time. You should be able to see that. You told me you were upset about the egg donation process but hardly talked about it at all. If you see him again, it may muddy the waters. Your response in the past has been to compartmentalize. With such serious matters, I don't think you should be doing that. Peter in one compartment, motherhood in another, and in the third, an unstable, potentially threatening relationship."

"It's not that simple."

"I know," responded Dr. Geiger. "But we're out of time for today."

* * *

The library had been good to Peter that day. Perhaps it was because Elise was in the city, where he knew she would be holed up with her shrink and one of her writer cronies for most of the day. Or maybe his conversation with Celia, and her faith that he was capable of greatness, lay behind his inspiration. For that was the impression she gave him during their breakfast together: unconditional support and encouragement that he had real stories to tell. Today the Firestone

Library felt like home, and he had managed to work successfully not in his cramped carrel but at a shared table in the reading room, surrounded by students who would be there long after he left, reading late into the night, and into their bright, guaranteed futures. The reading lamp cast an otherworldly sheen onto the pages of text spread out before him, and the tapping chorus of students typing on their laptops energized him. On days like this he never wanted to leave, wanted to stay in the library until it closed. He was nearly done writing his chapter about the women carpet weavers, discovered by the colonial explorers and then destroyed as if by mutual agreement by the Spanish regime and the Moroccan sultan. He had found legal documents suggesting this: a formal pronouncement by a regional governor that all inheritance (and other family laws) henceforth had to follow Islamic and not African tribal customs. A letter dated at about the same time between a regional Spanish administrator and an official from French Morocco suggested that "in applying native laws and customs, for uniformity's sake, it is better to remove all traces of the primitive African ideas. As the natives progress from paganism to Mohammedanism to Christianity, at least the second contains consistent (and codified) rules, thus easing our duties."

The day's unexpected productivity made his scheduled coffee breaks feel well deserved, the paper cup filled with Small World Coffee warming his hand as he smiled charitably at the group of smokers clustered on the stone wall outside the library. Since last Saturday's race the weather had been overcast and rainy, which made leaving the dullness of the outside world for the warm earth tones and wood paneling of Firestone Library even more delightful. At this moment he loved being at Princeton, loved the sense of being a part of this high-powered, hallowed institution. The freedom of unscheduled days, of being a student again, of creating and disseminating knowledge: all were unparalleled privileges that his old friends, tied to the working world of nine to five schedules, could not possibly understand.

He would not allow himself to browse the Internet or look at Facebook during his breaks, though he did allow himself to jot down some resolutions regarding Elise during one of his breaks late in the day. *Make more time to do things together. Cook dinner more. Go into city, see play, dinner.* Elise had been so cooperative over the past few days that it made him want to be a better husband as well. In therapy, she told him, she had been making some breakthroughs. Elise insisted on the fragility of her mental state, and sometimes it was easier for Peter to attribute their marriage problems to her mental chemistry than to any real issues in their lives together. Despite his nostalgia for the intensity of his feelings for Leila, in his more confident moments he recognized that the reality of marriage was difficult and would have been with anyone. Although he was aware that he and Elise were going through a rough patch, he was confident that they would be out of it soon enough, especially now that she was getting closer to her goal of having children.

By five o'clock Peter had completed an astonishing amount of work. This productivity, he decided, should be celebrated. Breaking his routine, he decided to leave the library a little early and surprise Elise by making dinner. He picked up some hors d'oeuvres from the Mediterranean delicatessen and a bottle of good French wine at the liquor store. At home, he began to arrange the table, lighting candles and placing the appetizers in the little Portugese serving dishes that bore drawings of frolicking rabbits. Elise would arrive at any minute. She had planned to have lunch with Ciara Silverman, a loud-voiced confessional author who spelled women with a "y" and wrote sprawling novels about heroines facing weight crises and unfaithful husbands to find peace in religion, art, sensitive, ponytailed Renaissance men, or a combination of all three. He suspected his wife was trying to reconnect with some of her more successful writers, perhaps as a prelude to returning to work full time.

Her weekly visits to Dr. Geiger, seemed to sustain and reinvigorate her, much in the way religion did for other people. Peter knew that Princeton could be a difficult place for the spouse of an academic, especially for the husbands and wives of graduate students who had agreed to sacrifice several years to their spouses' dreams of academic grandeur in a town where there were few interesting jobs for non-academics. When they first moved to Princeton he tried to encourage her to make friends with some of his colleagues' wives, but Elise never seemed particularly interested in forming attachments with them.

"Why would I?" she'd said once. "We have nothing in common. They're all ten years younger than me. Or Bulgarian."

"Is there something precluding a friendship with a Bulgarian?" Peter asked.

"Oh, come on. I'm talking about Boris's wife. She looks like a blonde supermodel, always tripping around in high heels and tiny skirts, even in the middle of winter. Plus it's always the wives who are still here with nothing to do. It's like nothing's changed - the man gets the doctorate, the woman faithfully accompanies him."

"That's not true - there are some male spouses."

"Yeah, but for the most part, they're all women. They're all dissatisfied about something. Being around them might convince me that I've made a big mistake by coming here." Peter had launched a virtual campaign to get them to move to Princeton, and Elise relinquished life in New York with some reluctance. He understood her unwillingness to leave, knowing that achieving a successful life in the city had not been simple. Leaving a rent-stabilized apartment, a regular group of friends, and her favorite bars and cafés had not been easy. Now that they lived in Princeton she had allowed her friendships to drop one by one, except for her best friend from college. Why she rarely saw Caitlin was something Peter never quite understood. They spoke on the phone frequently, and it would have taken them both only an hour to get into the city to meet each other. Caitlin herself must have been lonely, since her own husband was rarely home and presumably unfaithful, yet on some point of pride neither woman could bring herself to leave the suburbs and visit the other's turf.

Peter heard the key turn in the lock, witnessing the private, unguarded look on his wife's face as she entered, not realizing he was at home. She looked beautiful, her cheeks pink, her eyes bearing a thoughtful, almost faraway look. What wisdom had she garnered from Dr. Geiger today? They did not talk much about her meetings with her psychiatrist, this being one of those inviolable zones of Elise's life that she protected from his view. He tried not to be suspicious of Dr. Geiger's influence in her life but hoped that the doctor was well disposed toward him. It seemed strange that she confided more about herself to a stranger than to her own husband; he wondered how the generations of people who lived before the advent of psychiatry would have considered this. Probably, he reasoned, they had fewer expectations for marriage and lived in separate worlds. Not like today, when your wife was supposed to be everything to you. His spirits sagged for a moment.

Elise started when she saw him at the table, her eyes taking in the plates of food he'd carefully assembled. "I wasn't expecting you to be home. It's early for you."

"Aren't you happy to see me?" he asked, getting up to kiss her. Her cheeks felt as smooth as porcelain from the chilly weather.

"Of course I'm happy, I just wasn't expecting you." She took off her coat and tossed it on the sofa, and Peter fought his immediate response to tell her to hang it up.

"Want a glass of wine? You must be tired."

"On the contrary, I'm filled with energy," she said. "But I'll take some wine. What's the occasion?"

"I made some good progress today on my work."

He poured her wine, and she sipped it thoughtfully.

"Enjoy these last few drinks," he told her. "Pretty soon you won't be able to drink anymore."

She looked at him, uncomprehending.

"The pregnancy," he explained. "Aren't you and Celia about to get started with the meds to synchronize your cycles?"

"Oh," she said. "Of course. I guess I'm not thinking that far ahead right now."

"I didn't think it was so far ahead."

"It may not be. I don't want to think about it too much. I could jinx it. Bring the evil eye upon myself."

Peter laughed. "Since when do you believe in the evil eye?"

"You never know. Might be superstitious, might be something to it."

He was puzzled. Over the years they had argued about this idea, Elise always taking the opposite position that Western science represented the apex of progress, Peter asserting that traditional cultures possessed useful indigenous knowledge that Westerners ignored. The Peace Corps had made him a firm believer in this idea.

Elise bit into an olive. "So tell me about your work."

"Well, now I'm thinking about textiles."

"Textiles?" She looked skeptical. "What does that have to do with the Sufi mystics you were working on before? Or the Arab explorers who described the Sufis in the medieval literature?"

"I'm focusing now on the colonial period," Peter explained. "We have French, English, even Spanish sources who wrote about their travels in North Africa. And we know that when they wrote about women, they would write about the royalty, the women of the harem, but even there what they wrote about was a projection of their fantasies of how great it would be to have a lot of women all lounging around, constantly in wait for you."

"That's nothing new," Elise said, sipping her wine. "Edward Said's theory of Orientalism pretty much covered that."

"Right," Peter said. "So they imagined a world where beautiful women spent the day bathing and perfuming themselves for men, and you see how they pictured it in the paintings of Delacroix and Ingres. But what were the average women doing? Has anybody asked this question?"

"I'm sure they have," Elise said. "But go on."

"I found some pretty radical evidence in the colonial literature that these women in Sidi Maarif were up to something very unorthodox. Weaving sumptuous carpets. But also running the community. Inheriting property according to some African tribal customs I haven't figured out yet, and not according to Muslim laws. Respected as leaders. And get this - the men were veiling themselves, just like the Tuareg people do, but the women were not."

"So your idea for a three hundred page dissertation is..."

"I want to show how colonialism destroyed all of this. I was thinking I could go back to Sidi Maarif and study a few other places where the travel literature describes a world that the colonizers systematically destroyed, along with the help of the Moroccan sultan. I want to see if I can recreate that world from the memories of the oldest citizens. I can interview people to find out what they know about life before colonialism, and what they remember."

"Is this not something you can do from the texts you have available here in Princeton?" Elise did not conceal her disappointment. "This sounds like a project you should have proposed two years ago. You'll have to spend a lot of time conducting fieldwork, maybe even living abroad for a while. Do you really want to start over at this point?"

"It wouldn't be starting over," he pleaded. He was getting defensive. "It would be following something I'm passionate about. The last few years have been full of false starts. Sure, it might take another one to two years to gather data and conduct fieldwork. But I'm realizing now that this is what I should have been doing all along."

Elise sighed, draining her glass.

"Okay, but I hope you can find enough evidence to support an entire dissertation on this. And soon, so we can move on with our lives. I didn't realize this PhD would turn into a ten-year affair. Does this mean you won't have a real job until you're over forty? Is this normal?"

"It is, actually," Peter said. "I know plenty of people who took at least ten years to finish."

"That's okay if they started when they were twenty-two. It seems normal to you because you're living in this world of overgrown adolescents who all feel like they're going to produce something brilliant after hiding away for seven to ten years of their life. But how many of them really do?"

"Is that what you're saying I am, an overgrown adolescent?" He was stunned at her nastiness.

"No, but some of your colleagues are."

"Do you think I can't get a good job? You know our department has a pretty decent rate of job placements. Last year alone, we had people doing post-docs at Yale and Harvard."

"And that's exactly what you need. A post-doc. Take ten years to finish and then spend another four hiding out in other campus libraries."

Neither of them had touched the food he'd set out. Elise refilled her glass with wine. The warmth and certainty he'd felt just a few hours before had dissipated.

"I wish you wouldn't undermine my confidence like this," he said.

"I'm not trying to do that," Elise said. "I'm just trying to get you to think about us. Marriage is a compromise. I didn't sign on to this marriage to live in Princeton forever."

"We could travel. If I do fieldwork, we can go to Morocco for a year."

"Since when do you do 'fieldwork'? You're not an anthropologist. I don't want to go to Morocco. I want to have a baby and get back to my own career." Elise was getting annoyed. "Maybe you should show your work to Dr. Kronenberg, to be sure you're on the right track."

"He's not my editor. It's not like this is college. Our professors assume we're pretty well-motivated at this point."

"Maybe they don't want you to finish. They don't want you out there in the academic world competing with them, writing things that contradict what they've written. They encourage this continual infancy."

"I don't think that's the case," he protested. "They want us to produce competent, quality work. For that, it's a long apprenticeship."

"Whatever," Elise said. "In the world I'm coming from, you'd better produce a book every couple of years or so, or else the money stops coming in. But then, at least in the fiction world, people actually read what you write."

Although Peter was usually capable of keeping his anger at the simmering point, this was too much.

"You think my work is worth nothing?" he shouted. "And you're surprised that I've gotten so little done when I have the world's best editor and critic constantly hanging over my shoulder."

"How can I be critical when you never show me anything? I just want you to finish so you can get out of this world. It's not healthy."

"Well, you're certainly not helping things. You're being a real bitch."

"Don't call me that!" Elise screamed. "I cannot believe you would use such a degrading word!"

It was impossible to win with her. He could feel the heat rising up his neck and filling his collar. He hated her right now for doing this to him, for slapping him down when he'd been feeling so positive about everything. Feeling her eyes on him, he walked over to the closet, pulling out his coat and slamming the closet door shut. Leaving the house would be the only way he could show her how angry he was. She knew he was a creature of routine, and that once he came home for the night, he almost never went out again.

"So much for trying to do something nice for you." He gestured at the table, the candles, and the wine.

"I don't recall that you've ever considered it exceptional when I greeted you at the door with food," she replied, her voice low. "You just took it for granted. This sudden interest in the underappreciated women of North Africa certainly has no basis in any liberated thinking on your part."

Peter did not respond. He was already out in the hallway, slamming that door, too, for emphasis. Once outside he realized he'd forgotten his wallet, but he did not want to spoil the effect of his exit by returning to retrieve it. It didn't matter; he could still walk to the library, and the guard on duty would recognize him and let him in. But forgetting the wallet did diminish the effectiveness of his dramatic departure. Before she went to bed Elise would find the wallet sitting on the nightstand, and she would know he had to come back. The wallet would be yet further evidence of how she must see him: predictable, incapable of spontaneity, prone to delusions of academic significance. What mattered suddenly was proving her wrong, though he was not yet sure how he might do this.

CHAPTER NINE

Celia sat down at the rectangular conference table, placing her coffee in front of her and pulling a sheaf of papers from her messenger bag. The coffee was a habit Celia had adopted from observing Nicole Sumner, who sipped double skim lattés as she offered thoughtful observations about the work of her peers. Decent coffee was a necessary accoutrement to sophistication, and not the Folger's that Celia's father drank, but specialty roasts from Yemen and Costa Rica, with added preferences that offered glimpses into the coffee drinker's personality: skim or soy, half-caf, a shot of amaretto.

She was fifteen minutes early and wanted to compose herself before the other students arrived. The stack of papers contained extra copies of her short story, ready for consideration in workshop that day, and several poems by Nicole. All twelve students had to take part in at least two workshops during the semester, and it was Celia's second turn. In her first workshop she had shared a forgettable story about running for the track team in high school. Her peers' comments were polite but neutral, and most of them seemed to find the piece too innocuous to merit any serious criticism.

"I want to see a little more life in the subject matter," said her writing teacher Carla, the first professor Celia had known who asked the students to call her by her first name. "More passion. You can write well, but you still haven't discovered your voice, and you're holding back. Don't censor yourself. Show us why this subject is so crucial, so necessary." Holding back! How did everyone seem to get this impression from her? Celia knew she was capable of doing better work but had been afraid, scared of revealing traces of her true feelings. What if she wrote about something that really mattered and they criticized it mercilessly?

Shutting out the voices of her imagined critics, as Carla Lopez-Ibarrez had told them to do, she had worked non-stop on her most recent story. What rose to the surface was the story of a man whose wife had just left him, a character not unlike Michael Lenhart, in a town that bore more than a passing resemblance to Deer Bluff. Celia struggled with describing the man's emotions, then decided not to describe them at all. Her character became someone who repressed everything, a man whose primary hobby had been attempting to build a dream house for his never-satisfied wife in the hopes that it would keep her from leaving him. In the final scene of the story Celia placed the man in a living room with cathedral ceilings, toying with a book of matches.

As the other students filed into the classroom, she realized how nervous she was. Her work might suffer from comparisons to that of the class star, whose series of three poems were stunning as always. Celia's mild obsession with Nicole had dwindled somewhat, distracted as she was with Elise and Peter, but when she was in the classroom with her she could feel it returning, an almost overwhelming ache of longing to be someone else. She looked down at a random section from one of Nicole's poems: "Tiny stars/their distance mirroring/ the space between us." Nicole had already published several of her poems in the *Nassau Review,* Princeton's student literary magazine. A bit of Internet sleuthing revealed a Boston upbringing, boarding school at Exeter, and a father who was vice chairman of one of the largest banks in the Northeast. Nicole managed to pull off a classic wardrobe that on someone less attractive might have come off as too old or frumpy for a college student. On her the sweater sets and pencil skirts just seemed to enhance her ethereal features. Celia imagined her composing her poems in a dorm room decorated with Ralph Lauren bedding and William Morris wallpaper. Yet there was an edge to her, visible in her poetry if not in her appearance, a hint that she had experienced more than her share of what Fitzgerald called "dark nights of the soul."

Celia had glanced at the comments Carla Lopez-Ibarrez wrote on Nicole's papers as she passed them back to her, Carla's loping, lowercase handwriting praising her work with comments like, "elegant, spare. as always, beautifully crafted." Carla's comments on Celia's own work had echoed what she'd said in class: "don't hold back! seek out the uncomfortable truths in what you know." What did she know? What were the uncomfortable truths? That was harder to figure out. She looked up as Nicole slid into the seat across from her, her eyes meeting Celia's, holding her gaze with interest. Celia blushed and looked down again at Nicole's poem: "your fingertips/leaving blue tattoos on my body/marks that I will still be excavating/years into our sullen future." Her blush deepened as she pictured Nicole in the intimacy the poem described, wondering what it would be like to be a man who loved her. She imagined writing such a poem, then tried to imagine a man whose fingertips would leave their marks on her own body. Unbidden, Peter's face flashed in front of her, and she remembered one moment over that breakfast at the pancake restaurant when he'd reached out impulsively and touched her arm as he spoke, the gesture stopping her in her tracks. Since their meeting she found herself replaying the conversation, thinking of particularly elegant ways Peter had expressed himself, the hand on her arm, gentle, steadying. She was having crushes on all sorts of inappropriate objects these days, those crushes small fires that threatened to burn out of control if she didn't find some way to contain them.

Celia was pleased with the way the dynamics had shifted with Elise; she was much more in control of the situation than she'd thought. But Peter she had not yet figured out. Despite his insistence that he had no imagination, he possessed a writer's sensibility for detail, and his evocative descriptions of the mythical Moroccan coastal town made her want to join the Peace Corps, or at the very least, to buy a one-way ticket for Morocco and see what happened when she got there. While Elise had portrayed her husband as regimented and obsessed with routine, to Celia Peter seemed both idealistic and dreamy, the type of person who would need someone to listen patiently to whatever bit of inspiration struck his fancy. She doubted that Elise, who was all hard edges and practicality, indulged him in such whims.

The steady hum of her classmates' voices snapped her out of her reverie. Her heart began to pound as Carla Lopez-Ibarrez shuffled casually through her papers. The professor's crimson fingernails matched the giant beaded necklace she wore over a beige linen tunic and pants that looked intentionally wrinkled. Carla's novels, which Celia had read the summer before, were humorous portrayals of life in the Cuban-American community, set in New York, Miami, or the mythical Havana of the pre-Castro era (which Carla herself could not possibly have remembered, since she was born in Miami).

"Let's start with... Celia. Celia Cruz, the Queen of Salsa." Carla always related their names to popular music, a mnemonic device to help her remember who her students were, which was, this late in the term, growing a little annoying. At least she was the Queen of Salsa, someone whose music was both exotic and respectable. Another student named Margaret had become Maggie May, after the Rod Stewart song, and even worse was Bruce, whom Carla addressed as "Bruce... the Boss," after Bruce Springsteen. And then there was poor Brittany Philips, who never spoke up, probably since she was the unfortunate namesake of Brittany Spears. When Carla did not call on her by humming a few bars from "Hit me baby, one more time," her name almost always triggered diatribes about the sorry decline of popular music.

In a low, careful voice, Celia read the last few pages of her story out loud. For two minutes afterward, there was to be no talking. This was how Carla conducted workshops, allowing the two-minute pause for the final words to sink in, for the students to prepare their comments. Comments were always supposed to be in pencil, and never in red ink, which introduced a severity Carla did not approve of. The writer herself was also not allowed to speak, or to defend her work, until everyone else had finished talking. Celia tried not to read the expressions on her classmates' faces, shutting out the sound of the soft scrawl of pencils on paper.

"Begin," said Carla, who would not go first, so as not to prejudice the other students with her opinion.

"I liked your main character," said one of the male students. "I liked it that he didn't talk a lot about his feelings. You did that well, even though you're a girl." A few of the students giggled. Carla frowned at the word 'girl,' but said nothing.

"I'm not sure about the tone," said a student named Manuel. "Like, at first I thought, what's wrong with this guy? His wife just left him, but where's the emotion? But then I realized he was repressing it. I guess it works."

"It was a lot better than your first story," another student said. "It's almost like this one was written by a different person."

"I don't know about the ending," someone said. "Is he going to burn the house down? Is that maybe too melodramatic?"

"It's ambiguous," Bruce 'the Boss' piped up. "There are other allusions in the story to smoking, and how he used to be a smoker but he quit. He's thinking about smoking too, so he's either taking up a bad habit or about to burn the house down."

"Your title is funny," the first student said. "Home Improvement."

"Did you notice other elements of humor in this?" Carla asked them. "Is the humor consistent? Maggie, we haven't heard from you." She broke into song. "'Wake up, Maggie, I think I've got something to say to you!'"

"I like it," answered Margaret. "The setting is good. Sometimes the humor makes it seem ridiculous, but also tragic. Faulknerian."

Nicole cleared her throat, the other students' heads swiveling around to hear what she would say. She was the only one Carla did not address with a mnemonic.

"I think the sense of place in this story is incredible," she said. "I've only been to Atlanta, so I don't know what the South is really like, but I can picture it like this—it's not romanticized. And I love this: 'Outsiders believed in the South's gothic beauty, but they were wrong—it was a ruin. Those who live in ruins cannot afford to be nostalgic.' I wish I'd written that line." Heat traveled throughout Celia's body at this compliment.

"I also suspect," Nicole continued, "that this suburban wasteland she describes is engulfing the entire country. The protagonist spends his weekends wandering the aisles of giant home improvement stores. They promise these elusive fantasy homes that will make life perfect, and all the while he forgets that the relationship with his wife should be central to this vision of home."

The other students nodded and looked at her, afraid for a moment to speak up, since following Nicole's comments with something equally as intelligent was a challenge few of them wanted to take. Celia tried to commit her words to memory.

"Overall, I'm pleased with this," Carla Lopez-Ibarrez finally said. "Your story is quite strong. Worlds away from your last piece. It has some fine moments." She passed her copy of the story down the table to Celia, who looked down discreetly to see what she'd written.

"<u>very</u> nice work. keep writing," the paper said. "submit to nassau lit review." Not as effusive as her comments for Nicole, but it was a start, and Celia felt immensely proud. The rest of the class period seemed to float by, Celia relishing Nicole's stunning poems and the awed silence they inspired in the other students. Carla had probably selected her to go first because Nicole was an act that couldn't be followed. It didn't matter; she'd written something decent, and she knew it.

Celia took her time gathering her belongings, wanting to savor this class for just a few moments longer. When she stepped out of the small brick building that housed the writing center, she saw Nicole standing on the sidewalk, smoking a cigarette. The cigarette seemed incongruous with her polished exterior.

"Celia," Nicole said, as if she were seeing her for the first time. "Good job today."

"Thanks. Your poems were great too, but then they always are." She blushed, embarrassed at how easily she'd offered the fawning compliment.

"I've had a lot of writing classes," Nicole said dismissively. "What about you, though? I haven't seen you in any of my classes before."

"This is just my second writing class. I'm an English major, but I'm planning to apply for the certificate in creative writing." The words tumbled out of her mouth with certainty, even though she had not fully decided until now that this would be her plan of study.

Nicole looked at her watch, which was silver and studded with small diamonds. Celia noticed she bit her nails. "I've got a train to catch in a little while. Want to have a drink with me? I'm all caffeined-up. I need to bring it down a few notches."

"Sure," she said casually. "But I'm not twenty-one."

"You don't have to be twenty-one to drink, silly," Nicole laughed. "Just not legally."

"I know that, I just don't have an ID." Celia felt like an idiot.

"I live off campus," Nicole explained. "We can have a drink at my place. Then I'll drop you off wherever you live on my way to the train station. Or maybe I'm going to walk to the Dinky. I haven't decided yet."

They walked to the house that Nicole shared with two other students, in a run-down two-story Victorian on the same street with a number of well-kept professors' houses.

"My roommates are grad students," she said. "You know, the neighbors don't like students to live on this street because they're afraid we'll throw loud parties. But we still do it anyway."

She followed Nicole up the wooden stairs to the second floor. Nicole turned her key in the lock, opening the door to reveal an apartment that was quite unlike anything Celia would have pictured her classmate living in. The walls and ceilings were stark white, the wood floors beaten up and badly in need of refinishing. On the hallway walls hung small, black-and-white photographs: a chair with three legs, the pointed top of a skyscraper, one side of a woman's face. They passed a living room empty of furnishings except for about twenty brightly colored cushions, two beanbag chairs and some low cubes for tables. A mobile of World War II-era model planes hung from the ceiling, and one wall was covered with a giant painting of an orange man with a silver bucket for a head. The combined effect of the objects in the room was intriguing, and she wondered about Nicole's roommates.

"Décor compliments of my roommates," Nicole said. "Architecture students. We hang out a fair amount."

At the end of the hallway, Nicole opened a door. Her own room was large, with none of the flowered décor Celia had imagined for her. The walls were spare, with only a small, framed woodcut hanging above an unfinished chest of drawers. The woodcut depicted an angel slumped in a chair, her head in her hands, a banner with the misspelled word "melencolia" in the distance next to a sunshine.

"Don't you just love Durer?" Nicole said, catching her looking at it.

"Oh, yeah!" Celia affirmed, trying to match Nicole's enthusiasm. "I love his stuff." She hoped Durer was a he. The print looked old, penitential; it had to have been done by a man. A double bed with a white down comforter was pushed to one corner, and a window overlooked the gravel parking lot in the back, where Nicole's green Vespa was parked. Celia lingered at the window, admiring the scooter, its color the same as the antique milkshake machines at Millie's Diner in Deer Bluff.

"Do you ride it in the winter?" she asked.

"The scooter? Nah. I keep it in a garage when it gets cold." At the foot of Nicole's bed sat an antique trunk, and a tall bookshelf held hundreds of thin volumes of poetry books. In the other corner of the room was an L-shaped red corduroy sofa. She motioned for Celia to sit down.

"What do you take?" Nicole asked, gesturing at a small refrigerator, on top of which sat several liquor bottles. "I've got vodka, tequila, beer, and wine."

"A Bloody Mary?" she asked. Nicole looked at her as if this were an odd request.

"No tomato juice. I can make you a screwdriver, though."

"That sounds good." Suddenly Celia was eager to drink, if drinking might forge further closeness between her and this stranger who had seemed unaware of her existence until today. From her days working at Sparky's, she tried to recall what a screwdriver was and was relieved to see it consisted only of orange juice and vodka.

"I'm going to bartend full-time next summer," Nicole said, stirring their drinks. "One of my friends has a place at the Vineyard. Just to have something to do. Work all night, sleep and go to the beach during the day, write."

"Restaurant work is tough. I worked at a place down in the Florida Keys one summer." Celia tried to think of some literary detail she could offer about Sparky's. "Serving fried fish and beer to drunk guys who all thought they could be Hemingway if they just spent their days getting sloshed in his old haunts." Nicole seemed amused, so she continued. "I had to learn to tell how many beers the regulars could drink before I'd need to stand at arms length, if you know what I mean."

"I don't mind that," Nicole said. "I can handle male attention." She fished around in her purse for her box of Parliaments. "Want a smoke?"

"No thanks."

"So, Celia," Nicole said, lighting her cigarette. "Where'd you learn to write like that?"

"You thought my story was good?"

"Better than good." She got up and walked across the room, returning with a glass ashtray. "How come you haven't submitted to Nassau Lit before?"

"I don't know. Wasn't ready to put myself out there, I guess."

"Princeton goes by quickly. Not a lot of time to make your mark." Nicole shook the ice in her drink and took a drag of her cigarette. "So what's your scene? How come I haven't met you before now?"

"I don't go out much," Celia said. "I don't really like that scene."

"Which scene? There are more than one. But I'm soooo over the Street. I'm more of a city girl these days." The Street was the tree-lined street of Tudor mansions housing Princeton's fabled eating clubs, whose keg-stand weekend antics Celia had avoided.

"You have friends there?" Celia asked.

"I'm seeing someone there. A photographer. That's where I'm off to after we finish our drinks." She surveyed her collection of liquor bottles on top of the small refrigerator, picking up an almost-empty tequila bottle. "Why don't we do a tequila shot? I need a little energy."

"Tequila shots on a Thursday afternoon?"

"The weekend's already started." Nicole put down her drink. "No classes for me tomorrow." She produced two shot glasses bearing a fraternity's Greek lettering. "I have salt but no limes. So drink it straight and chase it with the screwdriver." She lifted the glass to her lips and downed it in one swallow. Celia shuddered at the tequila's slimy taste, quickly reaching for her screwdriver to wash it away.

Nicole stubbed out her cigarette and jumped up again. Like Elise, Nicole was tightly wound, the kind of person who always needed stimulation. Or perhaps it was just the elation of the workshop. Throwing open a closet, she grabbed a pair of leather boots, which she tossed on the floor next to the bed. Unselfconsciously, she unbuttoned her tailored pants and let them fall in a silky puddle on the floor, walking over to the dresser in her underpants and sweater. As she bent over to open a drawer, Celia glimpsed the lace-trimmed strip of a pink thong. The guys in their creative writing class would kill to be where she was right now. Nicole kept talking, as if this were perfectly normal for her.

"My boyfriend's crowd is more Euro," Nicole announced, pulling on a pair of artfully ripped jeans that Celia knew must have cost her hundreds of dollars. Still wearing the cashmere sweater, she flipped her head over and began brushing out her hair. Her blonde hair shimmered with static. "I'm trying on different personas. Conservative, old Princeton here, something a little more continental there. I like to shake things up. Keep my lives pretty separate. It's all good for the poetry."

"How did you meet your boyfriend?"

"José?" she said, as if she had more than one. "He's a fashion photographer. A friend of mine from back home who goes to NYU does some modeling. That's how we hooked up."

"You're boyfriend's Spanish?"

"Colombian."

"I thought men in the fashion world were all gay." She wanted to kick herself as soon as the words came out.

Nicole laughed, as if Celia were hopelessly unworldly.

"Some of the models are. A lot of people in the fashion industry are just bi."

"Bisexual?"

"No, bipedal." She laughed again. "You're funny."

Outside of class, Nicole seemed not very serious, almost flaky. Celia was dismayed that their conversation had touched only on trivial subjects. She wanted to tell her this somehow.

"This wasn't how I expected our first conversation would be," she said, watching as Nicole applied mascara to her fine blonde lashes in a small mirror.

"What do you mean?" Nicole turned to her, blinking.

"I don't know, I guess I was thinking we'd talk more about writing or the class or something."

"Oh, I get it. You had this image from some movie set in a women's college. Two girls on a flowered comforter in a dorm room, bonding over our shared love for Sylvia Plath?"

"Talking about our Daddy complexes, for sure." She tried to be offhand, to turn it into a joke.

Nicole laughed.

"Can I ask you something?" Celia said.

"Sure. Shoot."

"How are you going to do it? This whole writing thing? Once you leave college, I mean."

"I'll get an MFA after I graduate, maybe Columbia or Iowa. Build my contacts. Then I'll just see where to go from there. I can always work in editing. There are a lot of possibilities."

Nicole returned to the sofa and sat down. The dark eyeliner and mascara hardened her doll's features, making her look almost like a little girl playing dress-up.

"You make it sound easy," Celia said. "I always imagined the life of a writer as being difficult and filled with failures."

"Life is going to be difficult no matter what," Nicole said. "You choose your difficulties." She picked up the tequila bottle again, noting how little was left. "Want some more? I'm just going to finish this off.

I can't stand the clutter of almost-empty bottles." She poured the tequila on top of the melting ice in her glass.

"How can you choose your difficulties?" Celia asked. "Seems to me that they just get handed to you."

"I guess some of them are. But with some things you have a choice. Like, you choose if you want to get married and have kids, or take a job where you make a lot of money, or try something riskier. Some people choose the path of least resistance. I wanna make things interesting. It's a choice. Difficult can be interesting."

"You seem like you can afford to take risks."

"In what way?" Celia wanted to say that it was all about money, that only people who took money for granted could create risks for themselves. Someone would always be there to bail them out after failed experiments. But talking about money was gauche, so she hedged.

"You don't seem to care what people think about you."

"A thick skin helps." Nicole had finished her drink and was pouring herself another. "Or at least you have to learn to pretend not to care." She tilted the vodka bottle over Celia's nearly empty glass, filling it almost half full.

"My dad's an alcoholic," Celia found herself confessing.

"That doesn't make you an alcoholic." Nicole shrugged. "I love your accent, by the way."

"I don't know what to say when people tell me that," Celia said. "I think my accent's kind of backward. I'm trying to get rid of it."

"When you said your dad was an alcoholic, I just thought about the whole southern writer thing. Tennessee Williams, Faulkner. Southern writers and alcoholism seem to go hand in hand."

"I try not to make risky choices," Celia said.

"Don't." Nicole pulled another Parliament from her packet of cigarettes. "My personal philosophy is to always make choices that are a little bit scary. You can't spend all your time worrying about your risk factors. It won't make you a better writer if you hide in your room."

"Staying home all day didn't stop Jane Austen from writing wonderful books."

"She's the exception. It wasn't until women were able to get out of the house and have the same adventures as men that they started to be taken seriously as writers."

"I'd like to have adventures. I just don't find the typical college sex-and-drugs experimentation to be particularly intriguing."

"You're right," Nicole agreed. "People do that because it's safe. It feels daring but you're still getting high in a room with your buddies, or sleeping with the guy you met in your political economy class.

People like to pretend they're having an adventure, but without real risks. A real adventure would be going to Trenton to try to buy some crack." Seeing Celia's shocked expression, she burst into laughter. "I'm kidding. I'm not saying you should do something stupid."

"I'm going to donate my eggs," Celia blurted out. There. She'd finally told someone. "Although I'm not really donating them. I'm getting paid a lot of money to do it."

"That's cool," Nicole said, unfazed. "My freshman roommate did that a couple times. Racked up some ridiculous change and used it to buy a closet full of clothes I would die for. I can give you her number if you want to join the support group."

"Support group?"

"You know, in case you get all worked up afterward about all the little Celias you're spreading around out there."

What did it take to impress Nicole, to offer up something that would surprise her? Celia could think of nothing else to say. Her eye fell on the single pearl set in platinum that Nicole wore on her hand.

"That's a beautiful ring," she said.

"You like it?" Nicole said, turning her hand over. "It belonged to my aunt, my dad's older sister. She was the black sheep of the family, made everyone angry by writing a memoir that exposed a lot of old family secrets. But she was also the family writer. Everyone says I take after her. Why don't you wear it?" She took the ring off her hand and slipped it on Celia's. The gesture was almost childlike.

"I can't take this," she protested.

"I don't mean permanently, just for a few days. I'll get it back from you the next time you're over here. We're having a party next Thursday."

"Party? Who's hosting it?"

"My roommates and I. I'm inviting you. We'll go to the Eric Babu reading and then load up on tequila shots. I'll introduce you to some interesting people. You'd get along well with my roommate Yves. I think you two would really hit it off." She winked. "You're exactly Yves' type. A willowy brunette. Innocent but corruptible." The adjectives came at her quickly, both insulting and flattering. But Eve? Nicole had it all wrong.

"I'm not gay," she protested.

Nicole looked confused, then laughed. "I didn't say anything about being gay. It's Yves with a Y. He's a man, and he's French. Not Eve, as in Adam and Eve." A man. The idea of a man, let alone a French one, sounded threatening.

"I thought you weren't allowed to have parties in this house."

"Allowed? This isn't a dorm. Or some noisy frat party. Just a bunch of grad students."

"So what do they do, sip absinthe and talk about Foucault?"

Nicole laughed again, as if she found Celia endlessly entertaining.

"And then when you come to the party, I'll give you a writing assignment. Your assignment is to do something that scares you a little bit, something worthy of writing about. If you write something, I'll critique it." Celia wondered what her options were. Hooking up with Yves? Doing lines of coke in the bathroom?

Nicole had finished her drink and was putting on her coat to leave. She picked up a round, red leather suitcase, which looked like something a flight attendant from the 1960s might carry, back when they used to be called stewardesses.

"This was my mother's suitcase," Nicole said, reading her mind. "Cute, isn't it? She got it when she was a student at Wellesley. Took it with her when she studied art in Italy after college, before she married my father. She used to be an artist. Of course she gave all that up for my dad, which was a huge mistake, but they didn't realize it back then. They never do."

Wellesley. Italy. Artist. The words leapt around Celia's mind, signifiers of a world whose contours she was beginning to grasp, certainly far removed from her own: *Deer Bluff. Textile mill. Millie's Diner.* She had to learn to speak the same language, to have her own powerful words to toss around that would, little by little, gain her entry. She took one last look around the room, taking in the objects Nicole surrounded herself with. Objects carried the essence of people, she thought, looking down at the ring on her hand..

"What was your aunt's name?" she asked. "The one who wrote the memoir."

"Mary Sumner Strauss," Nicole said. "She shocked everyone by not marrying a WASP. Those were different times." She opened the door to her room, and Celia followed her out into the hallway.

* * *

These were unpredictable times, Elise was thinking as she waited for Celia to arrive at the Small World Café. Small World, with its blonde wood floors and cheerful art, would be a better venue than the Annex, where perhaps the basement setting and the dark décor made for bad *feng shui*. Their last meeting had thrown her off balance, but she'd done what Celia had asked of her, putting in a phone call to a few people she knew at Smyth & Copperfield to inquire about summer internships. An old friend was starting a literary agency and agreed to take Celia on, just as an office assistant. Meanwhile, Elise had been getting the contracts for the ova donation prepared. The contract offered an advance of two thousand dollars, specifying the remainder would be paid once the ova had been extracted. They would wait to begin the synching of their monthly schedules until January, after the long winter break. Then if all went well, Celia would start her shots and the donation could take place in early February.

Being on a schedule made Elise feel uncharacteristically hopeful. The uncertainties produced by the previous week's fight with Peter about his harebrained new dissertation schemes and her confusing, exhilarating lunch with Eric Babu had momentarily dissolved when the doctor told her that all looked well for the synching of their menstrual schedules. When she called Celia to tell her the news, Celia sounded relieved and almost happy to hear from her, and they planned to meet in the early afternoon to go over the contract, before Elise would leave for the weekend to visit Caitlin in Connecticut. After several days of barely speaking to Peter and a few nightly phone calls to her best friend (in which she learned that Caitlin too was having problems with her husband and was feeling a little lonelier than usual), she'd decided to get out of Princeton for a few days.

Peter hardly responded when she told him, furthering her fears that with this last fight, she'd crossed some invisible line that she hadn't been aware of. But she still could not believe that her words merited him calling her a bitch. It was unprecedented. He knew how she felt about that word. After the fight he disappeared for a few hours, but she knew he would be back when she saw he'd forgotten his wallet. Although she had little appetite, she finished the bottle of wine herself and put away the appetizers he'd carefully laid out. Perhaps some of her remarks had been a little unfair. Her initial reaction when he told her of the new direction his work was taking had been distress at the thought of being in Princeton two years longer, and she'd lashed out. Imagining he wanted to go to North Africa to get away from her, she had attacked him out of defensiveness, but she saw now that this was a mistake. She should have been more supportive.

Peter was the sole subject of her conversation with Dr. Geiger the next week, and Dr. Geiger seemed to agree that she had gone too far. Her dissatisfaction with her life and regrets about her career were replaced with the fear of losing Peter. As Dr. Geiger had asked, she'd been thinking about their relationship and trying to remember why she married Peter in the first place. It was not difficult, especially when she began to imagine life without him. His positive qualities, which normally she gave little thought to, were easier to recall.

"So why," Dr. Geiger had asked, "was Peter the one you wanted to marry? What did he have that no other man had?"

"He was a good listener. And he was thoughtful. He was crazy about me, and I didn't have to worry about what I had to do to keep him guessing."

"And what interested you in his own qualities?"

"What do you mean?"

"Think about what you just said. You said he listened to you. He was thoughtful. He was crazy about you. Was he just a mirror who showed back a version of yourself you wanted to see? What did you find in Peter that you liked?"

Elise thought about it. Beyond the obvious (they had good conversations, they liked the same books), there was something comforting and safe about Peter. Where other men played games, and where Elise had to control her feelings for them lest they sense she liked them too much, Peter offered certainty. When they met, she was still caught up in her on-again, off-again affair with Babu, but she became aware of Peter's presence in the landscape of her life. He was the affable, handsome colleague who often stopped by her office with small gifts: small paper cups of Cuban coffee from the deli down the street, or a book he was reading that he thought she'd like. He was always there, like a familiar household object one goes for months without noticing until one day that object suddenly becomes indispensable.

When he finally asked her out, she could sense the heady effect she had on him. His own positive qualities kept his interest from seeming overbearing. He was good-looking, kind, and highly intelligent, if a bit confused about his direction in life. He had issues with his father, but who didn't? She knew he came from money, and while she did not believe this entered into her decision to marry him, it added to the solid, safe impression he gave. His ex-girlfriends were all attractive, confirming for Elise that if he'd chosen her, she herself must be good looking as well. In bed he was a skilled and attentive lover, and if she never felt any overwhelming passion for him, both experience and literature had taught her that an ardor of Titanic dimensions was not to be trusted.

Yet somehow she'd taken all this for granted, failing to see the danger she stood of losing him. Perhaps on a subconscious level her desire to have children was a product of this awareness, as if there was some age-old, evolutionary wiring that convinced women that babies were a good way to hold onto a man in danger of slipping away. Lately she knew she was pushing him away, but somehow she was powerless to stop herself from telling him the many small ways that he infuriated her. Dr. Geiger said she had strong levels of what Freud called the "death instinct," which manifested itself not in a desire to die but in the urge to dismantle everything that was good in her life.

"Remember: think 'productive' and not 'destructive,'" Dr. Geiger had urged. *Productive* only needed the 're-' before it, the new being whose existence would signal rebirth, taking their relationship into a new season. For a while, at least, Elise vowed to focus exclusively on their relationship, and on the baby.

When Celia arrived at Small World Café, she was out of breath and still in her running clothes. She went back to the counter to order her coffee, Elise noticing how healthy she looked, and how innocent.

"Do you know a writer named Mary Sumner Strauss?" Celia said as she returned to the table with some elaborate, frothy coffee drink.

"Of course. She wrote *The Feminist's Guide to Marrying Well*," Elise said. "It's a staple of women's studies programs. Very controversial, as you can probably guess from the title."

"A friend of mine is her niece," Celia announced proudly.

Elise noticed a ring on Celia's right hand. Celia never wore jewelry, and the ring stood out.

"That's pretty," Elise said. "Very classic."

"Thanks, it's not mine," she answered. "Same friend loaned it to me." She lowered her eyes.

"How are your classes going?"

"Pretty good. Excellent, actually," Celia said. "I had one of my stories workshopped in my creative writing class this week and everyone loved it. I'm over the moon about it."

"That's great news. I'd love to read it if you want to email it to me."

"Would you?" she said. "Carla liked what I wrote, for once."

"Of course. Carla Lopez-Ibarrez. I know her work. Have you read any of her books?"

"Yeah, they're good, but not exactly a style I'd aspire to."

"And what style is that?" Elise challenged her.

"Colorful immigration novels. She makes it sound like being a Cuban in New York is like being on Sesame Street. My own style is a bit darker." What did this girl know about dark, Elise wondered?

"Well, if you still want to work in the city next summer, I made a few phone calls. I set something up for you."

Celia reached over the table and hugged Elise impulsively.

"It's not going to be the most exciting work," Elise said. "A friend of mine just started her own agency. You'll basically be an office assistant. But we all start out this way. Getting coffee and helping to sort through the slush pile. But it will allow you to make some contacts and get a taste of what goes on in publishing." She reached into her bag and pulled out a sheet of paper, where she'd written down her friend's contact information.

"Is it a literal slush pile?" Celia wanted to know. "Like, just stacks of manuscripts, waiting to be read?"

"It's getting less and less literal. Probably a lot of your work will be going through email queries."

"Wow, this is really cool," Celia said. "Thank you. Maybe you can give me advice about how to find a place to live as well."

"Look on the Internet. Craig's List is a good place to start," Elise said. "You'll definitely find students looking to sublet for the summer. Check in the area around NYU. But you don't have to start thinking about it right now." She took out the contract the lawyer had prepared.

"And here's a copy of the contract. The lawyer who prepared it specializes in reproductive law. You can read it over, see what you think, and have it notarized when you sign it."

Celia flipped through the pages of the contract, her eyes falling on the monetary amount.

"Two thousand now? When does that happen?" she asked.

"Right now." Elise relished the way Celia's face lit up when she handed her the check. Being the bearer of money was a powerful feeling.

"This will really help. It's been a little tough since I quite my work-study job," she confessed. "The only times I've been out to eat have been with you. And forget about new clothes."

"Be careful with this, then. The rest won't come until after we do the transfer. If all goes well that could happen around February." She filled Celia in on her hormone treatments, explaining that she'd been tested for different combinations of hormones and that doctors had found the ones most likely to provide a suitable environment for the baby. She gave Celia the prescription the doctor had written out for the birth control pills that would synchronize their schedules. "Save your receipts from the pharmacy and I'll reimburse you."

"Thank you." Celia folded the papers, placing the check underneath a paperclip to secure it. Elise wanted to say more, to keep her in the café a little longer. She felt a sudden wave of melancholy wash over her. Even with all the money this was costing, the chances that it would work were still below forty percent.

"You seem sad," Celia said. "Is something wrong?"

"No." Elise weighed whether or not to confide in Celia. Before she had been confessional, but talking about her life was always more of a performance, not a reflection of her true emotional state. What would be the advantages of telling Celia how she felt? She would see Caitlin soon enough; she could tell her old friend everything. "Nothing's wrong, really. Things have been kind of crazy with work."

"I thought you were taking some time off," Celia said.

Elise forgot that Celia knew this. "Well, yes," she hedged. "That's part of the problem. Some of my most important clients have work for me and I'm not quite sure whether I'll get to take it, now that I'm no longer working."

Celia leaned forward, and Elise could see she had her attention again.

"Like, which writers? Who in particular?"

"Well, Eric Babu has told me he's nearly finished with something that promises to be stunning. Underground Islamic fundamentalism among Africans living in the outer boroughs. Over lunch last week, Eric just kept telling me how important it was that I take this project on. What could I do? I couldn't say no. He's under contract with Smyth & Copperfield, so he can't pull out if I don't work on it, but still, I'd like very much to honor his wishes. And he's not the only one." Elise felt satisfied that she had gained control of her performance again.

"That's amazing. You say it so casually—you had lunch with Eric Babu. Does Peter mind?"

"What do you mean, does he mind? Why should he care?"

"Because you used to be involved with him." Celia said this matter-of-factly, as if she'd known all along. Had Elise told her? She couldn't remember. She didn't think she had.

"Umm, I guess you could say we had a strong editor-client relationship."

"I thought when you told me he based a character on you, that it implied you'd been involved," Celia said. "In that book you gave me. *The Dam-builder's Apprentice.* The woman from Houston who works for Big Oil, Evangeline, her personality is so much like yours I knew he must have modeled her after you."

"You thought I was Evangeline? I think the resemblance is only physical. It ends there."

"Hmm, then he's got a hell of an imagination. Those love scenes were really intense. More like competitions for who could gain the upper hand in the relationship. I figured real life must have bled into what he was writing."

Elise tried to control the blush spreading over her face. "Beginning writers tend to be more autobiographical. But not seasoned writers like Babu."

"Carla told us that writers can never escape the self, and that she always draws on the self for material, no matter how many books she writes."

"You have to be careful not to get too obsessed with the self," Elise said. "Some writers do more navel-gazing than others. It gets old after awhile. Not Eric Babu. He's always reinventing himself as a writer."

"Some people think he keeps writing the same book over and over again, just with different characters."

"How many have you read?" Elise became defensive. "You can't possibly make a statement like that without years of acquaintance with his work."

"I've read three of his novels, and a couple of the short stories," Celia said confidently. "I'm working on a term paper about him for my postcolonial lit class, though, and a lot of the critics say he repeats himself."

"In what way?"

"Same archetypal characters, same old game of Blame the Colonizer for the mess Africa finds itself in. He's always got a noble protagonist who can't be corrupted, who faces the temptations of the West and of his own corrupt leaders but always makes the honorable and painful choice, even if it means death. They say he'll never win a Nobel, because he's just going over the same territory as Wole Soyinka and Chinua Achebe. Also, some of them think he's out of touch. Chris Abani does a better job describing the current Nigerian landscape. And Adichie writes with more heart."

"And you believe the critics? You're just going to copy their arguments out in your paper without thinking for yourself?" Elise tried to modulate her tone but her words came out harshly.

Celia drew back. "Actually, no. I was planning to argue that the critics are criticizing each other. They're really attacking postcolonial studies because they always look for the same themes in all these books. Sometimes I think the battles among critics are more about the critics than the works themselves. I don't really care what the critics think. I was just telling you what they've said about him."

"I'm sorry," Elise said. "I don't mean to sound defensive. Sometimes when I hear my writers criticized, I feel like I was the one who got attacked."

"Apology accepted," she said warily.

"It's very complicated. I was extremely close to Eric. So I'm sorry if I came across as snappish. It's not your fault. I just don't like to hear criticism of Eric's work."

"I'm only interested in whether his work is autobiographical because it's a question I keep asking myself," Celia said. "If writers are always writing about themselves, then what kind of a life should I choose for myself to make it more interesting? Is the imagination limited? Do I need to have lots of experiences before I can really be a writer?"

"That's a myth," Elise said. "Of course you need to grow as a writer through your experiences, but not everything has to be about you. Wasn't it Annie Proulx who said something like writing what you know produces really boring novels? And that you should write what you're interested in. Observation is just as important as throwing yourself into something. You read a lot, and that's good. You'll get ideas through that."

"Yeah, but people keep telling me that I'm too hesitant, and that I'll never be a good writer unless I'm being risky, or making dangerous choices. Embracing the world."

"I don't know what that means, 'embracing the world.' I can tell you from my own experience that I always threw myself into everything, and it often got me into trouble. But I'm not a writer. Be careful, though. There's a difference between experience and destructiveness."

Celia smiled. "I'll think about that."

"It's taken me fifteen years of therapy to realize that lesson. If you can get it now, you'll save yourself a lot of problems later on."

Elise looked at her watch and realized it was time to catch the train. Impulsively she hugged Celia goodbye, feeling like she was losing a little sister. Surprised, Celia returned the embrace, then quickly pulled away, not meeting Elise's eyes as she pretended to be busy gathering her things. As a college student Elise had also wanted to be a person to whom many things had happened; she imagined this would make her world-weary and wise. And for what? Had she imagined wanting someone like Celia to look up to her, envying the mark of sophistication she wore? Yet the experiences never brought the hoped-for wisdom. Therapy came somewhat closer, but with each session she still only took the smallest steps toward self-understanding. In therapy, small problems were solved, yet new ones presented themselves.

Lately, Eric Babu had taken to sending her suggestive emails. They were lines of text that might either be interpreted as snippets of the new novel he was working on, or as allusions to what had passed between them. Either way, they confused her, and she could not even tell Dr. Geiger, since he disapproved of her maintaining contact with her former paramour. She was listening to Dr. Geiger on one important count, though, pretending she had a real reason to be out of town tonight when Eric was scheduled to give his reading in Princeton. In New York, any reading he gave would have been well attended by people she knew. Here, she had not bothered to try to infiltrate the academic writing scene. Celia and her classmates would be there, and Elise would feel like a lone wolf, attending alone, speaking to no one, clearly without any sphere of influence whatsoever. She was worried about how it would look, both to her new protégé as well as to Eric.

Elise drove to the train station, parking her car in one of the commuter lots. She had hoped Peter might drive her to the train station, but he'd announced he could not interrupt his concentration until after six. Concentration was his baby now, and he spoke of it as something that needed to be coddled and disciplined, sacrificing everything else in his life to this mysterious concentration that produced nothing.

Although it was not quite four-thirty, the sun was already low on the horizon. She sat on the platform with her small suitcase at her feet, shivering in the cold air. On impulse she bought a pack of cigarettes on the way to the train station, an old habit Peter detested and which she had given up several years before. She lit a cigarette now, observing the people who waited for the train that would transport them into New York for the night. A few, like her, were sitting alone, but others gathered in small groups that seemed to radiate energy, talking excitedly of their plans. She saw a couple who might have been heading for dinner and a Broadway show, singing their favorite musical numbers. Disaffected high school students, their heads sprouting sculptural tufts and dyed various shades of black and red, smoked and tapped beats on their bodies as they waited. Elise caught snippets of conversation, hearing "That would be YOUR ex, not mine!" from a group of heavily made-up women in their late twenties who were dressed to go out, high heels and dark stockings peering out from beneath long coats, their end destination probably a club where they would dance, drink, and flirt with men, perhaps making a pact to be sure they came home together at the end of the night.

She envied them—each person a part of a group, their desires perfectly aligned with one another, certain of the course they would steer together for one night at least. They also seemed to belong here—bored suburban kids, suburban theatergoers, single women seeking the entertainment of the city. Bridge-and-tunnel types. But Elise did not feel as if she fit in this scene. She had no reason for being in Princeton except for her husband, who seemed to have lost interest entirely in weekend excursions to the city where they once both lived. It struck her as ironic that she wasn't even venturing into the city, she was heading toward another suburb, toward a friend who was just as lonely and alienated in her marriage as she was. The difference was that Caitlin had children to occupy her, to give meaning to what she did every day.

The light above the platform began to flash, passengers filing out of the station to meet the approaching train. Elise stubbed out her cigarette and threw it in the trash, entering the train's warm, brightly lit interior.

* * *

Since their fight, Peter's anger with his wife had been enormously productive. He had written almost sixty pages now. Already he could see that he would need to schedule a trip to the Spanish military archives in Madrid. Then he might wind his way down to Morocco, and, if he were brave enough, take the two-day trip down to Sidi Maarif to set up some oral interviews with some of the town's oldest residents.

A small, triumphant defiance, these plans constructed without Elise, though he intended to fill her in eventually. For the past week she had been quiet and unobtrusive, preparing food that amounted to peace offerings, dinners they ate silently before they both got up and staked territory in separate rooms, until it was time for sleep. He sensed she was beginning to feel remorse for the way she'd treated him, was starting to respect how different the dissertation-writing process was from the novels her clients tapped out on their keyboards, purely inventions of their imaginations. She had also been preoccupied lately with one of her writers; Eric Babu was working on something new, and Peter had caught a glimpse of emails between them. He hadn't meant to be nosy, but upon finding her laptop open on the desk one evening while she was in the shower, he clicked on one of the emails Babu had sent her. It contained only a few brief lines of text:

Strange to recall the way they had been with each other, before the towers fell. Their checkerboard bodies locked together, from a God's eye view, were either an advertisement for multiculturalism or a painful optical illusion.

That was all the email said, and he closed it quickly, not wanting to disturb any of the creative karma that must have flowed between them. At the very least, he felt happy that she was still in contact with her professional life.

He stayed in the library all day, finally printing out the now eighty-page document he had been composing at a lightning pace. Feeling uncharacteristically confident, he let himself into the locked offices of the Near East Studies department, where he placed his work in Youssef Kronenberg's box with a quick note that maybe they could meet soon to discuss his progress. Then he locked the office doors behind him and stepped into the bright, cold Princeton evening. Tonight he had plans. In his briefcase he carried a bottle of the nicest vodka he could find, a gift to celebrate his colleague Boris's completion of his doctoral work. Boris had successfully defended his dissertation that afternoon, a massive, five hundred-page work of social history about the everyday acts of resistance wrought by nineteenth century Bulgarians against Ottoman occupation. The defense had been a huge success, with Kronenberg praising Boris for the subtlety with which he had probed the historical records to unearth the voices of the oppressed. The success of Boris's defense could be measured in the number of faculty who actually attended. Even the legendary Mortimer Hayes-Blair had showed up, recovering from a stroke and speaking hesitantly but still managing to make a few searing remarks about the Bulgarians' constitutional inability to accept the gifts of Ottoman civilization.

To celebrate the event, Boris had invited his classmates in the Near Eastern Studies Department out for dinner at a restaurant on Nassau Street. From the façade, the brewery looked no larger than any of the other storefronts on Nassau Street, but inside it was cavernous, with tall ceilings, exposed brick walls and the type of brash yet nondescript artwork customarily reserved for contemporary restaurants. Encased in glass were thirty foot-high brass vats of beer, offering a sanitized view of postmodern factory life, absent of people, with only the giant machinery turning out endless batches of seasonal varietals like pumpkin lager.

At the bar Peter found his colleagues nursing tall pints of beer and waiting for a table. Nobody seemed to have brought presents, so Peter waited until the right moment to offer the vodka to Boris. The conquering hero stood in the middle, rehashing particularly triumphant moments in his defense, half in English and half in Bulgarian. He was surrounded by a group of students Peter did not recognize, members of Princeton's Eastern European contingent of grad students, most of whom were from the engineering department. Peter ordered a beer and walked over to Edgar, Mourad, and Yasemin, who had all started the same year with him. At first he had difficulty following their non-linear conversation, which was not so much a conversation as an attempt to figure out how far along the others were, or a way of dropping hints about where one was in the writing process.

"The collections at Harvard are the best," Edgar was saying. "If I spend next summer up there I should be able to finish by the winter."

"I used a lot of sources from UCLA for my third chapter," Yasemin said, thus letting everyone know she had not only a third chapter but Chapters One and Two as well. She winked at him. Peter still had not figured Yasemin out. She alternated between being standoffish and overly chummy, particularly at events like these, where she inevitably drank too much and made suggestive remarks that he had never bothered to exchange. On the surface she was attractive, with wild hennaed curls that sprang up all over her head, wide eyes lined Cleopatra-style with kohl, and an hourglass figure, but tonight she'd ruined the effect by wearing a fuzzy old sweater, ripped up army pants and Doc Martens.

"Boris has four job interviews at the Middle East Studies Association meetings," Edgar said. "Next year I plan to go on the job market myself, even if I won't defend until December."

"After graduating," Mourad announced, "I will have a better chance of finding work in Morocco than I would if I had done my PhD there."

"That seems crazy," Peter said. "You can get a better job after studying your own country in the United States."

Mourad nodded and started to speak, but Edgar interrupted him.

"I saw Joe in the library today, and he told me he just finished a chapter today about the rise of nationalism among the Druze of the Levant. His fifth. I believe he will be the next among us to finish."

Peter suddenly remembered why he disliked socializing with his fellow students. He belonged to a particularly competitive cohort, and the only person he'd really liked was Ali, the talented scholar who'd had a car accident and moved back to Jordan. At least Ali was a good conversationalist.

At dinner he sat next to Yasemin, who seemed unaware that her thigh kept rubbing against his. They had a long conversation about the difficulties of being part of an academic couple, which mostly consisted of Yasemin complaining about her on and off again boyfriend, who was finishing a PhD in electrical engineering at the University of Texas.

"It must be nice, being married to a nonacademic," she said.

"The grass is always greener," he said. "Just because my wife isn't an academic doesn't mean she's willing to follow me anywhere."

"I don't know," Yasemin sighed. "Sometimes I think about ending my relationship and going back to my old boyfriend in Istanbul. Still he is single, and he would like to come to the United States. In Turkey he is unemployed. Here he could perhaps find opportunity as a waiter."

After drinking two beers with nothing to eat, Peter was grateful when his food finally came, Chilean sea bass served with polenta and black beans.

"Did you know this fish was once called the Patagonian Toothfish?" Edgar, who had ordered the same thing, announced. "They renamed it to make it more palatable."

Peter ate slowly, concentrating on his sea bass and only paying slight attention to the conversations of his colleagues. At the other end of the table, Boris and his friends had begun speaking entirely in Bulgarian. Peter looked at his watch.

"You must not go," said Boris, when Peter finally announced he was leaving. "I have hardly spoken to you all night." Peter apologized, saying he was exhausted.

"Please at least come with me to the party of the century," Boris said. "Right now we are leaving. Everyone?" He stood up and waved to get the waitress' attention. "One last night, all of us together. You will come?"

"There's a party off campus," Yasemin explained. "The architecture students throw the best parties in Princeton. You should come, just for a few minutes."

"Or perhaps your wife is waiting for you?" Boris said. "She maybe gets angry when you are not in bed by ten, tucked under the covers." He laughed.

"No, nobody's waiting," Peter said, feeling challenged. "I'm coming."

It was just after ten o'clock when they finally left the brewing company, after a final round of vodka shots that Boris had ordered for everyone. The beer, which Peter rarely drank, had given him a buzz, but after a few minutes the vodka began to take its effect, and Peter realized that he was slightly drunk. The cold air no longer felt quite so bracing. When Yasemin linked her arm through his as they walked down Nassau Street, he realized with a jolt that she might be hitting on him.

"You know, I'm in an open relationship," she said casually, confirming his suspicions. He did not remove her arm, which clung to him like a barnacle, but wondered how, at a party filled with strangers, he would be able to escape.

The party was in a house a good twenty minutes in the opposite direction from his apartment, a beautiful old Victorian that did not look like it belonged to student housing. Peter looked at his watch, deciding that he would return to his apartment by midnight, which would mean setting out again at 11:20. Yasemin finally released his arm but looked back at him with anxiety as they climbed the steps to the second floor as if to make sure he was still there. At the top of the stairs stood a student Peter recognized from around campus, one of the legions of black-clad art and architecture students, a bald and angular man in his thirties wearing glasses with a heavy black frame and a faded black t-shirt.

"Welcome, welcome, I don't know you, but welcome anyway," the man said, visibly irritated at the size of their contingent, perhaps envisioning the drain on his beer supply. Peter handed him the bag with the vodka, hoping it compensated.

"Well, well. Thank you for this," he said, examining the bottle. "I'm Mark. The other hosts are Yves and Nicole. There are beers in the fridge. Have a good time."

Peter walked down the hallway, following the sounds of techno music to a spacious living room emptied out of its furniture, where a few students were dancing. A DJ stood behind a mixing board in the corner, one hand holding his headphones to his ears, the other flipping through a vinyl record collection. Tiny white lights had been suspended from the high ceiling, creating a roof of stars.

"Want me to get you a beer?" Yasemin said, still at his elbow.

"No, thanks," he said. "I want to see what they've got to drink." He wandered out of the room and down the hallway, passing two bedrooms that had been transformed into lounges where men and women sprawled on sofas and beds. The bedrooms all had tall bookcases, walls covered with student paintings and posters of counterculture heroes like Ché Guevara, Lenny Bruce and Serge Gainsbourg. Battered Salvation Army couches were mixed with modernist collectibles like an Ant chair and an Eames lounger, drink carts and barwear from IKEA. This was what a graduate school experience ought to be, Peter thought wistfully. A cloud of smoke enveloped one room, designated for smokers, and he walked past it toward the kitchen, where another group of guests had gathered. A blonde woman in a pink mohair sweater and black leather pants was cutting up slices of cheese and arranging them on a platter with grapes and crackers. A few people looked him over as he entered, but nobody spoke to him.

He took a beer from the refrigerator and looked around. The art and architecture students were more stylish than the average graduate students, for whom clothes were an afterthought, a secondary concern to the life of the mind. At least these students put more effort into their vaguely punk ensembles, generating the edgy cool of indie record store clerks, many of the women sporting individual touches like kilts or red vinyl boots. Yasemin had run into someone she knew and seemed momentarily to have forgotten Peter. His other colleagues were nowhere in sight, though when Boris and his now heavily intoxicated friends stomped into the kitchen, everyone turned to look at them. Peter slipped from the room before they noticed him, but Edgar detained him in the hallway, subjecting him to a drunken monologue about Foucault and the Panopticon.

He spotted Celia before she saw him, her dark hair twisted up on top of her head, a few strands curling around her face. She was wearing a pale green cashmere cardigan over a black slip-dress, looking nothing like her usual coltish, jeans and t-shirt self. The blonde in the pink sweater he'd spotted earlier in the kitchen was leading her to the room with the DJ, heads turning as they passed. They stood out, both very attractive and very obviously undergraduates. Most of the time grad students and undergraduates didn't mix. For a moment he continued to listen to Edgar, puzzled at her presence here, and then he excused himself to talk to her.

Her friend was dancing, piling her blonde hair on top of her head as if she were Bridget Bardot and twisting her hips while several male graduate students watched. Celia stood to one side, holding a martini glass and swaying slightly, a smile spreading across her face when she recognized him.

"It's nice to see you," she said. "I feel a little out of my league."

"With her?" he said, gesturing at the blonde.

"With everything," she said.

"You don't look out of your league," he assured her. "You look beautiful."

Celia looked down at the drink she held in her hands. "This is my fourth martini. Help me with it. I don't even like them that much." He took it from her and offered her his beer. The strength of the martini surprised him.

"Someone's trying to get you drunk," Peter said.

"That would be Yves. One of the guys who lives here." She gestured at her friend. "Nicole's been trying to set us up, and he pounced as soon as I walked in the door. I guess I should be flattered by the attentions of a graduate student, but he doesn't seem very discriminating."

"I don't think I know him," Peter said. "I just came here with some friends from my department. I don't know most of these people." Celia asked him about Elise, surprised to hear that he hadn't spoken to her at all since she'd left for Connecticut the day before.

"That's odd," Celia said. "Not even to check in?"

"Nope," he said, not wanting to talk about it. In the doorway he could sense Yasemin looking at him, and he turned away, pretending he hadn't seen her.

"Someone you know?" Celia said. "She's glaring at me."

"I think she's trying to hit on me. She's in my department. We had a department dinner earlier and I kept thinking the hand on my leg under the table was an accident."

Celia laughed. "I had no idea graduate school was such a hotbed of sexual innuendo."

"Neither did I." He sniffed the air, where the smell of cigarette smoke was now mixed with something sweeter. "Is that marijuana? God, I haven't smoked in years. I love that smell."

She looked skeptical. "You seem so straitlaced."

"Not when I went to Brown," he insisted. "I wouldn't turn it down if it were offered to me. I just don't have any friends right now who smoke."

"Let's go smoke some," she said impulsively. "I've never tried it."

"You can't just go up to people and ask them if you can smoke," Peter said. "There's an etiquette. You have to be invited."

Celia grabbed her blonde friend's hand as she shimmied past.

"This is Nicole," she said. She whispered something in Nicole's ear.

"Come on," her friend said, angling her head toward the hallway. He ignored Yasemin's vexed look as he brushed by.

Nicole led them into a back bedroom, where a few people sat on a red corduroy sofa. Peter thought suddenly of the effects that smoking might have on his training schedule, but his hesitations were outweighed by the novelty of the party, and the exhilarating sense that even being at this party was completely out of character for him. Elise would not be able to imagine what he was doing tonight.

"I need a few minutes of privacy," Nicole told the people in her room. "Would you mind leaving for a second?" The guests looked annoyed but got up and left the room, Nicole locking the door behind them. "It is my room, after all." She pulled out a shoebox from under her bed, producing a half-sized Ziploc bag filled with pot.

"Snack bags were the best thing to happen to the weed industry," she said, shaking the dried leaves onto a small square of rolling paper and expertly rolling it up. "They're the perfect size. It's almost as if they were invented expressly for pot. Who did you come here with?"

"Some grad students in the Near East Studies department," Peter said.

"How do you know Celia?"

He looked at Celia, unsure of how to respond.

"We're both runners," she said, saving him. "We met at some local running events."

"A running event, sounds cool," Nicole said, handing him the joint, and he took the lighter and lit the end of the twisted paper tip until it crumbled off. He sucked in deeply, then passed it to Nicole.

"Celia and I are in a writing class together," she explained. "Celia's quite the talented writer."

"I'm a hopeless novice," Celia said, fumbling with the joint as Nicole handed it to her and explained how to smoke it. She took a first tentative puff, blowing out the smoke. When nothing happened, she inhaled more deeply and started to cough.

"Then you have to pass it quickly," Nicole said. "If you don't, people will think you're trying to hog it."

"Don't Bogart that joint," Peter said, remembering some of the pot slang from his college days and fielding blank stares from Celia and Nicole.

"What does Humphrey Bogart have to do with it?" Celia asked, passing it over to him. The end of the cigarette was wet. He frowned, trying to erase the thought that had just flashed through his mind of a doctor mixing sperm and egg in a Petri dish. The harsh smoke filled his lungs.

"There used to be a song with that line in it," Peter explained. "I'm showing my age, I guess. But you know something? In Morocco, when you smoke a joint you hold onto it. It's like everyone gets one turn but you treat it like a cigarette, taking a little from it when you want but continuing with your conversation. Americans are always so intensely individualistic about it. We don't want to let the joint burn down without letting everybody have as many hits as possible. In Morocco it's a social thing."

"You could argue it's social here, too," Nicole said, "just representing a different idea of sociality. What were you doing in Morocco?"

"Peace Corps."

"The place where he was sounds like something out of Marquez." Celia slipped the sweater from her shoulders, and he noticed a spray of freckles across her collarbone. "The Spanish built the town and then abandoned it," Peter explained, telling them about the ruined bullfighting ring, the library that no longer had any books, the unknown saint. "They renamed it to Santa Maria of the Lost. When they left, the Moroccans changed the name back to Sidi Maarif, but it was already too late. Colonialism destroyed the culture and the history entirely."

"Fascinating," Nicole said, her blue eyes widening. He found Nicole attractive but not beautiful; she had the expensive good looks of so many Princeton students, but she was obviously trying to offset her childlike features by cultivating a hard edge, the dark makeup and black leather pants incongruous with her delicate features.

"I believe you two are both from Boston," Celia said, taking the joint again. Talking about their hometown confirmed what he'd suspected: Nicole was from an old, notable Boston family, had attended a boarding school that was a rival to Peter's, and summered at the Cape. Despite their wealth, Peter's family was not in the same league with Nicole Sumner's people. Although Peter's grandfather had made a fortune in timber, he had grown up poor, and money made in the last half of the twentieth century would still be, by the reckoning of a Sumner, new money.

"How do you feel, Celia?" he asked, changing the subject.

"Honestly, I don't feel much of anything," she said.

"Sometimes it doesn't work the first time," Nicole explained. "But if you want to feel something right away, Yves has something that will really pick us up." She winked.

"I'm all good," he said. Celia was looking at Nicole with an open, curious expression that seemed to indicate that she was up for anything. Feeling protective, he suggested they go back to the party.

Nicole closed the shoebox and slid it under the bed, and Celia followed Peter out of the room, but immediately she was intercepted by the man Peter assumed was Yves, another skinny architecture student with tousled dark hair and a turtleneck. Yves steered Celia toward the room with the DJ, his hand on the small of her back; it was a gesture of ownership, of intimacies to come. Nicole grabbed Peter's hand, her warm, sweet breath on his neck.

"Dance with me," she said, leading him down the hall to the living room. Yves and Celia followed them, and they carved out a little square for themselves amid the other dancers. By now the room was filled with people, the hip-hop music thumped relentlessly from the DJ's oversized speakers, and Peter saw from his watch that it was already almost midnight. So much for self-imposed curfews. He suddenly decided to get rid of his watch, to free himself of the oppressiveness of time. His own life was one gigantic, meaningless routine, both arbitrary and pointless. Taking off the watch, he looked over at Celia, the one person he knew he would see again. He handed it to her.

"Would you guard this for me?" he shouted over the music. "It's too heavy for me to wear right now."

"People keep giving me their jewelry," Celia laughed, fastening his watch around her wrist, where it slid around like a chunky, oversized bracelet. The delicateness of her wrists touched him somehow, so narrow and small; he imagined pinning those wrists over her head, wondering what she would look like beneath him, the lines of her body unbroken by clothes. Embarrassed, he felt his face flush in the darkness as she smiled up at him. He was more stoned than he'd thought.

Yves had disappeared; he returned now with more martinis, handing one each to Nicole and Celia, returning again with another for Peter and himself. Peter complimented Yves on the party, but it was too loud to hear his reply over the music. Unknowingly he seemed to have been paired up with Nicole, who touched him from time to time while they were dancing, and then Yasemin was at his side again, sliding up and down his leg like a stripper. Yves had backed Celia into a corner, one hand possessively cupped around her waist, her eyes lowered and head turned to the side so that Peter could not read whether she wanted Yves, wanted that hand against her so closely. Peter turned away, trying to enjoy his surroundings, the two women circling him in a pantomime of the sinuous, explicit movements of women in rap videos. Nicole was dancing ironically, laughing at herself, but Yasemin's expression was grim and determined. He could feel them pressing in on him, moving closer and closer until he was aware of the room for what it was: a sweaty mass of bodies, all of them pathetically longing for what they couldn't have.

"Back in a second," he said to both of them, placing his martini glass on the mantle of the fireplace and threading his way through the crowd and out of the room.

CHAPTER TEN

She did not know if what she felt was the effect of the marijuana or the martinis: both elated and light-headed, as if the weight of navigating her way in the everyday world had suddenly lifted. In Nicole's clothes she felt beautiful, the black slip dress from BCBG fitting her perfectly, expensively. Earlier that afternoon, to Eric Babu's reading, she had worn one of Nicole's pale blue cashmere sweaters, her Lucky Brand jeans and a pair of ballet flats. If clothes could make you someone else, certainly tonight she could feel herself breaking out of her cocoon, someone else's clothes transforming her into a person who could be careless, beautiful, and enviable.

Babu's reading in the packed James Stewart auditorium almost didn't happen. Twenty minutes after his scheduled appearance, he still had not appeared and the audience was murmuring about something the great writer was not happy with.

"Let's find out the reason for this rock star behavior," Nicole said, going up to the front rows to ask Carla what was wrong.

"Get this - Babu's throwing a fit because they put him in the Witherspoon Suite of the Nassau Inn," Nicole informed her. "Witherspoon owned slaves."

"Who's Witherspoon?" Celia asked. "I know Witherspoon Street, but I never bothered to find out who he was."

"One of our early presidents."

"So, they should get him another room."

"He wants a suite. All the other ones are full."

But the matter was apparently resolved, because in a few minutes Babu appeared. He was considerably older than Celia had expected, probably in his early fifties. Though tall, he was not quite the larger-than-life presence Elise had portrayed. He wore jeans and an African dashiki radiating with deep blue, tie-dyed coronas. When he read, he seldom looked up from his work. But his voice was mesmerizing, a deep, mellifluous baritone that lent gravity to his every word. He read from his last novel, the one Elise had given her, and from a new collection of short stories that had just been issued by his publisher. Elise had not mentioned the new collection.

After the reading, Celia and Nicole stood in line for an autograph.

"I'm nervous," Celia confessed.

"Don't be," Nicole said. "He's human just like the rest of us. I've met writers who are more famous. Derek Walcott. Mark Strand. Philip Roth."

Eric Babu looked up at her from his signing table with the unrecognizing eyes of a stranger, unaware of the tenuous links they shared.

"To whom shall I dedicate this?" he said in his British boarding-school accent.

"To Celia," she said. There was much she wanted to say: she might drop Elise's name, demonstrate her thorough knowledge of his work, or mention that she herself aspired to be a writer. But she was unable to speak.

"She's a huge fan of your work," Nicole said, nudging her. "And she's also a writer. You'll be hearing from her someday."

He suppressed a wry little smile as he scrawled something with a substantial fountain pen. How many apprentice writers he must have seen, at writer's conferences and college readings, how many people must have stood in line just like her, imagining what it was like to be on the other side of the table, a mythical presence spilling his ink into their books.

"Be careful, the ink is still quite wet," he said, handing her the book and looking behind her at the next customer.

They stepped away from the crowd, looking to see what he'd written. "To Celia, at Princeton, may the ink never run dry," she read.

"Nice," Nicole said, blasé as always. "Did you see his Mont Blanc?"

"His what?"

"The pen. It's a new Phillip Starck design. I'm going to ask for one for Christmas. He's got such a good eye for small luxuries. You can tell by the almost hungry way he describes rich people in his fiction. Although he could stand to upgrade his wardrobe a bit. That 'Empire Writes Back' look is so 1970s." Nicole might have been a society wife, downgrading the digs of a fellow rival, as if the beauty and achievement of the writing they'd just heard needed to be diminished, exposed as a product of a mind with commonplace desires.

Celia had wished she could go back to her room to think for a while about the reading, to let it sink in, but Nicole insisted she come home with her to help get ready for the party. She snapped out of her reverie now, a voice in her ear telling her that she resembled Audrey Hepburn. A *gamine*, Yves was saying, a word that probably meant the same thing in French as well, conjuring up images of slender, boyish models, Peter Pan, cigarette holders, and false eyelashes. The effect was due in part to wearing her hair up; if she pulled her hair down, she would become someone else entirely. Her hair was one of her strongest features, Nicole said. Men liked long hair, especially on college girls who wore it up, unpinning it to cascade over their shoulders at significant moments.

Celia was also conscious of her breasts, which Nicole had also admired; they made her not entirely a *gamine* and occasionally Yves' eyes strayed down to her chest, a little too obviously. Most of the other women at the party were not wearing dresses, and all night she could feel people staring at her, their eyes needing to fall on something, the women's expressions slightly annoyed, the men's approving. One woman even had the nerve to ask if she and Nicole had just come from a fraternity party, but Nicole had merely smiled and said in a voice that contained both humor and venom,

"Actually, I live here. I believe that gives me more reason to be here than you."

Yves was in his endgame, putting his final moves on her and acting confident that she would not refuse him. He was attractive in a consumptive, Byronic way but spoke in monosyllables: a few well-timed grunts when she said something, a "more?" now and then when her drink needed refreshing. Nicole said he was the type of person who communicated exclusively through his art, the painting of the man with the bucket on his head a representative example. The painting was too orange, the torso of the bucket-headed man gray and almost emaciated, perhaps a self-portrait of Yves, whose clothes were fashionable but seemed to conceal an excessive skinniness, as if he'd given up eating to focus exclusively on painting and cocaine. Celia decided she didn't like the Mick Jagger look. Pot was one thing, but the continued offers of cocaine from Nicole made her feel as if Nicole had brought her up to the top of a mountain and now aimed to throw her off. She was not swayed by Nicole's insistence that sex was infinitely better after a few lines, since she had no plans to sleep with Yves and was merely entertaining his attention until the ideal moment of escape.

"Remember what I said about doing something a little scary," Nicole said. "From what I hear, Yves is very good in bed."

She said it as if Yves were a magazine they were all passing around. Torn between admiring her worldliness and worrying that her new friend was more excessive than she wanted to be, Celia stopped trying to muster up the effort to convince herself of Yves' attractive qualities. There remained the small matter of escaping, but Peter's presence nearby was a comfort, and smoking the joint had given her the confidence to see she was just in a room full of graduate students, dancing awkwardly and taking themselves far too seriously.

She felt light, insubstantial; she was a mannequin in borrowed clothes, with the aunt's pearl ring and the comforting heft of Peter's watch on her wrist. Over the joint she'd noticed Nicole's suggestive winks at Peter, and when Celia told her he was married she only remarked casually,

"With most men the wedding ring is only a minor obstacle." But it looked as if Nicole had some competition from his colleague, who was unflatteringly dressed in waist-high jeans but could undulate impressively on the dancefloor. Nicole had so much more in common with Peter than Celia did, both of them affluent, both from Boston, probably able to trace their ancestors back to the Mayflower.

Then she noticed Peter was no longer there to anchor her vision. His presence had provided a familiar reference point that made her feel she could dance and drink without any ill befalling her. With him gone, her perspective on the party suddenly changed. Yves became a leering, smarmy presence who had trapped her into a corner and, if he were always this much of a player, might have any one of a number of diseases. She wondered if Nicole saw her not as someone to mentor but as a sort of science experiment, a modern day Eliza Doolittle with a small measure of raw writing talent who made an interesting subject for corruption.

She excused herself for the bathroom and found her way out of the room, wandering down the hall toward the kitchen in search of Peter. Unable to find him anywhere, she opened the door to the stairs leading out of the apartment, stepping carefully to avoid twisting her ankles in the high-heeled sandals she was unaccustomed to wearing. The apartment had been hot, jammed with people, and Celia was sweating, the cold air from outside jolting her awake. She saw him ahead on the darkened street, and she called out to him in relief.

"You forgot your watch," she said when he was close. "Will you walk me home? I don't want to go back there."

His look was one of concern, mixed with something else she could not read. "What about Yves?"

"Too aggressive," she said. She shivered as the air cooled the sweat on her skin, rubbing her arms to keep warm. Peter offered her his jacket. Nodding yes, she accepted the coat as he draped it over her shoulders. She slipped her arms inside it and wrapped it around herself.

"I felt fine when you were there," she told him. "I was actually having a good time. Then when you left I got nervous." He nodded and kept walking. "Why did you give me your watch?"

"Sometimes I get too wrapped up in where I need to be or what I should be doing," he said. "It all goes back to finishing the dissertation. If I don't get home by a certain hour, I won't get up tomorrow in time to be at the library early, and projects don't get finished without discipline."

"Why are you leaving, then, if you were trying to forget about time?"

"I needed to clear my head. For a minute I felt like I was in college again. I had that feeling I used to have when I was younger, like the future was stretched out in front of me, limitless. I didn't need the watch to remind me of everything I'd tied myself down to. Then I realized it was more complicated than that."

"You were just dancing. I don't see what's so complicated about that."

"The more you drink, the more you think about doing things you regret later," he said cryptically.

"When you left I started to feel claustrophobic," she said. "Surrounded by people I don't know or trust. For a little while I felt that same thing you're talking about, but for me it was more like I was cresting a wave. Like I had everything figured out, that I was playing my life out in exactly the right way. But then I started to think everyone was out to get me, and that I really have no idea what I'm doing."

"That's the pot talking," Peter laughed. "I'm flattered that everything was fine until I left, though."

"Only because I know where you live," Celia joked. "You're accountable." They turned onto Nassau Street, the storefronts bright with their ghostly nighttime illumination. At this hour the street was deserted.

"It's good to have doubts, though," Peter was saying. "I think that's healthy. When I was your age I was convinced I knew exactly what to do with my life, but look at me. For the entire decade of my twenties I had no clue what I wanted. Still don't."

"What did you think you wanted to do?" she asked. "When you were my age."

"It's a cliché," he said. "I'm embarrassed even to say it."

"Tell me. I won't laugh."

"I intended to save the world, starting with the Peace Corps. I was going to save Morocco first, and then I planned to amaze all the right people with my dedication and then be hired as a consultant in Washington. I don't know what I imagined consultants did. I guess I thought that two years in the Peace Corps made me an expert, and that I'd come back and people would be falling all over themselves to ask my opinion about how to solve Third World poverty." He laughed. "But I lost my initiative somehow. My parents also put a lot of pressure on me to get what they called a serious job."

"So you decided to save the world by becoming a professor?" she said. "There's nothing wrong with that. Teaching is noble."

"I guess so. Right now the prospect of teaching seems so far away. I don't know anyone who's excited about becoming a professor, or at least we never have these conversations in grad school. There's a whole dissertation looming in the middle, the pressure to publish. Sometimes I think Elise is right when she accuses me of choosing a PhD program so I could hide away for a couple of years."

"A PhD program seems an odd way to hide away. I would have chosen a beach somewhere, like in Mexico where nobody would find me."

"No, you wouldn't," he said. "You're a high achiever, or else you wouldn't be here at Princeton. You don't want to let down the people in your life. That's why I picked graduate school. I didn't want to disappoint my family. Princeton would shut them up for a few years, at least. Though I did just finish a pretty big chunk of my dissertation. I was inspired by that talk we had at PJ's."

"I'm glad I helped you somehow."

"More than you know. Maybe my father will never give a shit, but I'm thinking my advisor will be pretty excited."

She told him about her father then, about the summer they'd lived in Key West, and coming to the realization that adults possessed no magical roadmap for life.

"But it's not only my dad who's lost," she said. "It's my high school English teacher, you, Elise, everyone. I think that's why Elise wants to have children so badly. Maybe for the same reasons you're in graduate school. Having children to raise gives the illusion that your life is part of some larger plan."

"She never wanted children before," he told her. "When we got married, we both agreed we didn't want children. She only started to want them because the experts told her she couldn't have them. That's how she is. Conquering what she can't have and then forgetting about it."

"That seems pretty calculating," Celia said. "I don't think she sees it that way. She's just looking for meaning and purpose, like anyone else."

"You're too young to have developed my cynicism. And you don't really know Elise. But hold onto those illusions. And tell me more of them. I like hearing your Southern accent."

"I hate my accent," Celia said, aware that they were now flirting. "I'm so sick of people telling me it's pretty. I wish I had a neutral, Midwestern accent."

"You know, nobody at that party had any idea how we knew each other. Unless you told your friend."

"No, Nicole doesn't know anything." Celia was thinking that his presence there, at the party, was more than a coincidence. Something big was on the verge of happening, had to happen, and the universe had configured itself for this moment. "They didn't know that we're all set to have a baby with each other."

He laughed nervously. They stood still for a moment, waiting for the traffic light in front of the Garden Theater to change, the light blindly directing a street empty of traffic. The light changed and they crossed over, entering the corner of the campus.

"What does Elise say about me?" Peter's question came unexpectedly. "Tell me the worst thing she's told you about me."

"She says you're a slave to your routines." Celia felt like a tattletale. "Do you really get up at six every morning to run?"

"It gets me out of bed," he said. "Tell me what else she says."

"We talk about her, mostly," said Celia. "Sometimes we talk about her writers. I'm always prompting her for information about them. I want to know what they're like. They seem like demigods to me."

"They're not her writers anymore," Peter said. "She gave up her job. A few years ago she was really something. But by the end, she was just a glorified copy editor. She lost a lot of her status by switching to freelance."

"She doesn't make it sound that way," Celia said thoughtfully. "And she's still trying to hold onto the writers. Especially Eric Babu. I guess he was her favorite."

At the mention of Babu's name, the muscles in Peter's face clenched.

"Did she tell you she was still in touch with him?"

"She had lunch with him last week to see what he was working on. She also told me that he wrote about her in one of his books." Betrayal! Celia could feel herself hurtling down a course that now seemed almost natural. A few words had been enough from her to confirm Peter's suspicions.

"Did he, now," Peter said. It was more a statement than an expression of surprise. "Did she tell you she was once involved with him?"

"In so many words," Celia said. He did not look at her.

"You know we met because of Eric Babu. I always suspected they were lovers, but she never would admit it. I wouldn't be surprised if she was with him now in New York. I didn't think she would do something like that to get back at me, but you never know, the way things have been going lately." His tone was dispassionate, neither angry nor stunned. "He's been sending her these emails. I came across one the other day, and I think now that I was wrong about everything."

"I doubt she'd be with him now," Celia assured him. "I told you Babu was giving a reading here earlier tonight."

"But maybe he went home afterward," Peter said.

"No, I know for a fact he was staying at the Nassau Inn. Anyway, can you imagine him on the New Jersey transit, heading back home by himself?"

"No," Peter said. "They'd get him a limo, for sure. But Elise didn't mention he was reading here. I wonder why. I guess she wouldn't have wanted me to go."

They were at her dorm, and she ran her card through the reader. He followed her up the steps, steadying himself with the railing. She calculated that he was drunk, and that she had more power in the situation than she'd thought. With most men the wedding ring is only a minor obstacle, Nicole had said. And Peter. *The more you drink, the more you think about doing things you regret later.* And then there were Michael Lenhart's words. *If you give something, be sure what you take is of equal value.* At her door he stopped, murmuring that he'd get his coat back from her now if she didn't mind.

"Let me put something else on. I don't want to catch cold." Celia held open the door of her room. "Stay for a minute." She handed Peter his jacket and offered him a chair, fighting off a small voice that told her to send him away, put on her pajamas, and curl up in bed alone with a book. She walked over to the window and closed the blinds, her heart hammering in her chest. She felt amazed and elated at the way he sat there, dumbfounded, waiting to see what she would do. Mimicking a gesture from Nicole's playbook, Celia slipped her dress over her head and looked archly at Peter. "I just need to change." On Nicole's suggestion Celia had worn what Nicole termed "get lucky" underwear that night, just in case she was going to like Yves. She could feel Peter's eyes surreptitiously glancing at her breasts, which spilled over her lacy black bra. Walking to the small, institutional dresser, she bent over to the lowest drawer and took out a pair of shorts and a t-shirt. She remembered the image of Nicole bending over, the thin slip of thong bisecting her body like the cleft of a peach. How could a guy not go wild for that? Celia herself had even felt something like desire for Nicole, or at least, she knew what it must feel like to be a man completely at the mercy of such boldness.

When she turned, the expression on Peter's face was one she'd never imagined being directed at her: a look both transparent and elemental, one that telegraphed desire.

"Come here," he said, reaching for her. She looked at him for one long second, then dropped the clothes she held in her hands. She released her thick, dark hair from its clip, allowing it to tumble onto her shoulders as he pulled her onto his lap, her hips in his hands, his face close, his lips and tongue searching for hers. For a long time he kissed her, until she thought she might dissolve. Then he pulled back, smoothing a lock of hair away from her face.

"Would you excuse me for just a minute?" he said. "I need to use the bathroom." Celia maneuvered herself off his lap and looked away as he straightened his clothes. He turned and took her hand.

"I'll be right back, I promise," he said, kissing the inside of her wrist with gallantry.

At first she arranged herself on the chair in a way she imagined looked sexy: arms crossed over her chest, her long legs, also crossed, up on the desk. After a few minutes, he still hadn't returned. The chair began to feel hard and cold beneath her. She slipped on a t-shirt to wait, looking up at her alarm clock. Ten minutes had passed. Then fifteen. Twenty. Something was wrong. Out in the hallway, the boyfriend of one of her hallmates was bouncing a tennis ball against the walls, waiting for his girlfriend to come home from a party. Celia couldn't remember his name, but he was a constant presence on the hall and somewhat of an annoying guy.

"Did you see anyone come out of the guys' bathroom recently?" she asked.

"Ha, just my Arabic professor," he said. "Yeah. I couldn't believe I busted him like that. I caught him snooping around the RA's door, looking for condoms in that envelope she keeps there."

"Are you sure?" Celia's heart sank. "Did he leave?"

The guy narrowed his eyes, the pimples on his forehead knitting themselves together like a red constellation of stars. Kevin. That was his name, she remembered now.

"Was he here with you?" Kevin asked, laughing maniacally. "That's rich." Celia was beginning to piece things together now. Peter could get in tremendous trouble for this.

"No," Celia said firmly. "I don't know what you're talking about." She went back into her room and closed the door. She didn't have Peter's number. What should she do now? Throw on a coat and run out into the street looking for him? Get a taxi to his apartment? Obviously if he wanted to see her, he would find a way back. Or not. He was a passive guy, Elise had told her. It was up to Celia to take control of this. She'd brought him this far. The buzz from the liquor would wear off soon, and she'd lose her nerve, lose this opportunity forever. He needed to see her again in the party dress, which she slipped back on, throwing on her running shoes, a sweater and a coat this time so she'd be warm.

"You look like a real dork," Kevin laughed as she bolted out the door and ran past him in the hall. She didn't care, the shoes would get her there faster, and she didn't have the cash on hand for a taxi. She could only guess at which direction Peter was headed. Home, probably. Elise was, of course, out of town, and he could still be convinced. Countless times she had run by the graduate student apartments where Peter lived, on the road where Princeton's forested beauty gradually fizzled out into the ugliness of the ramps approaching Route 1. Her lungs burned, from the pot or the cold, she couldn't tell, but it felt good to be out here, her feet pounding the downhill slope past the golf course and into a wooded path where it had to be too freaking cold for rapists to be lurking. Ten minutes after she started out she was at his door, knocking frantically in case he'd gone to sleep. That was impossible, he would have just arrived. She knocked again, but no answer. Catching her breath in the ugliness of the institutional high rise hallway, she had the feeling that this was not her life, this was a movie, this was the kind of nonsensical scene she had imagined finding herself in, one free of the normally careful life course she steered for herself. Was Peter just behind the door, debating whether to answer, knowing that answering would mean defiling the bed he shared with his wife?

When it became apparent that he wouldn't answer, she suddenly got mad, enraged that she had run all the way out here, for someone who had just run out on her, who obviously wasn't man enough to acknowledge to an undergraduate that they were together. He'd taken a coward's way out. Why should she throw himself at him? No, but she had wanted to throw herself at somebody. It was embarrassing, really, that she had remained practically a virgin this far into her sophomore year, that she possessed only her lame high school encounters with Steven to relate in conversations with people like the more worldly Nicole, whose conquests numbered in the double digits. Nicole's list included not only the predictable WASPy types but also a longshoreman, the son of a Mafia don, and a film professor at NYU. What would Nicole do? She was already running away from the apartment building, and even though the return trip was uphill this time, her energy felt limitless. She sprinted back to her dorm, all the way plotting a new direction for the night, one that would take her places that would cause Nicole's jaw to finally drop with envy and surprise and that longed-for admiration that Celia sought so desperately.

* * *

It had to have been *mektub,* written, as the Arabs said, his fate that Kevin caught him in Celia's hallway like that, the very last person in the universe (aside from his wife) that he needed to see right then. If not fate, it was at least a certain sign that what he'd been half contemplating would have been a terrible, terrible mistake. Coming out of the bathroom, Peter had just paused to look at the brightly decorated door of the hall's resident assistant, his eyes drawn to a manila envelope surrounded by little penis-shaped arrows cut out of construction paper. Were there really condoms in there? And was this what he was doing with her, should he pick up a couple? He'd merely peeked down into the envelope to see if it was full, and then suddenly, at his back, the sneering voice he knew only too well from its owner's asinine classroom challenges.

"Hi, Professor." Kevin was grinning, his face lit up like a jack-o-lantern and just as horrifying.

"Kevin," he nodded, jamming his hands in his pockets as if they might have just happened upon one another in the library. Peter turned and began to walk quickly down the hallway, in the opposite direction from Celia's room. "See you in class," Kevin called after him.

And now there was no going back, with Kevin sitting sentry over the hallway. He walked away from the dorm, trying to figure out what he should do. He'd left behind his coat, and the air was freezing outside. He didn't want to go home yet, wondered if he should call Celia and tell her what had happened. No, he had no way of getting her number, and besides, this was a clear warning that he'd almost screwed up in the biggest way imaginable. Would Kevin turn him in? He hadn't done anything, really. There was no crime in being there. Celia had invited him to her room, and all they'd been doing was kissing. He would go back to the party, find Nicole, and get Celia's phone number. Then he could call her to apologize, to beg her not to say anything to Elise, and to make sure that nothing had changed between them. Everything needed to stay the way it was before the party.

The party had thinned out by now, though the few people remaining seemed to be generating even more noise, an effect of the lateness of the hour, and the amount of drinking they'd all done. He climbed the steps to the front door and pushed it open, not ringing the bell this time. The disco ball was still spinning, and the emaciated hipster in the turtleneck who'd been hitting on Celia earlier was now playing Eurotrash dance music, a set of puffy headphones held up to his ear, his body bending in time with the monotonous beat. Yasemin and Edgar were still there, dancing, but when they saw him, they both stopped and came out into the hallway as if Peter was their long-lost best friend.

"Hey amigo," Edgar said, patting him on the back.
"Where'd you go?" Yasemin asked.

"I've got to talk to the girl who lives here," he said, pushing past her and into the kitchen. Nicole's door was closed. He knocked a few times but nobody came out.

"I think they went somewhere to get something to eat," a guy standing near the refrigerator told him.

"Do you know where I could get Nicole's number?" Peter asked frantically. "It's important." Someone directed him to the third roommate, who did not look happy about the interruption of his bong hit, but the guy gave up Nicole's cell phone number without too many questions. Peter called, but it rang and rang before the answering machine finally picked up. He put his phone in his pocket, running his hand through his hair.

"Peter," Yasemin was saying. "Come here." She smiled at him. "Relax just a minute. Edgar has something for you." He was annoyed, but there was nowhere to go right now; he had to wait for Nicole to come home so he could get Celia's number. He followed her back into the room where Yves was DJ-ing. At the bar table now littered with mostly empty bottles, Edgar was pouring vodka into three shot glasses.

"Cheers," he said, handing Peter a glass. Peter gulped it down. Maybe this was what he needed, to bring back the good feeling from before, to put him in a better frame of mind before calling Celia. He could pass the time here for a while, with his two cohort members. Yasemin poured him another shot, which he drank just as quickly, enjoying the burn of the alcohol as it warmed his esophagus.

"What's the matter?" she asked him. "You look unhappy."

"I just had a run-in with an undergrad," he said. "It wasn't pretty."

"One of those girls you were dancing with earlier?" she asked.

"No, a guy in one of my classes."

"We're second-class citizens to the undergrads, this is for sure," she said. "I avoid them socially at all costs. I did not like it that those two girls were here. Have a cigarette." She reached into her back pocket, pulling out a silver cigarette case and offering him one. Hand rolled cigarettes, of course Yasemin would have an affectation like this. He declined, but Edgar accepted one. She lit it for him, and there was an intimacy in the gesture, the flame emanating from her slender hand so close to Edgar's mouth. She said something to Edgar in Turkish that Peter didn't quite catch, Edgar laughing and looking at Peter. He should have understood, Turkish was his second non-Western language in the department, but in truth, it was Ottoman Turkish that he was good at, not what was spoken today, in the twenty-first century. He smiled and felt foolish.

"There's a cure for that," Edgar said, as if Yasemin had just diagnosed him with something, but Peter didn't want to look stupid by asking. "Another shot." And it was the third one that put him over the edge, he'd stop now, really, but she was talking about Turkish tobacco, how it was sun-cured and would not cause cancer, so he took one, finding it stronger than she'd predicted, but still sweet as honey. Yasemin wasn't flirting with him anymore though something was up with Edgar, or had been up, clearly they had a whole story between them that he was intruding on, but she was different with Edgar there, hardly flirtatious at all, and it made him feel at ease at first but then want to know why she was so mercurial. Was he not interesting to her anymore? Or had Edgar beat him not just in dissertation writing but here as well? They kept drinking and talking about the department, about places they'd traveled, about nothing he could remember later, though what he did remember clearly was Edgar leaving the room to get a beer and Yasemin sliding her hand under his shirt, just for a moment, her fingers playing at the small of his back, but then moving away quickly as if nothing had happened at all and after that she wouldn't look at him and Edgar was there and Peter went outside to call Nicole again, who still didn't answer, and suddenly it was after one in the morning and they were in the pretentious grad student Dbar (D for debasement, since the bar was in the lowest level of the Harry Potter-esque stone castle built as an afterthought residence for grad students, but what a joke! As if grad students led debased existences). Boris and his friends had gone, and there were other people Peter knew there who kissed him on both cheeks and hugged him and said how glad they were to see him out, finally, and he felt a bit sad at being there because he'd avoided it since Ali's accident and the talks they used to have here, but this was obviously the place you went when you were single, with tealights flickering on the tables and he was obviously missing out on a whole social life and why hadn't he been coming here to escape the tension with Elise? And Yasemin had a room here, too, in another part of the dorm, which had been built at a remove from the rest of the campus, and he'd never liked being here or even seen a room but she offered to show him hers and it was warm with wood floors and she'd decorated it nicely with posters from Lebanese theater troupes and scarves draped on chairs and funny how easy it was to lift her and not Celia over into the bed, to pull off her fuzzy sweater and the army fatigues and find her soft and female and yielding beneath them. It was comforting, actually, how she was nothing like either Celia or Elise, and he had not, until now, cared anything for her and only cared for her now, in this moment, but still she had a stunning odalisque's body, big-hipped and narrow-waisted beneath the army fatigues, and those eyes staring at him like the knowing glance from the woman in the painting by Ingres.

Suspended over her, his entire body shuddered, and then he pulled away, his breath shallow and harsh in the darkness next to her. He closed his eyes for just a moment, but how long that moment was, he had no idea, until suddenly he woke up again, feeling the unfamiliar weight of arms clutching him in the darkness. He sat up, swinging his feet onto the floor, burying his head in his hands.

"Shit, shit, shit. I can't believe I just did this."

"It wasn't just you," Yasemin said. "I was here, too."

"I have to go." He sat up, glancing around the floor for his clothes.

"You can't make it unhappen."

He grew dizzy and lay back down, the vertical state too heavy to bear. The red numbers on her alarm clock swam together but he gathered that in the rational world where time was still kept, it was half past three. On a desk there was a red lava lamp he hadn't noticed before, and scarves everywhere, why so many scarves? She murmured something about performance art and a belly dance troupe, pulling one of the scarves off her bedpost and at first he thought she'd tie him up there but she didn't, she put it over her head and within seconds had tamed her curls into submission, completely hiding her hair under a *hijab*.

"Isn't this what you want?" she said, climbing on top of him. In the glow of the lava lamp she looked down at him, veiled, triumphant, and he almost would have preferred now that she'd tied him up, this was infinitely creepier. She leaned in, her beautiful weighty breasts and scarves brushing over his bare chest, her mouth tasting of wine and stale cigarettes. He would stay just a few minutes more and deal with the spinning of the world tomorrow.

But it did not stop. At dawn, awake again, Peter extracted himself from Yasemin's sleeping form, shuddering as he noticed out of the corner of his eye that she still wore the scarf. He left her room and went outside into the cold, crossing the barren winter golf course between the grad student dorm and his apartment. First order of business: to change into faded gray sweatpants and a thin t-shirt before sending himself on a punishing five-mile run, trying not to throw up the entire time. Back home again, he scoured his teeth and the alcohol from his breath with mouthwash and stood in the shower for a half hour, washing the night and all of its mistakes off himself. He drove to Route 1, wolfed down a breakfast from McDonald's, something he had not done in years, then he managed to plant himself in the library again, but he still was not thinking clearly. He wrote Celia an email but did not want to put anything too incriminating in print. *Can we chat? I owe you an apology.* He had done this because he had doubts about Elise's fidelity. Because she undermined him in so many ways. The madness of the act had reason, after all. And of course Yasemin was looking for him now, too, had already sent him two emails before the tentative knock at his carrel door came, of course she would know his exact hiding place. It was Yasemin and not Celia who wanted to see what he was working on, who searched hungrily for evidence of how far he'd come in completing his dissertation, though he played it coy, showing her a few of the travel fragments, reciting one or two of his favorite descriptions of Sidi Maarif. The carrel now seemed tailored for liaisons, with a beige sheet he'd rigged up in the window so that no one could disturb him. Yasemin switched off the light, biting his neck and pulling him onto his knees on the thin Moroccan *kilim* on the floor. After this he sent her away, begged her to go, to not bother him again. He lied that he'd been tormented by desire for her ever since their first year together at Princeton, and if nothing he was even more fascinated with her by now, but that he would be absolutely devastated if this were to end his marriage. He was not really surprised when she agreed, knew she was the kind of woman motivated more by competition with other women than by actual interest in him. Plus there was, she implied, something off-and-on with Edgar, and it was not in her interest to have this get any further either, to damage the fragile chemistry of their cohort. And so they made a pact: this would not happen again, they would not speak of it to anyone, and it was over, finished, done. Peter went home that afternoon and took two of Elise's Ambiens until he was knocked out, in a dreamless sleep that kept him dead to the world for the next eighteen hours, when he woke, famished and haggard in the light of the next afternoon, Elise due on the train any moment now.

* * *

If the very idea did not go completely against Peter's nature, Elise would have allowed Caitlin to convince her that he was having an affair. The signs were there: his growing impatience with her, his lack of interest in sex, the way he claimed to spend his entire day in the library without producing anything. Caitlin's own husband, Martin, was certainly cheating on her, especially since there were many nights he did not come home from the city at all, preferring instead to stay in his Soho loft when he was "working late." Working late meant attending to his nightclubs and restaurants, and Elise had seen tangible evidence of his indiscretions: photos of a red-faced, intoxicated Martin on the society pages of *New York* magazine, usually with one or two gaunt and coked-up models on his arm.

Caitlin advised Elise not to confront him, instead suggesting that she do what Caitlin longed to do but could not: get even.

"Don't let him get away with it. You've given up your career for him," Caitlin had said. "Remember what we used to say about monogamy being a way for society to take control over women's bodies? It's always the women who pay the price. We should be having some fun of our own instead."

Caitlin hated being out of commission: stuck in a large renovated farmhouse in Connecticut with her two small children while Martin had all the fun. Up close, Caitlin's situation no longer seemed enviable to Elise. Her children were little hovering, whining presences who buzzed around her all day, making demands, until they finally went to bed at night. They were exhausting, and Elise was utterly bored by the developmental games Caitlin played with them: the gluing of pipe cleaners on construction paper, the Sisyphean monotony of blocks stacked up, then knocked over, again and again. Elise hoped she would not feel this way about her own children.

"Once you have a baby, he'll become the doting husband again," Caitlin told her. "Martin did, for awhile. He was completely attentive for several months after the kids were born. Came home every night. Peter will, too. He doesn't have the same kind of lifestyle as Martin, where it's easy to go back to his old ways. With Peter, this will be a one-time thing. Men are like children, really, wanting to express their independence, to show that no woman can tie them down, even if they're married. He's probably just doing this because he's mad that you're pushing him to finish his dissertation."

"I don't know, I tend to think the affair is with his dissertation and not with a real flesh-and-blood woman," Elise said. Caitlin said nothing, but her look seemed to say, *you'll see*.

If Caitlin were correct (and Elise still had her doubts), she wondered whom he might be having an affair with. There was the professor whom Peter was a teaching assistant for, a Lebanese woman in her early forties. Samira Khoury possessed a classic, Lebanese beauty, with high cheekbones, arched eyebrows and sunken dark brown eyes fringed with an obscene amount of eyelashes. She knew he and Samira spent time together preparing for their class, but he'd also claimed that Samira was a lesbian. And then there was Yasemin, the overly flirtatious Turkish grad student, who always cornered Peter at parties and could barely bring herself to acknowledge Elise's existence. But Peter had always complained about Yasemin, the way she undermined the other students' work, her sniping comments delivered in a breathless little baby voice that belied how nasty and competitive she could be.

Although no other candidates came immediately to mind (and Elise had actually spent one day in the Princeton library checking up on him to make sure he was in his carrel when he said he would be), she continued to worry about their marriage. When Caitlin pressed her for details about her fertility struggles, Elise finally confessed everything, making Caitlin the third person, after Peter and Dr. Geiger, who knew. She did not tell Caitlin about Celia, implying instead that the donation would be anonymous. Perhaps Caitlin was right that she needed to speed up the egg donation process to draw Peter back into the marriage. When Celia finally signed and returned the legal documents, their transaction seemed a bit more secure. By February, if all went well, she would be pregnant.

In the meantime, Caitlin's offhand remark that she should also have an affair stuck in her mind. Having an affair could disrupt her equilibrium but, on the other hand, what equilibrium did she really have right now? With no small amount of guilt she concealed these thoughts of an affair from Dr. Geiger, preferring instead to focus in their sessions on Peter and the marriage. Dr. Geiger had offered numerous useful suggestions for strengthening the marriage, and some of them seemed to be working. After Elise returned from visiting Caitlin, she could detect some small but positive changes. He was less rigid about his daily run, only jumping up every other morning rather than every day, preferring instead to linger in bed in the cold of early morning until they got up to share a mug of coffee. Although he still did not reach for her in the night, at least he was a little more present in the relationship.

For Thanksgiving they had planned to go to his parents' house. The several hours they spent in the car together driving up to Boston were perhaps the most they'd talked in weeks. Elise tried to be supportive as he discussed the progress in his writing and his hopes that Youssef Kronenberg would like his chapter, while she admitted her own fears about giving up her career, hinting that she might like to go back to work full time if the egg donation business did not work out. Afraid that he might want to stop the process, she wasn't ready to tell him yet that she was willing to adopt. And after being around Caitlin's kids so much recently, she wondered if she was even ready to be a parent at all.

"Maybe we could rent a place between here and New York to make it easier for you to commute," he suggested. "Or we could move back there while I write. I could easily work in the library at Columbia."

She was surprised at the generosity of this idea, particularly considering his previous insistence that it was essential for him to be in Princeton for the entire time he was writing his dissertation.

Being around his parents, who sometimes seemed fonder of her than they were of their own son, made the relationship seem more stable. Unlike her mother, Peter's mother did not fault her for quitting her job, and Elise had hinted they were trying to start a family. Patricia affirmed her approval of this decision, as if Elise's efforts to get pregnant might be blocked by too much of a focus on other tasks. Patricia herself was an industrious woman, serving on the board of several museums, perfecting her cooking skills through classes at a local culinary institute, and volunteering at a homeless shelter. Observing Patricia's example, Elise, who had grown up being told by her mother that homemakers did nothing productive for society, felt better about her decision to stay home. Peter's father was fond of her too, though he was rarely around. At sixty-five Barry showed no signs of wanting to retire from his private practice, and he was often gone from seven in the morning until seven at night. They had one other child, a daughter named Adrienne, who was two years younger than Peter and worked in Seattle as a computer programmer. Adrienne lived too far away to come home much, and at any rate had inherited her father's devotion to work, disappointing her mother by showing no interest in marrying or having children.

As far as Elise could tell, Patricia and Barry's forty-year marriage was rock solid (they had met while he was in med school at Harvard, Patricia an undergraduate at Radcliffe), although Peter once confided that it had had its shaky moments. He thought Barry might have had an affair with one of his receptionists, years before, and as a result, Patricia had briefly veered toward dependence on prescription Valium. But those days were long past, and both Barry and Patricia had long since resolved the excesses of their youth.

Patricia's wine collection made their visits even more entertaining. The basement of their three-story house was a wine cellar, with special temperature controls and walls lined with blonde wood shelves that showcased their collection to great effect. Elise studied the labels, trying to memorize their names so she could look them up later on the Internet, ostensibly to learn what the wine experts had to say, but surreptitiously to check on the prices of the wines they'd drunk.

"Elise, you'll still have wine, won't you?" Patricia asked when they arrived. It was a not-so-subtle attempt to find out if she'd had any luck yet in getting pregnant.

"For the moment, yes," she said. Patricia poured her a glass of shiraz to go with the roast beef she'd prepared for dinner. Peter closely resembled his mother, whose dark eyes and chestnut hair suggested a hint of Mediterranean blood, even though Patricia insisted her ancestors had all been Scottish and French Huguenot. She was delicate and fine-boned, still beautiful in her early sixties and possessing a more aristocratic bearing than her husband. Barry had the build of a former quarterback, his sandy hair now turned a silvery gray, his blue eyes and ruddy complexion hinting at what Peter termed his Pennsylvania-Dutch farm origins, although by the time Barry was born his own father had long since left the farm to become a captain of industry.

On Thanksgiving morning Patricia and Elise started with mimosas while removing the turkey from its brine, then basting its skin with a mixture of apple juice, cognac and butter. Over cheddar-olive biscuits, they talked about books and culture, the art world and Patricia's volunteer work. Patricia uncorked a Riesling from the Pacific Northwest that she had just discovered, and they nibbled at crackers and camembert while putting together the oyster stuffing, asparagus with browned butter and shallots, and Patricia's homemade cranberry sauce. Elise placed a pumpkin pie into the cavernous professional oven, then helped Patricia toss a green salad with cherry tomatoes and avocado, taking the first sips of a 1988 *Lafite Rothschild* Bourdeaux that Patricia had uncorked for the occasion. Peter and Barry were largely absent from this domestic scene, having run a Thanksgiving Day Turkey Trot 5K before both retired to their separate rooms.

"Barry works so much that when he has time off, he just sleeps," Patricia said. "I wish he'd retire so we could travel more. Most of our other friends have stopped working by now, and they travel all the time."

"I can see where Peter gets his discipline," Elise said. "Every morning up at six thirty for his daily run, in the library by eight, home at seven every night."

Patricia was just as eager as Elise was for him to finish. At least Patricia could count on Adrienne's progress in her career to yield news to report to her friends. In his mother's eyes, Peter had spent the past several years treading water.

"I'd love to see him get an appointment at Amherst or Harvard," Patricia said. "But there are so many good schools around here that he could really have his pick. Middle Eastern Studies is such a hot field these days. It would be great to have one of my babies close by." Elise said nothing, but she knew Peter did not want to move back to Boston. They had talked about California, or maybe out west somewhere, just to have the experience of leaving the East Coast for a while. But the danger of academia was that he could not really have his pick of a particular region or place. If the jobs were in rural Missouri, he would go to rural Missouri. Elise wondered if she could handle this. But then, the South had produced Celia, who was whip-smart and possessed depths which Elise was only just beginning to fathom.

They set the table at four, Elise feeling pleasantly, warmly drunk, full of good will toward her in-laws and confident that she belonged in this family. At lunch she and Peter's parents talked about a new exhibit at the Isabella Stuart Gardner museum that Patricia wanted them to see, and Barry and Patricia's upcoming sailing trip on the Aegean.

"You'll have to give me a few book recommendations for the trip," Patricia said. "I'd love to read something set in Greece, just to get a feel for the place."

Barry, whose literary interests centered principally on works about investment and golf, put down his glass of wine.

"Find her a book like *The Da Vinci Code*, so she can fill me in about all the ways Greek civilization was secretly run and organized by the ladies." He looked at his son for approval, but Peter did not laugh. Elise wondered if his father had any idea about the latest subject of his son's dissertation. Peter said little during dinner, drinking only a single glass of wine and glancing from time to time at the minuscule portions of turkey that Elise had put on her plate.

"So much for eating on a day of abundance," he said at one point, when his parents' attention was elsewhere.

"I snacked a lot while we were cooking," Elise said.

"Right. Getting smashed with my mother is more like it."

She said nothing, but over the weekend his mood worsened. He refused to go with Elise and Patricia to see the new art exhibit, insisting that he could not spare even a moment from his dissertation.

"I've already wasted enough time," he said. "I lose two days just with the driving alone." Instead he spent the remaining two days of his vacation in the library at Harvard, coming home well after dark while Elise played the role of Patricia's surrogate daughter.

"His father has his moods too; he gets that from him," Patricia said over lunch at a bistro close to Harvard. They had chosen the restaurant because of its proximity to the library, yet at the last minute Peter had emailed, saying he was onto something and couldn't meet them for lunch.

"His moods seem worse than usual," Elise said. "I'm not sure what I've done to contribute to them."

"You've done nothing, darling. I know my son. He was like this when he came back from the Peace Corps. It's a phase, and it'll pass. You know, when he came back from Morocco he didn't speak to us for several months."

"Why not?" Elise said. Peter had never mentioned this before.

"He announced he wanted to do humanitarian work. He didn't feel we were being supportive of his plans, because we urged him to get a job first and become a humanitarian later. What did he know about humanitarian work? He could have gone to Washington and started by working there, but he didn't do that. He just got angry. We only felt his plans were ill-conceived, you know, but he was resentful."

"I've tried to be patient." Elise felt tears leaking from her eyes.

"I know you have," Patricia said, patting her hand. "This, too, shall pass. It hurt me to no end when he pushed me away, but he came back."

But Elise had never seen Peter sharing much affection with his mother, and she wondered if he had ever really come back. In the car on the way back home, Peter was still distant. Elise tried to get him to talk about it.

"We were actually communicating on the drive up," she said. "What happened?"

"Nothing," he said. "Do I always have to be communicative?"

"Your mother told me you were like this when you came back from the Peace Corps," she said. "Is it something I did?"

"You've been talking about me to my mother?" he said, keeping his eyes focused on the road in front of him. "You're always analyzing me with other people. It's bad enough you do that with Dr. Geiger. But my own mother? I didn't know you were both ganging up on me."

"I didn't do that. I just wanted some clues from her about how to understand you."

"She's the last person you should be approaching for advice about how to understand me."

"Who am I supposed to approach, then?"

"No one," he said. They were both silent for a few minutes, and then he spoke. "I don't know why you're suddenly so enamored with them. They're so bourgeois, and you used to hate that stuff. Like my mom with her wine cellar and her charitable pastimes. And my fucking father, absent and always working. They're the last people whose shoes we should want to fill. Although maybe you should start a wine collection. You certainly drink enough of it."

"I don't know where this resentment is coming from." She practiced what Dr. Geiger was always urging her to do, wording her discontent in the first person so Peter wouldn't feel accused. "I feel like this is undeserved." Ugh, the passive voice was so awkward and cringe-inducing.

He responded with silence. The rare and brief good mood he'd been in prior to the Thanksgiving trip was a fluke, and he was more intractable than ever. Elise was quiet the rest of the way home, thinking about what to do. He would never consent to couples' therapy, would see it as more pressure. Was the answer just to pull back entirely, to quit trying to talk about anything until he came around? Or should she do something else?

The answer came to her as she turned on her computer to check her messages. There was one email from Celia, a forwarded article about the risks of the follicle-stimulating hormone she would inject to produce more eggs. 3-5% of the ova donors developed a painful and dangerous condition from the hyper-stimulation of the ovaries. She hoped Celia wasn't planning to back out again. Another email was from Caitlin, asking if things were any better with Peter. *No*, Elise typed, adding a frowning face directly after it. *I'm still thinking about what to do about that. Am considering all options at this point.* Then she saw she had a message from Eric Babu, suggesting another lunch date. But this time, he said, how about reserving the whole afternoon? *I just got a new espresso maker, want to stop by for some coffee next time you are in the city?* Peter had gone out for a run, and she was alone in the apartment. She thought only for a second before writing him back. *Sounds great*, she typed. *You name the day.* Then she went on Facebook. Her husband's page, as usual, was blank. On her own page, she typed: *things are gonna change, I can feel it.*

* * *

The carrel had been defiled, cursed, and since they'd come back from Boston, Peter had not been able to write a single word. The usual scraps of archival fantasy failed to inspire him. He had made a terrible mistake by letting Yasemin into his workspace, altering the *feng shui* and forever disrupting its solemnity. At least he had a meeting planned with his advisor, and hopefully the positive feedback from what he'd already written might induce him to continue. In the meanwhile he would take some time off, spending the day at his desk rereading some of the weirder Sufi poetry, with all its references to wine-drunk, spinning ecstasy, the beauty of beardless boys and the impossibility of uniting with the Beloved, with the Obscure Object of Desire that was Unknowable Essence, Unstoppable Force, and Immovable Object.

Peter disliked the whole culture of therapy, but after several years of being married to someone who used the jargon incessantly, he found himself exhibiting many of the symptoms that might cause a psychiatrist to raise an eyebrow. He was "compartmentalizing," trying to place his infidelity into a separate part of his brain, refusing to admit that what happened affected his feelings about his marriage. The affair was a "reaction formation," which from what he understood meant committing the most unexpected, out-of-character act in an attempt to prove that he wasn't locked into his own stagnant behavioral patterns. Then there was the fact that he was following in his father's footsteps, which Elise and Dr. Geiger would have a field day over, if they knew or could discuss the issue dispassionately. (He could picture Elise and her bearded guru smugly commenting on his misogyny as a mask for all sorts of latent Freudian parental complexes). Finally his urge to categorize, to make order of his life (which he assured himself couldn't be "obsessive/compulsive," didn't OCD people wash their hands a lot?) had gotten worse.

He sat in his carrel, drinking a double espresso and trying to stay awake. That morning he'd woken up at four but could not bring himself to rise from bed until the red digital letters flipped from 6:29 to 6:30. On a particularly difficult run through the dark and icy drizzle, he'd fallen on a slippery bridge, his skinned and swollen knee further punishment for his indiscretions. Elise was still in bed, a pillow over her head, and he bit his lip to keep from cursing as he poured rubbing alcohol on the wound.

A part of him (there it was, the compartmentalization again) feared he had destroyed everything. His shock at seeing Kevin in the hallway of Celia's dorm almost made him believe in the "bad karma" Elise often talked about. Running into Kevin was his unlucky punishment, the evidence that could potentially destroy him, though he was not quite sure whether under University regulations he'd done anything wrong. Being in a dorm wasn't illegal, was it? And he wasn't a real professor, just a graduate student teaching assistant. But it did matter; she was still a student. He could be accused of abusing his power, even if people found out they'd only kissed. Kevin did not show up in his Arabic class the next day, and then school was closed for Thanksgiving, so it was still a mystery what action he might take. He wondered if Kevin had been following him all along, waiting for the slightest misstep, bent on his quest to destroy him.

Maybe the marijuana had destabilized him. He'd stopped smoking pot years before when the peaceful, easy feeling it gave him was replaced by a dull paranoia, a sense that the four walls surrounding his life contained no exit door and were shrinking in on him by the year. But at the party he felt wonderful, convinced that whatever he did was correct and almost fated, a feeling he'd been able to sustain for at least an entire week.

He realized he'd been wrong to think he could handle this. On so many levels his actions were reprehensible: he had intended to sleep with his wife's egg donor (even if it hadn't happened), she was only twenty, he should have known better. And then he had done something even more despicable with Yasemin. His misdeeds could be fodder for a daytime talk show, and he imagined himself confessing in a dispassionate, psychotic monotone to the rising jeers of an audience, Celia, Elise and Yasemin sitting on the other side of Maury Povich, clad in little sundresses, ready to begin ripping out tufts of each other's hair in a staged catfight. To punish himself he began watching these shows at night, along with the reality programs where people lived their sloppy, mistake-filled lives for an invisible audience. At least their destruction was public, shared, appealing to the human instinct that must have once led people to rally around public hangings or delight in watching gladiators spear each other into oblivion.

He checked his emails once he was safely back in the library, changing the password just in case Elise knew it somehow. Fortunately there was nothing from Yasemin. There was one email from Celia that had come over the break, which he had not opened. He had written to her, explaining that it was a good thing Kevin had been in the hall that night because otherwise they would have done something they would have both regretted. She had not responded until now.

Dear Peter,
I'm writing this from a deserted campus, since everyone seems to have gone somewhere for Thanksgiving except for me. Someone from student services actually called and invited me to a professor's house for dinner. I guess I should have jumped at the invitation to break bread with the Woodrow Wilson School prof who invented a mathematical formula to analyze the effectiveness of microcredit loans, but I said no. Instead I hung out with the international kids who'd also declined their invitations. It was fine. What better way to commemorate American genocide than with institutional gravy and charity cases from the former British Empire, right?

Peter frowned. He did not remember her being so cynical.

I left your coat next to the mailboxes in your department, just as you asked me to do. You don't have to worry about me saying anything. We can forget that anything ever happened. Money is particularly an issue for me right now, and I need for everything to go smoothly. If all goes well, we might be able to try for January to have the process completed before the beginning of the second semester, and I'd like to get it over with before the second thoughts I've been having get out of control.

I don't want to be the reason that everything came crashing down for you. Although, given what I heard from Nicole about the girl you finally did go home with, maybe I'm not.

Again, you can count on my discretion.

Her discretion. So Celia knew something had happened with Yasemin, too. If she had figured it out, could Elise be far from knowing? His father had spoken of discretion as well. Barry had known without asking that something was wrong. During his visit home, Barry took him aside one night and said,

"I don't know what's going on between you and Elise, but pull yourself together. We all get tired of our marriages sometimes. Men are not, by our nature, programmed to be with one woman for the rest of our lives. Do whatever you have to, but be a man about it. You haven't done enough yet to be having a mid-life crisis." Barry patted him on the back, an attempt at a fatherly gesture, but Peter was still dwelling on his father's comment about his accomplishments. "Try to be a little more discreet."

Barry's manner was almost smug, as if pleased that his son was taking his rightful place amid the pantheon of rogues who recognized monogamy as an impossible demand. Peter remembered how devastating his father's affairs had been for his mother. There had been more than one, but he only told Elise about his father's secretary, not wanting to prejudice her too much against his father. In fact, there had been numerous instances, and he sometimes found himself hating both his parents: his father for being so casual about it and his mother for putting up with it. Affairs were greedy things that took on a life of their own. He did not know how Barry could have been so certain, after all his dalliances, that he still wanted to be married. He remembered the bachelor party before his wedding when a friend had lifted his champagne glass and said,

"Congratulations on your starter marriage." Almost a curse, that one comment had been enough to end the friendship, but the former friend had succeeded in placing a small grain of doubt in Peter's mind that he constantly fought, even during the best of times. At first his feelings for Elise were strong and uncomplicated. She had allowed him to glimpse the side of her that was tense and fragile, which nobody at Smyth & Copperfield could have imagined lay beneath her confident, steely exterior. She had loved him, too, once, but he wondered if she still did. Celia had confirmed something he'd long suspected, that Elise had once been involved with Eric Babu (and possibly was again), which left him feeling fundamentally betrayed. Babu was, after all, the pretense that brought them together, but now that pretense was being revealed as artifice, a conspiracy on Elise and Eric's part to toy with him.

Peter pushed aside his books, pressing his temple against the cool metal surface of his desk. Somehow he fell asleep, waking with a start to look at his watch and see that it was half past eleven and that he'd missed the first half of his class. He felt panicked; what was happening to him? Dr. Khoury would be livid—he'd given her no warning, had not even excused himself as sick.

He sent a quick note to Samira Khoury, apologizing that he had suddenly come down with the flu and hadn't been able to make it to class. Surely he could miss one class. There were more emails he was ignoring, most significantly an ominous note from his advisor. *I know we're supposed to meet on Wednesday, but it would be better if you could stop by today. There's something we need to discuss.* Had Kevin reported him? Or was it something about his writing?

Avoiding everything was a tempting option. So was going home and crawling into bed to sleep, except that inevitably Elise would be there. Not in bed but lounging around the apartment, chattering on the phone with Caitlin or reading books about organic pregnancies and raising green babies. Green babies. In better days they would have laughed at the fact that a book about green babies would have meant nothing, fifteen years earlier. What was a green baby, a monster? A jealous infant? They would have had a discussion about the funny new ways language had changed in their lifetimes. To google someone. To have a staycation. To be meterosexual. Or was it metrosexual?

Be a man. Pull yourself together. He had stolen a sheet from his father's prescription pad and written himself a scrip for more Ambien. After all these years of experience as a doctor's son, at the very least he could copy his handwriting. But he needed something stronger. Locking his carrel behind him, he trudged up the stairs and walked across campus toward the health center. The trees were bare of leaves now, and above him the sky hung low, threatening snow. Snow would be good. The white would absolve him; he could go someplace wide and flat, like the Princeton battlefield, and gaze out at the white expanse in front of him, imagining the long-ago battles that people no longer cared about. At the health center he located the counseling office, asking the administrative assistant in a low voice if he could make an appointment. Although he didn't particularly want to talk to anybody, he knew that this was the drill: confess and we'll give you the pills. She gave him an appointment for later in the week.

At home he tried to be nicer to Elise, but he could not pull himself out of the tremendous gray hole that had sucked him in. The hole was gray and not black, he would tell the psychologist, it was indeterminate and nebulous, it was the grayness of the stone buildings, rain-soaked pavement, flat sky. All it would have taken were a few gentle words to Elise: *I'm sorry I've been like this lately, I'm going through a phase, it's not you, it's me,* but those were weak words, not the words of a Man Who Needed to Pull Himself Together or a Man Who Needed to be Discreet. At dinner he was morose and silent, barely managing to comment on the excellent food she prepared, the only sound the tinny ring of knives and forks striking against their dinner plates. Elise was doubling her efforts at being a good housewife: there was *coq au vin* one night, lamb *rogan josh* with fresh *naan* and *samosas* the next. He drank several beers to wash down the spicy food but it did not make him any more loquacious. By this point she'd given up trying to draw him into conversation.

On Wednesday he faced his Arabic class, sending them through drills and conjugations without much inspiration, answering their questions about a film Dr. Khoury had required them to see, one about the Palestinian Intifada. He ignored Kevin's usual inflammatory remarks, not even caring enough to craft a response.

"I don't study Palestine," he said. "You'll have to ask Dr. Khoury what she thinks. My focus is strictly on the medieval period, which contains all the lessons we need to understand the Middle East today."

"Isn't that what you would call a reductionist Orientalist argument?" Haley asked. "The idea that people have an unchanging essence that can be found in ancient texts?"

"You can call it whatever you want," said Peter. She was right, this was a good argument against his entire dissertation plan. "But it's no more ridiculous than other arguments that get printed in newspapers with wide circulations. Take Thomas Friedman's Golden Arches theory, for example. No two countries with McDonald's restaurants will ever go to war with one another. What a bunch of crap. Can you really learn anything about the world from that theory? This is a problem. We're too invested in stupid, simplistic theories."

They looked at him, saying nothing. They were a captive audience, a sea of eager, impressionable faces.

"Empires rise and fall. Look at the Ottoman Empire. They once controlled the entire Middle East and some of Eastern Europe as well. Bulgaria to Algeria. What if I argued that countries with names ending in *–ria* will never go to war with one another? Theories explain nothing. But anyway." He realized he was rambling. "We live in a dying empire right now and we're too stupid to see that it's ending. We can't see the signs." Some of the faces in the sea were no longer meeting his eyes. It was no longer clear that he had their attention. Kevin began to argue that their empire was not dying at all, that in fact that decline of the manufacturing sector had been replaced by American preeminence in the service sector.

"Kevin, this is way off topic," he said. "Let's review our conjugations."

After class, he braced himself for his meeting with Youssef Kronenberg. He worried that Kronenberg had received a formal complaint that Peter was seen in the dorms, kissing a half-naked undergraduate. He prepared himself for the worst, but at least his advisor would find something redeeming in his writing, he was fairly sure of that. His writing would reveal that he was still on track.

Kronenberg had one of the largest offices in the department, with a sumptuous blue Persian carpet on the floor, Arabic calligraphic art (four of Allah's ninety-nine names) in gold frames on the walls, and oak bookshelves that stretched nearly to the ceiling. A Moroccan lantern hung in the middle, casting the shapes of stars and moons on the ceiling. Kronenberg sat at his desk, reading by the light of a lamp.

"*A salam wa-alaykum*, Boutros," the professor said, greeting him by his name in Arabic.

"*Wa alaykum salam.*" Peter sat down. Kronenberg closed his book and looked over his eyeglasses at Peter for a moment before speaking.

"Peter. What happened?"

"I'm sorry?" The best approach was to play dumb, not to admit guilt until he was accused. Or maybe he did not need to admit his guilt after all. Celia would lie for him, would say it was Kevin's conspiracy to threaten the academic integrity of his professors.

"We missed you at the department research presentations last week before Thanksgiving." Oh. That. He'd been mortified at the thought of running into Yasemin.

"Something came up," he said. "Family emergency."

"And you couldn't let anyone know? That's not like you. I don't have to remind you that these meetings are important."

Peter said nothing.

"But this brings me to something else we need to discuss." Peter braced himself. Had he been caught?

"That writing sample you gave me. Is this something from your dissertation?"

"Yeah," Peter said, aware that he was supposed to introduce it somehow, to explain what he'd shoved into Kronenberg's mailbox that fateful night.

Kronenberg picked up the document and began thumbing through it. Peter could see the first few pages covered in red ink, but then it looked as if he'd stopped reading.

"Do you want to tell me what you were going for here?"

"It's a new direction," Peter explained. "I stumbled upon some archival material about the Spanish colonial occupation of Morocco. I think it's pretty significant."

"You can't write something like this. It's speculation. Your argument has no legs to stand on, so to speak. You base almost eighty pages of writing on a few fragments of text. This isn't scholarship. This is…" Kronenberg searched for a word, letting the manuscript drop on the desk with a thud. "Fiction."

"I've got more evidence to back it up," Peter said, trying to keep the panic out of his voice. "I just need to get to the archives in Madrid. And I've heard the French colonial archives in Nantes also have some relevant documents--"

Kronenberg cut him off.

"Listen, Boutros, I'm just calling it like I see it. This is not what you said you'd write about in your dissertation proposal, which the department approved. This is unacceptable. I'm going to need to see something better from you by the end of the term, or else--"

"Or else what?"

"Let's not take it there just yet," he said, his voice softening. "You know what to do. Back to the drawing board."

Kronenberg handed him the document, and Peter tried to control his hands from shaking as he took it. Although he was relieved that he hadn't been called out for his crimes, he felt a deep sense of despair that his professor had just dismissed the only thing he'd managed to write so far. He longed, suddenly, to ask Kronenberg his secret for Being In the World. How had he managed to get to this position of confident authority, sitting behind his gleaming wooden desk surrounded by his ridiculous souvenirs, his framed calligraphic prints of God's ninety-nine names, the decorative hookah and silver tea set atop his filing cabinets? But the distance between Peter and tenured professor was so vast it might have been the unbridgeable distance between stars.

Peter stood there for a moment, clutching his manuscript, but Kronenberg had returned to his desk, clearly finished with their encounter. Numb, Peter wandered over to the graduate student lounge to hold his office hours. He went through the motions of opening the Arabic textbook to prepare the next week's lesson, but he stared at the swirling Arabic script and could not bring his mind to translate.

"Professor."

Kevin stood in the doorway. Peter's heart sank even more deeply, and he wondered if his day could get any worse. Kevin sat down in the chair across from Peter, making an exaggerated gesture out of taking off his baseball cap.

"How am I doing in your class?" Kevin asked.

"From what I've seen, you've been around a solid B the entire semester."

"I'm planning to write a pretty stellar paper for the end of the semester," Kevin said. "Free of bias, or anything at all controversial. I'm going to write about the philosopher Averroes and his influence on Western thought."

"That sounds great," Peter said, without much enthusiasm. "So what can I do for you?" Kevin smiled innocently.

"I just wanted to let you know about my paper. To see what you thought of the topic."

"Your topic sounds very interesting."

Kevin leaned in toward Peter, lowering his voice. Peter braced himself. Up close, his student's face glistened with sweat, the pimples on his skin standing out in sharp relief against his white skin.

"I also wanted to tell you that I'm planning to go to medical school after college. It's really hard to get in these days. Your grades have to be perfect. I'm thinking my final paper will be so good that it will raise my grade to an A. I believe you're in charge of grading for this class, right?"

"There's also the final exam," Peter said. "Raising your grade is contingent on a solid performance on the exam, once we get back from the holiday break."

"That's something else I wanted to talk to you about," Kevin said. "I won't be able to make it to the exam. I'm going to be in Vail."

The nerve of this student! The heat rose in Peter's face.

"And your other exams?" Peter asked, trying to stay calm. "Will you be missing those as well?"

"No, they happen to be scheduled at better times. But your exam time is just not convenient."

"I'm sorry the timing of the exam interferes with your vacation plans," Peter said quietly. "But you will appear for it, or risk losing the B and failing entirely."

"I think you'll see my final paper more than compensates for missing the exam. You'll probably be too busy grading to notice I'm not in the room. If you did happen to notice, I might also remind you that there's already a complaint pending about your political bias in the classroom. If the administration heard you've also been… um, consorting with undergraduates, they might not look too kindly on that."

"This is bullshit," Peter said, shaking his head. "You'd better be at that exam."

"Is that a wedding ring you're wearing?" Kevin said. "Well, I guess I'd better be going. I look forward to seeing you in class next week."

Peter slammed the book closed, lowering his head onto his arms. His forehead felt hot. The enormity of everything that had happened pressed down on him. Had he done all of this? Had he willfully brought down his carefully ordered world? His only hope had been that brilliant kernel of wisdom he'd imagined lay at the core of his dissertation, but now Kronenberg had taken that away, too. How simple it would be just to give Kevin a good grade, to abandon what was left of his ethical principles. What did it matter? Tomorrow he would see the Princeton psychologist. By the time the January exam period rolled around (*in sha Allah*, God willing), he would find a solution.

CHAPTER ELEVEN

*In darkness, his foundling
is weightless, all apparition
and remote coolness. His hands
touch the sharp points of the blades
that carry her shoulders, the soft hollow
of her lower back. He is dreaming of towns
blanketed in white, drifting faces,
snow banks, the white sea parting before him.
Conscripted now in the service
of his own words, the girl a gift
or curse he has given himself.*

Celia put down the paper she was reading from and looked around at her classmates. Maggie was blushing fiercely, scribbling something on her paper. Bruce nodded his head and tapped his pencil on the table in front of him. Nicole had a half smile on her face, nodding at her in approval.

"Bravo, Celia," Carla said, clapping her hands together. "You've come a long way. Really, you've improved so much across genres. I look forward to your bright future in the writing program." It was the last reading of the semester, the last time her work would be critiqued. She knew the other students would have no idea what the poem referred to. This was for Nicole, it was all for Nicole, to whom she'd made allusions about a great many things happening that night, only half of them true. She had never actually lied about what had happened, in fact, had intended to tell her everything the day after Nicole's party when they met for brunch. Over pancakes at PJ's she was relishing her new role as Scheherezade, letting the suspense draw out, describing how she brought Peter back to her room.

"I keep thinking about what you said at the party. 'The wedding ring is only a minor obstacle with the married man.' I hardly had to do anything at all."

"I wouldn't know," said Nicole.

"You mean you've never been with a guy who was married?"

"It's something I'd like to do," Nicole said casually, as if sleeping with a married man were a career ambition. "Not out of any perverse desire to wreck someone's marriage. Just to see it from the other side, to understand why men are like that."

"But what about your poem? "The Eggshell Mistress." That one was all about sleeping with a married guy."

Nicole laughed.

"Celia, it's just a poem. Nobody said it had to have happened to me. You don't need to take a vow of truth when you write poetry."

Celia was quiet for a moment. She'd stopped the story at the point where they kissed, having said nothing yet about how Peter was part of the couple she was going to donate her eggs to.

"Anyway," Nicole sighed, "I think that he's kind of a player."

"What do you mean?" she asked. And as Nicole talked, she tried not to reveal how hurt she was when her friend reported that Peter had returned to the party, that he'd asked for Nicole's phone number, and that she'd seen him drunk off his ass and leaving with his arms around the Turkish girl. This was devastating, worse than what Celia imagined. Why had Peter felt it necessary to stick to his principles with her while abandoning them with the Turkish girl?

"What an asshole," she said, pretending to laugh it off. "Well, we didn't sleep together. He got up and walked out of the room and got busted by one of his students in my hallway. So obviously he ended up back at your place…" she trailed off. "But it didn't matter, because by then I was somewhere else entirely. You won't believe where."

"Tell me," Nicole said, breathless.

"In Eric Babu's hotel room."

"Holy shit, how did you end up there?" Finally she had succeeded in doing something to impress Nicole. Celia did not mention how she had humiliated herself in front of Peter's apartment door, before coming home to think up a way that she could redeem this night for some literary value. Wanting to do something brave and crazy, she remembered a small detail from the reading earlier in the night: Eric Babu's anger at being placed in a hotel suite named for a slave owner. The Witherspoon Suite. It had been easy enough to locate a map online of the suite layouts in the Nassau Inn, and then to fix her makeup and party dress, putting on Nicole's heels and walking over to the hotel, striding into the lobby as if she had a reason to be there. She did not know what she'd say, exactly, when she got to Babu's room. If she were really brave, she decided, she would tell him that she was an escort, sent by Elise to keep him company in her absence. But when he answered the door in plaid, flannel pajamas, rubbing sleep from his eyes and looking slightly alarmed at this apparition presenting herself in the middle of the night, what had seemed a brilliant plot from the safety of her dorm room now struck her as utterly ridiculous if not insane.

But she played the groupie, told him how much his words had meant to her, mumbling something about the significance of his work that she'd patched together from her classes and her conversations with

Elise. He thanked her, asking if she wanted an autograph. She agreed and followed him inside. The suite was subtly tropical by way of the British Empire, with a palm tree bedspread and 19th century prints of palm trees on the wall, a few faded safari colors here and there. Was it the décor that had offended him, on top of the connection between the suite's namesake and the suffering of African slaves? She wished she could ask.

"Drink?" he offered her, gesturing at a bar concealed in a cabinet. She had a feeling from the way he offered it that he didn't really mean it.

"No, thank you," she said, feeling stiff. What would Nicole do? Undoubtedly she would know a way to take this situation further, but Celia could think of nothing to say. Had she hoped all she needed to do was show up at his door, a pretty, silly white girl in her twenties, and he would magically try to seduce her? Eric Babu took the book from her and sat down, signing the book at the page she'd opened it to, fortunately never realizing that it was the same copy he'd signed earlier that evening.

"I'm sorry about everything," she told him as she got up to go. "Interrupting your sleep. And the incident with the suite they put you in. I don't think they meant to do it intentionally."

"People never mean such slights," he said. "At least today I am an African conscripted in the service of words and not body."

His last comment stayed with her, and she recited it all the way home so she wouldn't forget it, writing it down as soon as she got back to her room. *An African conscripted in the service of words*. She would steal it later for her poem. In the harsh light of the morning the entire episode seemed a dream, and she couldn't believe she'd had the nerve to go to him, or that he hadn't thrown her out for her impetuousness. Telling Nicole all about it had been her first impulse, but after learning what Peter had been up to, she decided to hold her cards close, to keep her mouth shut about what had really happened. She could become part of the James Frey school of memoir just as easily as Nicole could.

"Let's just say," Celia said to Nicole, "that his reputation as a man who knows *exactly* what to do with women is well deserved." And Nicole had howled with amusement, telling her excitedly that she had to write about it, maybe even a creative nonfiction piece if she was willing to share the truth with the world. She nodded and smiled and said that yes, she did, in fact, have a lot to work through on the page. After breakfast, she returned to her room and cried.

She thought of Elise, then, of the way her face lost its characteristic poise when Celia threatened to back out of the donation process, leaving only a sort of naked terror that Celia realized with a shock she was responsible for. Elise had been nothing but good to her and this was how she'd thanked her, by not only trying to sleep with her husband but also knocking on the door of her former lover in the middle of the night. Something had happened with Peter, too, which felt significant even if it wasn't sex, and his rejection hurt her as well. And she cried over how she'd allowed herself to be a foot soldier for Mr. Lenhart's disgust with the world, even if his cynicism had only been enough to carry her part of the way through her intended transformation into the role of a ruthless, acquisitive schemer, eager to avenge in one blow not only the injustice of her former teacher's failed marriage but also the particular circumstances that put Elise and Peter in one socio-economic position, herself in another. But now that she was alone again, she realized that nothing was like Mr. Lenhart said it was. And so, she'd scrawled off the poem, which she recited that day in class with relish, with Nicole in mind, knowing that she had finally succeeded in impressing her. If there was a contest between who we are in real life and who we are in our writing, she thought, the literary version will always be infinitely more interesting.

To avoid raising Elise's suspicions, Celia saw her once for coffee, trying to consider their interactions solely as a business deal in the final stages of the transaction. Seeing Elise-- oblivious, frantic, nervous about the upcoming process-- made her feel terrible. But she had also begun to wonder if a baby was what Elise truly needed. From her remarks about her friend Caitlin's kids, it was clear she was not particularly fond of children. But something about the success of the whole endeavor must have been crucially important to Elise. Perhaps she saw it as a way to anchor herself back into the marriage.

In January the final procedure would take place, and everything would be over. It was a convenient time, since after exams the second semester would not begin until February. After two weeks of taking pills, Celia would learn how to give herself shots to suppress her hormones. Twenty days later, the shots would culminate in the retrieval, when her eggs would be fertilized and then implanted in Elise a few days later. Her gift finally over, her relationship with Elise and Peter could be severed forever.

More than once the idea crossed her mind that if they'd followed through, she and Peter could have done all of this without the intervention of so much technology. If sex existed for procreation, then how had the two acts come to seem so separate? What did conception mean without sex? She wondered whether children could sense the conditions under which they'd been conceived, or if test tube babies were like so many plants in a nursery, incubated in the generative heat of greenhouses before being transplanted to different yards.

In the baggage claim area of the Columbia airport, Daniel waited for her. She searched for signs of distress, noting that his face lacked the ruddy glow from working outdoors that he'd sported over fall break. He hugged her, stepping back to look her over, and she could read her transformation in his face.

"Exams wore you out?" he asked. "You've got dark circles under your eyes."

"No, Daddy, the exams are after the break," she said. "A lot of schools up north do it that way."

"That sure is weird," he said, shaking his head. "Doesn't make for much relaxation over Christmas, does it."

"I guess not," she agreed. "But I'll be fine."

He took her suitcase from her and swung her bookbag over his shoulder.

"How come you're not staying longer?"

"I'm working with a professor on an editing project," she lied. "I'm getting paid to do it."

"I was wondering what you were doing for pocket money," he said. "They never did assign you to a different office after that professor got sick, did they."

"No, they didn't." She had almost forgotten these early deceptions, their combined weight increasing her sense of estrangement from her father.

The next morning Daniel did not get up to go to work, even though it was Friday. Celia rose to make coffee, but the door to his room remained closed. She opened the Deer Bluff Sentinel and began to read the headlines: a robbery at a check-cashing store, a Christmas parade down Main Street, a local pharmacy going out of business after seventy-nine years. At nine-thirty her father appeared at the kitchen table, bleary-eyed in his scruffy USC t-shirt and pajama pants.

"You're not going to work?"

"Work?" He scratched his head, as if not quite understanding the question. "Oh, I'm not with the landscaping firm right now. They don't have much for me to do in the winter. It's seasonal."

"You didn't tell me." He turned toward the coffee maker, pouring himself a cup.

"You kept saying you were busy with your studies. I didn't want to add to your stress."

"What are you doing for money, then?"

"I've been wrapping presents at Belk in the afternoons. It's just part time, but it keeps me busy."

"The pay can't be all that good," she said, unable to picture her father measuring out Christmas paper and tying ribbons. He sat down across from her.

"It's just until I find something else. I've got my resume in at a couple places."

"Dad, why don't you leave this place?" She was suddenly exasperated. "You don't have to go to someplace like Key West. You could just pick a big city, like Columbia or Charlotte, a place with more opportunities."

"Cee, you don't understand the curse of unemployment, especially for an older man," he said. "They read 'executive manager' on my resume, they look over the gaps, and then they see the landscaping work, and it just doesn't add up. They look at my age, and they ask themselves what's wrong with this man, why'd it take him so long to get back on his feet? And you know what? I don't even want that kind of job anymore. I don't need the stress. My bills aren't so high, you're on a scholarship, I own this house, and I don't have any other mouths to feed except my own. I do alright."

"I just wish you wanted more for yourself."

"Why should I?" he said. "I only wanted more for you. I've done right by you. That's all I wanted."

She had hoped for a better moment to tell him about the internship, but he might as well be disappointed now.

"I might have a job opportunity next summer in New York. How would you feel about that, if I didn't come home?"

Daniel shrugged, trying to smile, his shoulders slumping just a little.

"You do what you have to," he said. "Of course I'd love to see you, but I knew the day would come when you would leave the nest for good. Just come home when you can."

"We can still talk on the phone a lot," she said.

"Of course we can, June bug." He reached over and squeezed her hand.

"And maybe when I finally get settled somewhere after college, you could move there too, right?"

"We'll see when the time comes. How about we do breakfast at Millie's today?"

Daniel drove while Celia stared out the window, feeling depressed. The reality of Deer Bluff, the bare, yellowed tobacco and cotton fields outside of town, the strip mall parking lots filled with the Fords and Buicks of Christmas shoppers, made Princeton seem effete by contrast. Main Street was deserted except for the illuminated Christmas wreaths and candles tacked to the tops of lampposts, most of the storefronts empty. The parade that night would pass through a street that stood as a monument to the past, a pretty place that nobody cared about inhabiting. One hundred years before, Main Street had boasted an opera house. Downgraded to a dinner theater in the 1970s before finally going out of business, the building now sat empty. The progress of modernity had done nothing for civic life in Deer Bluff.

But Daniel did not turn into the crowded Millie's parking lot, driving instead past the diner and the Starlite Motel, turning his car onto the mill road that had been swallowed by weeds and kudzu, littered with fast food hamburger wrappers and crumpled beer cans.

"It's amazing how fast nature takes over," he said. "I didn't want to tell you this on the phone, but there's something you need to see."

When they entered the clearing where Anayo Mills should have been, Celia saw only a blackened hull. She drew in her breath sharply as Daniel switched the engine off. Charred bricks crumbled into the center, and the grass was higher in some places than the walls crumbling around it. The roof and high, broken windows were gone, and the chute that had once delivered merchandise to the waiting train cars lay in a twisted metal heap among the weeds.

"I was just out here the week before it burned," he said. "I used to come here when I wanted to think. If I came after dusk I might catch couples parking back here, but otherwise I never saw anyone. I never went inside. Never knew if I'd run into a crook or a bum, or a snake, to say the least."

He kept both hands on the steering wheel, staring ahead at the ruined building.

"Hard to believe we used to bring Japanese textile machinery reps down here in limousines. Do you remember that glass case with the statues, the ones you hated so much?" Celia nodded. Just inside the entrance to the mill, the glass case had contained two life-sized mannequins dressed as stereotypical Native Americans, the male resting on a makeshift hammock made out of a sheet while the female mannequin, clad in a short, buckskin robe, stood ready to serve, a stack of white towels in her hands. A sign read, "A well-spent buck on an Anayo sheet." Even as a child, Celia had sensed there was something offensive about that sign.

"I can remember when I'd walk down the rows to see how my workers were doing. I loved the sound of the machines humming. I tried to memorize one thing about each employee, and if I read in the paper that someone in their family had passed on or married, I'd mention it to them. But you know, that didn't change anything. They still held it against me when the mill closed."

"It wasn't your fault. You were just the nearest person for them to blame."

"They took me down to the police station for questioning," he continued, still not looking at her. "Patel out at the Starlite Motel had seen a brown Taurus driving back here. I told them what I told you—I came out here sometimes to think. I won't deny it. I asked them, now, why would I have set this place on fire? It was already useless. But they eventually figured it out. Someone dropped a cigarette into a pile of leaves. What do they know? It's not like they've got forensic experts here in the Deer Bluff PD. So they decided it was one of the high school kids who came back here to get high."

Celia felt very small, pinned to the seat of the Ford Taurus, the forest looming up around them, ready to reclaim this spot for nature. She wanted to remember everything about this moment: the catch in her father's voice as he talked, the way the mill had shrunk to less than half its size, the pale winter light filtering through the full pine trees and the bare arms of the deciduous ones.

"I knew it was stupid, but I'd always hoped I'd hear one day that they were opening it up again. But I have to tell you, I just feel a big sense of relief. Now that the damned place has been burned to a crisp, I can finally move on."

He turned the car engine on and circled the old parking lot.

"Let's get some pancakes," he said.

In the afternoon he left for his part-time gift-wrapping job at Belk. Celia felt tired, more tired than she'd been in months. She climbed back into her bed and fell asleep, and when she woke up it was almost seven. Her first thought was to cook dinner for her father, but the refrigerator contained only a few cans of Coors, a hard block of cheddar with a blue film of mold encircling it, and a single egg in a carton. Opening the freezer, she saw several Swanson's and Lean Cuisine frozen dinners, neither brand offering very much appeal. There had been one TV dinner she loved as a child, when her father cooked most of their meals, allowing himself only one night off a week to heat up the metal trays in the oven. She always wanted the same thing: fish filets, tater tots, and peas, all carefully partitioned into little sections.

"For my little astronaut," he'd say as he placed the silvery tray in front of her, knowing she liked to pretend this was what they ate on the space station. On those nights she was allowed to eat in front of the television, watching the news and Entertainment Tonight back-to-back.

"Your mother would turn over in her grave," he always said, shaking his head. "She'd say we were living like trailer trash." But the other nights of the week he honored Linda's memory, doing the best he could with spaghetti and Hamburger Helper and chicken cutlets dipped in egg and cracker meal, served with a lemon and a side of mashed potatoes.

Opening a can of beer, Celia sat down at the table with her laptop. She tried to describe the way the mill had looked, wondering how an artist would see it, but her description came across as wooden and one-dimensional, doing nothing to conjure up all the feelings and associations Celia had with the place, and with her father. Her next thought was to try and write about herself, but the substance of her words had the stilted, juvenile feel of a journal that didn't begin to capture how strange and empty she felt.

After several false starts she gave up caring how the words looked on the paper, as she remembered why she liked writing in the first place. She could never really know how she felt about something until she tried a thousand times to write it down. Her writing had gotten her into college, attracted Elise's attention, and pulled Nicole, whom she had never imagined would speak to her, into her orbit. So what if her talent was not staggering but merely promising? Surely she could get somewhere with hard work, even if she lacked Nicole's obvious gift with words.

Daniel came home after nine, pouring the first in his usual series of Jack Daniels and Cokes into the familiar, battered glass and switching on the television. She had given him a set of expensive tumblers, with little bubbles blown into the bottom of the glass, which he acknowledged with a thank you and a hug, placing them in their box in the china cabinet, alongside her mother's wedding china that they never used.

He liked documentaries, flipping the channels until he found one about the origins of space, the announcer intoning in a deep, soothing voice about the mysteries contained in clouds of cosmic dust, in black holes and dying stars. She studied Daniel as he eased back into his recliner, his dark hair graduating to gray at the temples, a hole in the toe of his white athletic sock, but for once she did not try to read the disappointment she'd projected onto him in these small signs. He was simply himself, and she was neither in danger of changing him nor becoming him, the alcoholic gene merely one possible inherited affliction among others. Whether he'd set the fire at Anayo Mills or not, she might never know. She was growing away from him, but this was part of the natural order of things, and her life would increasingly be filled with stories she would be unable to share.

Celia brought him his frozen dinner on a tray in front of the television, but for every night that followed until she returned to

Princeton, Celia cooked from an old copy of the *Joy of Cooking* that had belonged to her mother. Her mother's eyes had gazed down on the same pages, translating the words into food that nourished her family. The book contained all the instructions she would need to make roast chicken and potatoes, spaghetti with meat sauce, or homemade macaroni and cheese. Her mother had given her life, but her father had sustained it, and soon she would be leaving him.

* * *

With Eric, there would be no pretense the next time they met. Elise had planned to see him at his apartment in the city, her acceptance of his veiled invitation to try out his new espresso machine tantamount to agreeing to an affair. The trick was, of course, to pretend to be oblivious to this assent, to let the encounter play itself out as if there were some doubt about the outcome, and to enjoy the flattery and attention she had not received in quite some time. In truth, she was more excited about the process of the seduction than the affair itself. He mentioned he would cook something, and she imagined Eric plying her with course after course of exotic Nigerian food, making her as happy and sated as she was when he'd taken her to the African restaurant in Brooklyn that doubled as stage set for his latest novel. After all this, she still held out the possibility of refusal. The best part would be experiencing again what it was like to be desired.

She avoided discussing her plans with Dr. Geiger, who must have suspected something, for he continued to urge her not to create complications at a delicate time in her life, particularly with Celia coming back after Christmas to prepare for the donation. The doctors were aiming for delivery of the ova a few days before the beginning of the second semester. Caitlin, of course, was encouraging her, but she suspected Caitlin wanted to stir up more trouble so that she could live vicariously through her friend. Friends did not always have your best interests in mind, despite their usefulness as confidantes. She had never felt that her own marriage was in such dire straits as Caitlin's, so full of Martin's obvious infidelities, their children practically the only glue holding them together. But without that glue, what did Elise have? She dismissed the thought from her mind.

Elise would have to make her own decisions about what happened with Babu, since neither Dr. Geiger nor Caitlin truly understood what she needed to do for herself. This thought made her feel stronger, certain that when the time came, the right answer would be revealed to her. She was torn between thinking she and Peter had real problems and wondering if she'd only invented them out of paranoia, creating issues to have something to worry over now that she no longer had the responsibilities of work to distract her. Still, she could feel the gulf between them growing wider, and perhaps to compensate for this, she found herself dialing up Patricia every few days just to chat, on the pretense of asking questions about wine or offering a reading suggestion for her mother-in-law's upcoming trip to Greece. At least she could shore up her relationships with his family members.

Peter continued to act erratically. Underneath his carefully stacked piles of sweaters in the closet, Elise found bottles of Ambien and Xanax, and when he was home he had developed a fondness for vacuous reality shows involving groups of oversexed twenty year olds who lived in a garish, TV-set home. If that show wasn't on, he was watching the Travel Channel, staring comatose at shots of filmy white curtains drifting through tall windows framing a blue expanse of sea.

"What's gotten into you?" she asked him one night, after he sat in front of a three-hour marathon of one of the more contemptible reality shows. On the screen, three shirtless guys lounged on their sofas, gold chains nestled in the hard crevices made by their overly muscled torsos. Elise shuddered and wondered how many women in America this sight appealed to.

"Just relieving stress," he replied. Around the house they were civil strangers, talking politely of events that had nothing to do with them as a couple, such as the rising cost of gas or a new restaurant that was opening up in Hannibal Square. She refrained from reminding him that in a month he was going to have to take time out of his schedule to begin the daily trips to the clinic for sonograms, blood tests, hormone checks, and ultimately his own sperm donation. Perhaps his reticence was due to his fear of how their lives would change once a baby was on the way. Caitlin disagreed.

"It's an affair," she said for the hundredth time on the phone, the night before Elise was to meet Eric in the city. "Wake up, Elise, it's past eight o'clock, he still hasn't come home, and Christmas is in less than a week. Do you really think he's still in the library? If the students have all gone home, then he's probably having an affair with a townie. Or another professor."

Elise tried to picture him with one of the soccer moms, an SUV-driving, Gwyneth Paltrow look-alike who dropped her kids off at Pilates for Tots then waited for Peter at her mansion off campus, her husband always away on business trips. But where would he have met someone like that? At a film series or concert? A bar? Peter never went anywhere, and the only outings he took were for runs.

Running. That was it. He would have met her at a group run with the Princeton Running Club. He would have been drawn to her (real) blonde hair, pulled back in a ponytail, her gazelle-like stride, the fact that she belonged to another man. She was older, in her forties, and expected nothing from him, neither money nor children, only uncomplicated, athletic sex. They could go for runs together, and with all that heavy breathing there was no time to talk or ask questions, just silent bonding along the sandy towpath alongside the canal, a shower at her place afterwards with hubby safely on the train to the city, the kids off at Princeton Day School.

Although Elise knew her imagination was running away from her, it helped to have a theory, an explanation for why Peter withdrew further each day. He would be conducting the affair out of fear, she decided, one last fling before the realities of adulthood set in and he realized how ridiculous this stunted student lifestyle was, especially with a baby on the way.

But in the meanwhile, she would find ways to withdraw herself.

Anticipating the usual difficulties in deciding on an outfit that would bring good luck and convey the right message, she'd gone to J. Crew the day before and bought a new dress. Plum colored with a plunging v-neck, as well as a belt that tied in the back and held the dress together like a robe, it was a dress that begged to be untied. She'd made an appointment at the salon to have a cut and a touch-up of her highlights, and at the tanning place next door she tried the all-over bronze tanning mist, which made her look as if she'd just returned from a weekend in Miami. At home she examined herself in the full-length mirror in the bedroom, impressed with the way the dress slipped off her shoulders and fell into a heap at her feet. When Peter came home, he looked her over, then announced,

"You look like you just got back from the Jersey Shore."

A wet snow had begun to fall by the time she arrived in the city, and the weather was turning colder, threatening to be a real mess for the Jimmy Choo pumps she was wearing, which up until now were her lucky shoes (they had to be, since she'd spent a few hundred dollars on them back when she was still earning an income). Exiting the subway near Eric's apartment, she wrapped her heavy coat tightly around herself as she searched for his building. The prices for the lofts in the area had skyrocketed since he'd purchased this one over ten years before, yet another fortunate choice in his enviable life.

Eric buzzed the intercom and she pushed open the heavy door, walking through the clean, nondescript lobby that had not been remodeled despite the wealth of the building's inhabitants. For several years she had not seen the inside of Eric's apartment. She remembered the loft's minimalist décor, the shock of his darkness beneath her against the tableau of an unassuming bed with white sheets and a white down comforter. White offered absolution, purity; it was the perfect color for affairs, as neutral and anonymous as a hotel room. There was something satisfying about returning to this place, remembering that he was the last man she'd slept with before her marriage to Peter.

His door was already open, the smell of curry powder and fried peppers drifting out of the apartment. Eric was at the counter of his kitchen, stirring what looked like a large clay pot.

"Pepper and plantain soup," he said. He wore a soft, white woven shirt untied at the top, and loose pants that resembled pajamas. "Good for chasing off the weather." She took off her coat and hung it on a rack, glancing back to see if he was still looking at her, but he'd turned his attention back to the stove. The gleaming wood floors and tall windows of his loft always made her think of ballet studios, with their particular smell of sweat and chalk and exertion, and the memory of her developing body in a leotard, which had embarrassed her enough to cause her to quit just before she'd graduated to *pointe*.

"How did the Princeton reading go before Thanksgiving?" she asked. "I'm sorry I wasn't able to make it."

"Eh, it was nothing special," he said. "You probably read in Gawker about the commotion I caused."

"Honestly, I don't keep up with that website anymore," Elise said. "What happened?"

"I was accused of being a diva, simply for stating my objection to being placed in a suite named for a slave owner. And this colored the entire event. Right down to the young co-ed who arrived at my room in the middle of the night, ostensibly to apologize for the way I'd been treated."

Elise laughed. "Did you send her away?"

"Of course," he said, stirring at the soup. "With a smile and an autograph."

He kept no curtains on the windows, and Elise could see the grayish snow outside swirling against the sky like ash. In the corner of the room where she expected to see the remembered bed, a king-sized ebony platform bed now dominated the space, covered with a pumpkin-colored silk duvet and heaped with zebra-patterned pillows. A tent of mosquito netting was inexplicably draped around the bed itself. Behind the bed, barely visible around the tent, hung a Japanese cloth painting, featuring a few cherry tree branches and a woman combing her hair next to a brook. The decadence of the scene was embarrassing; it telegraphed seduction a little too obviously, except for the presence of a stuffed lion in the middle of the bed.

"What's that?" she said, gesturing at the toy.

"That is Simba. He belongs to my son," Eric said. "He gave it to me as I got on the plane. He never parts with it, so I'm certain it was no small sacrifice for him to give it to me."

There was affection in his voice, something she'd never noticed in the past when he spoke about his wife and children.

"I didn't realize malaria was such a concern in the city," she said, looking at the netting.

He smiled. "It's something that reminds me of my childhood, almost a fetish object that helps me to write. I think about the British, who brought the netting to Nigeria to protect them from malaria. Why don't you sit down?"

He pulled a bottle of red wine from a rack on the granite counter top, bringing it over to the glass coffee table with a wooden tray of cheeses. She read the label, noting that it was a less than impressive Australian vintage.

"At home we would be drinking palm wine," he said, "but perhaps Shiraz is the next best thing." He sat beside her on the white sofa, near but not too near, and for the first time his eyes took in her outfit.

"You are as luminous as always," he said. "As if you've just returned from the seaside."

Luminous. Elise let the words sink in, one by one. *Seaside.* Much better than the Jersey shore. His charming way with language, and not just in novels, was appealing, the British pronunciations uttered in a dark, lilting accent.

"So, how have you been?" she asked.

"You know how it is. One attends the usual parties, sees the usual suspects. I've given a few readings to promote the new book."

"What new book?"

"Short stories. Nothing particularly new. Nothing you have not seen already."

Elise frowned.

"Who was the editor?"

"Amy Barron." Elise knew of Amy, a younger woman who was rapidly moving up at Smyth & Copperfield. She did a quick mental calculation: Eric would have submitted the stories while she was still doing freelance work for the company.

"Why didn't you let me know you were working on something?"

"I was told you were not available," he said. "This was before you contacted me. Anyway, I didn't think it mattered. Most of these had been edited before. Only some minor copy editing was required."

"Still, you should have let me know," she said. He sliced a piece of cheese and placed it on a cracker, handing it to her.

"I was recollecting something the other day," he said. "The time when you were over here consulting with me on *Apart from Babylon*. You were different then, with long, dark hair, and at one point, you pulled out your clasp and your hair fell all around you, like this." He fluttered his fingers around his own head. "I found that gesture so arresting that I knocked a glass from the counter, and it shattered into thousands of tiny pieces."

Elise reached up unconsciously and touched her much shorter hair. She remembered the moment but not her own gesture, recalling that she leapt up to help him sweep away the glass, and how he had leaned in and kissed her when they were both crouched on the floor, searching for the last glittering fragments.

He watched her from over his glass of wine, studying her as if contemplating the right moment to pounce. Elise looked away. She could not enter into the flirtation. Her skill at playing this game had momentarily abandoned her.

"I embarrass you, perhaps," he said gently. "The short hair is also becoming. Long hair is for girls. You are a woman now. I'm surprised you still do not have children."

"Do you think I would be here if I did?" she asked. Eric's traditional reverence for motherhood, a theme in several of his novels, would have put her off-limits to him once and for all. "Other men's wives were fair game, but mothers were sacred, untouchable," he had written in *Holding the Center*, about one of his many tomcatting protagonists.

"You might not be here if you were busy with children," he said. "But I do not think you would come here at all if you weren't searching for something. What's missing from your life that I was once able to give you?"

"What did you give me? You were married," she said.

"Marriage and pleasure are two very separate things," he said, leaning in. "Why shouldn't you have both?"

She glanced over at the bed looming in the corner.

"Ideally one would like to find both in the same person."

"If you had that, you wouldn't be here." He looked at her pointedly. "Marriage dulls the senses, its daily porridge sustaining the soul yet starving the heart. We find ourselves longing for the taste of others."

She recognized it as a line from *Lagos Burning*. She was glad to recognize it as a line, to know that he'd spent some time composing it rather than coming up with it on the spot. Still smarting from the news of his new collection of stories, she was no longer in the mood to be impressed with his verbal abilities.

"In Nigeria, when people are married several years with no children, there is a problem," he continued. "Perhaps the man cannot perform his duties as a husband." Looking at her significantly, he got up and walked back to the open kitchen.

He held the ladle up to his nose and sniffed it, closing his eyes, before dipping it back into the pot and serving up two small terra cotta bowls of plantain pepper soup. Placing the bowl in front of her, he waited for her reaction. The velvety soup was excellent, the spices perfectly balanced, with a satisfying heat that set in at the end. She felt awake, recalling the surprising flavors of the food she'd eaten in Brooklyn.

"This is delicious; the spices are all so vivid," she said. "I'm reminded of the restaurant you took me to the last time we met. I'm dying to hear more about your new novel." Reverting to her professional self was also a tactic; she refused to be caught so easily.

"I did not invite you here to discuss business."

"It's not business," she said quickly. "I was just curious. The premise of the novel was so fascinating."

"And that, for the moment, is all I can share," he said. "The book is growing in new directions that I cannot discuss at the moment. You know how I work. Talking about it disrupts the delicate rhythm I must create for myself."

"I understand," she said. She watched him eat; he savored each bite reverentially, as if the food transported him to the lost places of his past.

They finished their soup and he filled their glasses with more wine. The warmth of the soup and wine softened her, making the smart of his having another editor for the collection not quite so intense. It was just copy editing, after all. He had still invited her here, prepared lunch for her. Suddenly she pictured herself standing at the stove of the apartment in Princeton, cooking dinner for Peter, her skin imprinted with the memory of Eric's hands. She wondered whether Peter would notice, whether he had a sixth sense for betrayal, a primitive awareness of territory violated.

Eric, with his writer's sensibility for detail, had noticed the small shift in her emotions.

"I sense something amiss with you," he said. "A sadness, a sort of heaviness about you."

She sighed, debating whether to tell him anything about her marriage, but this would end the game, placing her in a vulnerable position, which was not somewhere she wanted to be with Eric. The urge to confess was strong, and she wished she had someone she could talk to with whom there weren't all these subtexts and subterfuges, someone who would neither judge nor try to steer her in a direction she did not want to go.

The intercom rang, and Eric glanced over at the wall.

"I'm not expecting anyone," he said. "Deliveries may be left with the concierge. Can I make you some coffee?"

The offer of coffee felt rushed, the soup insubstantial. Was this all he planned to give her? Seductions were supposed to be accompanied by several courses of food, each new taste deferring desire until the lovers could not bear to keep their hands off one another.

"This is it?"

"I only had time to make the soup," he apologized. "I wanted to make something more, but I was caught up in work and could not pull myself away."

A loud, prolonged buzzing startled them again. When it became apparent the noise was not going to stop, Eric jumped up and went over to answer the old-fashioned wall phone.

"I'm sorry," he told the person on the other end. "I cannot see you now. I'm meeting with someone." He held his ear to the phone. "No, we will have to discuss this later. Right now I am occupied." Replacing the phone on the hook, he walked back over to the sofa.

"A fan," he explained. "They can be persistent."

"Maybe you need a bodyguard," she said. He laughed. The intercom rang again. Exasperated, he walked over to pick it up.

"What?" he said. "Claudia, please. I will have to talk to you later. No, I am not going to... Alright, then." He hung up.

"I must go downstairs for just a minute."

"The fan has a name," she said dryly.

"She will not leave me alone. I am considering an order of restraint against her. If I do not talk to her, she will continue to ring until someone else lets her in, then she'll be at my door. This fan is... how do you say it? A bit psycho. Give me just a minute."

He went out into the hallway, closing the door behind him. Elise walked over to the window overlooking the street and opened it, leaning her head out to try and catch a glimpse of Claudia. Heavily swaddled in a dark hat, scarf, gloves, and a coat, a woman paced in front of the building, but Elise could not see her face. Eric soon joined her, shivering in his light clothes, the woman arguing with him about something. No fan would have a reason to express herself with such intimacy, no stranger could produce the slightly ashamed demeanor

Eric assumed in talking to her. Snow pricked Elise's face, and she closed the window.

His workspace was in front of the window, a slim computer monitor rising up out of a glass desk, the keyboard in a clear drawer beneath. A screen saver spun fractal patterns in the background, and Elise decided to check her email. She moved the mouse until the screen returned and began looking for the web browser icon on his desktop. Something entitled "NY Novel-working copy" caught her eye, and despite her better intentions, she found herself clicking on it.

"Above a busy storefront in a forgotten corner of Brooklyn," the document began. The old excitement she felt whenever one of her favorite writers gave her something new returned, the thrill of receiving an electronic copy and printing it out to work on it at home. She returned to the window to make sure he was still downstairs. From this height the great writer was nothing but a tiny figure, pantomiming a gesture of apology to the woman, whose arms were crossed fiercely across her chest. Elise returned to the computer screen, her eyes scanning the page.

The document was short—only twelve pages of writing that seemed largely descriptive, characters half-introduced and not interacting with one another, and partial, broken sketches of places. At times the voice switched into first person. Eric never wrote in the first person. "What would these men do?" he wrote. "This writing is riddled with prejudice, not with the characteristic subtlety I am known for." Skimming through the pages, she found other passages that seemed to be responses to his critics. "Even now my characters are mere archetypes, as they have accused. Even in America I cannot get beyond my colonized identity." On the last page the writing dropped off abruptly. "I remember a time when a mere shake of the tree resulted in a rain of bananas. What is happening to me?"

Outside the window Eric was embracing the woman, which appeared to have silenced her. Elise felt only indifference; one large measure of his skill with women had been his talent at keeping them separate, all of them aware that others existed but unable to find evidence except for the rumors, which he neither confirmed nor denied. He was slipping. She closed "NY-working copy" and looked around the other folders on the desktop. A folder containing short stories was full, but another folder, entitled "Ideas," was curiously empty, save for a one-paragraph description of the hotel room snafu at Princeton, which trickled out with a half-written sentence on the legacy of slavery in American society.

Closing all the computer windows, she returned to the sofa, finishing her glass of wine and watching the snow fall outside. In a few minutes he was back, his hair and shirt wet with snow. In front of her he changed into a t-shirt. Elise took in the muscular curves of his back and shoulders dispassionately, aware suddenly and with great certainty that she did not want to be there.

"Sorry for the disturbance," he said. "She would not go away without the signing of an autograph, which I have now left her with."

"So many autographs to sign," Elise murmured. "I do have one question for you."

"What can I tell you?" he said.

"Do you have a title for your new book yet?"

"No," he said. "At the moment it is simply entitled New York. The title will reveal itself in due time."

"How far along are you?" she said. "Although I'm sure Amy Barron is quite capable of helping you in case I'm unavailable, I was hoping to get an idea of when you might be finished."

"I have written over 100,000 words," he said, and now she knew that he was lying. "The last part is most delicate, since I am uncertain how my characters would resolve the mess they have made for themselves. They are involved in a host of anti-government activities, and with the climate of fear these days, I'm not sure whether it makes more sense to have them caught or to have them blow something up."

"Don't you think New York has been through enough?" Elise said.

"This is precisely my dilemma."

"Maybe you're blocked," she said, getting up. "Maybe someone has given you the evil eye." She looked at him significantly before walking over to the coat rack and taking down her coat.

"Where are you going?" He stood up. "I haven't even made coffee yet."

"This was a professional visit." She began buttoning the coat, until not a glimpse was left of the purple dress. "To announce that I'll no longer be working with you. I'm going to have a baby."

He stepped back as if struck. Then he tried to recover, smiling and reaching out to her.

"Congratulations," he said. "I assume the father is your husband?"

She ignored the nastiness of his last remark.

"I wish you the best of luck with your new editor," she said. Before he could say anything else she was already out in the hallway, taking the stairs instead of the elevator so that he would not follow her. Holding onto the railing to support herself in the teetering pumps, she dug with her other hand through her purse for the cell phone, and finding it, punched Number 3 on her speed dial, the number for Dr. Geiger.

* * *

For Christmas Elise wanted to go to Boston again, but fortunately a snowstorm to the north of them had intervened, making the driving, although possible, treacherous. They might have taken the train, but Peter refused, and Elise, increasingly compliant these days, did not press him. At the last minute she'd decided to take the Amtrak to Baltimore to visit her mother, but Peter refused to go along with her. Elise's mother, never particularly fond of Peter, lived in a dingy rowhouse in a neighborhood that was supposedly gentrifying, although at night you could sometimes hear gunshots. And so he found himself gloriously alone, pretending, after the obligatory phone call to his parents and to Elise and her mother, that Christmas day was like any other day.

The library was closed on Christmas, and most of the residents of the apartment complex were gone. There was too much snow and ice on the ground to run, so he drove to the indoor track across campus whenever it was open, but otherwise he did very little. The low dose antidepressant that the Princeton shrink had prescribed him was beginning to take effect, making him feel curiously free of any worries or cares, content to order Chinese take-out and pizza every night without the usual fears about MSG or cholesterol. He ran, he ate, he watched television. If he ate too much he ran some more. He prepared salads to counteract the effects of the junk food, making sure that breakfast at least was full of vitamins and fiber. At night he sometimes took sleeping pills, though he avoided taking them every day to make sure he was not addicted. He looked at marathon calendars and thought about training for the Paris marathon. His compulsion to be in his carrel every day disappeared. When he did go to the library, he could now sit in the overstuffed sofas of the Victorian reading room for hours, enjoying its near-deserted state, closing his eyes and imagining a university without students, only books, the knowledge from all those books flowing into his brain by osmosis.

But then Elise came back and the worry descended again like a cloud, breaking through the illusory, protective barrier the antidepressant had created. He felt divided into two selves, one an earthly persona struck down by fear, emotion, and frustration, while the other self was more ethereal, allowing him to float up into the stratosphere and escape the earthly self entirely. The ethereal self gazed down at his life like a benign, uninvolved ancestor watching his descendants make costly, absurd mistakes. None of it really mattered, they were all such tiny, inconsequential specks on the face of geologic time, their petty concerns and worries erased by the immensity of the universe.

Whenever he could, he allowed himself to float upwards, but sometimes this was impossible. Sometimes he was rooted to the earth, panicked by the swift passage of time and the dullness of his mind that was impeding his progression in any direction. He had vivid, disturbing dreams of himself as a tree growing in the middle of a surging river, trunk slowly decaying, unable to move until the rush of water wore away his foundation and carried him off. Since Elise returned his earthbound self was constantly fighting off a creeping sense of panic, a fear that everything was about to come crashing down on top of him. He would be caught, Yasemin would renew her efforts to pursue him, or Kevin would have him dragged before some imaginary tribunal. Sometimes he thought about talking to Celia, who still had only heard his coward's explanation of why he'd run away that night through an email. But he did not try to arrange a meeting. For now his main goal was to make it through this time of panic and disorder. With luck he might once again reach a neutral plane of existence, insulated by comforting routines. Celia was only a name, a person whom Elise drove back and forth to the clinic.

"Is there something wrong?" he asked, but Elise said no, today's appointment was a routine check for cysts, since Celia was on her period right now and this was what the doctors did.

The doctor's report came back cyst-free. Then Celia and Elise were both taking pills, consulting on the phone every day. Elise's pills would blanket her uterus with hormones, creating a rich environment suitable for receiving the fertilized embryo. The estrogen made her maniacally cheerful, and Peter wondered if there might be some pharmaceutical love chemical that could enhance both their moods and enable them to be permanently well disposed toward one another. Meanwhile, Elise reported, Celia was off in her dorm room injecting herself with shots every night.

"The girl is absolutely fearless," Elise said admiringly. She had been there at the clinic when Celia learned how to give herself the shots. "Not squeamish at all. She would have made a perfect heroin addict." He imagined Celia poking at her skin, seeking a strong vein and thinking of eight thousand dollars.

But Celia also must have been studying for exams. By the ninth of January most of the students had returned, and exams began on the eighteenth. Peter spent a week preparing the exam for his Arabic class, one of the responsibilities Dr. Samira Khoury no longer had to attend to, now that she was an associate professor and he was her teaching assistant. As he crafted his questions he imagined Kevin hoisting his ski bag into the overhead luggage compartment of a plane headed for Colorado, smirking at the thought of how he had cowed Peter into giving him an "A" for the term.

The earthly self alternated between feelings of rage and fear that Kevin might try to destroy him, but as he created the exam, the simplicity of introductory Arabic sent him into the ethereal plane once again. He spent hours perfecting the exam, focusing on the purity of the unbroken letters, those letters that still kept the Qur'an in its original form while all the other world religions' holy books had been tainted by multiple translations. It was such a shame how inadequate the students' appreciation for the language's sacred quality was. In the background noise of his life, Elise's voice was distant static, addressing him earnestly in another language: sonograms and Lupron, bloodwork and retrieval.

On Friday morning he carried his perfect exams into the classroom a half hour early. The students shuffled in one by one, some still sleepy eyed and bed-headed. He took attendance. He passed the exams around.

"I want you all to note the absence of your classmate Kevin," he said. "Unfortunately the exam was a casualty of his planned ski weekend in Vail. Should I need to call on you later as witnesses, please remember that today he was not here." They nodded, their expressions unreadable; they had perfected their poker faces in front of teachers whose mental states must have been the subject of much gossip outside the classroom. They were largely a group who had learned the art of bullshitting authority figures while still in the cradle. Undoubtedly his evaluations would be horrible this term, but he did not care. One day at a time.

After the exams, he had another appointment at the Princeton clinic to talk to the psychologist.

"I can feel the medicine working a little bit," he said. "It's done away with the compulsiveness, but the problems are still there." He told the psychologist, a neutral blonde woman of middle age, about the split the medicine had produced in his personality. He told her about the floating self, adding that he would prefer to remain in this state at a possibly higher dosage of the antidepressant.

"Do you feel this is you, this 'floating self'?" she asked. "Or is it someone else entirely?"

"It's the me I would like to be," Peter told her. "The problems ultimately bring me back to earth again, but I'd like to do away with them entirely."

"And are the problems," she said, "related to your fears about your wife and the egg donation?"

"That and the pressure of my career," he said. "And also, I cheated on my wife."

The psychologist looked down at her tablet as she wrote, pressing the pen a little harder, perhaps, at this last revelation, but she had mastered the poker face as well and showed no signs of reaction.

"I don't think medication is the only answer here," she said. "Medication isn't there to obliterate our problems. We still have to deal with those problems one by one. The antidepressant is only supposed to help you feel less overwhelmed..."

Blah blah blah blah. The meaning of her words began to slip away, transformed into the blurry, megaphoned sounds of an authority figure from a *Peanuts* cartoon. But the floating self managed to convince her for a stronger dosage, and more Xanax too.

He was *in treatment.* Therapy. What would his father think? Old school, stiff upper lip, don't-let-the-women-run-your-life Barry, who considered psychiatry one of the lesser medical disciplines for those who didn't want to get their hands dirty. Peter took his stack of exams to the library reading room. For three solid hours he diligently marked papers, entering the grades one by one into his laptop until he had an average for each student. Kevin would receive a zero and his average in the class would fall to a D. But he did not submit the grades to the university just yet.

After lunch, he went to the pharmacy to fill his prescription. While he waited, he wandered around looking at discounted Christmas decorations and the aisle of red valentine trinkets already set up for the next holiday. On impulse he bought a heart-shaped box of waxy chocolates for Elise.

"It's early," he said when he handed her the box. A puzzled look crossed her face.

"A Whitman's Sampler?" she said, taking a bite of one. "These taste like they were sold at a truck stop. If I were reading this gift as a barometer of your affection for me, I'd be in real trouble. Why didn't you go to the Lindt store?"

"I don't know," he shrugged. "I was in the pharmacy and I thought I'd get them. I thought you might think it was funny."

"Okay," she said, looking at him strangely. "Thanks."

The new, stronger pills were an improvement. Within a few days, Peter was able to enter the floating state more easily. He turned in his grades, and afterward, went to Kronenberg and told him as gently as he could that they, and the entire Near Eastern Studies Department at Princeton, could all go fuck themselves.

* * *

  The needles made Celia feel tough. They were tiny but still menacing, resting on the sterile cotton towel each night like drug paraphernalia, along with the vial of Lupron, and more recently, little pen shots of FSH, the follicle stimulating hormone that would transform her body into an egg factory, causing it to go into overproduction mode. She'd become an expert, squeezing up the skin of her belly and plunging the needle at a ninety-degree angle. At first she used an ice pack to numb her stomach, but now she'd given up on that, liking the shock of the tiny pinch, which reminded her that she was doing work. She also had a folder of documents to confirm this: contracts written by a reproductive lawyer, 1099 forms, forms from the clinic bearing the number to her bank account, where the money would later be transferred by the clinic itself, after she was finished, the money neutral now that it was coming from somewhere else, laundered by the clinic. Celia tried to tell herself she had a job to do, and that she'd always been a responsible person and would go through with it, even though she was beginning to have second thoughts.

  They were nearing the end of the process, and for several days, Elise drove her to the clinic each morning for a blood test and an ultrasound. The doctor, an Armenian with a heavy mustache that covered up his lips and made his expressions practically unreadable, muddled around inside her with plastic, condom-covered probes. He marveled over the quality of her young, developing eggs, as if he might exhibit them later at a state fair. At this point Celia just wanted it to be over, and she dreaded the site of Elise's car idling outside the dorm each morning, waiting to pick her up for the drive down strip mall-filled Route 1 toward the clinic. Elise's desire to bond had grown even more intense lately, and in the car, Celia was a captive prisoner, forced to listen to the chattering radio that Elise had become. Yes, it sounded like Peter had been cheating. Yes, once they got pregnant everything would get better. Yes, it was a good idea you called his mother and told her he bought you cheap chocolates. Yes, it's weird that he watches so much television. Elise was considering disconnecting the cable without telling him, just to see how he'd react. Celia stared at her puffy hands in her lap, opening and closing them. They felt stiff, foreign, part of a body that, for the moment, didn't belong to her.

  One day, driving back in the car, Elise pulled off the road, into a parking lot for an abandoned doughnut shop. She locked the doors, and Celia noticed her hands on the steering wheel were shaking. She sat up slightly in her seat; this was uncharacteristic behavior. Had she found out something?

  "What are you doing?"

"Locking the doors. It's not the safest area. I wanted to talk."

Celia wanted to say that this was all Elise ever did, but she kept quiet.

"It's infuriating me that I can't read your expressions since I'm driving," Elise said, turning to look at her. "You just sit there and agree with me on everything. You're getting worse than Peter."

"I thought that was what you wanted," Celia replied. "Support."

"It's like you're stoned, almost. Have you been smoking pot?"

"Not recently. Why would I do something like that?"

"You never know. I just had to ask. You're not acting like yourself anymore. Nobody is." Elise studied her, as if trying to read something on her face. "I want someone to react to me. You and Peter are both like Stepford wives these days. And you know what? It makes me just want to talk more, to fill up the silence. I can see I'm pushing you both away, but I can't stop. And I'm so nervous this isn't going to work." She bowed her head over the steering wheel, hiding her face. For one long, awkward minute, Celia watched Elise's shoulders shake with sobs. Finally Celia reached over and put her arms around her. She could feel Elise's ribs, her body thin and fragile beneath Celia's hands. She felt the sudden urge to take care of her, to bring Elise home and put her to bed, maybe make some soup for her in her kitchen.

"It'll work, Elise. You'll get pregnant. I can feel it."

Elise lifted her head. She took a tissue from her purse and rubbed under her eyes, where her mascara had made raccoon trails down her cheeks.

"I almost don't want it to work. I can't picture what my life would be like. They're going to ask how many embryos to transfer. Two would give me a better chance. But I don't know if I could handle two. I don't even know if I can handle one, on my own."

"What do you mean, on your own? Peter will be there to help out." Even as she said it, she knew somehow that Peter would not be there, either physically or in spirit.

"I don't know, Celia. I don't know anymore. I'm almost 100% sure he cheated on me. And I'm pretty sure I know who with. That bitch Yasemin, from his program. But it doesn't matter. I was going to do the same thing. With Eric. I thought I might get back at Peter that way. I'd show him that infidelity could be a woman's game, too. But I couldn't do it."

"How do you know it was Yasemin?" Celia asked.

"I saw her in Small World Coffee one day and she made a comment. It was something weird, along the lines of 'I had to take care of your husband while you were out of town recently.'"

"Maybe he'd just had too much to drink."

"That wasn't how she said it."

"So why didn't anything happen with Eric?"

"Because I love Peter. I don't really know why, but I do. And it wouldn't have felt good. We'd be like the Israelis and the Palestinians, each side escalating the hostilities of the other. And there'd be no solution."

Later that day, Celia told Nicole about the conversation. Eventually she'd shared with Nicole that Peter and Elise were the couple she was donating to. It made the story better, after all, more complicated. They were in Celia's room, Nicole wanting to see her stash of medicines, to watch her inject herself. Nicole was writing a poem about it. Probably pretending that she was the donor herself.

"You're such a badass," Nicole said, her eyes on Celia's stomach.

"The needles don't really hurt."

"But I don't see how you can just be so cool about everything. Aren't you at least freaked out that you might have a kid out of this?"

"It wouldn't be my kid," Celia explained. "Biology isn't destiny."

"Well, in a way it is. It's your biology creating this kid's destiny. You should think about it a little bit. Your kid, growing up with Elise and Peter."

"I've already thought about it," she assured her. But thinking about it now was different from thinking about it at the beginning, when her only worry was whether she cared about her genetic material being "out there." Thinking about it now was different from thinking about it in the middle, when she was worried about exploitation and had demanded more money. Thinking about it now was different, now that she'd played a small part in destroying whatever fragile bonds of matrimony had still been in place before she came along.

"If you ask me," Nicole said, "Peter's the one I really wouldn't want as a parent. Elise is just a little neurotic. She might not be particularly maternal, and she certainly wouldn't let her kid displace her as the center of her universe, but she'd do her job. But something about him always struck me as off. I always see him at the campus center, all dressed up with his briefcase, just to go off to teach. And that time we hung out in my room... He seemed a little bit too eager, you know?"

"Come on," Celia said, wanting to defend him. "He's just trying to find himself. He's sort of a tragic figure, I think."

"Why would you defend him? He ran out on you like a coward."

Her remark stung. But Celia was determined never to let Nicole see her unruffled. She shrugged.

"He was just looking for an easy way out. Think of how much worse all this would be for him if we'd gone through with it."

When Nicole left, Celia continued to replay their conversation. She'd been wrong - she didn't really care whether her biological offspring was merely out in the world, but now she wondered about her responsibility to that nonexistent child. But she had entered into a contract. They would have chosen someone else, if not her. She needed the money, and Elise's connections, to ensure herself a career path away from South Carolina. She saw the importance of maintaining good relationships with people she didn't exactly like, since there was no telling how she might need them later. Mr. Lenhart's admonition to destroy the people who exploited you would not get her that internship in New York. But she could not stop thinking about the possible baby that might result from all this. She'd agreed to bring a child into the world without knowing what a bad marriage would mean to this new life. The thoughts swirled around in her head throughout most of the night, and she slept fitfully.

* * *

On two occasions Peter accompanied Elise to the clinic. In the waiting room he read magazines about parenting. He learned the importance of setting limits and choosing your battles. He learned how the sex life of couples could often suffer after the birth of a child, and how to Keep Things New.

"This feels like much more of a partnership," Elise told him, patting his hand. "I'm glad you made time in your schedule for this." Funny how the simple act of driving someone someplace could produce this impression. He could handle this. All that was required right now was that he simply show up. And then a bit of acting. He tried to demonstrate the strength of their partnership by feigning attentiveness, asking the doctors questions whose answers would not stay fixed in his memory. His natural expression must be one of concern.

Celia was having frequent sonograms so the doctor could see how the eggs were developing. Elise drove her to the clinic for these visits, and for a few days more he managed to avoid seeing her. The girl was taking some kind of drug used in prostate cancer patients that forced her ovaries into overdrive, causing them to produce multiple eggs. Peter's wondered dispassionately if the drugs would hurt her somehow, years down the road. Soon, he would be called upon to perform his role in this whole process. The eggs would then be fertilized to grow on their own for a few days, and then, a few days later, to be placed in his wife.

On the morning of the retrieval they picked Celia up at her dorm just after six in the morning. It was still dark outside, Elise urging Peter to blast the heat so they could make sure Celia stayed warm. Celia hesitated for a moment before climbing into the car, as if she had something to tell them.

"Get in, we don't bite!" Elise practically beamed at Celia. She was in a good mood. Celia wore loose warm-up pants and a sweatshirt, her face puffy from the water weight the medicine had caused her to take on. Still she was beautiful, though he found himself oddly unmoved by her. The floating self experienced no regret or desire, was both neutral and neutered. Turning his expression of practiced concern toward her, he asked how she was feeling.

"Fine," she said. "A little swollen, but otherwise fine." Her face was free of makeup, and she was holding a tattered, stuffed bear. He looked away, focusing on maneuvering the car out into the road.

"Are you scared?" Elise asked.

"Sort of," she replied. "But I'll be knocked out for most of it. I should be okay tomorrow." Peter asked about her exams.

"I did fine," she said. "The grades aren't all in yet, but it looks like I'll end up with a couple of A minuses, plus an A in my creative writing class."

"Peter, watch out!" Elise exclaimed. He swerved to avoid a deer, almost sending them into the oncoming path of another car. The deer darted into the woods, a flash of liquid eyes and white tail disappearing like a comet into the darkness.

"Don't worry," he assured them. "I saw it." For a second he imagined he had killed them all but was somehow protected from this knowledge. What if you could be dead but not really know it? He kept this thought to himself, exchanging small talk with Celia about the exam schedule, the weather, her classes for the next term. Elise was happy, unsuspecting. There was no reason to hurt her. He would atone.

The clinic was a forty-minute drive from Princeton, and Peter looked down at the fuel gauge, noting they were low on gas. He pulled into a gas station and handed the man at the pump his credit card.

"I've never gotten used to how they pump the gas for you in New Jersey," Celia was saying. Elise went into the convenience store to get drinks.

"Get Celia something," he called after her.

"I'm not supposed to eat until after the retrieval," Celia said. "I'm actually starving. I'm thinking about sausage biscuits. I should have put a rider in my contract saying you had to take me to McDonald's afterwards."

Peter forced out a laugh.

"I'll be happy to drive you anyplace you want to go," he said. In the rearview mirror her eyes met his.

"She seems happy," she said. "Like you're working things out."

"Yes," he said, nodding.

"You didn't tell her."

"Of course not."

She pulled her blanket up around her chin and sank back into the seat, staring out the window. "I almost didn't come this morning. When I got to the car, I was getting ready to tell you it was off."

Peter said nothing.

"You know," Celia started, "she suspects you were cheating on her with Yasemin. She was thinking about sleeping with Eric Babu, just so you could be even. But at the last minute she couldn't do it."

"She told you that?"

"Yeah. She realized she didn't want to be with anyone else. It wouldn't solve anything. She said getting revenge turns us into the Israelis and the Palestinians."

Peter laughed.

"That's a rather grandiose analogy. It's just a marriage. She should hardly have equated it with all the suffering—"

"I'm not one of your students," Celia snapped. "I don't need a lecture. It was just an analogy."

The gas station attendant knocked at his window, waving the credit card. He signed the form and put the card away in his wallet as Elise climbed back in the car, holding two coffees. Taking a cup, he glanced over at her. Her face was flushed, ecstatic; for once she was getting what she thought she wanted.

He settled in the waiting room while Elise went back with Celia, glad he wasn't present to see her going under. Elise had described how the needle would pierce the abdominal cavity, aspirating the eggs from their egg sac one by one. *Aspirating.* It sounded so brutal. In another room Elise would then receive a progesterone injection. And he himself would—

"Peter?" A nurse called out his name, leading him down the hall to a little room, handing him a cup and a paper bag. He knew the drill, had done it before for the failed IVF treatments, seen this joke played to death in teen movies. At Brown he'd had friends who regularly made sperm donations to pick up extra cash. It was so minor, really, compared with the elaborate process women went through, his buddies joking over bong hits in their dorm rooms about the kids they must have scattered all over Providence. A hundred bucks to Celia's eight thousand.

The pain and suffering were what made her gift the greater one, they said. After all, Celia had been giving herself shots every night now for twenty days. The compensation was for discomfort the sperm donor would never feel. A sperm donor would not seriously be haunted by the thought that he had any number of potential children out there. But she would worry.

The room was painted pink, an emasculating color under the circumstances. In front of him on a table sat a television and a VCR, and the nurse had indicated a drawer filled with magazines and videos. She encouraged him to take his time. Pulling open the drawer, he took out a magazine and began flipping through it. How many hands must have rifled through these magazines. At first he thought it wouldn't happen. The antidepressants had neutered him, the floating self was perpetually soft. In one photo a woman bent over a silver-haired businessman to serve a gin and tonic, her uniform hiked up around her waist. *Chandra is a flight attendant and a member of the Mile High club. She'd love to serve you from her beverage cart.* In another unlikely scenario, two women beneath a waterfall pressed twin silicone globes against one another as they threw their heads back in mock ecstasy. *We were hiking and we got so hot. Jenifer saw the waterfall and suggested we cool off.* He flipped the page to a photo of a schoolgirl in the obligatory plaid Catholic skirt, her outsized mammary glands spilling out over an unbuttoned white dress shirt, smacked her classmate's ass with a ruler. Were all men really closet pedophiles, desiring only hairless, servile young women with Photoshopped bodies? Was he a member of this tribe? The magazine was beneath the atmosphere of dignity the clinic conveyed, as a place where couples anguished over their fervent desire to continue the species.

He thought about exiting the room, informing the nurse he was unable to deliver, but then, reminding himself of what he had put everyone through these last several months, he decided against it. His father would have done it. Barry would have had no problem with the magazines, with the command to perform to the slick spectacle of horny camping lesbians. The image of Yasemin hovering over him, her hair pulled back in a veil, flashed into his mind. The floating self was horrified, but he could still channel his father, donor of half of his own genetic material.

Leaving the room, he was no longer embarrassed. The nurses saw men like him all day. Star quarterback, he handed off his contribution and returned to wait for Elise and Celia to come out. It seemed like hours later when they finally appeared, and this time Elise was supporting Celia for real, Celia looking drowsy and spent on his wife's arm.

"Fourteen. They got fourteen eggs," Elise announced. Celia slept on the ride home, not wanting McDonald's anymore, saying she wanted only to go home and sleep. He stopped in front of her dorm while Elise helped her up to her room, and then they drove home.

"No trouble, I hope?" he asked.

"None at all," Elise said. "She has to monitor her condition to make sure she doesn't get this ovarian hyper-stimulation syndrome, but other than that, she'll be fine. In a few days they'll call us to transplant the embryo."

"How are you paying her?"

"I'm not doing it, the clinic will transfer the money," Elise scrutinized him. "I'm surprised you're thinking of money at a time like this."

Elise went into the bedroom to lie down.

Flipping on the television, Peter settled back on the sofa. In one month he'd be thirty-seven. At first he had hoped that taking time off might help him to have more ideas, but the antidepressants cleared out his mind, removing cobwebs and productive thoughts alike. His eyes were heavy; neither he nor Elise had slept much the night before. Turning down the volume on the television, he closed them, just for a minute.

When he awoke, the Travel Channel was showing a beach. Not a tropical beach, palm trees flanked by white sands, but a place somewhere on the Atlantic, its dark waters spilling onto a shore where a shirtless, brown-skinned child dipped his hands down to catch their eddies. Desultory camels paced back and forth on their tethers nearby, humps mounted with saddles for the next group of tourists. The cameras panned down the shore until beach turned to rocky coastline, crumbling white castles rising up in the distance, and he knew immediately where he was.

Almost as if he were sleepwalking, the floating self got up and walked into the bedroom, looking down at his wife's sleeping figure beneath the comforter. He turned on the computer, and Elise stirred without waking. On the Internet, his fingers entered his destination into a travel website, the invisible engines humming and whirring until the prices displayed in neat rows before him. It was winter, low season in Morocco, and he found himself typing in "Agadir," then pressing *Buy*, pulling the credit card from his pocket, receiving the instant confirmation: he would depart on his birthday, one month from today. He did not book a return date.

* * *

Elise had read everything she could find on the Internet about how to maximize the embryos' chances for success. *Follow a healthy diet.*

Avoid caffeine on the day of the transfer. No smoking or alcohol. After the transfer, try to rest quietly. Make it a quiet day. Have hubby do everything for you. Do not lift anything heavy, and no vigorous exercise. Avoid hot baths, hot tubs or saunas. Avoid weight loss or dietary changes during your IVF cycle.

On the morning of the transfer, she brewed two cups of coffee, drinking one and leaving the other for Peter. They drove to the clinic together in silence. It was bitterly cold, and they both kept on their heavy jackets in the car, the fabric adding further layers of distance between them. The sound of the car's heater blasting out hot air was so loud it discouraged talking. Against Dr. Abassian's advice, she had started taking her antidepressants again without telling anyone. Except Dr. Geiger, of course. Along with Peter's Xanax, one of which she'd just popped before getting in the car, the medicine calmed her, made her feel she could handle anything. The world had taken on a soft glow again.

"We have several good quality blastocysts," Dr. Abassian's nurse had told her over the phone. "If you transfer two, you maximize your chances."

"One is enough," Elise replied. For the transfer, she asked Peter to stay in the lobby. He was only too happy to agree, and he opened up the copy of *Runner's World* that he'd brought with him. For what felt like the millionth time, she lay back on the fake leather table in the examination room. Dr. Abassian attempted a smile that merely lifted the corners of his moustache.

"Your donor has really good eggs," he said. Celia was a winner. "Minimal fragmentation. You can always transfer the frozen ones if this fails." He busied himself with some instruments on his table.

"I'll tell you every step of what I'm doing," he said. "Now I'm loading what we call a fine transfer catheter." The nurse had smeared lubrication jelly on her stomach.

"You look like you've lost weight," the nurse commented, moving the sonogram machine around her belly, which was almost concave. "Been eating all your vegetables?"

"Yes," Elise said. *To maximize the chance of embryo transfer, you should follow a healthy diet.* Last night she'd gone by herself to the Annex, ordering a glass of wine and a plate of jalapeño poppers. She brought Eric's new collection of short stories with her. As she ate, she read the stories slowly, savoring his haunting prose. Even if he never wrote another word, and even if these were pieces that had already appeared in magazines years before now, he had still produced an astounding body of work. She would be thrilled to work with writers like him again. She ordered a second glass of wine and thought about all the times she'd sat in the Annex with Celia, discussing what the future would bring. The future no longer scared her. It no longer seemed bleak or inhospitable, just mysterious. It wasn't something you could plan for, and this was okay.

"Now we're looking for just the right spot," Dr. Abassian was saying. "You'll feel a pinch from the catheter. No more painful than a Pap smear." What did he know what it would feel like? He was a man. He knew nothing about the phenomenology of women. After he'd finished, she was left to rest for a half hour. She remembered all those times after she and Peter had made love, when she'd contort her body into yoga positions that were supposed to help the sperm find its mark. The lotus pose ahead of time, to prepare the space. The legs-up-the-wall pose, *viprarita kirani*. *The lotus pose can enhance fertility. Avoid hot yoga when you are trying to conceive.* How easy she'd expected it would be.

"How do you feel?" Peter asked her in the car on the way back.

"Fine," she said. But it was her body now, not his. She didn't want to talk about it anymore.

After the transfer, try to rest quietly. Make it a quiet day. Have hubby do everything for you.

Peter left for the library. As she took some laundry down to the first floor of the apartment complex, she wondered whether Dr. Kronenberg had liked Peter's last chapter. He had said nothing about it. Elise made herself a sandwich and answered a few emails. She returned several times to check her laundry, taking the stairs instead of the elevator. When the laundry finished, she put on her yoga clothes and bundled herself up in her coat and hat. She drove to the yoga studio and checked the class schedule. A *bikram* yoga class was beginning in a few minutes. She took her mat into the yoga room, feeling a blast of one hundred degree heat as she opened the door to the room where the hot yoga class would take place. It felt good after the cold outside.

Later, after taking a long bath, she stood in front of the bathroom mirror. Her face was flushed from the exercise, and her hair was growing out, returning to its original brown at the roots. A new Elise emerging. She liked the outline of her small breasts and waist under her black tank top, her arms thin but muscled from yoga. In her hand she held the two pills: 400 milligrams of progesterone. She was supposed to take them every day now. To maximize her chances. She looked at the pills, glancing back at her reflection in the mirror as if to ask that other person what to do. Then she tossed them in the toilet, pressed the flush, and went into the kitchen to get herself a glass of wine.

CHAPTER TWELVE

"They're forecasting snow," Peter said, making small talk as he waited for her to dress. She had chosen to wear all black, the favored color of mourners and graduate students of architecture. He surveyed her choice of clothes, the thin sweater that would be too cold for this time of year, his brow furrowed with the intimate concern of a parent who has decided to stop giving orders, only to hint at the grave mistakes the child might be making.

This was the final betrayal, Celia driving him to JFK airport in the Honda that she would later leave in the parking lot of the apartment complex. By mid afternoon the traffic was already snarled on the Long Island Expressway, the sky full of high, puffy white clouds. She did not speak of her fear of driving in the chaos of city traffic, simply doing what he asked. He told her where to make turns and had prepared a detailed map so that she could find her way home again.

She imagined herself as his wife, taking him to the airport where he would fly away from her forever, and wondered how that would feel. They had conceived children together, after all, their offspring lying not in the barren womb of Elise but frozen in a laboratory somewhere in New Jersey. She thought of Sarah in the Bible, asking Abraham to bear children with her maidservant.

Elise would understand why he had to go, he told her. She would understand that it was no use to stay in a marriage where she was not loved as she deserved to be. Celia was not sure whether or not she believed him. She had seen Elise once since the donation, at the Annex. The two-week wait for the pregnancy test had been almost as agonizing for Celia as she imagined it must have been for Elise. A half-empty bottle of *pinot grigio* on the table in front of her, she jumped up and hugged Celia. The wine itself was a bad sign, although with Elise's lack of reverence for what she put into her body, she never knew. For a few minutes they exchanged small talk. Elise seemed to be relishing the suspense of keeping her waiting.

"So... do you have any news to share?" Celia asked.

"The embryos didn't stick," she said ruefully, fingering her napkin. Celia felt both relieved and sad, but Elise patted her hand briskly across the table.

"Don't worry, you're off the hook," Elise had said. "I don't know what's going to happen with Peter, but I have a plan. An exit strategy."

"You're leaving him?" she asked, surprised.

"No. But I am going back to work. And I recently came into some money from my father. More of my guilty inheritance. It's not a lot, but enough to get me started in a new direction. My dad heard through the family grapevine that Peter and I were having trouble, and *voilà*, a check appeared. At first I thought about burning it."

For the thousandth time, Celia was stunned at how casual Elise was with money, as if her father's gift were something she could simply refuse on principle. She should have considered it child support. But Celia made no comment. Her role, which was almost over, was to nod and agree.

And so, while she didn't believe Peter that Elise would understand (perhaps her exit strategy had been to leave him, too, only he'd done it first), Celia hoped Elise would be fine. That she needed to believe.

Marriage is a fluid state, Peter announced suddenly. It's like a current you're caught in for awhile until suddenly you find yourself needing to fight it, to get out and breathe again.

He looked at her significantly, as if she might want to write this down.

At the airport he asked her to go in with him, to stand there as he checked in, to watch him as he went through security, frustrating the other travelers with his slowness, the care with which he took off shoes and watch, emptying his pockets of change. Watching him merge with the flow of travelers and out of her sight, she was his surrogate wife, the one who would offer no resistance to his plans, who knew she had no right to ask him not to leave. On the drive home in the unfamiliar car she flipped through the radio channels, trying to find songs to distract herself from thinking of the airport, of Peter turning around and waving after he passed through the security checkpoint, wearing a hangdog expression that proclaimed he was being a good sport even though something too heavy for words was weighing him down. It was a look that reminded her of her father.

As he requested, Celia left the car in the apartment parking lot. It was dark already, and she had not yet opened the thick envelope he'd given her ("To pay for parking," he announced).

When she got back to her room she opened the envelope. As expected, she found the twenty-dollar bill he'd intended her to use for parking, but there was something else. A thick sheaf of photocopies, scrawls of handwriting she could barely decipher in an ancient, crabbed script. Some of the pages were in Spanish. Switching on the light next to her bed, she held the copies close to her face.

Sidi Maarif is locked in by mountains so stony and fortified as to seem impenetrable. To get to the village one walks for three days along mountain footpaths with a native whose feet are guided by such memory that even blindness could not lose them. Many are lost on these mountains, but if one perseveres, S. Maarif is said to amply reward the visitor with clean water, palm trees overflowing with fruit, and inhabitants who are as pleasant and hospitable as the most lavish of desert shaykhs. This is to say nothing about the rugs, which fetch a higher price in the markets of Marrakech than a caravan of gold. Even the famous Dacca gauzes of India pale by comparison.

With difficulty she worked to decipher the handwriting, reading page after page of the descriptions she vaguely remembered seeing in his library carrel. These were the impressions that inspired him, but they were nothing he would have been able to turn into anything substantial. The other document was heftier: his attempt at writing a dissertation based on those impressions. His advisor had hated it, he mentioned in the car, told him it was crap. This was one of the reasons he was leaving.

He'd single-spaced what he wrote and printed it in a tiny font, which she had to squint to read. He depicted the women weavers as almost Amazonian goddesses with a strange power over men. It was weird, disjointed but somehow lucid at the same time. But it wasn't particularly well written.

On the final page he'd written her a note.

The beauty of words is more dangerous than anything. More seductive. I am giving you these papers, which are worth more to me than all the money we gave you to give us a child. I am hoping you can do something with them.

How like those long ago explorers Peter was. He had escaped, and assumed that in doing so, he could erase his tracks. It was nervy of him, to abandon everyone and then to leave his precious photocopies with her as if he were bestowing some great treasure. She sat on her bed for a very long moment that seemed to stretch out into hours, until the phone rang. Daniel's voice rose up from the faraway dark of Deer Bluff. For the past month her father had been working for the Patel family as a night manager at the Starlite Motel. Vijay Patel's brother Sanjay had opened up a gas station, their son was off at Harvard, and until another family member could be found to do the night shift, they'd decided to hire someone temporarily.

"June bug, I've been thinking," he said. "You're going to think this is a crazy idea, but I'm determined to do it, and I need your help."

He paused, waiting for her approval to continue. She could hear the eagerness in his voice.

"Tell me," she said.

"I know you're planning to work in New York this summer," he said. "But I was wondering if you could spare a couple of weeks after school ends and come down here and help me move."

"Move where?"

"I've decided to sell the house and move to Key West. Go back into the timeshare business. When we tried it before, I wasn't ready, but now I'm certain that this is what I want to do."

"You're sure?"

"Absolutely. What's left for me here? You will never have a reason to come back to this place, and I don't want you to feel like you have to. Anayo Mills, Deer Bluff, it's all dead for me. Dead for a lot of people. Those jobs don't exist anymore. Service is the wave of the future. I talked to my old boss down in the Keys, and he's willing to give me another try. What do you think?"

Celia did her best to assure him. They were all such solitary creatures: she, her father, Peter. There was no way to rationalize what had happened, but it was over and done with, and now people were moving on. Celia thumbed through Peter's archive copies again, the life's work of long-ago explorers and ethnographers all looking for something elusive, who had no idea where people would read what they'd written later. She tried to honor their memory by falling in love with the beauty of those words, as Peter had, but all she could think about was the fact that the accounts were so one-sided, and that they described only the stories of those men privileged enough to travel, not the women who'd created the weavings. This was not over. She had so many stories in her, so many things she needed to tell the world. She opened her laptop and began to write.

Walking over to the stove, Elise turns on the gas, the blue flame leaping out with a reassuring crackle. She lowers her father's check closer and closer to the flame, picturing the way it might leap up into the paper, engulfing the check rapidly until it became something insubstantial, a charred black slip that would crumble into itself, releasing a burning smell into the air. She stands staring at the flame for a long time before finally switching it off. The check would allow her to do so much. Why should she have to struggle, after all? She's been through enough. She places the check carefully on the counter, then takes the wine bottle over to the sofa, where she pours herself glass after glass until she has finished the bottle entirely. Tomorrow there will be a headache that she will not allow herself to regret. Then she will begin again.

EPILOGUE

At a party celebrating the release of her new book, Celia recognizes the irony that Smyth & Copperfield has become her publisher. Ten years earlier, Elise might have been her editor, and present at this very party. Elise now has her own literary agency in Los Angeles (named the *Elise Matthews Agency*, of course), which Celia discovered on the Internet in her own search for an agent. She suppressed a laugh at the opening page of the website: Elise in sepia tones, looking slightly away from the camera, glamorous and intense. When Celia browsed the client list, she saw (and with not a small amount of relief) that Elise was doing quite well.

Tonight Celia is the center of attention, a role that still does not come naturally to her. Against the high white walls of the art gallery, voices take on an odd echo, and she hears everything as if from far away: the constant murmur of congratulations, her own voice answering with quiet confidence, making small talk about how she brought her book into the world. She looks up, conscious that the art on the walls also has its ironic echoes in her past. She recognizes a Rothko painting, a copy of which she'd once seen on Elise and Peter's wall and asked if one of their friends had painted it.

Celia's editor, a likeable and efficient woman named Amy, continuously brings over people she should meet. Next to her, Daniel is at her side, lovingly awkward and out of place, champagne flute in hand. Nicole flits about somewhere nearby, networking furiously, as always. Through Nicole, she has finally met someone: her boyfriend Miles, an earnest environmental writer who has just returned from writing a story about children damaged from lead pollution in the Dominican Republic. She catches his eye across the room and he returns her gaze, smiling and giving her the thumbs up. And she has managed, little by little, to make more friends, who are also here for support, people she's known since the internship that summer, friends from her MFA program, and from the investment firm where she worked to support herself through grad school.

So much of her life has gone into the book now carefully displayed on the table before her. She thinks back to the summer after "the gift," and the road trip she took to Deer Bluff with Nicole to help her father pack up the house and move to Florida. Through Nicole's eyes, Celia began to find elements of southern gothic everywhere: most obviously, in the ruined mill, but also in the illuminated sign for the Starlite Motel (Starlite missing an "e" so that it now wistfully proclaimed itself to be Starlit), and in The Diamond, where they ran into Michael Lenhart and enjoyed a rousing evening marked by too many rounds of Pabst Blue Ribbon and barbed conversations with Marxist overtones. While Nicole was in the bathroom, Mr. Lenhart teased Celia for bringing home the landed gentry. There was a suggestion in what he said of her preference for women: to prove him wrong, she let him kiss her, in one last, misguided effort at having writer-worthy experiences before she finally swore off such attempts. Celia has not been back to Deer Bluff since, and this final leave taking was what has remained imprinted in her mind when she thinks about home: the night with Michael Lenhart at The Diamond, followed by the careful loading of the set pieces from her childhood into a U-Haul bound for Florida.

In the memoir on the table, *Cracked: The Other Side of IVF*, it is Celia who gets the final word. She has written it all down: the small town girl escaping the desolate landscape of her childhood, the affluent and worldly couple who offer a way out. In the book, Babu is not referred to by name but is simply the Famous Writer. And she has not, finally, lied about any of it: she writes of losing her nerve at the door to his room, and of playing the incident up later for her friends, and in her writing. One advanced reviewer has called it an "unvarnished look at reproductive exploits and exploitation," while a renowned feminist critic has praised her for "asking why girls in America must always be defined by their sexuality, in one guise or another." The identifying details of Elise and Peter have been altered slightly, so that they might not be recognizable to others who knew them, but if they pick it up, they will know themselves. She is certain that at some point, Elise will read it, although Peter, at last Google, was still lost in translation somewhere in Morocco, possibly the proprietor of a bed and breakfast, though she wasn't quite sure.

Celia imagines Elise circulating at other book parties in her black cocktail dress, her profile framed against works of abstract modern art tethered to the high walls. She remembers the story of how Elise and Peter met, Elise oblivious that she had caught Peter's eye, and thinking only of Eric Babu, whether they might meet each other alone later. Returning to that scene, would Elise have changed her future if she could see it before her: Princeton, infertility, divorce? Were they hardships or gifts in disguise, gifts left behind on the way to something better? The very air around Celia seems to spark with possibility, and she wishes she could remain suspended indefinitely in the oblivious present, unaware of the potential mistakes she is making, which will be clear, someday, when she tries to count the things she wishes had happened.

*Rumi – Ode 2357, from Like This, translated by Coleman Barks. Ode 3079

Made in the USA
Charleston, SC
08 September 2013